The
Candy
House

ALSO BY JENNIFER EGAN

Manhattan Beach

A Visit from the Goon Squad

The Keep

Look at Me

Emerald City and Other Stories

The Invisible Circus

JENNIFER EGAN

The Candy House

corsair

CORSAIR

First published in the United States in 2022 by Scribner
First published in the United Kingdom in 2022 by Corsair

1 3 5 7 9 10 8 6 4 2

A CIP catalogue record for this book
is available from the British Library.

HB ISBN: 978-1-4721-5091-2
TPB ISBN: 978-1-4721-5093-6

Printed and bound in Great Britain by Clays Ltd, Elcograf S.p.A.

Papers used by Corsair are from well-managed forests
and other responsible sources.

MIX
Paper from
responsible sources
FSC® C104740
FSC
www.fsc.org

Corsair
An imprint of
Little, Brown Book Group
Carmelite House
50 Victoria Embankment
London EC4Y 0DZ

An Hachette UK Company
www.hachette.co.uk

www.littlebrown.co.uk

To my writing group—
Collaborators and compatriots,

Ruth Danon
Lisa Fugard
Melissa Maxwell
David Rosenstock
Elizabeth Tippens

The Brain—is wider than the Sky—
For—put them side by side—
The one the other will contain
With ease—and You—beside—

Emily Dickinson

For nothing is more unbearable, once one has it, than freedom.

James Baldwin, *Giovanni's Room*

BUILD

The Affinity Charm

1

"I have this craving," Bix said as he stood beside the bed stretching out his shoulders and spine, a nightly ritual before lying down. "Just to talk."

Lizzie met his eyes over the dark curls of Gregory, their youngest, who was suckling at her breast. "Listening," she murmured.

"It's . . ." He took a long breath. "I don't know. Hard."

Lizzie sat up, and Bix saw that he'd alarmed her. Gregory, dislodged, squawked, "Mama! I can't reach." He had just turned three.

"We've got to wean this kid," Bix muttered.

"No," Gregory objected sharply, with a reproving glance at Bix. "I don't want to."

Lizzie succumbed to Gregory's tugs and lay back down. Bix wondered if this last of their four children might, with his wife's complicity, prolong his infancy into adulthood. He stretched out beside the two of them and peered anxiously into her eyes.

"What's wrong, love?" Lizzie whispered.

"Nothing," he lied, because the trouble was too pervasive, too amorphous to explain. He chased it with a truth: "I keep thinking about East Seventh Street. Those conversations."

"Again," she said softly.

"Again."

"But why?"

Bix didn't know why—especially since he'd only half-listened, back on East Seventh Street, as Lizzie and her friends called out to one another through a cumulus of pot smoke like disoriented hikers in a foggy valley: *How is love different from lust? Does evil exist?* Bix was halfway through his PhD by the time Lizzie moved in with him, and he'd already had those conversations in high school and his first couple of years at Penn. His present nostalgia was for what he'd felt *overhearing* Lizzie and her friends from his perch before his SPARC-station computer linked by a modem to the Viola World Wide Web: a secret, ecstatic knowledge that the world these undergrads were so busy defining, in 1992, would soon be obsolete.

Gregory nursed. Lizzie drowsed. "Can we?" Bix pressed. "Have a conversation like that?"

"Now?" She looked drained—was being drained before his eyes! Bix knew she would rise at six to deal with the kids while he medi-tated and then began his calls to Asia. He felt a wave of desperation. Whom could he talk with in that casual, wide-open, studenty way that people talked in college? Anyone working at Mandala would try, in some sense, to please him. Anyone not at Mandala would presume an agenda, possibly a test—a test whose reward would be employ-ment at Mandala! His parents, sisters? He'd never talked to them that way, much as he loved them.

When Lizzie and Gregory were fully asleep, Bix carried his son down the hall to his toddler bed. He decided to get dressed again and go outside. It was after eleven. It violated his board's security require-ments for him to walk New York's streets alone at any hour, much less after dark, so he avoided the trademark deconstructed zoot suit he'd just taken off (inspired by the ska bands he'd loved in high school) and the small leather fedora he'd worn since leaving NYU fifteen years ago to assuage the weird exposure he'd felt after cutting off his dreads. He unearthed from his closet a camouflage army jacket and a pair of scuffed boots and entered the Chelsea night bareheaded, bridling at the cold breeze on his scalp—now bald at the crown, it was true. He was about to wave at the camera for the guards to let him back in so he could grab the hat, when he noticed a street vendor on the corner of Seventh Avenue. He walked down Twenty-first Street to the stall and tried on a black wool beanie, checking his look in a small round mirror affixed to the side of the stall. He appeared utterly ordinary in the beanie, even to himself. The vendor accepted his five-dollar bill as he would have anyone's, and the transaction flooded Bix's heart with impish delight. He'd come to expect recognition wherever he went. Anonymity felt new.

It was early October, a razor of cold in the breeze. Bix walked uptown on Seventh Avenue intending to turn around after a few blocks. But walking in the dark felt good. It returned him to the East Seventh Street years: those occasional nights, early on, when Lizzie's parents visited from San Antonio. They believed she was sharing the apartment with her friend Sasha, also an NYU sophomore, a ruse Sasha corroborated by doing laundry in the bathroom the day Lizzie's parents came to see the apartment at the start of fall semester. Lizzie had been raised in a world oblivious to Black people except those who served and caddied at her parents' country club. So frightened was she of their presumptive horror at her living with a Black boyfriend that Bix was banished from their bed during her parents' first visits, even though they stayed in a midtown hotel! It didn't matter; they would *just know*. So Bix had walked, occasionally collapsing in the engineering lab under the guise of pulling an all-nighter. The walks had left a body memory: a dogged imperative to keep going despite his resentment and exhaustion. It sickened him to think he'd put up with it—although he felt it justified, on some cosmic balance sheet, the fact that Lizzie now managed every facet of their domestic lives so that he could work and travel as he pleased. The legion of good things that had come to him since could be seen as recompense for those walks. Still, *why*? Was the sex really that good? (Well, yes.) Was his self-esteem so low that he'd indulged his white girlfriend's magical thinking without protest? Had he enjoyed being her illicit secret?

None of that. What had fueled Bix's indulgence, his endurance, was the thrall of his Vision, which burned with hypnotic clarity on those nights of slogging exile. Lizzie and her friends barely knew what the Internet was in 1992, but Bix could feel the vibrations of an invisible web of connection forcing its way through the familiar world like cracks riddling a windshield. Life as they knew it would soon shatter and be swept away, at which point everyone would rise together into a new metaphysical sphere. Bix had imagined it like the Last Judgment paintings whose reproductions he used to collect, but without hell. The opposite: disembodied, he believed, Black people would be delivered from the hatred that hemmed and stymied them in the physical world. At last they could move and gather at will, without pressure from the likes of Lizzie's parents: those faceless Texans who opposed Bix without knowing he existed. The term "social media" wouldn't be coined to describe Mandala's business for almost a decade, but Bix had conceived of it long before he brought it to pass.

He'd kept the utopian fantasy to himself, thank God—it looked comically naive from a 2010 perspective. But the Vision's basic architecture—both global and personal—had proved correct. Lizzie's parents attended (stiffly) their wedding in Tompkins Square Park in 1996, but no more stiffly than Bix's own parents, for whom proper nuptials did not include a mage, jugglers, or fast fiddling. When the kids started coming, everyone relaxed. Since Lizzie's father died last year, her mother had taken to calling *him* late at night when she knew Lizzie would be asleep, to talk about the family: Would Richard, their oldest, like to learn to ride horses? Would the girls enjoy a Broadway musical? In person, his mother-in-law's Texas twang grated on Bix, but there was no denying the zing of satisfaction her same voice, disembodied at night, afforded him. Every word they exchanged through the ether was a reminder that he'd been right.

The East Seventh Street conversations ended on a single morning. After a night of partying, two of Lizzie's closest friends went swimming in the East River, and one was carried away by a current and drowned. Lizzie's parents had been visiting at the time, a circumstance that chanced to place Bix near the tragedy. He'd run into Rob and Drew in the wee hours in the East Village and done E with them, and the three of them had crossed the overpass to the river together, at sunrise. The impulsive swim happened after Bix had gone home, farther down the river. Although he'd repeated every detail about that morning for the police inquest, it was vague to him now. Seventeen years had passed. He could hardly picture the two boys.

He turned left on Broadway and followed it all the way up to 110th Street—his first such perambulation since becoming famous over a decade ago. He'd never spent much time in the neighborhood around Columbia, and something appealed to him about its hilly streets and grand prewar apartment buildings. Gazing up at the lighted windows of one, Bix thought he could practically hear a potency of ideas simmering behind it.

On his way to the subway (another first-in-a-decade), he paused at a lamppost feathered with paper flyers advertising lost pets and used furniture. A printed poster caught his eye: an on-campus lecture to be given by Miranda Kline, the anthropologist. Bix was deeply familiar with Miranda Kline, and she with him. He'd encountered her book, *Patterns of Affinity*, a year after forming Mandala, and its ideas had exploded in his mind like ink from a squid, and made him very rich. The fact that MK (as Kline was affectionately known in his world) deplored the uses Bix and his ilk had made of her theory only sharpened his fascination with her.

A handwritten flyer was stapled alongside the poster: "Let's Talk! Asking Big Questions Across Disciplines in Plain Language." An introductory meeting was scheduled to follow Kline's lecture three weeks later. Bix felt a quickening at the coincidence. He took a picture of the poster and then, just for fun, tore off one of the paper tabs from the bottom of "Let's Talk" and slipped it into his pocket, marveling at the fact that, even in the new world he'd helped to make, people still taped pages to lampposts.

2

Three weeks later, he found himself on the eighth floor of one of those stately, faded apartment buildings around Columbia University—possibly the very one he'd admired from below. The apartment bore a pleasing resemblance to what Bix had imagined: worn parquet floors, smudged white moldings, framed engravings and small sculptures (the hosts were art history professors) hanging on the walls and over doorways, tucked among rows of books.

Apart from the hosts and one other couple, all eight "Let's Talk" attendees were strangers to one another. Bix had decided to forgo Miranda Kline's lecture (presuming he could have finagled entry); her antipathy toward him made it seem wrong to attend, even in disguise. His disguise was "Walter Wade," graduate student in electrical engineering—in other words, Bix himself, seventeen years ago. What gave him the chutzpah to pose as a graduate student all these years later was the confidence that he looked much younger at forty-one than most white people did. But he'd erred in assuming that the other discussion group members would be white: Portia, one of their art historian hosts, was Asian, and there was a Latina animal studies professor from Brazil. Rebecca Amari, the youngest, a PhD candidate in sociology (the only other student besides "Walter Wade"), was ethnically ambiguous and, he suspected, Black—there'd been a twinge of recognition between them. Rebecca was also disarmingly pretty, a fact heightened, not muted, by her Dick Tracy eyeglasses.

Luckily, Bix had marshaled other tools of identity concealment. Online, he'd purchased a headscarf with dreadlocks emerging from the back. The price was exorbitant but the dreads looked and felt real, and their weight between his shoulder blades was like the touch of a ghost. He'd known that weight for many years, and liked having it back.

When everyone had settled onto couches and chairs and introduced themselves, Bix, unable to repress his curiosity, said, "So. What was she like, Miranda Kline?"

"Surprisingly funny," said Ted Hollander, Portia's art historian husband. He looked to be in his late fifties, a generation older than Portia. Their toddler daughter had already charged into the living room pursued by an undergraduate babysitter. "I thought she'd be dour, but she was almost playful."

"What makes her dour is people stealing her ideas," said Fern, dean of the women's studies department and rather dour herself, Bix thought.

"People have used her ideas in ways she didn't intend," Ted said. "But I don't think even Kline calls it theft."

"She calls it 'perversion,' doesn't she?" Rebecca asked tentatively.

"I was surprised by her beauty," said Tessa, a young professor of dance whose husband, Cyril (mathematics), was also in attendance. "Even at sixty."

"Ahem," Ted said good-naturedly. "Sixty isn't so very ancient."

"Is her appearance relevant?" Fern challenged Tessa.

Cyril, who took Tessa's part in everything, bristled. "Miranda Kline would say it was relevant," he said. "More than half the Affinity Traits in her book have to do with physical appearance."

"*Patterns of Affinity* can probably explain each of our reactions to Miranda Kline," Tessa said.

Despite assenting murmurs, Bix was pretty sure that, apart from himself (and he wasn't telling), only Cyril and Tessa had read Kline's masterwork, a slender monograph containing algorithms that explained trust and influence among members of a Brazilian tribe. "The Genome of Inclinations," it was often called.

"It's sad," Portia said. "Kline is better known for having had her work co-opted by social media companies than for the work itself."

"If it hadn't been co-opted, there wouldn't have been five hundred people in that auditorium," said Eamon, a cultural historian visiting from the University of Edinburgh and writing a book on product reviews. Eamon's long deadpan face seemed to shield an illicit excitement, Bix thought, like a generic house containing a meth lab.

"Maybe fighting for the original intent of her work is a way of staying connected to it—of owning it," said Kacia, the Brazilian animal studies professor.

"Maybe she'd have some new theories by now if she wasn't so busy fighting over the old one," Eamon countered.

"How many seminal theories can one scholar produce in a lifetime?" Cyril asked.

"Indeed," Bix murmured, and felt the stirring of a familiar dread.

"Especially if she started late?" Fern added.

"Or had children," said Portia, with an anxious glance at her daughter's toy stove in the living room corner.

"That's why Miranda Kline started late," Fern said. "She had two daughters back-to-back, and the husband left her while they were in diapers. Kline is his name, not hers. Some kind of record producer."

"That is fucked up," Bix said, forcing out the profanity as part of his disguise. He was known *not* to curse; his mother, a sixth-grade grammar teacher, had heaped such withering scorn on the repetitive dullness and infantile content of profanity that she'd managed to annul its transgressive power. Later, Bix had relished the distinction that not cursing gave him from other tech leaders, whose foul-mouthed tantrums were infamous.

"Anyway, the husband is dead," Fern said. "To hell with him."

"Ooh, a retributivist among us," Eamon said with a suggestive waggle of eyebrows. Despite the stated goal of using "plain language," the professors were helplessly prone to academic-ese; Bix could imagine Cyril and Tessa's pillow talk including terms like "desideratum" and "purely notional."

Rebecca caught his eye and Bix grinned—as heady a sensation

as taking off his shirt. At his fortieth-birthday party last year, he'd been presented with a glossy pamphlet entitled "Bixpressions" that codified, with photographs, a system of meanings assigned to barely perceptible shifts of his eyes, hands, and posture. Back when he was the only Black PhD student in NYU's engineering lab, Bix had found himself laughing hard at other people's jokes and trying to make them laugh, a dynamic that left him feeling hollow and depressed. After getting his PhD, he cut out laughing at work, then cut out smiling, and cultivated instead an air of hyperattentive absorption. He listened, he witnessed, but with almost no visible response. That discipline had intensified his focus to a pitch that he was convinced, in retrospect, had helped him outwit and outmaneuver the forces aligned in readiness to absorb him, co-opt him, shunt him aside and replace him with the white men everyone expected to see. They had come for him, of course—from above and from below, from inside and from every side. Sometimes they were friends; sometimes he'd trusted them. But never too much. Bix anticipated each campaign to undermine or unseat him long before it coalesced, and he had his answer ready when it did. They couldn't get in front of him. He gave some of them jobs in the end, harnessing their wily energies to advance his work.

His own father had regarded Bix's rise with wariness. A company man who wore the silver watch he'd been presented at his retirement from a managerial role at a heating and cooling corporation outside Philadelphia, Bix's father had *defended* Mayor Goode's decision to bomb the house of the MOVE "slobs" who "put the mayor in an impossible position" (his father's words) in 1985. Bix was sixteen, and the fights he'd had with his father over that bombing, and the resulting destruction of two city blocks, had opened a chasm between them that never quite closed. Even now he felt the whiff of his father's disapproval—for having overreached, or become a celebrity (and thereby a target), or failed to heed his father's lectures (delivered liberally to this day from the helm of a small motorboat his father used to fish along the Florida coast), whose refrain, to Bix's ears, was: *Think small or get hurt.*

"I wonder," Rebecca mused a little shyly, "if what happened to Miranda Kline's theory makes her a tragic figure. I mean, in the Ancient Greek sense."

"Interesting," Tessa said.

"We must have the *Poetics*," Portia said, and Bix watched in amazement as Ted rose from his chair to look for a physical copy. None of these academics seemed to have so much as a BlackBerry, much less an iPhone—in 2010! It was like infiltrating a Luddite underground! Bix got up, too, ostensibly to help Ted search, but really for an excuse to look around the apartment. Built-in bookshelves lined every wall, even the hallway, and he ambled among these examining the spines of oversize hardcover art books and old yellowed paperbacks. Faded photographs were scattered among the books in small frames: little boys grinning outside a rambling house among piles of raked leaves, or snowdrifts, or heavy summer greenery. Boys with baseball bats, soccer balls. Who could they be? The answer arrived in a photo of a much younger Ted Hollander hoisting one of those boys to place a star upon a Christmas tree. So the professor had a previous life—in the suburbs, or maybe the country, where he'd raised sons before the arrival of digital photography. Had Portia been his student? The age spread was suggestive. But why assume that Ted had chucked his old life? Maybe that life had chucked him.

Could you start again *without* chucking everything?

The question intensified Bix's dread of minutes before, and he retreated to the bathroom to ride it out. An age-splotched mirror hung above a bulbous porcelain sink, and he sat on the toilet cover to avoid it. He shut his eyes and focused on his breathing. His original Vision—that luminous sphere of interconnection he'd conceived during the East Seventh Street years—had become the business of Mandala: implementing it, expanding it, finessing it, monetizing it, selling it, sustaining it, improving it, refreshing it, ubiquitizing it, standardizing it, and globalizing it. Soon that work would be complete. And then? He'd long been aware of a suggestive edge in the middle distance of his mental landscape, beyond which his next vision lay in wait. But whenever he tried to peek beyond that edge, his mind went white. At first he'd approached that pale expanse with curiosity: Was it icebergs? A climate-related vision? The blank curtain of a theatrical vision or the empty screen of a cinematic one? Gradually, he began to sense that the whiteness was not a substance but an absence. It was nothing. Bix had no vision beyond the one he'd nearly exhausted.

This knowledge arrived decisively on a Sunday morning a few months after his fortieth birthday as he lounged in bed with Lizzie and the kids, and the jolting horror of it made him bolt to the bathroom and vomit in secret. The absence of a new vision destabilized his sense of everything he'd done; what was it worth if it led to nothing—if, by forty, he was reduced to buying or stealing the rest of his ideas? The notion gave him a haunted, hunted feeling. *Had* he overreached? In the year since that awful morning, the Anti-Vision had shadowed him, sometimes barely perceptible but never entirely disappearing, whether he was walking his kids to school or dining at the White House, as he'd done four times in the year and a half since Barack and Michelle came in. He could be addressing an audience of thousands, or in bed helping Lizzie to achieve her elusive orgasm, when the ominous vacancy would begin to drone at him, harbinger of a void that harried and appalled him. More than once he'd pictured himself clutching Lizzie and whimpering, "Help me. I'm finished." But Bix Bouton couldn't say such a thing ever, to anyone. Above all, he had to maintain; fulfill his roles of husband, father, boss, tech icon, obedient son, major political contributor, and indefatigably attentive sexual partner. The man who longed to return to the university, in hopes of provoking a fresh revelation to shape the remainder of his life, would have to be a different man.

He returned to the living room to find Cyril and Tessa poring over a volume with carnal transport, as if it were a tub of ice cream. "You

found it," Bix said, and Tessa grinned, holding up a volume of Aristotle from the same "Great Books" set his parents had purchased along
with their treasured *Encyclopaedia Britannica*. Bix had reverently consulted the *Britannica* as a kid, quoting from it in school reports on
cannibals and hemlock and Pluto; reading the animal entries purely
for pleasure. Four years ago, when his parents moved into their modest Florida condo—having refused his help to buy a larger one, out
of pride (his father) and modesty (his mother)—Bix boxed up those
volumes and left them on the sidewalk outside the West Philadelphia
home where he'd grown up. In the new world he'd helped to make, no
one would ever need to open a physical encyclopedia.

"In my reading of the Aristotle," Tessa said, "—mind you, I'm a
dance professor, there are probably a million scholarly pages on this—
but Miranda Kline is *not* a tragic figure. For her to be Tragic-tragic,
the people who appropriated her theory would have had to be related
to her. That would increase the betrayal and the dramatic irony."

"Also, didn't she *sell* the theory? Or the algorithms?" Kacia asked.

"I think there's a mystery around that," Portia said. "Someone sold
it, but not Kline."

"It was her intellectual property," Fern said. "How could anyone
else have sold it?"

As one of the purchasers of Kline's algorithms, Bix squirmed in a
state of squeamish duplicity. He was relieved when Ted said, "Here's
a different question: Miranda Kline's algorithms have helped social
media companies to predict trust and influence, and they've made a
fortune off them. Is that necessarily bad?"

Everyone turned to him in surprise. "I'm not saying it *isn't* bad,"
Ted said. "But let's not take that for granted, let's examine it. If you
look at baseball, every action is measurable: the speed and type of
pitches, who gets on base and how. The game is a dynamic interaction
among human beings, but it can also be described quantitatively, using
numbers and symbols, to someone who knows how to read them."

"Are you such a person?" Cyril asked incredulously.

"He is such a person," Portia said with a laugh, slipping an arm around her husband.

"My three sons played Little League," Ted said. "Call it Stockholm syndrome."

"Three?" Bix said. "I thought there were two. In your pictures."

"Scourge of the middle son," Ted said. "Everyone forgets poor Ames. Anyway, my point is that quantification, per se, doesn't ruin baseball. In fact, it deepens our understanding of it. So why are we so averse to letting *ourselves* be quantified?"

Bix knew, from his cursory research online, that Ted Hollander's academic success had come in 1998, the same year Bix incorporated Mandala. Already midcareer, Ted published *Van Gogh, Painter of Sound*, which found correlations between Van Gogh's types of brushstroke and the proximity of noisemaking creatures like cicadas, bees, crickets, and woodpeckers—whose microscopic traces had been detected in the paint itself.

"Ted and I disagree about this," Portia said. "I think that if the point of quantifying human beings is to profit from their actions, it's dehumanizing—Orwellian, even."

"But science *is* quantification," Kacia said. "That's how we solve mysteries and make discoveries. And with each new step, there is always the worry that we might be 'crossing the line.' It used to be called blasphemy, but now it's something more vague that boils down to *knowing too much*. For example, in my lab we've begun to externalize animal consciousness—"

"I'm sorry," Bix interrupted, thinking he'd misheard. "You're doing what?"

"We can upload an animal's perceptions," Kacia said. "Using brain sensors. For example, I can capture a portion of a cat's consciousness and then view it with a headset exactly as if I am the cat. Ultimately, this will help us to learn how different animals perceive and what they remember—basically, how they think."

Bix tingled with sudden alertness.

"The technology is still very crude," Kacia said. "But already, there is controversy: Are we *crossing a line* by breaching the mind of another sentient creature? Are we opening a Pandora's box?"

"We're back to the problem of free will," Eamon said. "If God is omnipotent, does that make us puppets? And if we are puppets, are we better off knowing that or not?"

"To hell with God," Fern said. "I'm worried about the Internet."

"By which you mean an all-seeing, all-knowing entity that may be predicting and controlling your behavior, even when you think you're choosing for yourself?" Eamon asked with a sly glance at Rebecca. He'd been flirting with her all night.

"Ah!" Tessa said, seizing Cyril's hand. "This is getting interesting."

3

Bix left Ted and Portia's apartment ablaze with hope. He'd felt a shift in himself at points during the discussion, an arousal of thought that seemed familiar from long ago. He rode the elevator down with Eamon, Cyril, and Tessa while the others lagged behind, looking at some plaster reliefs Ted had bought on a trip to Naples decades before. Outside the building, Bix idled in a circle of small talk, unsure how to break away without seeming rude. He was reluctant to let it be known he was heading downtown; would a Columbia graduate student *live* downtown?

It turned out that Eamon was walking west and Cyril and Tessa were taking the train to Inwood, having been priced out of the neighborhood around Columbia and unable, as assistant professors, to get faculty housing. Bix reflected guiltily on his five-story townhouse. The professors had mentioned that they were childless, and one side of Cyril's wire-rimmed glasses was held together with a paper clip. But there was a crackle of conductivity between these two; apparently, ideas were enough.

Buoyed by a sense that he could go anywhere as Walter Wade,

Bix strode in the direction of Central Park. But the half-bare trees silhouetted against a sallow sky put him off before he reached the entrance. He wished it were snowing; he loved snowy nights in New York. He longed to lie down beside Lizzie and whichever kids had been washed, by nightmares or nursing, into their oceanic bed. It was after eleven. He doubled back to Broadway and got on the 1 train, then noticed an express at Ninety-sixth and switched, hoping to overtake a faster local. From his Walter backpack, he unearthed another disguise element: the copy of *Ulysses* he'd read in graduate school with the explicit aim of acquiring literary depth. What the tome had delivered concretely was Lizzie, in whom (through a calculus Miranda Kline surely could have explained) the combination of James Joyce and waist-length dreads provoked irresistible sexual desire. The calculus on Bix's end had involved a pair of tan patent-leather boots that went higher than Lizzie's knees. He'd kept *Ulysses* as a romantic artifact, although its worn look derived more from the passage of years than rereading. He opened it randomly.

"—*Eureka!* Buck Mulligan cried. *Eureka!*"

As he read, Bix began to feel that he was being watched. The sensation was so familiar from his normal life that he was slow to react, but at last he looked up. Rebecca Amari sat at the opposite end of the subway car, observing him. He smiled at her and raised a hand. She did likewise, and he was relieved to find that it seemed okay to sit apart in friendly mutual acknowledgment. Or was it okay? Maybe it was antisocial to follow several hours of lively group discussion with a distant nonverbal greeting. Bix so rarely had to contend with questions of ordinary social etiquette, he'd forgotten the rules. *When in doubt, do the polite thing*; he'd internalized this dictum from his scrupulously polite mother too decisively to unlearn it. Reluctantly, he put away *Ulysses* and crossed the car to Rebecca, taking the vacant seat beside her. This felt instantly wrong—they were touching from knee to shoulder! Or was total body contact the norm for people who took the subway? Blood flashed into his face with such force it gave him vertigo. He rebuked himself: When mundane social inter-actions became heart-attack-inducing, something was wrong. Fame had made him soft.

"You live downtown?" he managed to ask.

"Meeting friends," she said. "You?"

"Same."

In that moment, Bix noticed his stop—Twenty-third Street—flying past the window; he'd forgotten he was on an express. He won-dered if Rebecca would alight at the next stop, Fourteenth Street, en route to the district known as MALANDA, for Mandala-land. Bix had opened his new campus there the year after 9/11, and in eight years it had expanded into factory buildings, warehouses, and whole stands of rowhouses, until people joked that when you turned on the taps below West Twentieth Street, Mandala water poured out. As the train approached Fourteenth Street, Bix considered getting out and just walking home, but crossing his own campus in disguise seemed perversely risky. A downtown local was pulling in; he decided to take it one more stop and double back on an uptown local.

"You getting out here?" Rebecca asked as they both left the train.

"Just switching."

"Oh—me, too."

They remained standing on the southbound 1 train. Bix felt a wisp of suspicion; was it possible that Rebecca knew who he was and was following him? But she seemed relaxed, not starstruck, and his suspicion yielded to pleasure at riding the subway beside a pretty girl. A fancy seized him: He could get off downtown and walk to the old apartment on East Seventh Street! He could look up at his and Lizzie's windows for the first time in well over a decade.

Preparing to alight at Christopher Street, Bix noticed Rebecca also making shifting movements suggestive of departure. Sure enough, she got off. "I wonder if we're going to the same place," she said, laughing as they climbed the exit stairs.

"Unlikely," Bix said.

But Rebecca, too, turned east onto West Fourth Street. Bix's suspicion flared again. "Are your friends at NYU?" he asked.

"Some."

"Cagey."

"It's my personality."

"Paranoid?"

"Careful."

He was grateful for city noise to fill the silence. Rebecca walked looking straight ahead, which allowed Bix to enjoy, in sidelong glances, the delicate symmetry of her face, her freckled cheekbones bringing to mind a pair of butterfly wings. Maybe being so pretty was what made her careful. Maybe the Dick Tracy glasses were a beauty disguise.

She glanced over and caught him gazing. "It's freaky," she said. "How much you look like Bix. You could be brothers."

"We're both Black," Bix said with a grin, quoting the line he'd prepared in advance for a white questioner.

Rebecca laughed. "My mom is Black," she said. "Half Black, half Indonesian. My dad is half Swedish, half Syrian Jew. I was raised Jewish."

"Don't you win some kind of prize for all that? In the race combination sweepstakes?"

"Actually, I do. Everyone thinks I'm like them."

Bix stared at her. "You have the Affinity Charm," he breathed with awe. It was a term from *Patterns of Affinity*. According to Miranda Kline, the Affinity Charm was a potent asset, granting its rare possessors the trusted, enviable status of Universal Ally.

"Wait a minute," Rebecca said. "You weren't even at her lecture."

"I . . . did the reading."

They'd been waiting for the light to change at Bowery, and walked the next block in silence. At the corner of Second Avenue, Rebecca turned to him suddenly. "My last year at Smith, three years ago," she said, in a kind of rush, "Homeland Security interviewed all the high academic performers of 'indeterminate race.' Especially if we studied languages."

"Whoa."

"They were pretty insistent," she said. "Didn't want to be told no."

"I can imagine. With the Affinity Charm, you could work anywhere."

As they neared First Avenue, Bix began recalling favorite landmarks: Benny's Burritos; Polonia with its incredible soups; the newsstand along Tompkins Square Park that sold egg creams. He wondered which of them were still there. At First Avenue he paused to say goodbye before turning left—but Rebecca, too, was heading north. Suspicion reared up in him, impossible to ignore. He quickened his pace and gazed up the long gray avenue, wondering how exactly to confront her.

Rebecca spun around to face him. "Promise me you don't work for them," she said.

He was blindsided. "Me? That's crazy. Work for who?" But he was keenly aware of being in disguise.

Rebecca stopped walking. They were nearly at the corner of Sixth Street. Searching his face, she said, "Can you swear that you really are Walter Whatever, graduate student in electrical engineering at Columbia?"

Bix stared at her, heart bucking in his chest.

"Shit," Rebecca said.

She swerved right onto East Sixth, Bix matching her stride. He had to fix this. "Look," he said under his breath, "you're right. I'm . . . who I look like."

"Bix Bouton?" she cried in outrage. "Give me a break! You have dreadlocks, for fuck's sake." She sped up, as if trying to escape him without breaking into a run.

"I am," Bix insisted softly, but making this claim while he half-chased a beautiful stranger through the East Village, after midnight, caused him to doubt himself. *Was* he Bix Bouton? Had he ever been?

"I gave you that idea," Rebecca said. "Remember?"

"You noticed the resemblance."

"This is, like, classic." She was smiling, but Bix could feel that she was afraid. There was trouble in this situation. To his relief, she stopped run-walking and scrutinized him in the acid streetlight. They had somehow lurched their way almost to Avenue C. "You don't even look that much like him," she concluded. "Your face is different."

"That's because I'm smiling, and he doesn't smile."

"You're talking about him in the third person."

"Fuck."

She gave a scornful laugh. "Bix doesn't swear, everyone knows that."

"Holy shit," Bix heard himself exclaim, but then his own suspicions swerved back into view. "Wait a minute," he said, and something in his tone made Rebecca stop and listen. "You're the one who came out of nowhere. I think you followed me all the way from Ted and Portia's. How do I know you didn't say yes to Homeland Security?"

She gave an outraged laugh. "That's psychotic," she said, but he heard a tremor of anxiety in her denial, the mirror of his own. "I wrote my master's thesis on Nella Larsen," she said. "Ask me anything about her."

"I've never heard of her."

They eyed each other with mistrust. Bix felt spooked in a way that brought to mind a bad mushroom trip in his teens when, after an Uptones concert, he and his friends had briefly scattered in fear. He took three long breaths, the basis of his mindfulness practice, and felt the world settle back around him. Whatever else Rebecca might be, she was a kid. He had fifteen years on her, at least.

"Look," he said, standing at a respectful distance. "I don't think either of us is a dangerous person."

She swallowed, looking up at him. "I agree."

"I accept that you're Rebecca Amari, graduate student in sociology at Columbia."

"I accept that you're Walter Whatever, graduate student in electrical engineering at Columbia."

"All right," he said. "We have a contract."

4

It turned out that Rebecca had circumvented her destination, a bar on Avenue B, which she returned to after they reached their fragile accord. Bix declined her invitation to join. He needed to reflect on their scrape and assess the damage. Was there any way he could return to the discussion group? Would Rebecca return?

He'd overshot the East Seventh Street apartment by several blocks and now was close to the Sixth Street overpass that led to East River Park. He mounted its stairs and crossed the FDR to find the park transformed since he'd last seen it: There were sculpted bushes and a picturesque little bridge and joggers still out, even at this hour.

He went to the rail and leaned over the river, watching its surface toggle the colored city lights. His overnight walks often had concluded here, sunrise skidding off the oily river into his eyes. Why would anyone swim in it? The question made him aware that he was standing in the place where he'd stood with Rob and Drew on the morning Rob drowned. "Gentlemen, good morning," he suddenly remembered saying to them, an arm around each. An impression of Rob returned to him: a stocky athletic white kid with a smart-aleck grin and pained, evasive eyes. Where had that memory been? And where was the rest: Rob's voice, and Drew's, and everything they'd said and done on that last morning of Rob's life? Had there been a clue Bix had missed, when he said goodbye, of what would happen next? He felt the mystery of his own unconscious like a whale looming invisibly beneath a tiny swimmer. If he couldn't search or retrieve or view his own past, then it wasn't really his. It was lost.

He stood up straight, as if he'd heard his name aloud. A connection quivered in his mind. He looked up and down the river. Two white women jogging toward him seemed to veer away when he turned. Or had he imagined that? He replayed the moment—an old, disquieting conundrum that clouded whatever new thought had been trying to form. Abruptly, he was exhausted, as if he'd been walking for days—as if he'd wandered too far from his own life to reenter it.

He speed-dialed Lizzie, wanting to close the distance between them, but ended the call before it rang. She would be asleep, likely with Gregory at her breast, her phone charging out of reach. She would scramble for it in fear. And how exactly would he explain his bizarre whereabouts at this hour?

His parents? They would think someone had died.

He dialed his mother-in-law. Bix almost never initiated calls to her, and doubted she would pick up. He found himself willing her not to.

"Beresford," she answered.

"Joan."

She called everyone else "darling" and they called her "Joanie." But Bix and his mother-in-law called each other by their real name.

"Everyone all right?" she asked in her laconic drawl.

"Oh, yes. All fine."

There was a pause. "And yourself?"

"I'm . . . fine, too."

"Don't shit a shitter," Joan said, and he heard her lighting a cigarette over sounds of lawn mowers. Apparently, they mowed their lawns at night in San Antonio. "What's on your mind?" she said, exhaling.

"Nothing much," he said. "Just wondering . . . what should happen next."

"Aren't we all."

"I'm supposed to know," he said. "It's my job."

"That's a lot to ask."

He stared at the colors moving and melting on the river. Joan's cigarette crackled in his ear as she took a long drag.

"I hear worrying," she said smokily. "That's a worried silence."

"I'm afraid I can't do it again."

It was the first time Bix had said these words, or any like them, to anyone. In the pause that followed, he recoiled from the confession.

"Horseshit," Joan said, and he could almost feel the hot blast of cigarette smoke hitting his cheek. "You can and you will. I'll bet you're a lot closer than you think."

Her words, spoken casually, brought a wave of unaccountable relief. It might have been her use of his given name, which he rarely heard, or the fact that she wasn't generally the booster type. Maybe hearing anyone say *You can and you will* at that moment would have made it seem true.

"I'm going to give you a piece of advice, Beresford," Joan said. "It comes from the love in my heart. Are you ready?"

He closed his eyes and felt wind on his eyelids. Tiny waves lapped the parapet below his feet. There was an ocean smell: birds, salt, fish, all of it mingled, incongruously, with Joan's whistling breath.

"Ready," he said.

"Go to bed. And give that crazy daughter of mine a kiss."

He did.

Case Study:
No One Got Hurt

1

Nobody, including Alfred Hollander himself, is certain of when he first began reacting violently—"allergically" is the word he uses—to the artifice of TV. It started with the news: those fake smiles. That hair! Were they robots? Were they bobbleheads? Were they animate dolls he'd seen in horror-movie posters? It became impossible to watch the news with Alfred. It became hard to watch *Cheers* with Alfred. It became preferable not to watch anything with Alfred, who was apt to holler from the couch, still with a slight lisp: "How much are they paying her?" or "Who does he think he's kidding!" It broke the mood.

Turning off the TV wasn't enough; by age nine, Alfred's intolerance of fakery had jumped the life/art barrier and entered his everyday world. He'd looked behind the curtain and seen the ways people played themselves, or—more insidiously—versions of themselves they'd cribbed from TV: Harried Mom. Sheepish Dad. Stern Teacher. Encouraging Coach. Alfred would not—could not—tolerate these appropriations. "Stop pretending, and I'll answer you," he would inform his startled interlocutor, or, more bluntly, "That's phony." His family cat and dog, Vincent and Theo, went through their days without pretense. So did the squirrels and deer and gophers and fish that populated the lake-abundant region of Upstate New York where Alfred grew up and where his father, Ted Hollander, taught art history at a local college. Why did people have to pretend to be what they already were?

There was an obvious problem: Alfred was difficult—or "a fucking nightmare," to quote several witnesses. And there was a deeper problem: He poisoned his world. Many of us, wrongly accused of, say, spying for the Department of Homeland Security, or stalking a famous person whom we haven't actually identified, will respond with guilt, anxiety, and attempts to telegraph our innocence. We behave, in other words, exactly as a surveilling Homeland Security agent, or surreptitious stalker, would behave. Likewise, adults charged by Alfred to "stop using that fake voice" would strive to act more natural and wind up acting less so: Parents played parents; teachers played teachers; baseball coaches played baseball coaches. And they got away as quickly as they could.

Family life was the epicenter of Alfred's discontent. At dinner, he felt "asphyxiated" by the quiet supremacy of Miles, his oldest brother, who was organized and accomplished, and by the studied vacancy of Ames, the middle brother, who came and went invisibly and whose real thoughts were always out of reach. In reply to his parents' innocuous questions about his day at school, Alfred often would bark, "I can't have this conversation," upsetting his mother, Susan, who treasured family time.

At eleven, Alfred began wearing a brown paper bag with eyeholes over his head during holidays with extended family. He kept the bag on throughout the meal, tweezing forkfuls of turkey or pecan pie through a rectangular mouth slot. His goal was to create a disruption so extreme that it jolted genuine responses—albeit negative—from those around him.

"What is Alfred doing?" a grandparent would ask.

"I'm wearing a bag over my head," Alfred would reply from inside the bag.

"Is he unhappy with his appearance?"

"I'm right here, Grandma, you can ask me."

"But I can't see him . . ."

Certain rare individuals had the gift of *inducing* naturalness, and these were the sole recipients of Alfred's regard. Chief among them was Jack Stevens, the best friend of his brother, Miles. "Wear the bag, Alf," Jack would beg, chortling in anticipation, but the bag was unnecessary with Jack present—he made the whole family relax. Jack spent many nights at the Hollander home, his mother having died of cancer when he was young. Alfred describes Jack as having been rowdy, spontaneous, greedy for stimulus, a bringer of kegs to "the beach," a shingle of sand on the site of a defunct summer camp that was a popular party spot for local teens. Jack was known for deflowering cheerleaders in the old camper cabins, but broken hearts were assuaged (to Alfred's mind) by Jack's goodwill, high spirits, and occasional flashes of motherless heartbreak, discernible (again, to Alfred) in his tendency to gaze out across the lake, which was deep and cold, formed by glaciers, and populated by thousands of Canada geese in fall.

Miles and Jack Stevens remained close through college but had an angry rupture soon afterward. With his brother and his idol no longer speaking, Alfred lost touch with this fixture of his childhood.

As an undergraduate at SUNY New Paltz, Alfred formed a small cohort of friends who shared his contempt for the "bullshit" surrounding them. But after graduation in 2004, he grew disillusioned with these same friends' "pseudo-adulthood." On completing law school, they pretended to be lawyers, or to work at marketing firms or engineering firms or Internet firms that were just getting back on their feet after the dotcom bust. When a friend from college lost weight or got a nose job or began wearing colored contact lenses, Alfred corrected for these "disguises" with queries like: "Do you see yourself as a fat person who just happens to be thin right now?" or "Do you ever wonder if you chose the *right* nose?" or "Does my skin look green through those contacts?" Name changes were null to him; "Anastasia" was still good old Amy despite her threats to disinvite Alfred from her wedding if he persisted in calling her that, which she finally did after several warnings.

College friends drifted away at high speed, and Alfred was relieved to be rid of them and bereft without them. He'd taken a room in the apartment of an elderly couple on West Twenty-eighth Street in exchange for organizing their weekly pill dispensers, reading aloud their email, and typing their dictated replies. He worked in a bicycle repair shop and poured his every resource into making a three-hour-long documentary about the migratory patterns of North American geese. Entitled *The Migratory Patterns of North American Geese*, it was narrated in a voice completely free of artifice—that is to say, devoid of all expression. The film proved coma-inducing to all who attended the private screening Alfred paid for in Manhattan. Miles, a notorious insomniac, had to be forcibly roused when the film ended. Miles begged Alfred for a DVD of *Geese* to bring home to Chicago and watch at bedtime. Enraged and crushed, Alfred refused.

2

I first learned of Alfred Hollander in 2010, a year after *The Migratory Patterns of North American Geese* was completed. Alfred's father, Ted, hosted a discussion group with his second wife, Portia (Alfred's parents divorced the year he left for college), that I participated in while I was in graduate school at Columbia. I emailed Alfred several times requesting an interview for my dissertation, an examination of authenticity in the digital era. When he failed to reply, I sought him out at the bike shop where he worked. I found an affable strawberry-haired guy whose cheeriness had a hostile edge.

"With all due respect, *Rebecca Amari*," he said in a tone that made me wonder whether I'd invented that name, "why would I let you co-opt my ideas into some phony academic bullshit, just so you can get tenure?"

I explained that I wasn't at the point of seeking tenure, just my PhD and hopefully a teaching job somewhere, and assured Alfred of my intention to acknowledge his story as his own even as I worked to codify and contextualize the phenomena he described.

"No offense, but I don't really need you for that," he said.

"With all due respect," I replied, "I think you do."

"Why?"

"Because the only thing you've managed to produce so far is an unwatchable film about geese," I said. "No offense."

He put down the tool he was holding and tilted his head at me. "Have we met before?" he asked. "You seem familiar."

"We both have freckles," I said, and got a first genuine smile out of him. "I'm guessing I remind you of yourself. Plus, I'm the only person in the world as obsessed with authenticity as you are."

It was a year before I heard from him.

I already knew, from Alfred's father, that he had embarked on a project even more alienating and extreme than his middle school paper-bag-wearing had been. Its impetus dated to a morning in late summer when Alfred walked his dog, an adopted dachshund named Maple Tree, to a local elementary school on enrollment day. He informed two women who worked for the Department of Education that he wished to enroll Maple Tree in pre-K, then settled in to relish their bewilderment.

"She's really smart," he said. "She just learns differently."

"She doesn't have language, but she understands everything."

"She'll sit quietly and listen as long as you throw her one of these treats every few minutes."

The ladies, whose curved fingernails had been lavished with the nuanced paintwork normally reserved for museum-quality surf-boards, listened with barely repressed hilarity. "You want to enroll your dog in school," one intoned, her mouth twitching.

"What happens when the other children want to bring their pets to school?" the other rejoined.

"Is she potty-trained? We can't have anyone weeing on the floor ..."

"Does she know her letters or her numbers?"

Alfred noticed the ladies exchanging crafty glances and began to smell a performative rat. After surreptitiously applying lipstick, one said, "All right, honey, we've got a whole line of people waiting outside. Time to break through that fourth wall."

"What are you talking about?" Alfred asked, clutching Maple Tree to his chest.

"Is it on you, the satchel, or the dog?"

"I hope it's the dog," said the first. "I've been giving that puppy my best side."

At the discovery that Alfred had no hidden camera with him to record the absurd encounter—that they'd just wasted twenty minutes humoring a dolt, with no prospect of YouTube fame—the ladies tossed him out on his ass.

Thus Alfred's awakening to our Self-Surveillance Era.

Back in his room on West Twenty-eighth, he gazed despairingly into Maple Tree's amber eyes. In this new world, rascally tricks were no longer enough to produce authentic responses; authenticity required violent unmasking, like worms writhing at the hasty removal of their rock. He needed to push people *past* their breaking points. Even Mr. Quiet Supremacy had a breaking point, as Alfred learned when his oldest brother called him at SUNY New Paltz in a drunken, anguished state during Alfred's senior year—the first time he'd ever heard Miles sound hammered.

At the time, Miles was in his second year of law school at the University of Chicago and living with Jack Stevens, who had a job in banking. Their mother visited often—dating someone in Chicago, she told Miles, who liked that she kept the refrigerator stocked with fresh fruit. But the person she was sleeping with, it turned out, was Jack Stevens.

"Are you sure?" Alfred asked when Miles hurled this thunderbolt over the phone from a Holiday Inn he'd decamped to immediately upon discovering the truth.

"I can never think about high school again," Miles slurred. "Or home. Everything is ruined. It's . . . finished. Because it was all leading up to this."

"Look," said Alfred, thrust into the uncharacteristic role of Calming Agent, "it's not like anyone died."

"It is . . . One. Hundred. Percent. Like someone died," Miles said, tightroping the words. "It's like all of us died. You. Me. Mom. Dad."

"What about Ames?" Alfred asked, in an effort at levity. They all had a tendency to forget Ames.

Miles's enraged yell made him hold the phone away. "You don't get it, Alf! You're too weird, you're like Mom. Nothing means anything to you." And Miles began to weep, the first time Alfred could remember hearing his older brother cry. "They ruined everything," Miles sobbed. "There's nothing left."

The next day, Alfred received an email from Miles: "Hey Alf, sorry about the emotionalism on the phone. Who would've taken me for a nostalgic? Life goes on. Yours, Miles."

Miles didn't speak to their mother for over a year, at which point her relationship with Jack had ended. In the eight years since, Jack Stevens's name had not been spoken in Alfred's hearing. But he'd heard Miles cry in pain, and treasured the memory.

In some middle school science class there had been a unit on pain. Scientists studying pain had to inflict it without causing bodily harm, which they did using cold; hands thrust into frigid water hurt unbearably but are not damaged. This detail had so fascinated Alfred that he'd filled a bucket with water and ice cubes in the family basement and held his forearms under the surface until their acute aching almost made him puke. Yet none of it left so much as a mark.

Not long after the Maple Tree pre-K debacle, Alfred heard a scream outside his West Twenty-eighth Street window—not a yelp or a cry but a full-throated shriek that swamped him with shivery fear. He sprinted outdoors and found a woman cradling a brown Labrador puppy that had slipped its leash and run amid the wheels of a truck before managing to bumble free unscathed. Alfred stared at the puppy and its owner. There had been volume, emergency, terror. But not even the dog was hurt.

3

Alfred began, on occasion, to scream in public: on the L train, in Times Square; at Whole Foods; at the Whitney. He can recall, with remarkable clarity (for someone who was screaming), the tableaux of chaotic reaction that followed, although these descriptions are curiously inert for the listener, like hearing someone recount a dream. The exception is Duane Reade on Union Square, because of what happened after: Escorted brusquely from the store by two security guards, Alfred encountered a girl whose look of rapt curiosity had stood out among the panicked shoppers inside. Now she leaned against a wall, apparently waiting for him.

"What were you doing in there?" she asked, the very question thrilling Alfred. Most people would have said he'd been screaming, but Kristen had seen beyond that.

Over latkes and hot apple tea at Veselka, Alfred explained his screaming project. Kristen's enormous pale blue eyes blinked at him like the wide-open beaks of baby birds as she listened. She was twenty-four, still in the adventure phase of her move to New York City to work for a graphic design firm. Alfred was almost twenty-nine.

"How often does it happen?" she asked. "The yelling. On average."

"I prefer 'screaming,'" Alfred said. "Sometimes twice in a week. Sometimes not for a couple of months. Overall . . . maybe twenty times a year?"

"Do you do it with friends?"

"Most people can't tolerate it."

"Family?"

"Zero tolerance. That's a direct quote."

"As in, someone used the phrase 'zero tolerance' to address the issue of your screaming?"

"As in, they used it all together in an intervention to address the issue of my screaming."

"Wow. What happened?"

"I see less of them."

"Because you can't scream?"

"Because it depresses me to know they're using phrases like 'craves negative attention' to explain my project."

"Families," Kristen said with a roll of her beautiful eyes. Then she asked, "Do you? Crave negative attention?"

The café had mostly emptied and the apple tea had gone cold. Alfred sensed that his answer was important. He was vaguely aware of having left out the *need* he felt to scream at times, like an urge to yawn or sneeze. He hoped this went without saying.

"Actually, it's the opposite," he said. "I put up with negative attention in exchange for something else that matters more."

Kristen watched him alertly.

"Authenticity," he said, unfurling the word like an ancient, holy scroll. He almost never uttered it, lest overuse diminish its power. "Genuine human responses rather than the made-up crap we serve each other all day long. I've sacrificed everything for that. I think it's worth it."

He was encouraged by Kristen's look of fascination. "Do you do it during sex?" she asked.

"Never," he said, then added, with heady boldness, "That's a promise."

Eight months later, Alfred and Kristen were passengers on an Avis bus at Chicago's O'Hare Airport, en route to pick up their rental car. The bus was jammed with people trying not to topple against each other as it pitched around curls of highway and swerved to yet another stop to take on more passengers. Alfred and Kristen stood near the back.

A familiar tickle rose in Alfred. He tried to suppress it; after all, he was bringing his possibly (hopefully) serious girlfriend to a gathering at Miles's home to celebrate the christening of his second child. Their mother was flying in, and the plan was for Alfred and Kristen to stay at Miles's house and sightsee in Chicago for the weekend, including an exhibit of Japanese anime at the Art Institute that Kristen was dying to see. But invoking Miles made the ticklish urge impossible to repress.

Alfred released a short, ambiguous spurt of sound somewhere between a moan and a bark. Even Kristen, attuned by now to his screaming and well past the point of finding it charming, wasn't entirely sure he'd been the source. Only when she saw his face— the single face devoid of curiosity—did her blue eyes contract into a threat. But Alfred was already savoring the two opposing forces at work in his fellow passengers: a collective wish to shrug off the unaccountable sound, and a contrary intimation of dread. Thus the Suspension Phase, when everyone floated together on a tide of mystery whose solution Alfred alone possessed. He could have stopped there—had, on rare occasions when mystery and power alone had felt like enough. But not today. When mystery deliquesced into renewed bitching over the cramped ride, Alfred issued a second moan-bark: longer, louder, and impossible to ignore.

Now came the Questioning Phase, when everyone within range (except Kristen, who stared fixedly ahead) tried, discreetly, to assess the nature of his complaint. Had the sound been inadvertent, best met with polite oblivion? Or was it a cry of distress? Thus preoccupied, his fellow passengers fell into a childlike state of reception that was breathtaking to behold. They *forgot that they could be seen.* Alfred basked in their unselfconscious wonderment while also sucking in breath to the brink of explosion; then he disgorged the contents of his lungs in an earsplitting emission that was part roar, part shriek, which he drove like a stake into the unguarded faces around him. He howled like a wolf howling at the moon, except he wasn't looking up, he was looking *out* at his fellow travelers, whose panic, horror, and attempts to escape evoked the hysterics of passengers on an airplane plunging nose-first into the sea.

To observe such extremes in the absence of any real threat was not a delight. It was not a pleasure. It was a *revelation*. And once a person had had that revelation, he returned to daily life awakened to the fact that beneath its bland surface there gushed a hidden tumult. And no sooner had that awareness begun to fade than the seeker longed, with mounting urgency, to witness again that coursing cataract. Why else did Renaissance painters keep painting Christ on the cross (to use an example of Alfred's) and only in the distant background add diminutive folk hunched under loads of rocks and hay? Because transcendent death is what people want to see—not the hauling of heavy loads! And Alfred had found a way to achieve that revelation whenever he wanted without having to die, or kill anyone else!

There was nothing quite like that first scream, so said Alfred, who likened it to the initial gurgling sip of wine on the palate of an expert. But the last bit was important, too, and to get at that, he had to keep screaming. He had only one rule: *Don't interact*. His job was simply and only to scream and await the Something Happens Phase—"something" usually taking the form of a physical incursion. Alfred had been slapped, punched, tossed out doors onto sidewalks; had a rug thrown over his head, an orange wedged into his mouth, and a shot of anesthesia administered without his consent. He'd been Tasered, billy-clubbed, and arrested for disturbing the peace. He'd spent eight separate nights in jail.

About thirty seconds after Alfred's first scream, the Avis bus veered to the curb and the driver, a tall African-American man, parted the flailing crowd and strode to the back. Alfred braced for physical confrontation, being guilty of prejudice about Black men and violence despite a passionate belief that he was free of it. But the driver, whose name patch read "Kinghorn," fixed upon Alfred the laparoscopic gaze of a surgeon teasing muscle from bone as prelude to excising a tumor. His invasive scrutiny prompted a discovery for Alfred: Being studied, while screaming, was actually more uncomfortable than being thrown or punched or kicked. And that discovery yielded a second: Physical assaults, while painful, gave him a way to end his uninterrupted screaming. Which led to a third discovery: Screaming is *not* uninterrupted. In order to scream, one must breathe; in order to breathe, one must inhale; and in order to inhale, one must interrupt one's screaming.

"Did someone hurt this man?" Mr. Kinghorn inquired sharply during the first such interruption. Having discerned a united denial and noticed a pale, distraught face close at hand—Kristen's—he addressed her quietly. "Are you traveling with this man?"

"I was," she murmured.

"Does he have psychological issues?"

"I don't know," Kristen said wearily. "I think he just likes to scream."

Mr. Kinghorn injected into Alfred's next several inhalations: "Sir, you've made your racket for going on two minutes now . . . I'll allow you thirty more seconds . . . at which point you'll either have to stop hollering or leave my bus . . . Am I making myself clear?"

Alfred found himself nodding his compliance, a heinous breach of his "don't interact" rule. Mr. Kinghorn consulted his wristwatch— a big chunky diver's watch, or a skydiver's watch, a watch that could make you an omelet or teleport you into another millennium. Then he waited. But Alfred couldn't keep screaming in quite the way he had; Mr. Kinghorn's authority soothed the ravaged passengers, neutralizing the screams' effects. Alfred had a sensation like a tent collapsing; awash in fabric, he fell silent.

Mr. Kinghorn gave a curt nod. "Thank you, sir," he said. "I appreciate your willingness to pipe down. Now let us proceed."

His voice rose with these last words, a sonorous baritone filling the bus and apparently also people's hearts, for there was a round of applause. The bus swung away from the curb and soon was hurtling toward the Avis rental lot buoyed by communal jubilation that knew only three exceptions: Alfred, who drooped in mortified exhaustion from his bar; Kristen, who stared furiously at the bleak airport landscape; and Mr. Kinghorn, whose expertise at subduing disruptive passengers made it clear there was nothing so special about this one.

"I wonder what Mr. Kinghorn is like in real life," Kristen mused dreamily as they sat in their Avis rental, enmeshed in O'Hare traffic.

"Why don't you call the Avis office and ask for him," Alfred said sourly.

"You're not in a very good mood," Kristen said. "You've just indulged in your fetish; isn't that supposed to leave you flushed and a little high?"

"Let's forget it happened."

"I wish!"

Alfred sighed. "You used to like my screaming."

"I wouldn't say *like*."

"You used to believe in it."

"True."

"What changed?"

Kristen considered this. At last she said, "It got boring."

4

The misery of the drive to Miles's Winnetka house was surpassed only by the misery of being there: eating sandwiches on his brother's deck overlooking Lake Michigan, leaves sashaying from the trees and settling on the water like yellow lily pads. His mother had enfolded him in her jasmine-scented embrace. Introductions to Kristen had been made (followed by pointed, questioning looks that translated to: "She's lovely; it's a miracle; she must not know him well; or maybe she's off in some way we can't see . . . ?"). Inquiries about the travel from New York had been satisfied (vaguely), and there was the new baby, of course, and he was tiny, of course, and everyone wanted to hold him, of course, and although Kristen had been nervous to meet Alfred's family, now she seemed glad just to be away from people who were screaming. Alfred had forgotten that Ames was coming. But Ames was here, along with the usual amorphous tension that arose from the shadowy mystery of his career. That mystery had swelled in direct proportion to Ames's muscle mass starting a couple of years after 9/11, when he advanced from enlisted soldier to Special Ops. Now, at thirty-one, he was allegedly retired, but he'd bulked up yet more, spent most of his time overseas, and, at a mention of Bin Laden's recent assassination, seemed briefly unsure who that was.

Miles's Quiet Supremacy had hardened over the years into an exoskeleton, growing stiffer with each honor until he looked barely capable of motion, much less spontaneity. His every gesture seemed to Alfred an act of pretense, even concealment—why else did Miles's only genuine smiles seem to come when Trudy was taking pictures with her iPhone? Trudy was an avid Facebook poster, a touter of family vacations and toddler artworks, a coiner of sappy hashtags like #motherdaughterlove and #thankgoodnessforgrandparents that Alfred logged on to Facebook specifically to be enraged by. His antidote to such artifice was usually the memory of recent screaming, but today that led him to the Avis bus and his public defeat. It was impossible to imagine screaming again. The project was dead without warning, leaving—what? What could Alfred do or say or even think that would make it possible to sit on Miles's deck for one more fucking minute?

And then it came to him. He could ask a question.

"Hey, Miles," he said. "Are you in touch at all with Jack Stevens?"

Miles paused infinitesimally in the act of eating, like a jump in a video. "No," he said with deliberation. "I am not."

A heavy silence followed, which Kristen tried to alleviate by asking brightly, "Who's Jack Stevens?"

Miles's mouth made a grim line. Trudy looked at the deck. Alfred felt Kristen's panic at having said the wrong thing.

"Oh, honestly, Miles," their mother said. "Can we please be done with this drama?"

Susan (as Miles and Alfred had started calling their mother) looked younger than fifty-seven, lithe and ashy-haired in her blue wraparound dress and soft white sweater—younger, somehow, than she'd looked when they were children. Then she'd been Harried Mom, the kind who runs onto the baseball field between innings to rub sunscreen on your nose. Those moms were always a little comic in their bright clothes and oversize fanny packs, hacking up watermelons for the team. After the divorce she grew quiet, watchful, as if she no longer knew what role to assume. But with time she'd acquired a more knowing air and begun doing what she pleased. There was nothing funny about her.

"Jack Stevens was Miles's childhood friend," she explained to Kristen. "They were inseparable all the way through college and even after."

"I see," Kristen said gravely. "Did something . . . happen to him?"

"You could say that," Miles said with a mirthless laugh.

Their mother set her glass hard on the picnic table. "I'm sorry, that is a ridiculous thing to say."

"Oh. You're sorry?" Miles asked with mock surprise.

"You'd think we'd murdered someone, Jack and I!"

"I misunderstood. You're *not* sorry."

"Don't talk to Mom that way," Ames said very quietly. He was holding the newborn; cradled in his burly, veiny arms, it looked like a mouse engulfed by a python.

"Oh. Now I'm the bad guy," Miles said.

Alfred felt a sudden absence of pain, like the cessation of a toothache. "Does he still live in Chicago? Jack?"

Miles looked at his watch. "How long have you been here? Forty minutes? Forty-five?"

"Thirty-seven," Trudy said.

"You timed our arrival?" Alfred asked.

Miles and Trudy exchanged a glance. "We wondered how long it would be before you did something provocative," Miles said.

"Thirty-seven minutes is an improvement," Ames said, and everyone laughed except Miles.

"I don't think he's funny," Miles said.

"*I* was funny," Ames said.

"Portia is almost thirty years younger than your father," their mother said, addressing Miles. "Your half sister, Beatrice, is the same age as your daughter. But none of that is a problem. Gee, I wonder what the difference could be?"

"We didn't know Portia before Dad married her," Miles said.

"You're lucky I didn't marry Jack."

"*You're* lucky you didn't marry Jack. Or you wouldn't know your grandchildren."

Ames was on his feet with martial swiftness. "Don't. Talk. To Mom. That way," he said in a barely audible murmur. Trudy plucked the infant from his arms.

"Careful," Miles checked Ames. "His next topic might be what you do for a living."

"Now who's being provocative?" their mother said.

"I'm retired," Ames said with a smile. "More than happy to talk about it."

Miles tossed his sandwich over the rail of the deck. "Thirty-seven minutes," he said. He looked exhausted, dark swatches under his eyes, as if the idiocy of other people were sapping his life force.

"You haven't answered my question," Alfred said. "About Jack."

"Yes. As far as I know, he still lives in Chicago," Miles said acidly. "Why, are you planning to visit him?"

"I think I will," Alfred said, and stood up. "I think I'll visit him right now."

There it was: frank surprise in the faces around him, unguarded and pure—like kicking open a door and finding golden light behind it.

Alfred retrieved his satchel and glanced at Kristen, half expecting her to stay behind. But she joined him at the door.

"Wow," she said as they left the house. "Is it always like that?"

5

Back in the rental car, Alfred tried to avail himself of the vaunted intelligence of his new phone, but it seemed capable of telling him only that hundreds, perhaps thousands, of Jack Stevenses lived in the Chicago area. His momentum stubbed against this fact.

Kristen became gloomy. "Now what?" she asked. "Our luggage is inside your brother's house. Are we even going back?"

"Of course we're going back," Alfred said. "After we visit Jack Stevens." He was scrolling among Jack Stevenses fat and scrawny, young and ancient, grinning from real estate websites and glowering from mug shots. He had a smoldering worry that Jack was a nickname for John.

After a while, Kristen leaned over to look with him, and her curiosity energized Alfred. "There!" he said suddenly, after several more minutes. They peered together at a face: rakish, big smile, blurry in a way that suggested motion, or indecision. "That's Jack."

Kristen winnowed away possible addresses associated with this strangely obscure and scantly photographed Jack Stevens until one emerged as most likely: a western suburb that might not have been a suburb at all, Alfred thought, when they reached it forty-five minutes later, so much as a low-slung extension of Chicago. Modest freestanding houses lined the streets, identical in every detail down to a staggered trio of rectangular windows cut into each front door. The house was in the middle of the block. A red toy lawnmower and a small pink scooter rested on its square of grass.

They stepped from the car into a smell of lawn clippings and motor oil. The quiet felt abrupt, as if children had been playing there just moments before. Alfred experienced an old, prickling anticipation. Jack Stevens. Why had he waited so long to seek him out?

"I'm nervous," Kristen said as they approached the door. "What if he's angry?"

"Why would he be angry?"

"Some people don't like it when you show up at their houses unannounced."

"Jack isn't like that."

"You don't really know what Jack is like," she pointed out. "You haven't seen him since high school."

The doorbell made a three-tone sound, like actual bells. They waited, and Alfred pressed again. "He isn't home," Kristen said with audible relief.

"He can't be far. There's stuff on his lawn."

They sat on the front steps to wait. Alfred was surprised by the neighborhood's uniformity; it wasn't what he would have expected for Adult Jack. As if sensing his thoughts, Kristen said, "What's so special about this guy, anyway? Other than, you know. The thing with your mom."

"Jack was, like, legendary," Alfred said, but the word was a poor vehicle for the legendariness he wished it to convey. "People just— loved him. He brought out the best in everyone, and sort of . . . completed every situation he was in." He stopped, confounded by the difficulty of invoking Jack's magical effect.

But Kristen nodded in recognition. "I guess every high school has a guy like that."

She was wrong, Alfred wanted to say—*no* high school had a guy like Jack Stevens, only theirs and only him, but he hesitated to contradict her now that they were getting along again. She would have to see for herself.

After thirty minutes, a worn-out gray Buick pulled into the driveway, its driver hard to discern, small faces peeking from the back windows. The car passed close to Alfred and Kristen on its way to a garage behind the house. They heard an electric door judder open, then a flotsam of children's voices and the twang of a screen door. The family had gone inside through the back.

"This is so awkward," Kristen said. "Why didn't he stop?"

"He was parking," Alfred said, but he'd experienced a flicker of cold as the car drove past. He took Kristen's hand and felt her sweating. "Would you rather wait in the car?"

"No way."

A slightly older, slightly heavier, slightly balder, slightly more weathered variant of Jack Stevens opened the front door, eyes narrowed in the manner of a man anticipating conflict. He was holding a translucent pink-and-blue life preserver. "Help you folks?" he said tersely through a screen door, which he left shut.

"Hi, Jack. It's Alfred."

Jack's face underwent an evolution of expression, as if he were deciphering a rune. "Holy fuck," he said at last, pushing open the screen door and squinting out at them. "Hollander?"

"That's me," Alfred said, and reached out a hand, but Jack ignored it and clapped him in a bear hug. To enable this, Kristen took the life preserver. "Alfred Hollander?" Jack said, pulling away to look at him again. "What in Christ are you doing here?"

"This is Kristen," Alfred said. "We're visiting Miles, and we got curious about you."

Jack took the life preserver back from Kristen and shook her hand. "Come on in," he said. "Mi casa tu casa, if you don't mind my ex coming by pretty soon to pick up my kids."

They followed him into a dim carpeted living room. A boy and a girl sat on a couch in bathing suits, fiddling with a TV remote.

"No TV," Jack said. "I told you."

"But we swam," the girl pleaded.

"You swam great. But no TV."

"Twins?" Kristen asked.

"Yes, ma'am. Sally and Ricky. Kiddos, say hello to my old friends—well, old and new," he said with a wink at Kristen.

"Pleased to meet you," the children intoned, eyeing them warily.

"They're sad because it's almost time to go. Right, kiddos?"

"We're sad because we want to watch TV," the boy said.

"Story of my life," Jack said with a laugh.

He brought Alfred and Kristen each an Old Style, and they sat on folding lawn chairs in the paved space between the back door and the garage. Alfred gave a blunt accounting of his father's remarriage to Portia, a fellow art historian hardly older than Miles, and fatherhood to a toddler. Jack already knew of Miles's ascendency in Chicago's legal world. When it came to their mother, he nodded stiffly and said, "Good lady."

"What about Ames?" Jack asked, for Alfred had forgotten to include him. "Still the army?" He chortled when Alfred cataloged the "retirement" from Special Ops and cryptic overseas activities. "Go, Ames," Jack said.

For his own part, he told them, he couldn't complain. He'd been laid off a year into the recession and was doing part-time work to cover the bills, collection agencies perpetually on his ass, but he liked the easier hours, had sharpened up his bowling game and played in a league three nights a week, but most of all he just loved his kids, although he had to fight for time with them—his ex was greedy, everything was about her; unfaithful, too, but that was another story, and look at those beautiful kids, they were part her, he supposed, though it was hard to see. He wished he could move with them back upstate; Christ, he missed the lakes, Lake Michigan was more like an ocean, there were shipwrecks at the bottom, but he couldn't leave Chicago, no way—he'd camp out in his ex's lobby just to be near his kids . . . and then the three-toned doorbell sounded and the children cried, "Mommy!" and there was a sound of stamping feet inside the house. Jack set his can of Old Style in the chair's fitted cylinder, stood up heavily, and went inside.

Alfred and Kristen sat in silence as a murmur of voices drifted through the house from the front door to the back. He felt Kristen watching him. Finally, she said, "Alfred, this guy is a mess."

The voices grew strident. Alfred caught *Dan and I want to go away next month* and felt a tightness approaching pain in his chest.

"Can you not see that?" Kristen asked.

"Of course I see it."

"So? Why aren't you screaming? Or demanding that he cut the bullshit and admit he's a failure?"

The suggestion shocked him. "Why would I do that?" he said. "The truth is right there."

"Isn't it always?"

The argument crescendoed, then cut off. The front door shut decisively, and the removal of children's voices to outdoors left a vacuum inside the house. Car doors opened, closed. Alfred pictured Jack watching their departure through the small rectangular windows in his front door.

After a while, Jack reemerged with three more Old Styles. The grin flashed, and he eased himself onto the chair and took a long drink. The sun had dropped, leaving the sky a worn-out pink. A moon was already up, soft and translucent as a sea turtle egg.

"Sunsets are weird here," Jack said half-heartedly. "Compared to the lakes."

"Nothing is really like the lakes," Alfred rejoined with energy.

"What are they like? The lakes of Upstate New York?" Kristen asked, and turned her hungry bird's-beak eyes upon Jack.

He took another long sip, as if mustering the will to respond. "Well, the sky is bright," he said at last, "but there's this ring of dark trees around each lake. So even at night, you're looking up from inside that darker ring at a lighter sky."

"And the geese," Alfred said.

"Oh, the geese!" Jack said. "Christ, those geese."

"I made a film about geese," Alfred said.

Jack turned to him, alert to bluffing. "You did not."

"It's called *The Migratory Patterns of North American Geese*."

Jack began to laugh. "Come on."

"I spent five years on it," Alfred said. "But it didn't really work. I see that now."

The disclosure had a revivifying effect upon Jack. He leaned forward in his folding chair. "Okay: Act One, Scene One," he said. "Walk me through."

"'Strange as it may seem to humans,'" Alfred recited from memory, "'for whom performance has become an essential part of everyday life, animals are focused entirely on survival.'"

"You haven't got the tone right," Kristen said. "Too much expression."

"She's right," Alfred said. Assuming a robotic monotone, he went on, "'To a human, a goose's wish to return to its Canadian home may seem sentimental, but "wish" and "home" don't mean to a goose what they mean to a human.'"

Jack convulsed with laughter. "Was it all like that?"

"Three hours and seven minutes," Kristen said.

Alfred went on narrating without inflection until Jack wiped his eyes and begged him to pause. "Gotta take a—you know," he said, and went inside.

Alfred had been trying, impulsively, to cheer Jack up. But when Jack returned with a whole cooler full of Old Styles and Alfred resumed his parody, it felt different. He proceeded with a sense of perilous intention, as if he were dismantling *The Migratory Patterns of North American Geese* and setting it afire for Jack to warm himself.

It was then, in the act of parodying his life's work, Alfred told me later, that he decided to contact me. Maybe he'd known he would; he'd kept my card in his wallet for the year since we'd met. Now that he was junking and repurposing failed endeavors, why not offer up his screaming project for "some phony academic bullshit," after all? For that, he needed me.

But I needed him, too. Why study authenticity if not to seek it—try to wring some last truth from that word before it's so leached of meaning that it becomes a word casing: a shell without a bullet; a term that can be used only inside quotation marks? I needed Alfred to help me *avoid* writing some phony academic bullshit. This collaborative chapter, hybrid and unorthodox as it may seem in an academic context, represents that attempt.

In retrospect, then, there were three of us sitting with Jack Stevens behind his house on that midwestern fall night. Darkness swooped down and the moon rose and hardened and turned white. The hiss of highway sounded like wind, or the sea. Alfred wanted to sit there forever. He drew out the hilarity as long as he could sustain it, staving off the moment when Jack would say he needed to get to bed, and the party would stop.

A Journey

A Stranger Comes to Town

MILES

My cousin Sasha had lived in the desert for twenty years before I discovered she had become an artist. I was looking at her kids' social media stories, as I often did with people I used to know, to see how they'd aged and try to gauge their happiness, when I saw a post from her son: "Proud of my Mom," with a link to an article about Sasha in *ARTnews*. The picture showed dozens of hot-air balloons suspended above rambling, colorful sculptures stretched out across the California desert. According to the article, Sasha made these forms out of discarded plastic. Later she melted the sculptures down to create compressed bricks that had been displayed and sold, along with aerial photos of that same plastic in sculptural form, at art galleries.

Sasha! What the hell!

If anyone had required proof that life's outcomes are impossible to predict, this development would have supplied it. Sasha had been a fuckup all the way into her thirties: a kleptomaniac who'd managed to pilfer countless items from countless people over countless years. How did I know? Because right before she married Drew, in 2008, she started returning things. Everyone in the family received an item or two, sometimes of so little value that it was amazing Sasha remembered what belonged to whom. My dad got a Bic pen, the kind they sold in bags of twenty at Staples. I, too, received a pen, but mine was a Montblanc worth several hundred dollars. I'd nearly had a brain hemorrhage when it vanished after a family dinner at a Korean restaurant while I was visiting New York. I'd phoned the restaurant, the taxi authority, the MTA; I'd retraced my steps through Koreatown, bent at the waist to scrutinize gutters. When that very same pen showed up in my mailbox a couple of years later with a handwritten note that began, "Since my teenage years I have struggled with a compulsion to steal, which has been a source of great anguish to me, and of loss and frustration to many others," I called my dad.

"I know," he said. "I got a Bic. I'm not even sure it's mine, it might have belonged to the restaurant."

"Can we please be done with her, Dad?" I asked. "Once and for all? She's incorrigible."

"She's the opposite of incorrigible. She's making amends."

"I don't want her amends. I want her to disappear."

"What makes you say things like that, Miles?"

I remember exactly where I was standing when we had that conversation: on the deck of the lakeside Winnetka home Trudy and I had overleveraged ourselves to buy (she was pregnant with Polly, our first) and painstakingly decorated together: the site of a planned domestic idyll of children, holidays, and family reunions that we'd rapturously envisioned since meeting in law school at the University of Chicago. Holding my phone, looking out at twinkling Lake Michigan, I understood with sudden clarity that doing the right thing—*being right*—gets you nothing in this world. It's the sinners everyone loves: the flailers, the scramblers, the bumblers. There was nothing sexy about getting it right the first time.

Fuck Sasha, I thought.

I'm fully aware that Sasha emerges from these descriptions as sympathetic, whereas I come off as a moralizing prig. I *was* a moralizing prig, and not just toward my cousin. My father, who treated Sasha as a daughter and whom I saw as her enabler; my mother, whose romantic adventures since my parents' divorce I found sickening; my younger brothers, Ames and Alfred, both of whom I'd deemed "lost" before they turned twenty-five—no one escaped the roving, lacerating beam of my judgment. I can access that beam even now, decades later: a font of outraged impatience with other people's flaws. How had the human species managed to survive for millennia? How had we built civilizations and invented antibiotics when practically no one, other than Trudy and me, seemed capable of sucking it up and just *getting things done*?

If anything can be said in defense of the person I was in 2008, the year Sasha made amends and Polly was born—the year I turned thirty—it can be only that I was least forgiving of myself. Every move I made was aimed at harrying myself toward greater excellence. But certain things, like sleep, resist rigid control. In high school, my insomnia had made it possible to excel academically while also playing three varsity sports, working for a tree pruning company, and pleasing a finicky girlfriend. I bridged the gaps with peanut butter, which I ate by the jar, and teenage energy. But Polly was colicky, and by then I was the youngest partner in my law firm's history, and the workload was crushing. I started taking sleeping pills at night and Adderall in the morning to get me going—and eventually throughout the day to keep me sharp. When the Adderall made me jangly, I'd calm down with Xanax or Percocet in the afternoon before knocking myself out with more sleeping pills at bedtime. I saw this metabolic tinkering as nothing more than taking care of business, and the ease with which I chemically managed my deficits, coupled with a slight drug nausea I often felt, made me doubly impatient with everyone else. I became, as they say, "irritable"—hard to work for and harder to live with. My high standards intensified the pressure I felt personally, which meant that I wasn't home with our kids enough (three in five years, in keeping with our plan) or much of a partner for Trudy—who had suspended her law career to enable our childrearing—sexually or in any other way. All of which made me *more* irritable, because I sensed that I was failing when all I'd ever done, my whole life, was try to succeed.

To the naked eye, things still looked fine at that point. I was bringing in business and seeing it through, albeit at the cost of some popularity at my firm. At home, everyone seemed happy, as I reminded myself daily by checking Trudy's Facebook—later, her Instagram feed. She was a genius at capturing offhand moments and making them look iconic. Scrolling through her trips to the beach, the park, the zoo (often with our neighbor Janna and her four kids)—ice cream dribbling from chins; a video of crayoned pinwheels twirling in the breeze—I could actually feel my heartbeat slow, my blood calm. Any fragment of time I'd managed to wrest from work and spend with them was always front and center, and I gorged on Trudy's shots of Polly hugging me; of Michael, our older son, throwing me a ball; of me spooning mashed bananas into the mouth of Timothy, our baby. Everything was fine, I told myself, drawing deep breaths at my cherrywood desk in my towering, glassy office. They were still there, still happy—*we* were happy, all five of us in our beautiful home by the lake, exactly as Trudy and I had fantasized after making love between law school classes—just waiting for me to come back.

In 2013, with the opioid crisis exploding, my doctor—until then a trusting prescriber of whatever I told him I needed—abruptly put the screws on. The prospect of being cut off from my prescriptions awakened in me a naked terror: I could no more function without those pills than I could without oxygen. My sleep, my focus, my ability to work and relax—all of that would end; *I* would end. With a sense of having swallowed a stick of live dynamite whose fuse was rapidly burning down, I lurched through actions that seemed alien to me even as I took them: first groveling for my doctor to renew my prescriptions; then raising my fist at him and being dismissed as his patient; drawing skeptical looks from potential new doctors when I cataloged my needs (two sent me away with literature on treatment programs); driving to pill mills in surrounding towns where doctors who looked more strung out than I was wrote scripts with shaking hands; and finally, on learning that Illinois would soon be enacting a prescription drug registry to keep people like me from collecting scripts from multiple doctors, forking over several hundred dollars to a pill mill doc in exchange for an introduction to a bona fide drug dealer.

Damon and I would meet in our cars at an appointed corner and drive until we were able to stop side by side at a red light under one of several sets of elevated tracks whose dappled shadows obscured what took place below. We rolled down our windows and I tossed an envelope full of cash into his car. Damon, who could have passed for a junior litigator at my firm, tossed a baggie full of drugs through my window, flashed a grin, and off we drove. It was a triumph of efficiency! Why had I wasted so much time wrangling doctors? Damon sold the same brand-stamped pills I'd been taking from the start, and I had enough disposable income not to have to economize by chopping and snorting them, much less resort to hideous cheaper alternatives like crack and heroin.

I might have gone on indefinitely like that but for an unforeseen shift: The hidden life I'd been forced to cultivate seemed to open up a new, secretive channel inside me. I began to look forward to meeting Damon on Chicago's moldering underside; its rusted railways and exhausted yellow brick struck me as a more authentic substrate of the glass-and-steel towers where my lawyering took place. With Damon, there was neither pretense nor judgment. I needed drugs; he sold them. The thing itself—how often do we see it? Damon had clear skin, blue eyes, good teeth. He drove a brand-new silver Nissan Rogue. There was something familiar about him, and I wondered if we might have met before, in some other context. I wondered about the rest of Damon's life, even imagined trying to start a conversation with him in those few seconds when we both had our car windows down. I hadn't had a close friend since I fell out with Jack Stevens, and found myself craving male companionship.

Groping for a less transactional relationship with Damon, I texted him one Friday afternoon: "Plans this wknd?"

He responded immediately: "Anything u want bro."

"I meant u."

"Grls? Prties? U tell me & Ill make it happen."

"Tks," I wrote. "Good to know."

Apparently, it was hard to avoid a transactional relationship with one's drug dealer.

Our neighbors were having a cocktail party that night. At one point, looking for the bathroom, I opened the door to one of the kids' rooms by mistake. Janna, the hostess—Trudy's friend—was snuggled in a chair with three of her four kids, reading *Puff, the Magic Dragon*. She grinned at me, embarrassed, and said softly, "They sleep better when I do this." I closed the door and then stood in the hall with my forehead pressed against it, my eyes shut, listening to her husky voice.

. . . Together they would travel on a boat with billowed sail . . .

I'm aware that, in the telling, my love affair with Janna is hopelessly clichéd—its components so familiar from life, or Lifetime TV, that it could be written out mathematically. How to explain the enthrallment of living it? My family and work—so long the crux of everything I did—became thin topsoil over a deep, bitter root system where my real life took place. Once I'd entered that system, it was all I cared about. As with Damon (whom I patronized on an accelerating schedule), there was no pretense with Janna, no restraint. The thing itself. Seven kids and two spouses between us were nothing against our mutual longing, and we fucked in bathrooms, on cold sand by the lake after dark, and in Janna's basement rec room during the small hours when neither of us could sleep. I adored her with a heedlessness poor Trudy had never glimpsed in me; I'd never seen it in myself. I told Janna I would die for her, and I think I assumed I would have to; for all the fervor of our passion, it was death-infused from the start.

Four months into the affair, Trudy confronted me on our deck after the kids were asleep. Dry-eyed, she explained that she had tolerated my distraction and absence for years, believing it was all to the purpose of our shared domestic vision, but she'd mistaken my character. There was no room to negotiate; she had already filed for divorce and wanted me out of our house by the end of the week. As I listened, the pilot light of my terror roared into flame, and I was engulfed by a sensation of apocalypse. My hands shook too hard to hold a glass, so I shoved my head under the bathroom faucet and swallowed several Xanaxes to try to calm down. I texted Janna and waited outside her house in my car. It was October 16, 2014. With Janna beside me, I hurtled toward Chicago while trying to explain that the time had come for the two of us to run away together, but my speech was garbled and I was driving erratically and way too fast, which led to Janna pleading, then screaming, to be let out of the car and my refusing, all of which culminated in a single-car accident at ninety miles per hour on Lake Shore Drive. My car flipped, flew, and plunged into the shallow lagoon just south of Diversey Harbor. Mercifully, the water rose only to our chests and likely squelched the explosion of my nearly empty gas tank. But Janna's left leg was partially severed and crushed beyond repair, and had to be amputated at the thigh.

I have a metal plate where part of my skull used to be. My whole head aches before a rainstorm, and a taste of metal fills my mouth and gives me gooseflesh.

I never tried to reenter my old life. In fact, with each year—fifteen before Timothy went to college—I grew more incredulous that I'd ever lived it. I would gaze up at the glass office buildings in the Loop in a state of wonder. Had I really gone inside one every day? Parked my car in an underground garage? Doled out Christmas checks to security guards? When I passed my former partners on the street, or associates I'd once hounded, I would duck and cower to avoid being recognized. But gradually, I found that, with my longer hair and civilian clothes, the baseball cap I always wore to hide my metal plate, I was invisible to my former colleagues. No one gave me a second look, as if I'd fallen through a trapdoor into a parallel world. There seemed no way to cross back over. It was Trudy who drove to the Loop each day for work and made partner in one of Chicago's biggest tax firms.

Trudy soon remarried, and I took over with our kids. She largely supported me while I slowly paid off my debts; although Janna hadn't pressed criminal charges against me, she and her husband reunited and sued. I gave them everything, and more, in a negotiated settlement.

I worked as a counselor at a methadone clinic not far from where I used to make my drug buys from Damon. My studio apartment was nearby, and as I walked to work under those same shadowy overpasses where Damon and I used to roll down our windows, I often wondered what had become of him. I didn't have to wonder, of course—thanks to Own Your Unconscious™, we can track down a person we've glimpsed just once in our lives. My dad was a big proponent of Own Your Unconscious when it first came out, in 2016; he'd gotten to know Bix Bouton, who invented it. I had no interest in externalizing my consciousness to a Mandala Cube and revisiting my memories, or—worse—filling in what I'd managed to forget. Still, my curiosity about Damon gradually wore away my scruples. Doesn't it always? If my life has taught me anything, it's that curiosity and expediency have a sneaky, inexorable power. Resisting them is easy for a minute—a hundred minutes—even a year. But not forever.

In the thirteen years since Own Your Unconscious had been released, one of its ancillary features—the Collective Consciousness— had gradually become central. By uploading all or part of your externalized memory to an online "collective," you gained proportionate access to the anonymous thoughts and memories of everyone in the world, living or dead, who had done the same. Finally, I caved and bought Mandala's Hey, What Ever Happened To . . . ?™. The process was frictionless, as promised: thirty minutes with electrodes attached to my head as I closed my eyes and pictured my interactions with Damon (thereby releasing those specific memories to the collective); then a twenty-minute wait while my "content" churned in the collective gyre, searching for facial matches. As I watched the wheel spin on the desktop computer in my studio apartment, I noticed I was gritting my teeth; I wanted Damon to have achieved something great! What that meant, I wasn't sure: Stockbroker? Managing partner at my old law firm? Governor? (Illinois joke.)

I had the story soon enough in the form of scattered "gray grabs" from the Collective Consciousness: people's anonymous memories that included Damon. I watched teenage Damon in prep school slacks, whittling the underside of a desk; then slightly older Damon hyperventilating in a teen group therapy session in deep woods, firelight lapping his anguished face; young-adult Damon gazing out the window of a college classroom at a crisp white steeple, and around the same time (same haircut, sweatshirt), Damon hawking stolen stereo equipment from the rear of a Toyota hatchback; Damon as I knew him, a young man toiling for a drug dealer to pay off some kind of debt. The last gray grab, dated the previous year, showed Damon in orange, doing push-ups in a penitentiary yard. The smile he sprang at the anonymous viewer was the very same I remembered seeing through our open car windows. I realized that the person Damon had reminded me of was myself: another white male who'd managed to blow through countless advantages and opportunities and fail catastrophically. The knowledge that he'd fared worse than I had was depressing, literally. I became depressed. I hadn't realized how badly I'd wished for Damon to thrive.

In the recovery world, we often speak of outcomes: who succeeds in treatment; who relapses or disappears or dies. My ability to stay sober was more than explained by my ACE score, the metric for Adverse Childhood Experiences, which in my case was an almost unheard-of zero. Loving family; no incarceration, addictions, or domestic violence—all of which raised the question of why I'd turned to drugs in the first place. Was there some trauma I'd repressed? That was entirely possible; Own Your Unconscious has turned up all kinds of repressed brutalities, and thousands of abusers have been convicted based on the evidence of their victims' externalized memories, viewed as film in courtrooms.

But what I kept coming back to was my cousin Sasha. Her ACE

score would have been high: Her father, an embezzler, vanished when she was six. As a teen, she'd fled the country and drifted through Asia and Europe for a couple of years before my father tracked her down in Naples and persuaded her to come back. I saw now that Sasha's stealing was an addiction like my own. Yet she and Drew were still married, and their kids—even the boy, Lincoln, whom I remembered as being impossible—were reportedly fine. How had Sasha done this? Curiosity: I had to know. So I asked my dad to put me in touch with Sasha and wrote to her out of the blue, asking if I could come to San Bernardino County and see her sculptures. And she wrote back, more graciously than I deserved, and invited me to visit.

DREW

On our way to pick up Miles at the airport, Sasha and I try to figure out how long it's been since we last saw her oldest cousin. We both remember the occasion: a gathering at Sasha's mother's, in L.A., maybe a year before Miles's accident. I never liked him. He was the opposite of his dad, Sasha's uncle Ted, whom we both love. If I could pick a single expression to capture Miles Hollander's relationship to the world, it would be a wince. Sasha's tortured history made him wince. Our son, Lincoln, who was a difficult kid, made him wince. It was something to do with Lincoln that prompted my ultimatum: We were finished with Miles Hollander. Looking back, I see my own pathology on display: I hated having an "abnormal" son, a son who made people wince, because I thought it revealed something wrong in me. And it doesn't get much worse than being responsible for another person's death. I was an excellent swimmer—a lifeguard—but I'd just had a fight with the friend who followed me into the East River in our sophomore year at NYU. I was ignoring him. And by the time I realized that a current had pulled him out, he was too far away for me to reach him.

It might startle the average person to know how unremittingly these facts are still with me. You'd think the guilt would relax over thirty-six years, and for a time I thought so, too. But I hadn't counted on the circularity of life: the way it delivers us, with age, back to the beginning. I dream of Rob's drowning, I weep over it, would do anything to be exorcised of it. But how? Mandala's MemoryShop™ only really works for recent traumas: You externalize the portion of your memory containing the "event" and then reinternalize it with that part erased, overriding the original. But how can I erase awareness that has permeated every minute of my life since the event itself? I'd have to erase the life I've built, and I can't. I love it all too much.

Rob's folks passed away in the pandemic, just a few weeks apart. Before that, Sasha and I used to go to Tampa every couple of years to visit them. Rob was their only son (an older sister lives in Michigan), and it seemed to mean a lot to his mom and dad to see his college friends moving through our lives. They believed Rob and Sasha had been a couple, and we never corrected them—our goal was to give comfort, and our presence in their living room seemed to do that. The room never changed: clean white shag, cut-crystal ashtray, porcelain cats tumbling porcelain balls of yarn. Framed pictures of eighteen-year-old Rob in high school graduation pasteboard; at prom with a girl in gauzy pink; in football regalia, stripes of dark grease under his eyes. Only his folks altered with the years, their hair going silver, Robert Sr., a high school football coach, ultimately on oxygen for emphysema, both of them seeming to shrink on the couch cushions in a way that made the crystal and porcelain artifacts look bigger each year. It took me days to recover from those visits—to stop asking myself, and Sasha, how the Freemans' lives would have been different if their son were still alive.

"You assume it would have been better," Sasha said once. "But Rob's dad was really homophobic."

"Having someone alive is always better," I said.

Bix Bouton was the last person to see Rob and me before our East River swim. He got in touch with me out of the blue in 2016, when Own Your Unconscious was blowing up. Bix wrote that it was his memory of Rob, and that morning, and those years—his difficulty remembering them—that first spurred him to try to mass-produce a memory externalization device. It filled me with relief to know that Bix, whom I hadn't seen since NYU and who'd become, in the interim, a tech demigod on a first-name basis with the world, was still moved by Rob's death.

Not long after Bix got back in touch, Sasha and I went to New York to visit him and Lizzie. The four of us watched Bix's memory of April 6, 1993, on separate headsets. Bix started rolling as we arrived at the East River, at sunrise. "Gentlemen, good morning," came Bix's voice, and there were Rob and me through Bix's eyes: two shaggy-haired nineteen-year-olds. *Kids,* was my first thought. As a parent, I saw Rob with aching clarity through the screen of his reddish stubble: his exhaustion and worry, an edgy eagerness to please that his irony couldn't conceal. At one point he lifted up his arms in a stretch and I caught the old football bulk, the ridges of pink scar tissue inside his wrists. And then there was the part I'd failed—or maybe refused—to see at the time: a tenderness when Rob looked at me, a trusting admiration that was obviously love. I wished, fleetingly, that Bix hadn't silenced the thought-and-feeling portion of his consciousness; I wanted to know if he'd seen it. Would Bix have recognized the fumbling proposition Rob made to me, some twenty minutes later, as inevitable?

But the real torture was watching my nineteen-year-old self: cocky and full of hope, unaware that *within the hour,* I would begin the "after" portion of my life, in which I would try, endlessly and futilely, to atone. *Gentlemen, good morning.* We watched the memory again and again. I was clutching Sasha's hand, and I felt her weeping. But repetition dulled her response, and at some point she and Lizzie removed their headsets and took a bottle of wine up to the roof deck.

I had to keep watching. There was something I needed to pinpoint in the lull, that last pause before Rob and I waved goodbye and began walking south along the river in the blinding metallic early-morning sunlight. And then we were out of sight; Bix had turned and was walking toward the Sixth Street overpass, heading to his apartment on East Seventh Street.

"Wait. Stop," I couldn't keep myself from exhorting him. "Turn around! Call us back—stop it! Stop it! Stop it!"

I realized I was shouting only when Bix switched off my headset and lifted it gently away.

We wait outside a chain-link fence for Miles to come off the plane. He was bound to look different after fifteen-plus years, but the sight of him stooped under a faded Cubs cap is a shock. As he makes his way toward us, smiling nervously, I notice a slight thoracic scoliosis, a hint of jaundice in his eyes. I'm trying to break the diagnostic habit now that Sasha and I are in our mid-fifties. Friends and acquaintances have begun to be unlucky, and I've learned the hard way that detecting illness early puts me in a bind. "You saying I look like shit, Doc?" I've been asked, only half in jest. And there was my close friend and tennis partner, Chester, who was treated successfully for a lymphoma I suspected before anyone else. But for reasons I can't comprehend, our friendship suffered. Chester avoids me now and plays tennis with other people.

Conversation is easy in the car, with Miles catching up on the extended family. I'm surprised at how out of touch he is with most of them. As he stares through the backseat window, I wonder if he's ever seen an American desert. I never had.

Back at the house, we chat about improvements we've made to the place in the twenty years we've lived here. Miles points his questions at me, and when I defer to Sasha—he's her cousin, after all—she replies to me rather than Miles. I feel like a diplomatic translator.

This watchful, tentative version of Miles is so unlike the wincing jerk I recall, it's like a stranger has come to stay with us. Leading to the question: What is he doing here?

I'm itching to get to my medical clinic, where there's always more to do and it always matters. But I've learned to resist that impulse. Years ago, when Sasha and I were struggling with Lincoln, my habit of "fleeing" to my clinic almost cost me my marriage. Since then, I've subjected my impulses to leave for work to a three-step protocol: 1) Is it necessary that I go *at this moment*? 2) Is there something at home that I want to avoid? 3) Will I be letting anyone down by leaving right now?

A quick application of my protocol informs me that I won't be going to the clinic until tomorrow.

I carry Miles's small suitcase—its size hopefully indicating a short stay—to our guest room and check the corners and under the bed for scorpions. I find Miles alone on our back porch, staring into the distance. "They're so quiet," he says, and I realize he means the hot-air balloons floating a few miles to the west. "Are they all up there to look at Sasha's art?"

"Not necessarily," I say. "The art looks beautiful from above, but so does the desert."

"Can you look at the art without being in a balloon?"

"Absolutely," I say, lunging for some way to pass the time. "We can take a look now, before dinner, if you don't mind a walk."

MILES

We left Sasha chopping vegetables in the kitchen. She looked the same—willowy figure, eyes narrowed against the sun, red hair gone pale with gray. But I was uncomfortable around her, and I sensed that she felt the same. My journey to visit Sasha, to *understand* Sasha, had been the focus of weeks of anticipation, but the logic for my visit seemed to evaporate the second I got off the plane. Why come all this way to see a cousin I'd never really known or liked?

In what she clearly meant to be a happy surprise, Sasha told me that Beatrice, my half sister from my father's second marriage, would be coming to dinner that night. Beatrice had graduated from UCLA the year before and become close to Sasha's family in her time there. But the prospect of seeing Beatrice filled me with shame. I hardly knew my half sister. And what could she know of me beyond my spectacular failure?

Once Drew and I left the house, I began to settle down. The sun was low, the light rosy, the scrubby flora a parched, iridescent silver. The emptiness of the desert felt biblical, as if nothing had ever happened there—as if all of history were yet to come. To my relief, Drew seemed content to walk in silence. Maybe we shared an impatience with small talk, being a heart surgeon and a drug counselor. The body and its needs: the thing itself. Beyond the tragedy of Drew's college years, I knew little about him, but the not-knowing was comfortable. I found that I wanted to know him.

My first thought, when we happened on a flailing assemblage of colored lawn chairs, was that someone had dumped a pile of trash in the desert. Then I got it. "Is that a . . . sculpture?"

Drew laughed. "Part of one. They connect over a large area."

"And it's . . . all plastic?"

"Yep. Refuse from our whole county."

"Sasha . . . attaches it together?"

"She designs a lot of it," Drew said with evident pride. "But she and the other fabricators are a co-op; when collectors or museums acquire the bricks and photographs, everyone divides the proceeds."

We followed a tributary of bright blue pipes that seemed a lurid blot upon the landscape. Eager to conceal my reaction, I asked, "How did she start?"

"Well, she's always liked collecting things," Drew said, and then, as if overhearing my caustic internal reply—*Oh yeah. She collected a few things from me*—he said, "I'm guessing you know what I mean." I nodded, chastised.

"When the kids were little, she made sculptures out of their old toys," he said. "Also collages out of paper artifacts: receipts, ticket stubs, to-do lists. And it just sort of evolved from there."

Acid commentary bubbled up in me as we followed the trail of trash:

Recycling: how original!

The only thing more beautiful than these "sculptures" would be the desert without them.

We reached a section of plastic bags: bags inside bags inside bags inside bags, tens of thousands of crinkled plastic membranes crammed inside huge cracked plexiglass boxes that resembled gargantuan ice cubes.

"It all gets melted?" I asked.

"Everything. Monitors gauge the breakdown of the plastics with surface swabs to make sure they don't leach."

Hey, I have an idea: How about recycling this crap WITHOUT spreading it all over the desert in the first place?

Is there a direction we can walk where I DON'T have to look at this stuff?

The balloons floated overhead like silent sentinels. I had a guilty fear they were reading my thoughts.

You're sure they're not up there trying to ESCAPE from the art?

But I kept my mouth shut.

DREW

By the time we get back to the house, I'm having an uneasy feeling about Miles. I have to keep slowing my pace not to leave him behind, and he's still breathing hard: troubling in a guy who was once such an athlete. I can't tell whether he hates the art or doesn't know what to say, and it irks me to have to wonder. All of which awakens a Pavlovian wish to go to my clinic, followed by the knowledge that I can't—that my patient is right here, panting beside me after a two-mile walk. But I don't know what's wrong with him, or how to fix it.

At dinner he hangs back, watching the rest of us laugh around the firepit. I'd looked forward to showing off Lincoln—graduated early from Stanford and working nearby in tech—and Alison, who everyone loves, a junior at UCLA. But Miles's awkward solitude makes me feel petty for having craved these triumphs. He hardly interacts with Beatrice, his half sister, and I wonder if it's shyness—whether Sasha and I should be asking him more about what he's doing. But Miles's history makes those questions feel loaded, or patronizing, and anyway, we're all in our fifties—do people even ask what we're "doing" anymore? Hasn't that already been decided?

The young people drift indoors, and the topic turns to a group of art collectors visiting tomorrow, from Virginia. They're what I call the hardy rich—the types who climb Kilimanjaro, occasionally even Everest. They'll want to do the predawn balloon launch, no question. Afterward, they'll walk the sculptures with Sasha and decide how many pieces they want to buy.

"I'd like to try riding in a balloon," Miles says. "Do you think there might be an extra spot?"

"I doubt it," I say. "They book up months in advance."

I feel Sasha's perplexity. "There's usually a no-show or two," she says.

"I wouldn't know," I say. "I've never done the predawn launch."

"Why don't you both go?" Sasha suggests, and it's like the old days—Sasha urging me toward our difficult son, me frantic to escape. I feel a blast of frustration with Miles for bringing all of that back.

"No need on my behalf, Drew," he hastens to say, and I suspect my resistance must be palpable.

"Not at all! Let's go together," I say with a heartiness only Sasha will know is forced.

Later, in bed, she smooths my forehead with her cool hand. "He's had a hard time, Drew," she says. "Is it too much to ask you to be patient with him?"

"He's not our son. I don't know him, and neither do you."

"He's family," she says. "Isn't that enough?"

Two hours before dawn, Miles and I meet in our dark living room and head to the car for the hourlong ride to the balloon staging area. I'm not inventing a need to be in my clinic; overnight texts have persuaded me that I can't take time for a balloon ride this morning. I'll get Miles situated and continue on to work.

Miles's excitement crowds the car. "I've never ridden in a hot-air balloon," he says. "Is it scary?"

"Not like skydiving."

He turns to me suddenly. "I haven't done something new in a long time," he says. "Can you believe I've never been to France?"

"One step at a time."

We park by a big stretch of gravel where around twenty semi-deflated "envelopes" droop against the ground, barely illuminated by small fluorescent lights. The Clubhouse is both spartan and lavish—the tricky balance required by the hardy rich. My distrust of the wealthy and the famous is prejudice, I'm well aware. But my patients have so little—they'd inherit the earth today if there were any justice. It's a godsend that Sasha likes dealing with collectors. She dresses up and paints on eyeliner like when she worked in the music industry, and the Sasha I fell in love with back in college is resurrected. No one can resist her.

Miles is told he's first in line for an empty spot, and he shakes my hand goodbye. "Thanks so much for the ride, Drew. I hope I haven't cost you too much sleep."

"Not at all," I say. But as I'm leaving the Clubhouse for my car, I consider what will happen if Miles *doesn't* get a spot. Everyone at home is still asleep; who will come get him?

So I wait with him, drinking excellent Colombian coffee while the hardy rich congregate in their costly cold-weather layers and fine haircuts. When they begin dispersing to their assigned balloons, Miles learns that everyone has shown up—there's no room for him. He can try again at one p.m. Visibly crestfallen, he shakes my hand and urges me on with my day, insisting he'll wait. I'm faced with a choice between driving him back to the house, directly out of my way, or leaving him to idle here for hours.

The balloons have begun to inflate, their bright patterns flattened by the dim fluorescence into shades of gray. I go to the desk. "I'm Drew Blake," I tell the shining young person seated there. "Sasha Blake's husband. I'm here with her cousin from Chicago. Any strings we can pull to get him a ride?"

Her face, initially shuttered, springs open in welcome, and she promises to try. I ask myself which feels worse: knowing people or not knowing anyone.

"Good news, Dr. Blake," my new friend tells me a few minutes later. "We're sending up one more. There's room for both of you!"

"I can't go," I tell her shortly. "I have to get to my clinic."

At her fleeting disappointment I repent my curtness. "Well, it's balloon five," she says. "He'll have it all to himself."

Miles's happiness is so palpable that I feel it, too: a burst of physical relief at exchanging letdown for adventure. "Number five," I tell him. "Have fun."

He shakes my hand for the third time and hurries outside. A first intimation of blue pulses along the mountaintop. I follow Miles to make sure he finds his balloon. Most of the baskets hold several passengers, but number five is empty except for a pilot, who helps Miles climb in.

The pilot turns to me. "I'm not coming," I tell him, and the man's momentary surprise, coupled with the solitary slope of Miles's shoulders (his back is turned), impales my heart like a spear. Even as I remind myself, wildly, that I've more than fulfilled my obligation,

I find myself aping the motions of a man overcome by irresistible temptation: I seize two of the cables and hoist myself up and over the top of the balloon basket, almost kicking the pilot in the head. "What the hell," I bellow. "You only live once!"

Miles whirls around, startled and visibly nonplussed. The indifferent pilot brushes dust from his coat with a gloved hand. Neither gives a shit what I do; I've imagined that entire drama. And now we're off.

MILES

From below, hot-air balloons look very still. So the first surprise—after Drew came crashing into the basket—was our swaying, shuddering rise. I felt nauseated as we pitched in the wind, and remembered that all I'd had that morning was coffee. I opened the breakfast box I'd taken from the Clubhouse and crammed a granola bar into my mouth. As we pendulated up, our relationship to the light began to shift, and I realized that all staged brightenings—in movies, in plays—are efforts to capture this first brightening: day dawning on earth. The thing itself. The desert sneaked into view in patches still devoid of color. I ate an egg burrito and gazed down, dimly aware of Drew and the balloon operator chatting behind me. I decided it was a good thing Drew had come along after all: They could talk to each other, and I could sightsee in peace.

By the time the sun nudged at the mountaintop, we were high above the desert. It felt strange to be in the open air at such a height; the intermittent hum from the balloon's burner wasn't like an engine noise, and I could hear birdsong from below. As I drank from my water bottle, the sun's upper edge cleared the mountain and dropped its light on the world below. In that instant, a skein of brilliant color snapped into view: Sasha's sculpture. From the ground, it had seemed a hodgepodge, but from my new height, it acquired structure and logic, like random scribbles aligning into prose. Skipping lines of color raced through the desert, skittering and twisting, backtracking, thickening, then scattering almost away: a skylarking utterance of surpassing joy that rushed up from the land and encompassed me. Where the sculpture gave way, the desert looked empty.

Tears broke in my eyes, and I pulled down the bill of my cap. "Look," I said to Drew. "Look what she did."

Drew, too, appeared spellbound. "I can't believe I've never seen this at sunrise," he said.

As I gazed down, reading Sasha's buoyant testimony, my mind broke free like our hot-air balloon lifting away from the earth. From my new height, I saw my life with brute simplicity; my overweening pride and contempt, and then my failure, so much failure—failure everywhere I looked. I had tried, Lord, I had tried. But it wasn't enough; it was nothing. My children were grown and whole and didn't need me; were perplexed by me, I often felt. I was alone, had been ebbing away for years in a purgatory that seemed, from this height, more dire than death. There was nothing to go back to.

Tears muddled my vision, blurring Sasha's sculpture. Each time I blinked, its colors winked back at me in code: *Here. Now. Enough. GO!*

I seized one of the braided steel cables and hoisted myself over the basket's edge, a mix of cold and warm air splashing around my dangling legs. For a fraction of a second I balanced there, my mind vacant with hypnotic purpose. Then I let go. There was a brief, horrifying drop, my body beginning to accelerate, and then something—the crook of an arm, it seemed—caught me under the chin and clamped my head against the side of the basket. I cried out, choking and flailing from my neck. Gravity gulped at my legs and seemed about to tear my body from my head when I felt whoever was holding me begin to tip out of the basket. Then a metal hook, or brace, caught me under my left armpit and jerked me up and over, flipping me backward into the basket, where I smashed headfirst on the bottom. My skull plate juddered, and a rush of metal singed my mouth and nose and eyes. I blinked through a strobe of stars and saw Drew leaning over me, panting like a madman. He hit the side of my face and sat down hard on my chest.

"No, you don't, you fucker," he breathed, and hit me again. "No, you don't."

"Get off him," the pilot yelled, yanking at Drew. "He's passing out."

"Let him."

"You saved his life and now you're gonna kill him?"

Through the windows of the psych ward, where I was transported by ambulance, the scrubby desert mountains resembled a painted backdrop. I stared at those mountains to avoid looking at my shaken children and frightened parents (now both in their seventies); my brothers, Ames and Alfred; Trudy, who held my hand and asked if I needed more money. All of them wanted to help, and their tenderness filled me with despair for having brought them yet more sorrow and disappointment. Failure upon failure. I wept uncontrollably, and the doctors scrambled for some better way to stabilize me. It took almost three weeks.

There was one exception to my remorse: the man who'd saved my life. I hated Drew for having thwarted my bold urge, which now had abandoned me. Drew hated me for, as he put it, trying to kill him within twenty-four hours of my arrival. Now we shared the booby prize for his heroic act: a person no one wanted, not even me.

Our blunt exchanges of enmity began while I was still an inpatient, but it was after I was discharged and back in Drew and Sasha's guest room (whose windowsill she had lined with flowering cacti to cheer me up) that we gave full vent to our mutual loathing. I shouted at Drew through the desert silence, and he shouted back at me. Sasha begged us to stop, demanded we stop, and stormed out of the house when we ignored her. We couldn't stop. One night, as we raged at each other across their deck, Sasha began spraying us with a garden hose the way Trudy, back in Winnetka, used to douse fighting cats. Stunned, we covered our heads until, helpless and waterlogged, we both began to laugh. That was a turning point. "Do I need to get the hose?" Sasha would ask when she sensed us drifting into conflict. Drew had begun forcing vitamins on me in the hospital; at his house, he imposed a high-protein fresh-food diet and enrolled me in a punishing course of physical therapy. As my color improved and I worked on my limp, I caught Drew eyeing me now and then with a look I struggled to name. Then I got it: curiosity. I was fifty-one. Whatever I did with the rest of my life would belong to Drew as much as me. My actions mattered immediately and directly. This discovery roused my old ambition; I felt it prickle to life like a limb so long asleep, I'd forgotten it.

I returned to Chicago nine weeks after leaving. On the ride from O'Hare to my apartment, I gazed at the sparkling buildings downtown and felt my failure and exile slide back around me. Nothing had changed. The act of entering my studio was forensic, like visiting a crime scene. The stale air had a faint toxic sweetness. I was afraid that if I went to sleep there, I would never wake up. So I stayed awake, organizing my possessions overnight and arranging for them to be boxed and shipped to Drew and Sasha's house. I left keys and instructions and money in an envelope for the super, and hoped for the best.

Dawn had barely broken when I got back on the Blue Line to the airport. As I watched the illumination of the Chicago sky, I was dreaming of the desert. I wanted to fill its emptiness with a different story than the one I'd lived so far. Like Sasha had.

I rented a room in town and began studying for the California bar, feeling a rumbling return of my old appetite for arguments and statutes. Within a few months, I was doing legal work for some of Drew's indigent patients. At the end of my first year, I was elected mayor of our San Bernardino town. If these victories seem improbable, I invite you to recall the narrative power of redemption stories. America loves a sinner, lucky for me.

Drew and I never talk about our odd history, but I think my "success," and any good I've managed to do, have brought him gladness. Sasha tells me, during her long hugs that I've come to depend on, that I've helped him to relax. After our twice-weekly tennis games, Drew usually stops and has a beer with me rather than bolting straight back to his clinic. When the balloons are out, as they often are, we raise our glasses at the sky before we drink.

Rhyme Scheme

M has four primary freckles on her nose and approximately twenty-four secondary freckles. I say "approximately" not because her secondary freckles can't be counted—few things in this world can't be counted—but because I can't stare at M's nose for long enough to count her secondary freckles without making her uncomfortable. Her hair is thicker than the hair of 40 percent of the women who work among us and longer than 57 percent, and she wears hair bands 24 percent of the time, scrunchies 28 percent of the time, and her hair loose 48 percent of the time. She is exactly one week older than I am—25.56 to my 25.54—a fact I learned from the icebreaker our team leader, O'Brien, conducted during a taco party he hosted at his house for our whole team when we first became a team. Each of us gave the date, time, and place of our birth, and O'Brien plotted our data on a dynamic 3D Earth model and slowly rotated it so that we could see all forty-three team members ping into existence over the course of our aggregate age span. In the model, M and I seemed to come to life at the same instant.

I've crowdsourced M's prettiness casually among members of our team's larger unit under the pretense of trying to decide, as a single heterosexual male, whether or not she is pretty, but in actuality to gauge the breadth and strength of my competition. Of the 81 percent who found M pretty, 64 percent are not competitive, being males or nonbinaries attached to or interested in other people, or else females—of whom the 15 percent who identify as gay or bi are not a threat because M is "straight." Obviously, I recognize the existence of a spectrum of desire between straight and gay, but placing M on this spectrum would require either an honest reporting of her sexual history, which I am in no position to acquire, or gray grabs of M's sexual memories and fantasies from the collective—an act of such grotesque personal violation that she would justifiably revile me afterward, thus defeating the point.

Of the remaining 36 percent male or nonbinary respondents who might conceivably compete with me in pursuing a relationship with M, fully half possess at least one possibly-to-likely-disqualifying personal trait: 14 percent = noticeable body odor or other personal hygiene violations (nose picking, ear drilling, etc.); 11 percent = online warlordry; 9 percent = old (over thirty-five); 7 percent = radically self-obsessed; 6 percent = obsessed with Bix Bouton; 3 percent = prone to miscellaneous offenses, including engaging in Iraq War re-enactments, telling sexist jokes, smoking cigarettes, or wearing bandanas. Okay, that last one is a pet peeve of mine but probably not M's. I hate bandanas.

Now to the remaining 18 percent of poll respondents who represent possible competing contenders for M's affection. And here is where the data begin to fail, because how can I calculate whose chances are best? The key to M's heart may lie in something quirky and impossible to predict without intimate knowledge of her background and memories and psychological state—which, again, I could acquire only invasively. Maybe the person who brings M a blue stuffed hippo will be the one she falls in love with, and which of us will do it? *I* will do it. I see a blue stuffed hippo at Walmart and think, *Maybe this is* x: *the unknown value required to secure M's love.* And then I have the same thought about a small ballerina music box. And then I have the same thought about some really long tulips that are actually made of silk. And then about a packet of rubber bands all different colors, and then about some things I pick up off the ground and even from the trash, always with the thought, *Any one of these may be* x—that ineffable, unpredictable detail that makes one person fall in love with another person.

Now, given that I am a counter—or, to put it professionally, a senior empiricist and metrics expert—it is reasonable to ask whether, by taking enough random cracks at assigning a value to x, I will statistically improve my chances of making M fall in love with me. The answer is "yes and no." Yes, because perfect bone marrow matches can be found between total strangers by sorting through enough random donor data. No, because I would have to devote the rest of my life (assuming an average American male life span) plus eighty-five more years solely to the task of acquiring random objects before I would increase my statistical likelihood of finding the "right object," at which point M and I would both be dead. And all of this assumes that x is an object, which it may not be!

And acquiring a large box full of random objects, as I now have done, presents hazards of its own. Suppose M is a minimalist who regards acquiring heaps of objects as a disqualifying personal trait the way that, for me, bandana wearing would be? She may react like my sister, Alison, who sees the box containing the hippo, etc., in my living room and says, "What the hell, Lincoln, you're turning out to be exactly like Mom." And although we adore our mother, Alison does not intend this observation as a compliment. What she means is that I'm stockpiling random meaningless objects, and she is right, but she is also wrong, because every object has a history and a relationship with other objects and is therefore meaningless only until you have assigned a meaning to it.

Assigning meanings to my heap of objects would require handing each one to M and asking whether it caused her to fall in love with me. But honest reporting is hard to achieve without anonymity, and a person falling spontaneously in love with the lanky (but *very* fit) bearded empiricist and metrics expert currently handing her objects from a box in his living room might not want to admit it to his face—might not even be able to assign language to the storm of feeling within her when he hands her a blue stuffed hippo (for example).

In order to neutralize M's self-consciousness, I would have to veil my project in the guise of a study. I'd say, "M, I'm hoping you'll participate in an experiment that involves graphing your physical responses to a seemingly random array of objects, using several sensors that you may attach privately and by yourself in my extremely clean bathroom that makes me a statistical anomaly to the crowdsourced opinion that twenty-something-year-old bachelors are slobs: one sensor on your carotid artery, three around your heart, one midtorso, and one inside your vagina. Okay?"

No, that's going too far. We'll stop at the midsection.

"Sure, Lincoln, no problem," M replies (in my fevered imagination). And so we begin. And what does x turn out to be? The rubber bands? The hippo? The small china cat I found at a garage sale and bought because of crowdsourced data that girls like cats? Maybe none of it works, maybe I'm watching a series of lines whose fluctuations are all within the range of normal, and at last I say, "Okay, we're done here; would you like some cookies and milk?" And the cookies are homemade because I like to bake—another way in which crowdsourced data on twenty-something bachelors fails to describe me—and I pour M a glass of milk and put two cookies on a plate, oatmeal–chocolate chip, because by eliminating the raisins you can merge the two genres perfectly, and I bring the cookies and milk to M, and she takes a bite, then a sip, and she says, "Thanks, Lincoln, these are really delicious," but I can hardly hear her voice over the ringing alarm on my seismograph, even though it wouldn't be a seismograph and they don't have alarms it makes a better fantasy, and the lines are swerving off the graph because M has fallen in love with me *right at that moment*, it was the cookies and milk that did it! And now x has a value and the equation can be completed and M is mine, to hell with the rest of that 18 percent, to hell especially with the single member of that 18 percent who is truly, undeniably threatening: namely, M's boyfriend, Marc.

Why does it feel significant that both their names start with M?

M has been dating Marc for five months, six days, and 2.5 hours, setting the inception of their relationship at the moment Marc walked into her cubicle and asked her to lunch and she said yes. At the six-month mark, they will have a 32 percent chance of taking a more permanent step such as marriage, so I am tracking the days carefully—in part because a permanent step in the relationship between M and Marc will prompt my immediate death. I have no data to back this up, but I'm certain of it.

Knowledge is power, so they say, and yet any counter will tell you that merely possessing data, in itself, is neither useful nor predictive. Does it help me to know that, in the roughly 5.224 months they have been dating, M and Marc have spent the night together approximately one out of three, or 53.07, nights? Assuming that they're having sex on all of those nights, and twice on, say, half of those nights, it's likely that they've had sex in the neighborhood of 79.6 times. Note that I've moved from observations to estimates despite the fact that my cubicle and M's cubicle share a partition. I made this switch in order to free myself from the need to note whether M and Marc arrive at work together. I have chosen (with Alison's help) to desist from this particular data collection for two reasons: 1) It was distracting me from the data collection that is my actual job, thus compromising my performance to an extent that prompted my team leader and friend, O'Brien, to speak to me about it twice. 2) Because this data collection was edging me into the role of creepy voyeur.

Last Halloween, M came to work in a teacup costume. It says a lot about a person that she could come to work dressed as a teacup. I wondered whether Marc would come to work dressed in a complementary costume, like a teapot. I spent the morning in a state of frenetic dread, eager to see what Marc would be wearing, yet afraid to see. *If he is dressed as a teapot,* I thought, *I will give up my crusade to win M's love.* But it turned out that Marc wasn't wearing any costume at all. I became elated when I saw this. *It's over,* I thought; *there's no hope for this relationship. Marc cannot understand this teacup-costumed woman.*

If I were dating M, I would have come to work dressed as a teapot.

I don't want to be a creepy voyeur. I want to be an actor in my own drama. And there are reasons to believe that I could be, although listing them involves dangerous immodesty, because although I always preferred math to English, I know what hubris is and where it gets you. So I will now transcribe the list of my assets compiled by my sister, Alison, to give me hope on a down day, accompanied by parenthetical commentary of my own:

—Handsome (To those who favor these dimensions: six-one, dark blond hair and beard, gangly muscular build)
—Good athlete (Baseball, soccer, basketball)
—Popular (A vexed assertion, given the vagueness of that term. In this case it means two male friends, one of whom is my boss and team leader, O'Brien, plus the usual thousands of "friends" who I don't know and never see.)
—Kind (Love parents and sister, and they love me)
—Sexy (How can a sister say such a thing, you may ask! Well, she is basing her statement on nine shows of interest and affection from colleagues as reported by me during the two-year period I have worked at Harvest, including an invitation to drink schnapps, a small bouquet of daisies on my birthday, a bag of carrots at lunchtime [I love carrots] and, most intriguingly, a note left anonymously on my desk that read, "You have a great ass and a great personality.")
—Amazing at your job (This is not something Alison is equipped to evaluate. She is an impressionist: a typical who tends toward the romantic. She is the opposite of an empiricist, in other words, which has led our parents to jocularly speculate on whether Alison and I are one person split into two parts. But whereas Alison is a complete human all on her own, I have a feeling I would be a more complete human in combination with Alison. She is basing "Amazing at your job" on two data points, advancement and

rewards, both of which have come to me faster than to my colleagues. There is even a plan afoot among my unit and team leaders, Avery and O'Brien, to move me to an individual office. I have resisted this move because it will take me physically away from M and create a difference of rank between us. Alison insists this will be a good thing, or at least not a bad thing—but, being Alison, she has no data to back up her assertion other than a vague claim that "people always have crushes on their superiors," and a single data point to back *that* up: herself. And yet, despite Alison's impressionism, her predictions have a perplexingly high success rate.)

I have left till last Alison's most vexatious assertion:
—You're funny.

Humor is the bugbear of those in my business and therefore the thing that obsesses us. Humor is impossible to quantify. For that reason, it is one of our chief tools in spotting proxies: vacant online identities maintained by a third party in order to conceal the fact that their human occupants have eluded. Lucrative "brand" identities are often sold (the first documented instance being a fashion model named Charlotte Swenson), and a squatter will occasionally take possession of an abandoned identity chassis. But most proxies are animated by "hermit crab programs" that maintain the established patterns of an individual's online activity—communication, commerce, and social media—as a way of hiding the reality that the original occupant of that identity has vacated it. Most proxying is orchestrated by Mondrian, a not-for-profit based in San Francisco. Mondrian's most sophisticated proxies are live professionals—usually fiction writers, I'm told—who impersonate multiple identities at once. Humor is our best tool for identifying them; it's very hard even for a human proxy, much less a hermit crab program, to successfully mimic an eluder's sense of humor. Unfortunately for us counters, it is equally hard for

a program to detect failed humor mimicry, making proxy identification both time-consuming and labor-intensive. It can be done, but
it is work for typicals. In fact, spotting proxies and eliminating them
from our count is the only realm of our business where typicals have
an advantage.

But how is it possible that humor *can't be quantified*? Simple: Because we lack a basic set of definitional terms for what is funny. And
yet some people are funny and others are not. Some of those who are
funny may be funny in ways they didn't intend. I am certainly in this
category, as are many of us counters. We are quantifiers. As children,
we were perceived as off-putting. To this day, I can tell you the exact
length of the pause in any piece of pop music you'd care to name,
beginning at Elvis. This fixation did not endear me to anyone except
my family, and only because I was already dear to them. My fixation
was social poison—as were, I'm told by fellow counters, their habits
of measuring neighbors' fences, cataloging Arthurian suits of armor,
mapping and reporting on solar storms, or—in M's case—tending
268 houseplants in her childhood bedroom, not counting the grass
with which she seeded her wall-to-wall carpet, and which forced its
roots into the (it turned out) decayed floorboards underneath said
carpet until, after a vigorous watering, a large chunk of the ceiling in
the room below M's (the kitchen, as it happened) broke free and fell
into the middle of the dinner table.

Now, that is funny for sure, at least it was when M told the story
at O'Brien's taco party when each team member shared a childhood
anecdote. And yet embedded in the comedy are both sadness and
triumph—sadness because M was already isolated, friendless, and
at odds with her family, and the ceiling debacle resulted in the dismantling of her plant system, and—when she afterward refused to
eat—hospitalization and tube feeding. Triumph because now she is
M!, gorgeous and sexy and well paid, and the world has bent her way.
Most of the stories we tell—my fellow counters and I—have both
these components, sadness and triumph, because the world has come

around to us. It's unbelievable. I still can't believe it. And while our ranks are fortified by typicals whose adolescence may have included popularity and statistical expertise limited to sanctioned realms like baseball stats, the fact is that we are simply better at counting—we are native speakers, if you will, many of us having understood numbers before we did language.

This morning, our entire unit—six teams in all—is summoned for an unscheduled meeting in the Sand Garden. Based on past experience of unscheduled unit meetings, this one has an 86 percent chance of indicating a problem, a 9 percent chance of indicating an unexpected reward, and a 5 percent chance of indicating a personal tragedy in our ranks. All 273 of us file into the Sand Garden and lounge there, waiting for Avery to arrive. When the waterfall that normally trickles over the pile of sharp black stones is switched off, our team members exchange worried glances. Something big is afoot. O'Brien looks as confused as everyone else.

Our unit leader, Avery, is a nonbinary I have never seen display emotion of any kind in a public setting. Now visual indications of stress are evident all over their person: hair hanging lank and unwashed, dark circles under their eyes, sweatshirt stained with egg on one cuff; and mascara and lip gloss, the only makeup they wear—absent from their face.

"We've completed a deep analysis of recent proxy bafflement," Avery tells us, "and have determined that a new generation of hermit crab programs has been designed specifically to elude our proxy filters. That fact suggests the direct involvement of one or more members of this unit actively working to help eluders exempt themselves from our count."

Bafflement refers to the specific ways that proxies avoid our detection. Eluding and proxying aren't illegal, but if someone at Harvest is working to help the eluders baffle us, thereby tainting our data with a statistically significant number of vacant identities and thus compromising the quality and accuracy of our work, that would fall under the rubric of industrial crime. Which explains why Phil and Patrice, our ombudsmen, are flanking Avery, looking more like cops than I've ever seen them look.

"We will be conducting an investigation," Avery says. "We will interview each of you individually, and we would welcome any confidential information you'd like to impart at any time. While I don't want to sow seeds of suspicion, I must ask you to adopt a certain watchfulness. If you have reason to doubt the commitment or loyalty of anyone on your team, please share that information with us."

Avery is using a code that only I and other native counters are likely to comprehend: The defector is a typical—likely an impressionist—beguiled by a fantasy of freedom and escape. It is a state of mind I can grasp only theoretically. There is nothing original about human behavior. Any idea I have is likely occurring to scores of others in my demographic categories. We live in similar ways, think similar thoughts. What the eluders want to restore, I suspect, is the uniqueness they felt before counting like ours revealed that they were an awful lot like everyone else. But where the eluders have it wrong is that quantifiability doesn't make human life any less remarkable, or even (this is counterintuitive, I know) less mysterious—any more than identifying the rhyme scheme in a poem devalues the poem itself. The opposite!

Mysteries that are destroyed by measurement were never truly mysterious; only our ignorance made them seem so. They are like whodunits after you know who did it. Does anyone reread a murder mystery? Whereas the cosmos has been mysterious to humans since long before we knew anything about astronomy or space—and, now that we do, is only more so.

Decoded, Avery's message boils down to this: An impressionist is fucking up our data out of some romantic notion that by doing so, they are helping to foment a revolution—when really all they're doing is screwing up our count and jeopardizing our jobs. So keep your eyes peeled for typicals who seem to be up to no good, and let's get the fucker out.

6.28 months ago, or approximately three weeks before M started dating Marc, I was working in my cubicle when she rose up over our shared partition slowly, her eyes appearing first and then the rest of her face. Her eyes, when those were all I could see, looked like the eyes of a golden cat. As I was staring, transfixed, her whole head bobbed up and she said, "Peekaboo," and began to laugh, and I laughed, too, and the fact that I was laughing made her laugh more and the fact that she was laughing made me laugh more, and I strove to calculate the exponential effect of mutual laughter because I felt like I was drowning, and a little illustrative math would have grounded me. But our laughter was too much to illustrate. That was the beginning.

M's boyfriend, Marc, is a typical—a misleading term because, among counters, typicals are atypical and always a minority. At times I'm cheered by the thought that M can't possibly have as much in common with Marc as she does with me. On the other hand, my parents and sister are typicals, and not only do I love them, but I specifically love *the fact that they are typicals*! Last month, when I hiked with my sister to a waterfall and we sat side by side on some rocks, I liked knowing that Alison was thinking something as simple as "how beautiful," rather than trying to calculate the density, speed, distance to the rocks below, and the volume of water falling. But the glow of appreciation that I felt for my sister swerved into torment at the thought that the same glow of appreciation must be what M feels for Marc! She must think, *It's easy and relaxing to be with Marc.* She must think, *Being with Marc reminds me that there are other ways of seeing the world.* She must think, *When Marc looks at me, I know that he's thinking I'm beautiful, rather than trying to count the secondary freckles on my nose.*

This succession of thoughts so distressed me that I had to lie down beside the waterfall and curl in a ball.

That was when Alison made the list of my assets.

Later on the same day that began with our unscheduled Unit Meeting with Avery, I see M eating lunch by herself in the rock garden. Normally, she eats her lunch with Marc—in fact, eating lunch together is how their relationship began—so M's presence alone in the rock garden is a rare opportunity for me.

I stare at M through the window in a state of extreme anxiety about how to proceed. If I approach her, there is a 100 percent likelihood that I'll have to initiate conversation, and of course a significant possibility that this conversation will not be spontaneous or interesting—especially since nervousness, a certainty for me in M's presence, will diminish by at least 50 percent my ability to speak naturally. But my dad has always said, "Doing anything really interesting requires a leap," meaning that boldness, by definition, flouts the math that precedes it. And because Dad is a mathematically inclined typical and a "political junkie" deeply involved in the metrics of our cousin Miles Hollander's bid for state senator, I take his analysis seriously.

The small stones I cross toward M are roughly 35 percent sharp-edged gray shale striated with white and another 25 percent rounded clayish stones. The remaining 40 percent are my favorite: dense, smooth black stones that soak up the sun's heat. The large furniture-like rocks appear to have solidified from a liquid state just moments before and are said to be meteorites. M is leaning against the largest one, looking up at a sky that is roughly one third fast-moving clouds and two thirds desert blue.

"Hi," I say.

"Hi," M says.

Having employed retroactive math on a multitude of my past interactions, I've arrived at a predictive formula that has proved infallible so far: If a two-person conversation remains awkward for eight lines of speech—four lines each, not counting salutations—it has an 80 percent chance of remaining awkward, whereas if a conversation becomes natural *within* those first eight lines of speech, it is likely to remain so, and—surprisingly—to leave an impression of naturalness *despite* up to ten additional awkward lines! The trouble with this predictive math is that conversation becomes harder to generate when you're feeling pressured and nervous, and the threat of an irrevocably awkward conversation with a girl you're in love with is stressful, especially since escaping the conversation will require that you walk away across fifty feet of stones, thereby granting her a prolonged opportunity (while watching your receding back) to reflect on how dumb it is that you crossed the entire rock garden to talk to her when you had nothing to say, how you obviously have a crush on her, how this is a shame because while she has enjoyed sharing a partition with you, she doesn't feel *that way* about you; how she might have, 6.28 months ago when she rose up over the partition and said "Peekaboo" and you both laughed so unbelievably hard, but after that you acted weird and distant and then Marc came along and she loves him now, and even if, say, 13 percent of her thoughts, as she watches your receding back, involve the fact that you're in excellent physical shape, in the winner-take-all system that is operative in the choice of a monogamous romantic partner, that 13 percent will wind up being statistically irrelevant.

So. Pressure.

And if more than eight lines of awkward dialogue threaten irrevocable awkwardness, silences like the one now elapsing between M and me are an even greater peril. And I am a guy who knows how to measure silences. But whereas in music, a prolonged pause adds power and vividness to the refrain that follows it, pauses in conversation have the opposite effect, of debasing whatever comes next to the point that a perfectly witty riposte will be reduced to the verbal equivalent of a shrunken head, if too long a pause precedes it.

Leading to the question: How long has it been since M and I exchanged our "hi"s?

3.36 seconds.

What! How can so many thoughts and observations possibly have elapsed in so brief a period? An impressionist will answer along the lines of "The distortions inherent in our perception of time," but to us counters, time is a bore—and not just because too much has been said and written about it. Time is irrelevant to math. Note that I did *not* say math is irrelevant to time; we hurl math at time in the vain hope of understanding it. The fact that so many thoughts could have gone through my head in 3.36 seconds is testament to the infinitude of an individual consciousness. There is no end to it, no way to measure it. Consciousness is like the cosmos multiplied by the number of people alive in the world (assuming that consciousness dies when we do, and it may not) because each of our minds is a cosmos of its own: unknowable, even to ourselves. Hence the instant appeal of Mandala's Own Your Unconscious. Who could resist the chance to revisit our memories, the majority of which we'd forgotten so completely that they seemed to belong to someone else? And having done that, who could resist gaining access to the Collective Consciousness for the small price of making our own anonymously searchable? We all went for it on our twenty-first birthday, Mandala's age of consent, just as prior tech generations went for music sharing and DNA analysis, never fully reckoning, in our excitement over our revelatory new freedom, with what we surrendered by sharing the entirety of our perceptions to the Internet—and thereby to counters, like me. Strict rules govern the use of gray grabs by data gatherers, but there are occasions when I'm obliged, in my professional capacity, to search the psyches of strangers. It's an eerie sensation—like walking through an unfamiliar home and being surrounded by objects that radiate significance I can't decipher. I grab what I need and leave as quickly as I can.

The good news, vis-à-vis 3.36 (now 3.76) seconds having passed, comes via retroactive math: A conversational pause can last a full four seconds before it bursts, as it were, releasing its toxic contents. Up to that four-second mark, it is merely an expanding, tautening bubble of catastrophic potential.

"So," I say, "what did you think about Avery's speech?"

"Why are you asking?"

While I'm taken aback by M's somewhat aggressive tone, I'm also aware that six additional lines of dialogue need to be uttered to get us to the safety of eight, so I hurtle forward: "Well, because you and I work together, and this was kind of a big announcement. I wanted to talk about it with someone."

"You think it's Marc."

"That actually hadn't occurred to me," I say, "until this moment."

"It isn't Marc."

"Okay," I say. "It isn't Marc. There are two hundred and seventy-three people in our unit—why would I assume it's him?"

While our exchange is not entirely friendly, there is the encouraging fact that we've reached line seven without awkwardness, defining awkwardness as conversation consisting of a series of futile attempts to solve the problem of what to say next.

"Who do you think is helping the eluders?" I ask.

"An impressionist," she says.

"My sister is an impressionist," I say.

"Mine, too. But you can't change your siblings."

"I love my sister," I say.

"You might not love her if she wasn't your sister."

"I might not know her if she wasn't my sister."

"Exactly," she says.

I sit down on the stones beside M. "Do you mind if I sit with you?" I ask.

"You already did."

"I can stand up again."

"Don't bother."

"It's no bother," I say. "I have strong legs."

"You just want to show off."

"The ability to stand up from a sitting position is unremarkable," I say, and I stand up again to prove it. "Tell me how this is showing off."

"I can see your muscles."

I look down at my jeans and T-shirt, but I do not see any muscles. "Is that a problem?"

"No," she says. "Sit down again."

I sit back down with my heart in an uproar. This is flirtation, plain and simple. The exhilaration I feel, flirting with M, is precisely what is always missing when I try to date typicals: I never know what's going on, and because my attempts to find out lack the tactful goo that typicals smear all over their actions and words to blunt their real purpose, I come across as lurching and off-putting.

"I like you," I tell M. "I always have."

"Thanks. I didn't know that."

"What about Marc?"

"I'm in love with him," she says.

"Will he mind that we're sitting here together?"

"No. He trusts me."

"Do you trust him?"

She hesitates. "Yes and no."

"That means no. Trust is all or nothing."

"No," she says. "It's a winner-take-all accounting system in which various gradations come into play."

"Such as?"

"I trust his feelings for me," she says. "But he could be helping the eluders."

"Why do you say that?"

"Sometimes his mind seems far away."

"The fact that someone's mind is far away doesn't mean they've defected to a secret network bent on destroying our business."

"But it could," she says.

"'Could' and 'is' are so far apart as to be opposites."

"No," she says. "'Is' and 'isn't' are opposites."

"I have an idea," I say. "Since you're attracted to me and I'm attracted to you, why don't we go to my house and have sex and see what happens next, no strings attached?"

"That would be a betrayal of Marc."

"You could call it that, or you could call it adding another gradation into the field of your trustworthiness."

"Having sex with you would turn me from being trustworthy into being untrustworthy."

"Not necessarily," I say. "If we sleep together once and it's not incredible, you'll be *more* trustworthy and committed to Marc from that point on, because when you see my muscles through my T-shirt and feel attracted to me, you'll think, *I've already had sex with Lincoln and it wasn't that great, so who cares about those muscles?*"

"You're cloaking your lust in logic."

"My lust is logical."

"Lust is never logical," she says. "It's biological."

"My lust for you is totally logical," I say. "Your combination of attractive properties makes it all but impossible for me to resist you. In fact, it takes a constant expenditure of energy to keep from reaching out and touching your hair right this minute."

"Don't," she says sharply.

"I won't. I'll continue to expend energy resisting that impulse. But it's not easy."

"You could walk away. That would make it easier."

"True. But we work near each other, so I'll continue to be aware of how badly I want to touch your hair."

"You'll be moving to an office soon," she says. "That will make it easier."

I'm stupefied by how quickly things have gone from good to bad—how, despite M's attraction to me and her suspicions of Marc, she's going to stay with him and be loyal to him. I understand now that nothing will ever happen between M and me, precisely because it has just come so close to happening and yet not happened. There are clear mathematical reasons for this, but explaining them requires a three-dimensional model that I'm too tired to deploy, even for myself.

"I can't walk away," I say, "because the energy I'm expending to resist the urge to touch your hair leaves insufficient energy for walking or even for standing up from a sitting position. Maybe you should walk away."

"Yes," she says. "I think I will."

She stands up and walks toward the building. I watch her go. Then I lie back against the small warm sharp stones punctuated by hot smooth black stones. I look at the clouds spinning in slow-motion helix patterns and wonder whether the fact that M will never love me is the result of the conversation we've just had, or whether our conversation merely revealed a preexisting fact that M will never love me. Was the mathematics of our conversation causal or merely illustrative? Wondering is the realm of impressionists, and as I watch the clouds, I feel my mother and sister in me. I wonder if I'll ever love someone the way I love Alison, but with the other stuff thrown in. I wonder if I can survive without that love. I wonder whether the misery of my childhood and adolescence will return and knock me back into despair that no mathematical ladder can lift me out of. I notice the pearlization of the cloud helixes overhead, and the blue behind them, and I realize that what I'm looking at *is* a mathematical ladder. But I cannot seem to climb it.

The next week, at our team's morning meeting, M and Marc announce that they are engaged. M looks shy and overjoyed, and there is a tiny diamond on her finger like a pinprick of flame.

I go straight to Alison's apartment after work to deliver the news, along with supplementary data suggesting an extreme likelihood—85 percent!—that M and Marc will marry.

"You're saying . . . engagement increases the likelihood of marriage," Alison says.

"Drastically," I wail. "Annihilatingly." And then I lie down on the floor and begin to cry.

I spend the next few days on health leave at my parents' house, the house where I grew up. I lie in my old bed with my eyes closed, and Dad takes two days off from his clinic and sits beside me, reading. It's a one-story house, and outside the window, I hear Mom nailing and gluing and attaching things together to make her sculptures. I occupy my mind with making a list of the 273 employees in my unit in order of likelihood that they are the defector—really 272, since I know that *I* am not the defector and therefore place myself last. Then I empty the list and begin again, like shuffling a deck of cards. With another part of my mind, I consider the detrimental impact of large numbers of hermit crab programs we cannot screen out. As a counter, I want, above all, my data to be accurate. The idea of false data tainting my analyses in the form of large numbers of undetected proxies posing as live human beings makes me feel dizzy and ill. But the bigger picture of the eluders doesn't worry me. If they achieve such numbers that their alternate network rivals the dominance of the one from which we derive our data—if they, in effect, secede undetected from our society and form a new one, with a separate economy and currency and even language (all the while appearing, online, still to be their old selves)—new counters will soon arise within their ranks to count their data. At first that counting will merely be a residual effect of connection and communication and access to one another. Even when recognized, the eluder-counters will seem to be benign neutral entities. But gradually, it will come to light that, while the counters *themselves* have no use for the data they passively acquire, they are lending, leasing, and selling it to other entities who use it in ways enormously profitable to themselves. And so the eluders will find themselves, once again, accounted for—in other words, right back where they started. And the older ones will be too exhausted to start another revolution and too cynical to believe it will work. But the younger ones will—you guessed it—try to elude the counters. They will vacate their identities and form a new secret network, thus seceding into yet another parallel invisible nation where, they believe, they will at last be free. And the same thing will happen. And the same thing will happen. And the same thing will happen.

Several days after I return to work, the eluder-ally is revealed to be O'Brien, my direct boss and team leader and one of my two male friends. The news ripples through Harvest like the sound of scary music in a movie. Up till now, there has been a fizz of excitement around the mystery of who the saboteur might be, but the revelation of whodunit is so shocking that mystery is replaced not by knowledge but by further mystery.

Why?

O'Brien is a native counter—and yet he has helped an untold number of eluders to elude our count.

O'Brien was tortured as a kid over his knowledge of wind currents—their speed and direction and seasonal fluctuations—and yet he has helped the eluders to elude us.

O'Brien joined the wind industry and thrived there as an executive, then left behind that success to join the ranks of us counters, where he moved up quickly and was well liked and an incredibly nice guy—and yet he has enabled a new generation of hermit crab programs to baffle our detection.

Clearly, O'Brien joined our ranks specifically to undermine us. From the beginning, O'Brien was in league with Mondrian.

And because of his deep knowledge of our systems, O'Brien's allegiance to the eluders will prove disastrous, throwing off our data to such an extent that three quarters of our clients will leave us.

But none of that is the really troubling part. The really troubling part is that O'Brien, who is not even a typical, much less an impressionist, believes so strongly in enabling the eluders that he has infiltrated Harvest and brought us down.

Which means that eluding is *not* a notion that appeals only to impressionistic typicals who romanticize the idea of becoming someone else. If O'Brien supports it, then it must also make *mathematical* sense.

The day he is found out, O'Brien is herded by a dumbfounded crowd to the Shinto torii gate that marks the entrance to our campus. Avery is in tears, something none of us could have imagined. Before passing through the torii, O'Brien stops and addresses all of us:

"Hey, I'm sorry for fucking you over. You're my friends and my family because I don't have any other friends or family. If you consider what I've gained by enabling so many proxies to function undetected, and thereby so many eluders to successfully elude—that is, nothing—versus what I've lost—everything—you'll understand that only one thing could justify that appalling cost-benefit analysis. That thing is belief. I believe in what the eluders are doing, I believe in their right to do it, and the force of my belief more than compensates for the fact that acting on it will cost me everyone and everything I love. I have no regrets, even now," O'Brien concludes, "much as I will miss you."

And then he walks out through the torii gate.

The chaos that follows this revelation takes many forms and strains. An inquiry begins into whether the man who made that speech was really O'Brien, or whether the real O'Brien was kidnapped by eluders and animated holographically beside the torii gate using gray grabs from the collective to capture his workplace tones and gestures and speech. Another hypothesis has it that the eluders somehow breached O'Brien's skull with a weevil—a burrowing electronic device that can interfere with thought—and were controlling his behavior and speech from afar. It is difficult to disprove either of these theses, and

I owe it to trusted typicals who persuade me of their unlikelihood on two bases: 1) Such actions would entail the use of the very invasive technologies the eluders abhor and are trying to elude. 2) Interventions like these are beyond the eluders' technological range; they simply could not pull them off.

In the reductions and restructuring that follow O'Brien's defection, 78 percent of Harvest employees are laid off, including M and Marc. I survive by a hair, I think because Avery likes me.

Eight months later, I am appointed leader of a new team: smaller and leaner than the one O'Brien led, but a team nonetheless. And while O'Brien is obviously not a leader whose example I would emulate, I can't help but remember fondly the taco party he held for all of us when we first became a team. So I force myself to plan a barbecue for my new team at my home—an undertaking that would be simple if I weren't dogged to the point of sleeplessness by questions like: Will people have fun? Will it be my fault if they don't have fun? Will they hold it against me forever if they don't have fun? Will they tell others who weren't present that they didn't have fun, and will that knowledge permanently reduce those others' opinions of me? Etc. Dad got me a new grill for Christmas as an inducement to conquer my fear of entertaining, and Mom accompanies me to the supermarket over the weekend to buy meat and veggies. On the night itself, Alison drives to my house to provide moral support. I introduce her to everyone as "Alison" rather than "my sister, Alison," because as team leader, I'd rather not have it known that I can't throw a party without familial help.

With Alison present, I relax, as if a protective spell has been cast and nothing can go seriously wrong. The spell is put to an immediate and severe test when Tom shows up with M as his date. I heard a few months ago that M and Marc did not marry, but by the time this news reached me, a welcome layer of distance had formed between me and everything M-related, to the point that my first thought, on learning that she and Marc had broken up, was that their behavior as a couple had gone from statistically compliant to statistically aberrant. Always surprising, even to a counter like me.

To my relief, my distance from M holds fast even now, with her physically in my presence—or is it my sister's protective spell? Alison takes my arm, and I feel her warmth and strength and calm flowing into me. She brought a keg of beer in her car, and we all drink a fair amount. I make a fire in my firepit and we sit around it and Tom holds M's hand and kisses her cheek but I feel nothing; memories of my agony over M are like gray grabs from a stranger's life. My sister keeps her arm around me while also pouring drinks and maintaining happiness among my guests—it's one of her impressionist's gifts to know when people are happy or not happy just by looking at them, whereas I'm more likely to speculate about how many hairs their eyebrows contain. I often notice that M is not smiling as we sit beside the firepit, but does that mean she's unhappy? People don't have to smile to be happy—sometimes they smile to hide unhappiness. But I don't know what percentage of smiles are happy smiles versus unhappiness-cover-up smiles, and self-reporting would be inherently flawed, since a person smiling to mask unhappiness would be unlikely to admit, when asked, that they are unhappy.

When it's late and dark and I've had several cups of beer and am in a giddy state over the obvious verdict that the party has gone well—people are clearly having fun, it's already a success even though it's still going on, so there is nothing left to worry about, and I can relax and have fun, too—I run into M coming out of my bathroom. I don't mean that literally, but there's a funny moment when we stand in my hall looking at each other.

"I like your girlfriend," she says.

"She's my sister."

"Oh," she says. "Tom isn't my boyfriend, either."

"He may not realize that."

I'm aware, even through my new distance from M, of how strange it is to see her inside my house—a situation I imagined for so long and with such longing. Deep in my closet, I still have the box full of possible x values I acquired last year in hopes of making M fall in love with me.

"Hey," I say. "Can I show you something, just for the hell of it?"

"Sure."

She stands in the middle of my bedroom while I dig out the box. "Here," I say. "This is a box of seemingly random items. I'm wondering if, when you look at them, anything in particular happens."

I'd meant for M to pick up the objects one by one and plug them into the socket of the equation that is *her*, to determine, hypothetically, whether any one of them happened to be x. Not because it matters, but because I hate to leave an equation unsolved. Since I haven't instructed M to remove the items one by one, she just leans over the box and stares at the jumble: the rose-crocheted dish towel; the small porcelain cat; the rainbow yarn sculpture on a Popsicle-stick cross; the oversize marble with a splash of turquoise in it.

"What is all this?" she asks, laughing.

"Just random stuff."

"What's supposed to happen when I look at it?"

"If it happened, you would know," I say, laughing, too.

"How were the objects acquired?"

"I mostly bought them. At Walmart."

"Then they aren't random," she says. "They represent a series of choices made by a particular person in a particular place. They could be diagrammed mathematically."

"So can randomness," I say. "After the fact."

"That's retroactive math."

"History is retroactive math," I say.

For some reason, we both look at the window, which is right beside my bed. It would be more accurate to say that the bed is right by the window, because I rented the house specifically so I could place my bed beside that window and look out at the starry desert sky. In the equation of my love for this house, the bedroom window is x.

The sound of the party is far away. I'm alone in my room with M, and my sister is outside keeping everyone happy. I take M's hand and lead her to the bed. "Let's look at the stars," I say, and we lie down side by side and look at them. All that math, glittering and shimmering back at us.

"I'm jealous of O'Brien," M says. "I want to feel the belief he felt."

"Me, too," I say.

"Was he really the O'Brien we knew, or someone else?"

"I guess he must be both," I say.

I know from the pulse in M's hand that her heart beats seventy-five times in the first minute we lie there, eighty-five in the second minute, and the third minute, the one we're in now, promises a hundred beats or more. M's body is accelerating, and mine is doing the same. My heartbeat swishes in my ears like someone wildly mopping my eardrums. I count both our heartbeats and wait for them to coincide. They seem to, for a moment, but mine always gets ahead—a statistical likelihood, given that I'm male. In the stillness, I realize that M is counting, too.

The vaginal sensor is allowable after all. Maybe that was x.

Or maybe the stars were x, in which case you could argue that the window was x for the second time. Madeleine says that for her, seeing me with Alison was x. For me, "Peekaboo" will always be x.

Not that it matters; it's all just retroactive math. The random walk of a drunk is of geometric interest, but it can't predict where he'll stagger next.

At our wedding, officiated by State Senator Miles Hollander, we release five hundred biodegradable balloons into the sky, where they float among the hot-air balloons already hovering there. My parents and sister cry from happiness, but because weeping is more or less continuous, and because theirs occurs on and off over many happy hours, the tears are impossible to count.

BREAK

The Mystery of Our Mother

Long ago, she told us, when we were just a hope in her heart or not even that, because she never wanted children (or thought she didn't), a higher power touched our mother's head and said: *Stop what you're doing! Two little girls are waiting to be born, and you need to have them right away, because the world is desperate for their brightness.* So she stopped studying anthropology, which she really did love and maybe would study again someday, *when you're all grown up and don't need me anymore.*

We'll always need you!

I'll always need you two, that's for sure. I'll try not to drive you crazy with my mommy needs.

Tell the end.

Well, I stopped going to anthropology school and I married your daddy and we brought you into the world. And here you are! It all worked out perfectly.

Where is Daddy?

You'll see him next week. He's taking you to ballet.

Last time he never came.

I'll be here. Just in case.

He can't make a bun.

That's not important, honey.

Before ballet . . . ?

Don't whine, sweetie.

He threw Tam-Tam out the window of the car. He said she was moth-eaten.

That was unfortunate.

How could you marry him?

Love is a mystery.

Does Daddy love you?

He loves *you*. That's what matters.

He said we were young spendthrifts.

Did he, now.

He said—

Can we not talk about what he said?

We're just telling you . . .

I don't need to be told. I know your father very well.

How did she endure these conversations? Of course our father didn't love her, any more than she loved him. He was fifteen years older than our mother, twice divorced when they met, with four kids—two by each ex-wife. How's that for a rotten prospective husband? But he was charming, a famous record producer, and above all (we later surmised), he wouldn't take no for an answer. Why he wanted our mother to say yes is another mystery; they had nothing in common beyond a taste for beauty (his) and beauty (hers). But she never lived by her beauty—she was the kind of mom who rarely wore makeup, who let her hair grow wild and didn't bother to shower on Sunday, her day off from the travel agency where she went to work after our father stranded her without any money to raise us.

The sun-gnawed apartment complex where we lived with our mother starting as toddlers in the late 1970s—the first home we remember— seemed to be populated entirely by females: aging B-movie actresses who took deliveries of Gallo wine in gallon bottles, and aspiring starlets whose much older boyfriends had white stripes on their ring fingers. The apartments surrounded a "garden" containing a single gargantuan palm tree—either a relic of some agricultural prehistory of that patch of land or a decorative feature that had bloated grotesquely out of scale with the modest complex it was decorating. The bedroom we shared with our mother faced a canopy of fronds like the fingers of a dozen hands. Even on sunny days, it made a sound like rain.

On Sunday mornings, we climbed into our mother's bed to "be the monster," which meant lying with our chests on top of hers so that all of us could feel our three beating hearts. Our hair tangled with her hair, and our breath melted into hers, until we were one creature lying under the moving, whispering hands of another creature, the palm tree. The tree had a name, we told our mother: Herbert.

What if it's a girl tree?

A girl can be Herbert.

Our mother propped herself on one elbow and studied us. There aren't a lot of men around here, are there? Do you wish you saw more of your daddy?

No!

He loves you very much.

We love *you*.

You can love us both, you know.

No. We can't.

Our parents' marriage collapsed when a San Francisco high school student washed up on their Malibu doorstep, having run away from home and hitchhiked south after our father seduced her on a business trip. We were three and four years old. Our father managed, on paper, to appear penniless. He left our mother with nothing but us—which, by his calculation, probably meant less than nothing. But for our mother, who had little else, we were infinite. She loved us infinitely in return, and gave us that rare thing: a happy childhood. She never told us why she'd left our father. Much later, he did.

•   •   •

On the occasions when our father showed up to take us to ballet, we walked grimly down the cracked outdoor steps from our second-story apartment to one of his many cars.

Hello, girls. One of you want to ride in front?

We shook our heads. It wasn't safe, everyone knew that except him.

How about something to eat? We've got time before your class.

We don't eat before ballet.

I can't do anything right with you two, can I?

We shook our heads, and he laughed and began to drive. But when he pulled up in front of the strip mall where the ballet studio was, he turned around and peered at us in the backseat.

I'm your father. You understand that, don't you?

We nodded in stony unison.

That's not nothing. That means something. He searched our cold eyes. You don't like me. Why?

It was not a rhetorical question. He was curious, awaiting a reply.

We looked at our father closely for perhaps the first time: his weathered surfer's tan and longish blond hair, his crooked front teeth. He watched us watch him, and then he laughed.

How would you know? You're just two little kids.

Some girls might have adored a father who came along occasionally in a showy car—pined for him, tried to be pretty for him and distract him from his girlfriends who were closer to their age than his; and ultimately become the playthings of other men with similar tastes. That's roughly how it went with our three older half sisters, Charlene, Roxy, and Kiki. Roxy was the one we idolized as little girls: Lithe and kinetic, cast in dozens of music videos, she'd achieved such notoriety by age seventeen that you could hardly fathom what kind of future it was all prelude to. But it turned out to be prelude to almost nothing: Roxy's promise was her main act. She ended up on methadone, with hepatitis C. Eventually only we could still see the flickering specter of her young self, flashing and bird-featured, like an antic ghost haunting a tumbledown mansion. The mannerisms of heroin, the dull eyes and sleepy movements, became her mannerisms. The old Roxy was invisible to everyone but us.

One day after ballet, our father told us that we weren't going straight home.

We glowered. Does Mommy know?

Of course your mother knows. What do you think I am, a kidnapper?

He drove grimly, our lack of enthusiasm clearly needling him. We played rock paper scissors in the backseat and pretended he wasn't there.

Hey. Try looking around for a change.

We were driving along a cliff, the ocean shivering enormously below. It seemed a different world from the parched flat one we inhabited with our mother, full of glittering cars in broiling asphalt lots.

Eventually, we descended the cliff and pulled into the driveway of a house with tiled roofs and magenta flowers overflowing its walls. There were no other houses around it. Rock and roll crashed from inside the house, but our father walked us straight past it to a beach whose fine white sand was different from Venice Beach, where our mother often took us on Sunday afternoons.

Where are the people?

It's a private beach. We're the only ones who can be here.

Is it yours?

Yes, it's mine. Go ahead. Run around. Have some fun.

We stood watching him.

Come on. Play.

When we failed to move, he said, I've never seen a pair of kids who wouldn't play.

It's your beach.

I'm your father. My beach is your beach.

We like beaches with people.

You're very tough, you two. Does your mother ever tell you that?

We shook our heads.

Ah. So I'm seeing the real you. The real you, plural.

No, she is.

She may think so. But I know better.

Visibly heartened by this notion, he unbuttoned his Hawaiian shirt. Our father wore shorts year-round, day and night, but we'd never seen him bare-chested. It turned out that today—maybe always—his shorts were actually swim trunks.

C'mon, kiddos, he said, taking our hands and trotting us over the powdery sand toward the sea.

We don't have bathing suits!

You're wearing leotards. That's the same thing.

It was true. We each wore a sleeveless Danskin with an elastic-waisted ballet skirt pulled over it, and the soft leather ballet slippers we'd gotten for Christmas.

Wait! We need to take off our skirts!

He paused while we slid them off and folded them neatly on top of our ballet slippers: two little piles in the blinding white.

I like that. The way you take good care of your things.

We stepped into the shimmering water with our father. The absence of a crowd, of music playing on boom boxes, of roller skaters and dogs and cigarette butts and Popsicle sticks buried in the sand, made it seem like an imaginary beach.

We swam with our father. We were seven and eight years old, and we remembered that swim as the first nice time we ever had with him.

The music had stopped by the time he brought us inside his house, which was big and airy with warm tile floors and ceiling fans slowly spinning and bright flowers in vases and a swimming pool in the middle of everything. We had lived in that house, which might have been why we felt comfortable there, despite its grandeur. A maid showed us how to work the fancy shower and gave us huge fluffy towels to dry off with. We kept the towels around us while our Dan-skins dried in the dryer.

Tell me when you're dressed, our father called from outside the bathroom door. Only after we chanted, "We a-are!" did he open it.

On the drive home, we looked out over the cliff at a dusty orange sunset. We felt fresh and clean and enchanted, like we were returning from a land in a fairy tale.

Down below, where our apartment was, it already seemed to be night. Our mother was waiting for us outside. Gosh, you're even later than I thought! she said.

We ran to her and threw our arms around her waist. We missed you! We went to the beach!

Our father stood in the shadows until we remembered to turn and say goodbye.

I'd like to spend more time with them, he said.

He learned pigtails, ponytails, even ballet buns, which he sculpted fastidiously, insisting on starting over again if hairs were stray or sloppy or caught. Other parents smiled at the sight of him pinching bobby pins between his lips. Everyone knew who he was; he'd made the careers of enough rock stars to be a star himself. People joked with him and tried to act like they knew him better than they did. Our father froze them out. He was prim in our company, as if his fame were a dull encumbrance he would have liked to be rid of.

Our father's swimming pool looked nothing like the garish turquoise tubs we'd glimpsed in apartment complexes near ours, littered with palm tree debris. His pool was the color of stone, full of lightly salted water, accessible from almost every room in the house. The pool was to his home what the palm tree was to ours.

On our second visit, he evaluated our swim strokes, found them dangerously wanting, and arranged for twice-weekly lessons with an instructor in his pool. Occasionally, we stayed for dinner. Eduardo, our father's cook, made fajitas and guacamole and pitchers of margaritas for whoever was around—usually some combination of our four half siblings (whom we barely knew) and musicians our father was working with. Under a cast-iron chandelier whose fat candles dripped wax into the middle of a massive slab of dining table, our father grew loud and loose, a showman we didn't recognize, or like.

Look at Lana and Melora, he said one night. They don't approve.

Everyone turned, and we felt our faces get hot.

They're tough customers, those two. They've got me doing pigtails. And buns.

Incredulous laughter. I don't believe you, said Charlie, our oldest sister. She dragged her chair next to our father and offered him her golden hair, which fell almost to her waist. Make a bun, she dared him.

Our father gathered Charlie's hair in his fists but seemed unsure at first what to do with it. Girls, he roused us. Get me the pins and brush.

Serious! Stickler! came the table howls.

Our father brushed Charlie's hair until it crackled in the candlelight. Then he herded it into a shimmering bundle and looped it expertly around, pins pursed between his teeth. Silence fell on the room as everyone watched. Our father slid the pins into Charlie's hair and anchored in place a beautiful, shining bun. It made Charlie look like a little girl, although she must have been in her twenties by then. Laugher broke at the table, and everyone clapped.

Charlie's eyes brimmed and overflowed. I don't know why I'm crying, she kept saying as she flicked away the tears. But they wouldn't stop.

We knew why. We were getting the best of him.

2

At some point during the past year, 2024, our mother disappeared. This fact is not yet widely known beyond (presumably) the circle of colleagues and graduate students who would have normally expected to see her in person. She is seventy-four years old and in excellent health. She may be in another hemisphere or hiding in plain sight.

Her proxy, so far, is doing the job. Professional proxying is still new, but the best ones manage to infuse their client's utterances with enough randomness and spontaneity (while staying "in character") to seem authentic even to those who know them well. If you're thinking *we're* somehow acting as our mother's proxies, think again; we discovered her absence well after those close to her already knew of it—had probably known for months. That's how far she had drifted from us.

Proxies are such quick responders, such deft evaders, that even in an intimate group chat, it can be hard to know for certain that you're dealing with one.

Hi Mom.

Girls!

We miss you.

Miss you too. Sry I've been so busy. Hoping things'll calm down soon.

But when?

Have to get through a few conferences/papers.

Whr?

Singapore, Reykjavik, The Hague . . .

Names of conferences? We don't see online.

They're private. Il send you everything ltr today, w/links. Mbe you can meet me at one!

What about HERE in LA? Where we all live!

Throw out some dates. You grls r busy too!

We need you, Mama.

I need you too, JBs.

We need to *see* you.

We'll make it happen soon, I promise. Meanwhile, you know you're in my heart, don't you?

Are we really, Mama? You seem far away.

Always are, always will be.

Without an immediate expectation of seeing someone physically, it can take a while to be certain you're dealing with a vacant identity. A proxy has access to every digital utterance a person has ever made, along with gray grabs from the Collective Consciousness—although there won't be many of those in our mother's case. We haven't shared our externalized memories to the collective, and she never would have externalized hers at all. The omniscience of the Collective Consciousness is what the eluders want to escape so desperately that they're willing to leave their identities behind. Some liken eluders to trapped animals gnawing off their own legs as the price of freedom.

In the end, a proxy's job isn't deception so much as delay, like leaving a body-shaped pillow in bed before a prison break. The goal is to buy enough time before you're found (through facial recognition or some other sleuthing) that you can rightly claim: I'm not that person anymore. She doesn't exist.

Proxies succeed because people want to believe. Even as our mother's proxy deflects and circumvents us, some part of us longs to think that we've dreamed her disappearance; that we'll throw out some dates and she'll pick one and we'll drive to a restaurant we all used to love and there she'll be, waiting for us: our magical, beautiful mother.

3

Our father must have had a part in our mother's decision to resume her anthropology studies, for her return to graduate school required that he pay our living expenses and pick us up from school three afternoons a week. We were ten and eleven. Embarrassed by his showy cars, we asked him to meet us down the street.

You're ashamed of your old man?

The cars.

He next appeared in a faded Plymouth Fury, the first car he'd ever owned. Our father never abandoned a car. The Plymouth was burgundy and had a convertible top that we always begged him to put down.

One day he drove us to his office, roaring along the highway so our hair was matted from the wind when we arrived. In the lobby, our father put an arm around each of us and said to everyone we passed, My daughters, Lana and Melora. These are my daughters. He seemed to love saying the words. My youngest daughters, Lana and Melora, aren't they gorgeous? And tough!

We rode an elevator to the very top: a sun-soaked office that over-looked the low, scuffed city and gray sea twinkling like static. It was only the tenth floor, but we had never been inside a tall building. We had never flown in an airplane. The glass went all the way to the floor.

Could the window break?

Hasn't yet.

The walls were covered with gold and silver record albums inside frames.

Can we play those?

They're not real, they're trophies.

You won a lot of trophies!

Everywhere we looked were pictures of our father with musicians: at concerts, in recording studios, at parties. His age varied, the surfer's shag retracting into stringiness, but he was always wearing shorts, always in motion. That was *why* he wore shorts, we realized—to move freely. Standing in that office, we recognized a link between our father's restless, incessant motion and the trophies on his walls. One had produced the others.

Rolph was the only one of our half siblings that our mother ever asked about. "That sweet boy," she called him, with a catch in her voice that perplexed us. Was it sympathy? Guilt? We found nothing sympathetic about Rolph; we feared him. He and Charlie were full siblings but nothing alike; where Charlie was easygoing and devoted to our father, Rolph's strident black eyebrows telegraphed his perpetual outrage. He shared our father's love of cars and arrived at the house with a shriek of tires and a hawking up of gravel that sometimes sprayed the windows. According to Roxy, Rolph raced cars in the desert, which our father had forbidden.

Rolph rarely looked at us directly. His gaze would wander into our vicinity, then swerve away as if from something painful.

Once, as we waited outside our father's house to go home after swimming, we heard anguished cries coming from his fleet of cars. Thinking there might be a hurt animal, we crept among the cars to look. We discovered Rolph hunched in a backseat with the windows rolled up, sobbing with such hopeless abandon that he'd fogged the glass. Astounded, we stood watching him, and then Rolph caught sight of us through the window and went still. His face looked pale and tender, like a little boy's. Years later, after his suicide, we would return again and again to that face through the car window, his misery and surprise. We gazed at Rolph and he watched us back: three sentient life-forms observing one another as if through aquarium glass.

Then our father called us, and we ran.

•   •   •

Rolph's distress was one of many mysteries whose answers our father hid from us. He didn't want us to know that drugs were consumed in his house; that he himself had a coke habit; that Roxy had dropped out of high school and that Kiki, at sixteen, had run away with her youth-group leader; that Charlie had joined a cult in Mexico that our father had to extract her from with hired gunmen; that Rolph, his only son and favorite child, did not speak to him even in his house. Above all, he wanted us not to know that Jocelyn, the beautiful Asian woman who often sat with us at dinner, was the very person who'd brought an end to our parents' marriage back when she was still in high school. And there were things our father may have hidden from himself, like the fact that Rolph, who was Jocelyn's age exactly—born the same day—was in love with her, too.

Our father took us straight home after dinners at his house. We never stayed overnight. He controlled what we saw of his life, and our blindfolded vision of it seemed to bring him relief.

As high school approached, we overheard our father tell our mother that he wanted to send us to boarding school. *To get them away from the madness.*

There's no madness in their lives, Lou, unless you're supplying it. Are you?

Of course not.

I'm not sending them away to get them away from you, if that's what you're asking.

I want the best for them. That's all.

If you want them to have a grown-up father, then grow up.

Talking with our mother, our father seemed furthest from the loosey-goosey famous dad he became at night in his own house after several margaritas. He spoke to her in subdued tones, and she watched him evenly with her hazel eyes that seemed to blink less than most people's. He was always the one to look away.

Once he told us, in her presence: The only mistake your mother ever made in her life was marrying me.

That's silly, Lou. If we hadn't married, we wouldn't have these two perfect creatures.

You're right, he said. Thank God.

So we stayed in Los Angeles for high school. After ten years in the palm-tree apartment, we moved with our mother into a two-bedroom near the UCLA campus, where she was finishing the coursework for her PhD. We were all students together. When we came home after parties, she was always there, in cutoff jeans shorts, surrounded by textbooks: an orb of feverish concentration in the sprawling, frivolous city. Only when she cut off her hair did we understand that our mother had been a beauty. No more. She was a Serious Student now.

Before she met our father, our mother had had an anthropology professor at UC Berkeley named Nair Fortunata. Professor Fortunata had written a classic ethnography about his years of living among a tribe in the Brazilian rainforest in the 1960s—that tribe's first contact with the outside world. A number of Fortunata's students later traveled to Brazil intending to locate this tribe. All but one returned disappointed, and that one—a twenty-six-year-old named Leslie Weiss—did not return at all. When months passed without a word from her, Professor Fortunata went to Brazil in search of Leslie Weiss and disappeared, too. This occasioned State Department involvement and a private search underwritten by Weiss's desperate family. It emerged that a man matching Fortunata's description had staggered from the jungle into the tiny village of Albaís, too sick with fever to be saved. He carried no identification, and when locals offered to contact his family, he seemed not to understand. He was buried just outside the village. When the man's skull was exhumed, dental records revealed that it was Fortunata's.

All of this would have been merely tragic except that Albaís is a coastal town several thousand miles from the rainforest dwellers Fortunata originally described. A cloud of suspicion amassed around the late professor. Had he fudged the location of his original subjects so that others wouldn't be able to find them—thus sending multiple students, including the still-missing (and ultimately presumed dead) Leslie Weiss, on a doomed goose chase? Or had there never been a tribe with the characteristics, and extreme isolation, of the one that had made Fortunata's reputation?

These events occurred during the palm-tree years, as we'd come to think of them, when our mother was so removed from academic life that she barely registered the controversy. But on returning to her studies, she rejected every suspicion of her former professor with a vehemence that intrigued us. Fortunata appeared quite striking in the black-and-white jacket photo on his famous book: thick hair, barbed teeth, a nose that clearly had been broken more than once. He looked like a man who'd been pummeled, accidentally, into handsomeness. We snickered that our mother had been in love with him, but she claimed barely to have known him when she was a student; although Fortunata was charismatic in public, she said, he'd been agonizingly shy one-on-one, incapable of small talk. It was the *mystery* of Professor Fortunata that captivated her. She read everything he'd written, including the handwritten notes from his original fieldwork. At night, surrounded by sheets of the professor's spidery cursive, she used an eight-track player our father unearthed for her to listen to Fortunata's recordings of the tribe's song cycles: deep, rich vocals arising from a mesh of ambient noise that suggested trees and rain and muttering beasts. We listened raptly, gazing at the professor's beaten-looking face.

· · ·

Our mother stepped deeper inside this mystery in 1991, in our sophomore and junior years of high school. She was forty-one. Her goal
was not (she insisted) to locate the descendants of Fortunata's original subjects but to test and strengthen a theory she was developing
about human "affinities," or what made people like and trust one another. She needed to spend time inside a community whose members'
histories were mutually known in their entirety, and that mass media
had never touched.

We moved into our father's house two days before our mother
flew to Brazil to begin what she projected would be eight or nine
months of fieldwork. We were excited and nervous, having never
spent a night with our father, but our mother was deeply hesitant to
leave us. She called each night from São Paolo and we tried not to
cry on the phone. When had we ever been without her? She was like
the palm tree in our old apartment complex, and her absence gaped
like the void that uprooted tree would have left.

You're strong girls, she told us on the phone in those first days.
Stronger than you know. Be strong for each other, and for your father.

Then the calls stopped, and she was lost—that was how it felt
after a week, two weeks, without her voice. We had lost her. Anticipating our bereavement, she'd written a series of fifty letters addressed to "My Jellybeans," intending that we open them at weekly
intervals. But we were too old to be comforted by such a ploy and
stopped reading after the first three. The letters reminded us of the
warm circle we'd shared with our mother all our lives. Reading them
made our longing for her unbearable.

Rolph's suicide had taken place several months before our mother left
for Brazil. We learned of it when we found her weeping inconsolably
in our apartment one evening. Weeks passed before we saw our father
again. Rolph was twenty-eight when he died. If there was a funeral,
a memorial—any of that—we never knew.

We'd seen less of our father in the months since Rolph's death, and he had seemed much the same as before. But he wasn't the same—nothing was the same, as we came to understand within days of moving into his house. The parties had stopped, the visitors were gone, and Jocelyn had taken off for good. Rolph had shot himself in our father's house. We weren't sure how we knew this, didn't want to know it, but his violent extinction hung over the place like a curse. We looked at the water fluttering in the gray swimming pool (which our father had ceased to use) and asked each other, Did it happen there? Did it happen in the kitchen? In the TV room? In the exercise room? In one of the halls? In one of the bedrooms? In the room we shared? Amid the pounding, dreadful silence, the grim truths our father had concealed from us began to crawl into view.

One night, Charlie got drunk and screamed at our father that it was his fault Rolph had done it. She locked herself in a bathroom with a pair of freshly sharpened shears, and our father, thinking she would slit her wrists, hurled himself against the door until his shoulder dislocated. Shrieking in terror, we called 911. Before the police arrived, Charlie opened the bathroom door and emerged with her head shorn like a prisoner's, her white skull bleeding where the shears had nicked her. Her long golden hair, the same that our father had spun into a glittering bun years before, lay streaked across the bathroom floor.

"My name is Charlene," she told all of us flatly. "Don't call me Charlie anymore."

Roxy nodded off by the pool one afternoon, and her lips and fingertips turned blue. No one could rouse her. Our father called 911 and rode away with her in the ambulance. Left behind in the death house, we crumpled onto our beds and keened for our mother. She alone could protect us from these abominations. We now understood that she had done it all our lives.

· · ·

And then, in the span of a year, we grew up—or maybe we'd grown up already and perceived it only then, without our mother to care for us. We turned sixteen and seventeen the year she was in Brazil, and found that we were capable in combination—more so than our grief-riven father and our broken sisters. We had each other, and in each other we had our mother. We felt her calm logic guiding us as we swept Charlene's lustrous hair into a bag and sent it to a wig maker for cancer patients. We drove Roxy to recovery meetings after school. Over our father's objections, we hired a vaunted family therapist to come to the house. Dr. Kray turned out to be a giggly, profane man with wings of Bozo-the-clown hair and a collection of sock puppets he wanted us to use to talk to one another. The debacle of our one session with Dr. Kray provoked the first genuine laugh we'd heard from our father since Rolph's death. He laughed until tears ran down his face. And with that laugh, a scrabble of new life began to assert itself.

Our mother's first and only real letter arrived seven months after her departure, on a thin membrane of airmail stationery. She'd written it over weeks, perhaps months, in tiny script in black ballpoint pen that had withstood water stains and all manner of organic smearing. She relayed no direct information; rather, each sentence contained an impression or a thought:

> *The forest is like a sentient creature drawing breath around me.*
> *The moon's brightness has a sound. It rings in the sky.*
> *I've had a fever, which has been hard, but it has left my mind clearer than before.*
> *There's another way of seeing the world, like looking through the bottom of a glass.*

We read the letter beside our father's swimming pool. Sunlight was key to deciphering our mother's cramped script, which also must have been written in sunlight. We alternated reading passages aloud, and when we finished, we both sat quietly, listening to the waterfall trickling over the Portuguese tiles. Then we looked at each other and said, She found them.

Our mother's return took place in stages: first her long-distance voice on the phone from Rio, then a gravitational shift as we timed the progress of her flight to Los Angeles. Though we'd thirsted for her, we felt unexpected reluctance to have her back. Some of it was petty; who wants to return to an apartment full of highway noise after hearing the ocean at night? Who wants to give up midnight swims? And our father had finally begun to flourish. He swam his morning laps again. He listened to music again—was selling music again. After school, we drove to his office, where our role had evolved from trying to animate a grief-gutted husk to real collaboration. Listen to this; what do you think? They're playing tonight; shall we go have a listen? What do you think? Good bet? Bad bet? Worth the risk?

Unlike rock stars, who emerged before other passengers from airplanes we'd gone to meet with our father, our mother was the last to disembark. Holding our pink helium balloons and "Welcome Home!" sign, we grew increasingly bereft.

She looked small, older than we remembered. Her entire person appeared to be a single hazel-olive tone: clothes, skin, hair, eyes—all registered on that same narrow spectrum. She smelled faintly of charred wood. How could this small monochromatic woman be our mother?

Then she gathered us into her arms and we held her, feeling the heat from under her skin, and we were the three-headed monster again, with its three yearning hearts. We held our mother as long as we could, and then longer, until she started to laugh.

My beautiful grown-up daughters, she said.

. . .

To our relief, there was no question of our moving back into the old apartment; our mother hated it now. I can't listen to traffic all day, she said, and I feel the dirt in my lungs.

She moved to a smaller place: a one-bedroom where highway sounds were more muted. She bought a big pullout couch and said, You two can share it when you want to stay over.

We had no wish to stay over, and our mother seemed to know this. Sorrow hung about her.

What's the matter, Mama? Why are you sad?

Who says I am?

We can tell.

I'm not sad, I'm just adjusting. To being back.

How long will it take?

I don't know. I've never done it before.

Solitude eked from the single coffee cup and plate and fork in the drying rack by her sink. One wineglass with a dark red ring. One plant with spiky leaves. A bird feeder leaned on the windowsill, but the tree turned out to be too far away for her to hang it.

Tell us about the tribe, we said, fingering the plant, whose spiky leaves were unexpectedly soft. How did you talk to them?

Through signs at first, and gradually, with language.

Were they nice?

I'm not sure what that means.

Were they nice to *you*.

Yes.

Why don't you like talking about them?

It's like trying to make myself heard from the bottom of a well.

Who has the energy to deal with a small sad woman at the bottom of a well? We sizzled with impatience we couldn't hide, in part because our mother knew us too well. But also because of the strange new way she watched our movements, our glances—even (it seemed, at times) our thoughts. She had always been observant, but now her watchfulness was exaggerated to the point of aberration, like a distended limb. She was the opposite of our father, who feinted and bragged erratically, even lied outright, yet was legible and easily controlled.

Three or four months after our mother's return, a skin formed over her sadness and new zeal seized her. She'd begun working on her book. The apartment was awash in her notes. She opened the couch into a bed to make space for more materials, ran strings across the living room, and clipped pages to them with clothespins. There were long mathematical equations; clearly, this was a book no one would read. Our mother had gone mad.

After a year she began to travel, presenting bits of her work in progress at academic conferences. Before leaving, she always called us at our father's house, where we'd chosen to live rather than decamp to student housing at USC, where we were in college.

Hi, Mom! we'd cry with a violent brightness we'd adopted in the hope of slapping away her solitary sorrow—though it had only seemed to deepen it. Now she used that same bright tone with us.

Getting on a plane, girls!

Where to?

Ann Arbor!

Say hello to the snow!

Will do! Love you both!

We love you, too, Mama.

There was an echo under all that brightness, a cavity left by the deep entwinement that once had sustained us. We were nothing like our mother, it turned out. We were our father's creatures. We loved his music empire and the characters who populated it; we'd made an office next to his and geared our college coursework toward recording industry expertise. We loved the messy tragedy of his life, the

loose ends and failed children; the enemies and sports cars and out-
bursts and midnight inspirations; his obtrusiveness even as he swam
his morning laps, snorting in breath and, when he emerged, flinging
water from his head like a dog. He couldn't function without us;
would not undertake a major decision without our help. It was deeper
than love, it was need. All our lives, we had needed our mother; now
our father needed us.

There came a night when we arrived at our mother's apartment for
one of our occasional dinners and found it empty of papers. Her
book had been done for over a year, but she'd awaited its publication
surrounded by the fluffy detritus of its creation, like a gerbil or some
other nest-building creature.

Are you moving? we asked.

I have a new office at the university. They've given me a tenure-
track position on the basis of . . . this!

From the windowsill, where the unused bird feeder still rested,
she took two slim hardcover volumes and handed one to each of us.
Patterns of Affinity, by Miranda Kline. There was no image on the
cover, just a quiet geometric pattern. We were mesmerized.

Miranda.

That is my name.

But everyone calls you Mindy.

You don't use a nickname on a book.

Kline?

I've kept that name. As you know.

But on a book?

I don't want a different name from yours. Even on a book.

Our mother had become the author Miranda Kline. We carefully
brought the two books home—or to the wing of our father's house
he'd ceded to us. When we showed him the books, he instantly par-
took of our reverence.

She did it, he said. He opened a bottle of champagne and poured each of us a glass at the wax-spattered table where we now presided, among friends and boyfriends, as often as he did. To your mother, he said. A remarkable woman. She said she would do it, and by God, she did it.

We toasted Miranda Kline and drank. She'd done it. But none of us had the slightest notion of *what* she'd done.

We placed the books proudly on a shelf without opening them.

4

Four years after *Patterns of Affinity* was published, in the summer of 1999, our father's friend and protégé Bennie Salazar came to visit from New York with one of his bands, the Conduits. We were out of college by then, working full-time for our father. At the office, Bennie wanted to play us a song we didn't have on CD. We asked one of our summer interns, Keisha, to drive to Tower Records and buy it.

You don't have to do that, Keisha said. She logged in to Napster and played us the song.

Do that again, our father said.

Keisha used Napster to play several more songs, some of whose copyrights we owned. Thanks, doll, our father said, apparently having grown bored with the lesson. That was very instructive.

Later, after Bennie and the Conduits had dinner at our house, our father asked the two of us to take a walk on the beach. That usually meant he'd had an idea.

Our beach could look many ways at night; sometimes the water was bright and the sand dark, other times the reverse. That night, the sand had a lunar fluorescence, making inky shadows around our bare feet.

Without preamble, our father said, In five years, not a single person is going to pay for music. He was peering toward a horizon impossible to make out in the hazy dark. I'm watching a tidal wave, he said. The complete annihilation of my business.

You're overreacting, Daddy.

If you think so, you've learned less than I thought.

We fell into chastened silence. We were learning something right then: People project their internal states onto the landscape. Our father was sixty-five. He'd been through a lot. He still had plenty of vitality, but not enough to reinvent his business. All he could see was an end.

And us? We were twenty-three and twenty-four, still near enough to college that functioning as adults felt like pulling something off. We saw the same facts our father did, but differently, *through the bottom of a glass*—that image came to both of us, we discovered later. People were letting the Internet go inside their computers and play their music, so that they, too, could play songs they didn't own without having to buy them. The idea made us squeamish; it was like letting a stranger rummage through your house—or your brain! Once the Internet was inside your computer rifling through your music, what else might it decide to look at?

No, we thought, our father was wrong. Once the novelty wore off, no one would be dumb enough to do this.

Our mother's reputation had grown since *Patterns of Affinity* was published, in the invisible (to us, though we'd only just left it) world of the university. She got tenure quickly and was beloved by her students, whom she fed pots of beef-and-lentil stew at the bungalow where she lived with Marco, a colleague she'd fallen in love with.

Shortly after the music industry went into free fall exactly as our father had predicted, he had a stroke that left him dragging his right leg. Our mother shared our woe at seeing him in such a state. Your poor father, she said. How can I help? On weekends, she and Marco brought nuts and oranges and cracked crab to the house—gifts for us as well as for our father.

You girls are too young to shoulder all this, she kept telling us, but how could we not try? In frantic league, we flailed for ways to end the "sharing" that was dismantling our father's business and our father. We contemplated a nationwide billboard campaign to remind people of that eternal law, *Nothing is free!* Only children expect otherwise, even as myths and fairy tales warn us: Rumpelstiltskin, King Midas, Hansel and Gretel. *Never trust a candy house!* It was only a matter of time before someone made them pay for what they thought they were getting for free. Why could nobody see this?

Our father's strokes—six in all—seemed a barbarous enactment of the assault that mass-marauding theft was visiting upon the industry he'd helped to shape. First he limped; then was paralyzed on one side; then confined to bed, hardly able to speak. Our house became a hospital and finally a hospice, with round-the-clock care and opium drips. We enlisted Bennie Salazar's help to bring people who had loved our father to say goodbye. Even Jocelyn came. She and a high school friend wheeled his bed to the pool and stood beside him as he eyed the gray water.

At some point in the course of our grief and frustration—our helplessness at watching our father reel, then buckle—we drifted from seeking ways to warn people of the Faustian bargain they were making, to hungering for their punishment.

Neither of us remembered who read *Patterns of Affinity* first. It may have been simultaneous, as so many things were for the two of us, for so long. Nor did we recall what moved us finally to open those slender volumes that had lain untouched on a shelf since 1995.

Patterns of Affinity introduces, with elegant simplicity, formulas for predicting human inclinations. In order to work, the algorithms require intimate knowledge of the individuals in question: a breadth of information that our mother could acquire only in a remote, insular community where the history of each member was known to all the rest. At the book's conclusion, she speculates that her formulas' predictive powers could, theoretically, be applied to people living in a complex, mobile environment . . . *but doing so would require exhaustive personal information that would be impossible to acquire in a modern setting without posing an array of intrusive questions whose answers few people, if any, would be willing to supply.*

Wrong, we thought. They're giving it away for a song.

Let the record show that we did nothing without our mother's explicit permission.

Whatever I've done belongs to you, she told us. Use it any way you like, and by all means, try to help your poor father.

In fairness, she had no idea what we were asking.

But she never retreated from that position—at least not to our faces—even after we'd patented her algorithms and sold them to the social media giants whose names we all know. Later, she spurned the credit that Bix Bouton and the others tried to give her, and she used her unwanted pop stardom to rail against the invasiveness of data gathering and manipulation, to insist on the deeply private nature of human experience, etc., etc. Still, she kept us out of it. She never once spoke our names in public or acknowledged, even to us, that we'd made a tragedy of her career by perverting her theory to bring about the end of private life.

But we grew apart.

In the end, the monster's three hearts yearned for different things. I, Melora, the youngest, carry on our father's legacy. Most of the music you hear passes through my hands, and I've absorbed innumerable companies along the way, including Bennie Salazar's, although I call him my partner out of respect.

Lana broke away in 2025, the year after our mother did. She, too, has joined the eluders—that invisible army of data defiers. The two of them are likely together, much as it hurts me to think of this.

Winning has its price, like everything else.

I've wondered endlessly—obsessively—when and how Lana's perspective began to diverge from mine after so much shared history. If we'd uploaded our memories to the Collective Consciousness, I could pinpoint the moment exactly. But we both knew better than that.

Our father's office belongs to me. His trophies, and mine, line the walls, and sunlight splinters on the ocean outside my windows. As I stare at it, I sometimes imagine eluding myself: selling off Melora Kline or consigning her to a proxy (now a booming and specialized business) and starting over as someone else. I wouldn't go far. In fact, my favorite fantasy involves returning to Venice Beach on a Sunday, something I haven't done in many years. I imagine threading my way among Rollerbladers and dancers and grifters and stoned teens, past acres of sunbathers shielding their eyes to study their screens while invisible entities study them in return. I wend my way to a nondescript bench where two women are already seated, familiar strangers, and sit down beside them at last.

Where have you been? I imagine asking as I fold them into my arms.

Right here, they say. Waiting for you.

What the Forest Remembers

Once upon a time, in a faraway land, there was a forest. It's gone now (burned), and the four men walking in it are gone, too, which is what makes it far away. Neither it nor they exist.

But in June 1965, the redwoods have a velvety primeval look that brings to mind leprechauns or djinn or faeries. Three of the four men have never been in these ancient woods, and to them the forest looks otherworldly, so removed is it from their everyday vistas of wives and children and offices. The oldest, Lou Kline, is only thirty-one, but all were born in the 1930s and raised without antibiotics, their military service completed before they went to college. Men of their generation got started on adulthood right away.

So: four men moving among trees whose musculature resembles the thighs of giants. When the men throw back their heads to search the sunlight for the trees' pointed tips, they grow dizzy. That's partly because they've just smoked marijuana; not a common practice in 1965, especially among squares, as anyone would agree these four are. Or three of them. There is a leader—there is usually a leader when men leave their established perimeters—and today it is Quinn Davies, a tanned, open-faced man accoutered with artifacts of a Native American ancestry he wishes he possessed. Normally, Quinn would wear a blazer, like the rest of them, but today he's donned what strikes his pals as a costume: a purple velvet coat and heavy moccasins that prove far better suited to navigating this soft undergrowth than the oxfords they're sliding around in. Only Lou manages to keep pace with Quinn, despite the fawnlike skittering this feat requires of him. Lou would rather look spasmodic than risk falling behind.

These men all moved to California recently, driven by a lust for space that can't be satisfied by old cities with their tinge of Europe and horse carts and history. There is an ungoverned feel to California's mountains and deserts and reckless coast. Quinn Davies, the only bachelor in the group, is homosexual, and was on the lookout early for a graceful exit from Bridgeport, Connecticut, where his family has lived for generations. After the navy, he followed the Beats to San Francisco, but now that he's here, they've proved maddeningly elusive. Still, there are always sailors who share Quinn's view that a man can be a multitude of ways, depending on circumstances. He has a flickering hope about one of the other four: Ben Hobart, from Minnesota, married to his high school sweetheart, a father of three. But it's too soon to tell.

All four work in San Francisco in banking, doing their part to feed an expansion that will draw more restless folk like themselves to the city. Over drinks on Montgomery Street a few weeks back, they got to talking about "grass," as marijuana is known even to those who have never seen it. They know grass is around, but what *is* it, exactly? What does it do? All four like to drink. Quinn Davies drinks so that those around him will drink, too—which occasionally makes possible an unexpected adventure. Ben Hobart drinks because it subdues a greedy energy that can find no outlet around his wife and kids. Tim Breezely drinks because he's depressed, but that isn't a word he would use. Tim drinks to feel happy. He drinks because, after several bourbons, he's overcome by a sensation of soaring lightness, as if he'd finally set down a pair of heavy valises he didn't realize he was carrying. Tim Breezely has a complaining wife and four complaining daughters. Inside his small Clement Street house, he drifts in a tide of shrill feminine discontent that followed him here all the way from Michigan, ranging from aggrieved and exhausted (his wife) to shrieking and infantile (the baby). A son would have made the difference, Tim is convinced, but drinking helps—oh, it helps. Well worth the two bent fenders, the broken taillight, and the multitude of dents he's made in the Cadillac.

No matter how much Lou Kline drinks—and he drinks a lot—a part of him is always removed, watching with faint detachment as the men around him get plastered. Lou is waiting for something. He thought it was love until he married Christine, whom he worships; then he thought it was fatherhood; then moving west, as they did two years ago. But the sensation of waiting persists: an intimation of some approaching change that has nothing to do with Christine or their kids or the house in Belvedere on a man-made lake where Lou swims a mile each morning and sails a little Sunfish. He's become the social impresario of their cul-de-sac, organizing cookouts and cocktails, even a dance one night last summer, dozens of neighbor couples swaying barefoot by the lake to Sinatra and the Beatles. At Christine's urging, he unearthed his sax and played it that night for the first time since his jazz-combo days at the University of Iowa, mildly electrified when everyone clapped. Life is good—it's perfect, really—yet Lou is haunted by a sense of something just beyond it, something he is missing.

Charlene, whom they call Charlie, is six. This morning she scrutinized Lou, wrinkling her sunburned nose, and asked, "Where are you going?"

"Short trip north," he said. "Some fishing, little duck hunting, maybe . . ."

"You don't have a gun," Charlie said. She watched him evenly, her long tangled hair raking the light.

Lou found himself avoiding her eyes. "The others do," he said.

His little boy, Rolph, clung to him at the door. Pale and dark-haired; Christine's coloring, her iridescent eyes. It's the strangest thing when Lou holds his son, as if their flesh were starting to bind, so that letting go of him feels like tearing. He has a guilty awareness of loving Rolph more than Charlie. Is that wrong? Don't all men feel that way about their sons—or those lucky enough to have sons? Poor Tim Breezely!

There will be no fishing, no hunting. What Quinn divulged, that afternoon on Montgomery Street as they drank and smoked their Parliaments and roared with laughter before driving their big cars home to their wives and kids, was that he knew of some "bohemians" who *grew grass* in the middle of a forest near Eureka. They welcomed visitors. "We can go overnight on a weekend sometime, if you like," Quinn said.

They did.

How can I possibly know all this? I was only six, and stuck at home despite my fervent wish to come along—I always wanted to go with my father, sensing early (or so it seems, looking back) that the only way to hold his attention was to stay in his presence. How can I presume to describe events that occurred in my absence in a forest now charred and exuding an odor like seared meat? How dare I invent across chasms of gender, age, and cultural context? Trust me, I would not dare. Every thought and twinge I record arises from concrete observation, although getting hold of that information is arguably more presumptuous than inventing it would have been. Pick your poison— if imagining isn't allowed, then we have to resort to gray grabs.

I got lucky; all four men's memories are in the Collective Consciousness, at least in part—surprising, given their ages, and downright miraculous in my father's case. He died in 2006, ten years before Mandala's Own Your Unconscious was released. So how could my father have used it? Well, remember: Bix Bouton's genius lay in refining, compressing, and mass-producing, as a luscious, irresistible product, technology that already existed in crude form. Memory externalization had been whispered about in psychology departments since the early 2000s, with faculty speculating about its potential to revolutionize trauma therapy. *What really happened? Wouldn't it help you to know what you've repressed?* Why does my mind (for example) wander persistently to a family party my parents took me to in San Francisco around the time this story takes place? I remember scrambling with a bunch of kids around the roots of an old tree; then being alone in someone's attic beside a white wicker chair. Again and again: scrambling with those children, then alone in an unfamiliar attic. Or not alone, because who brought me there, and why? What was happening while I looked at that chair? I've wondered many times whether knowing those answers would have allowed me to live my life with less pain and more joy. But by the time one of my father's caregivers told us about a psychology professor at Pomona College who was uploading people's consciousnesses for an experimental project, I was too wary to participate. A gain is a loss when it comes to technology—my father's imploding business had taught me that much. But my father had little else to lose; he'd had five strokes and was expiring before our eyes. He wanted in.

Lana and Melora were consumed with trying to save our father's recording empire, Roxy had moved to San Francisco, and Kiki lived in Connecticut. Rolph had been dead for many years. So it fell to me to greet the young Pomona professor, who wore red high-top sneakers, along with his two graduate students and a U-Haul full of equipment, early one morning at my father's house, in 2006. I parted the sparse remnants of my father's surfer shag and fastened twelve electrodes to his head. Then he had to lie still—asleep, awake, it didn't matter and there wasn't much of a difference at that point— for eleven hours. I'd moved his hospital bed to the pool so he could hear his artificial waterfall. I sat beside him for most of the time; it seemed too intimate a process to let him undergo with strangers. I held his floppy hand while a wardrobe-size machine rumbled beside us. After eleven hours, the wardrobe contained a copy of my father's consciousness in its entirety: every perception and sensation he had experienced, starting at the moment of his birth.

"It's a lot bigger than a skull," I remarked as one of the graduate students wheeled over a hand truck to take away the wardrobe. My father still wore the electrodes.

"The brain is a miracle of compression," the professor said.

I have no memory of that exchange, by the way. I saw and heard it only when I reviewed that day from my father's point of view. Looking out through his eyes, I noticed—or, rather, *he* noticed—my short, uninteresting haircut, the middle-aged gut I was already starting to amass, and I heard him muse (but "hear" isn't the right word; we don't hear our thoughts aloud, exactly), *How did that pretty little girl end up looking so ordinary?*

When Own Your Unconscious came out, in 2016, I was able to have the wardrobe's contents copied into a luminous one-foot-square yellow Mandala Consciousness Cube. I chose yellow because it made me think of the sun, of my father swimming. Once his memories were inside the Cube, I was finally able to view them. At first, the possibility of sharing them never crossed my mind; I didn't know it was possible. The Collective Consciousness wasn't a focus of Mandala's early marketing, whose slogans were "Recover Your Memories" and "Know Your Knowledge." My father's consciousness seemed like more than enough—overwhelming, in fact—which is maybe why, over time, I began to crave other points of view. Sharing his was the price. As the legal custodian of my father's consciousness, I authorized its anonymous release, in full, to the collective. In exchange, I'm able to use date and time, latitude and longitude, to search the anonymous memories of others present on that day, in those woods, in 1965, without having to invent a thing.

Let us return to the men scrambling behind or alongside (in my father's case) Quinn Davies, their guide. The introduction to grass took place at the trailhead, where Quinn passed around a small pipe, refilling it several times. Most people didn't get high on their first exposure (this was good old-fashioned *pot*, mind you, full of stems and seeds, long before the days of hydroponic sinsemilla). Quinn wanted to get this first smoke out of the way, to prime his pals—Ben Hobart in particular—for getting well and truly *wasted* later on.

A river flashes in and out of view far below, like a snake sliding among leaves. As they climb, the men's stumbling and guffawing yields to huffing, wheezing, and struggle. All four smoke cigarettes, and none exercise the way we think of it now. Even Ben Hobart, one of those preternaturally fit guys who can eat anything, is breathing too hard for speech by the time they crest the hill and glimpse A-Frame, as the house is known. Tucked in a redwood clearing and built from the cleared redwood, A-Frame is the sort of whimsical wood-and-glass structure that will become a cliché of 1970s California architecture. But to these men, it looks like an apparition from a fairy tale: *Is it real? What kinds of people live here?* Compounding the eeriness is Simon and Garfunkel's "Sound of Silence" welling from hi-fi speakers facing outward on the redwood deck. A-Frame's mastermind, Tor, has somehow managed to wire a house in the middle of a forest, approachable only on foot.

Hello, darkness, my old friend . . .

A hush of awe engulfs the four as they approach. Lou falls back, letting Quinn lead the way into a soaring cathedral of space whose vast triangular windows reach all the way to its pointed ceiling. The scent of redwood is overpowering. Quinn introduces Tor, an austere eminence in his forties with long prematurely white hair. Tor's "old lady," Bari, is a warmer zaftig presence. An assortment of young people mill about the main room and deck, showing no interest in the new arrivals.

This odd setup leaves our three newcomers unsure what to do with themselves. Lou, who can't tolerate feeling like a hanger-on, is abruptly angry with Quinn, who speaks quietly and privately with Tor. *What the hell kind of greeting is this?* Nowadays, a man ill at ease in his surroundings will pull out his phone, request the Wi-Fi password, and rejoin a virtual sphere where his identity is instantly reaffirmed. Let us all take a moment to consider deeply what isolation was customary before these times arrived! The only possible escape for Lou and his friends involves retracing their steps through the forest without breadcrumbs to guide them. So Lou paces around A-Frame in a way he cannot seem to help (though he feels its disruption), barking occasional questions at Tor, who sits aloft on a tall wooden chair that looks irritatingly thronelike: "Nice place, Tor. What sort of work do you do? Must've been hell getting pipes laid this far out . . ."

Lou opens doors and peers inside redwood-smelling nooks that are what pass for rooms in this kooky place. He's stopped cold in one room by the sight of a dark-haired girl sitting naked on the floor, cross-legged under a small window, her eyes shut. Tree-filtered light dapples her flesh and the dark spread of her pubic hair. Her eyes open slowly at the intrusion. Lou chokes out, "Beg pardon, I'm awfully sorry," and slinks away.

The desultory group begins, at last, to congregate around Tor in preparation for getting high. The Yardbirds are playing, but the world of their music is too far from Lou's own world for him to enjoy it. Still, he welcomes the sense of incipient coherence, a fresh structure of meaning. Tor has a knack for orchestrating such moments. Intimate of Kerouac, occasional lover of Cassady, future provider of LSD for Kesey, Wavy, Stone, and the rest, Tor is one of those essential figures who catalyze action in other people and then fade into nonexistence without making it into the history.

By my count, there are seventeen revelers: Tor and Bari, our four, the naked girl Lou was surprised by, now clothed in a loose flowered dress and meeting his gaze without embarrassment, and sundry others who look to be in their late teens and early twenties, who live in A-Frame's several outbuildings and farm Tor's marijuana crop.

Lou vastly prefers Tor's totemlike bong to the diminutive pipe he smoked with Quinn. Over the course of an hour's communal smoking and music changes, the group wafts into a state of blinkered absorption that is unprecedented for Lou, Tim, and Ben, who until now have known only booze as a means of consciousness alteration. Basic exchanges elongate like time-lapse fruits ripening and dropping into outstretched hands.

"This . . . grass . . . was . . . grown . . . around . . . here . . . ?" (Ben Hobart asking Tor)

"Yeah, the . . . crop . . . is . . . walking . . . distance . . ." (Quinn answering Ben Hobart)

"You . . . live . . . up . . . here . . . full . . . time . . . ?" (Lou asking Tor)

"We ... finished ... building ... a year ... ago ..." (Bari answering Lou)

Tor, you may notice, says virtually nothing. He has a story, too, but I can't tell it—he and Bari are childless, and there are no intimates' memories in the collective to scavenge from. Since Tor will pass away long before the era of Own Your Unconscious, we have only these glimpses of him through the eyes of his acquaintances.

There are still some mysteries left.

When widespread intoxication has been achieved, the group gathers at a long table. Or, rather, the men gather. Bari and the other women ferry to and from the kitchen, assembling a lavish vegetarian meal in bowls and on platters. To midwestern men whose days start with pork sausage and end with beef stroganoff or corned beef hash (or, better yet, steak or roast), the phrase "vegetarian meal" is an oxymoron. What can it mean? For Lou, it means the most delicious repast he has ever imbibed in his life—although, given the stoned arousal of his appetite, hardtack and warm water would have prompted similar raptures. Bari serves squash and turnips and tomatoes from her garden, along with "tahini sauce," something none of our visitors have ever tasted but can well believe was harvested from the Elysian Fields. Then come bowls of sorghum and buckwheat, chewy and wet and warm, served in towering piles that they devour in spoonfuls, with tufts of alfalfa sprouts and sliced avocados and Bari's fresh-baked whole wheat bread.

As I watched all of this through my father's eyes, I found myself asking a question he was likely too stoned or disoriented to ask for himself: *Why?* Why are Tor and Bari—and Quinn, for that matter— giving the red-carpet treatment to three squares who are entirely on the consuming end of the business? Well, how many reasons can there be? Money or sex: Pick your poison! For Quinn, it's sex, which he's had before with men at A-Frame (including Tor once) and which he's hoping he'll have tonight with Ben Hobart, based on nothing more than a hunch. For Tor, it's money. He's run through most of his inheritance building this place and planting ten acres of marijuana; he could use an investor or two. But there's a deeper reason: Tor has thrown himself into creating an alternate world, but hardly anyone has seen it. As a person who feels most alive in the act of awakening others, he longs to witness his vision ablaze in new eyes.

Toward the end of the meal, the sun drops behind the mountains, leaving the redwoods silhouetted like iron cutouts through the windows. As if at a signal, the younger revelers leave the table and begin pulling instruments from the nook where Tor and Bari stow them: bongos and castanets, shakers and recorders and ukuleles, plenty of options for those who can't carry a tune. The formerly naked girl appears with a clarinet that must be her own. Several people have guitars, and Tor carries a flute. They begin to leave the house, walking in twos and threes along a path that leads uphill through the redwoods. Lou and his friends are swept along into the cool, fragrant woods. Quinn dares to sling an arm around Ben Hobart's shoulders, causing a rogue flash of electricity to judder down Ben's spine. He glances at Quinn, deeply startled, and doesn't move away.

Tim Breezely trudges along in the rear. He'd like a drink. Smoking grass has drained his vigor, and added to the weight of his invisible valises is that of a mandolin someone handed him to carry. He's last to reach the hilltop. When he does, the redwoods give way to cleared land and it's sunny again, final rays browsing among the serrated leaves of a waist-high marijuana crop. Tim Breezely's mood lifts in this openness and light. The air has a dry, tart snap. A circle has already been cleared for bonfires on cold nights, and the group assembles there as if by habit, each putting down their instruments to take the hands of those adjacent before they sit. Emboldened by his earlier success, Quinn seizes Ben Hobart's hand, eliciting jolts of sensation in Ben that approach the orgasms he has with his wife. Lou happens, just happens, to find himself beside the formerly naked clarinetist, but his legs won't really cross; he hasn't sat "Indian-style" since boyhood.

Once seated, they close their eyes as if in meditation. I've witnessed this silent period from every available consciousness in the collective, and I have glints of what ran through each mind as they sat together in the dregs of sunlight: First Communion on a rainy morning; scooping black goldfish from a pond; a ringing in his ears; the sensation of landing a backflip . . . But my problem is the same one had by everyone who gathers information: What to do with it? How to sort and shape and use it? How to keep from drowning in it?

Not every story needs to be told.

Tor breaks the silence with the first and only sustained utterance his guests will hear from him today. In a thin voice, he asks them to feel the presence of a higher power in the food they've eaten, in the land beneath them and the sky above; to feel the uniqueness of this moment of the twentieth century—to forget, briefly, the scourge of wars and apocalyptic weaponry in favor of this beauty, this peace. "Feel it, my friends," Tor says, "and be grateful for our blessed convergence."

A vibration seems to roll up from inside the warm earth. The sun slips behind the mountain with a click of cold, an intimation of the Pacific Ocean snarling at cliffs just a few miles west. Tim Breezely finds that his eyes are wet. He wipes them discreetly as the others begin to play their instruments, and then he gives the mandolin a tentative strum. A guitarist with a fledgling beard leads the group, along with the clarinetist, through "Michael Row the Boat Ashore." It's a song these two know from their church growing up. They're an older sister and younger brother, like Rolph and me.

The array of instruments and harmonizing voices has a rousing effect. Bari floats to her feet and begins to dance. The others do the same, still playing their instruments. Quinn and Ben Hobart dance together, hands vehemently clasped; Tim Breezely dances with his mandolin. All of them move and sway, together and apart, in the fading light.

Lou and Tor alone remain seated. For Lou, my father, the music and dancing provoke a riot of alarmed awareness, as if he were remembering a flame left on, a door left open, a car left running beside a cliff. With a prescience that will distinguish him to the end of his life, Lou understands that the change he's been awaiting is now upon him. He has reached its source, can feel it in the soles of his feet. But he knows he's too old to partake. He's thirty-one, an old man! At the surprise thirtieth party he threw for Christine a few months back, a friend gave her a cane painted with polka dots! But Lou Kline won't tolerate being left behind. He must catapult himself into a producer's role, like Tor—who's older than he is, for Christ's sake! Not by growing grass; agriculture is too redolent of the Iowa terrain he left behind. But the music, there he can do something. He remembers the night in his cul-de-sac when everyone danced by the lake. Different dancing, different sound; the Yardbirds and their ilk have nothing to do with the life Lou Kline planned for himself, the one he's living now. They belong to the life he'll live next. He watches the brother-and-sister musicians and imagines them together on a stage. He thinks: *I can put them there.* And he does. We all know their music today.

Late that night, after Tor and Bari have gone to bed and Quinn and Ben Hobart have disappeared to parts unknown and some others have returned to the cleared land to make a bonfire (fire danger being a threat even then), Lou and Tim Breezely and the sibling musicians and their young friends descend the mountain to the river for a night swim. Lou leads—he is always drawn to water. He goes barefoot, a big improvement over his oxfords and downright sensuous on this carpet of velvety decay, as if sharp objects don't exist.

The river is smooth and still, pressed between walls of redwoods and so cold that their fingers throb when they dip them in. Could it harm them to submerge? Lou has heard of very cold water causing heart attacks, and feels responsible, having led everyone here. As they're mulling over the safety of swimming, Tim Breezely suddenly strips off his clothes and dives from a log, buck-naked. The smash of cold stops his breathing; he has a brief blackout sensation of death. But when he surfaces, howling, what's died is his gloom—he's left it on the river bottom. Freedom! Joy! Tim Breezely will soon divorce—they'll all divorce—everyone will divorce. An entire generation will throw off the fetters of rote commitment in favor of invention, hope—and we, their children, will try to locate the moment we lost them and worry that it was our fault. Tim Breezely will become a dedicated jogger before anyone jogs who isn't being chased. He'll write books about exercise and mental health that will make him a household name, and will receive thousands of letters from people whose lives he has transformed, even saved.

Cursing himself for not having jumped in first, Lou sloughs off his clothes and hurls himself into water so frigid it sends his nuts into his throat. There are splashes and screams as everyone follows him in. But when the agony passes and they've paddled around a bit, the cold reverses itself and becomes radiant heat. They leave the river tingling and euphoric, fused by their adventure, and scramble back up the mountain to A-Frame, naked and unashamed.

We waited at the window, Rolph and I, for our father to come home. Eventually, we went outside into our cul-de-sac. Our mother let us go barefoot, although we'd already had our bath. It was warm summer twilight. I wore a paisley brown-orange bathrobe, but I don't think I truly remember that. I have "memories" that are really just pictures from the albums our mother loved to make, telling our family story in small square photographs, still mostly black and white, with an occasional blaze of color as if everyone had woken up in Oz. That paisley bathrobe came back to me only when I watched our father's approach to the house through his eyes. I felt him note the blue beauty of the hour and experienced the surge of love that overwhelmed him at the sight of Rolph, in his cloth diaper, running toward him on stumpy three-year-old feet.

We seized our father's legs, and he put a hand on each of our heads, cupping Rolph's and holding it against him. Then he looked up at our mother, Christine, who smiled at him from beside the front door in a blue sweater, her dark hair falling from a clip. All around her were the spindly saplings they'd chosen together at a greenhouse and planted outside their brand-new California home, assuming they would live there forever.

Bright Day

In the last months of her life—she would die of an overdose at fifty-seven, in 2025—Roxy Kline turned philosophical. It was not what anyone would have expected. In the family calculus that allots roles based on childish inclination, Roxy had been classified early on as "wild"—mostly in contrast to her younger sister, Kiki, who collected rosaries and made the sign of the cross at their mother's boyfriends when they stayed over. In the course of her life, Roxy had more than fulfilled her "type"; in fact, she'd said that word—"wild"—so many times in recovery that it meant nothing to her.

In the Thursday-morning Dungeons & Dragons sessions at Bright Day, her treatment center, Roxy is fascinated by the way characters are made: A player rolls a few dice to assign values to traits like Charisma, Dexterity, and Intelligence, and then to acquired skills like Stealth and Animal Handling. A few die rolls, a list of scores, and boom—you have a Rogue or Wizard or Fighter with strengths and skills and weaknesses, exactly like a human being. Roxy once asked Chris Salazar, who leads the Dungeons & Dragons group with his friend Molly Cooke, if he ever scored real people that way: Generosity, Coordination, Immune System Strength, Sex Appeal . . .

"I don't," Chris said, "but the counters do. And the corporations who buy their numbers do. And the people who measure their own value in clicks and views do."

"That sounds bad," Roxy said anxiously.

Chris took her hands and squeezed them. He's thirty years younger than Roxy, still in his twenties, and treats her with loving indulgence. "Don't you fret," he said, kissing her cheek. "There's a way out of every labyrinth."

That conversation took place in the cramped apartment Chris shares with his girlfriend, Samantha. Roxy was there for Passover. Chris Salazar has come to feel more like family to Roxy than most of her family members, and she is included in his holidays. Chris is the son of Bennie Salazar, whom Roxy's father mentored and loved from the time Bennie was in high school. Like Bennie, Chris is beautiful, dark-eyed and olive-skinned, although Bennie's hair is silver now. Bennie first brought Chris and Roxy together ten years ago, when Chris came to the West Coast for college. But only in the past three years, since Chris started the Dungeons & Dragons group, have he and Roxy become close.

D&D happens in the early mornings at Bright Day, so working people can play for an hour after their dose. Normally, you would play in the evening, Chris says, after work, but drug treatment centers are not nighttime places. Bright Day closes in the afternoon.

All of the regular players are male except for Roxy, who doesn't actually play but likes to watch. Each week, Chris invites her to create a character and enter the game. You're never too late to join—there is no such thing as "too late" in recovery, as long as you're breathing. But Roxy is afraid of doing it wrong or not understanding. One of her "if onlys"—which take the form of spinning out the life you might have had if a certain bad thing hadn't happened (*if only I hadn't gotten in that car, if only my mom had walked into the room, if only I didn't care so much about being cool*)—is, for Roxy, *if only I wasn't dyslexic*, which is a way of saying, *if only I'd been born in 1998 instead of 1968*. According to videos she's watched, dyslexic kids do just fine nowadays—they write books and run schools! For Roxy, school was a prolonged episode of not understanding: sentences, paragraphs, chapters. Mathematical equations broke apart before her eyes. Had she learned to read for real, rather than the pecking way that's still the best she can do—had she happened to read Carson McCullers's *The Member of the Wedding*, for example, which Molly Cooke read aloud at Bright Day in three installments—she would have discovered that the *exact* emotions she experienced after a trip to London with her father, at sixteen, a trip that broke her, had been felt by others. She was not unique, but neither was she alone. Reading might have saved her.

"You look happy, Rox," Chris remarks, giving her a hug before she slides into one of the chairs around the gaming table in a small meeting room at Bright Day. She's just swallowed her dose at the window and returned the empty cup, and now she swishes water in her mouth to keep the methadone residue from eroding the enamel on her teeth. "What's your secret?"

"Who, me?" Roxy raises her hands in mock innocence. Everyone knows she's an incorrigible dabbler, trying to earn her way back to take-home doses after yet another dirty urine.

Chris watches her closely. He's empathetic to the point of telepathy. Roxy *does* have a secret this morning: Her Mandala Consciousness Cube—a present from her sisters for her fifty-eighth birthday next week—is supposed to arrive today. Her reason for requesting Own Your Unconscious is *not*, as it has been for many people she knows, to use the Collective Consciousness to solve a mystery: *Who was that kid who beat me up? Where is that teacher who touched me? Who killed my friend?* Or, more hopefully: *What happened to the guy I shared a beer with at Cafe Trieste in the 1990s? Who gave me that back massage during the Green Day concert in Golden Gate Park?* The love-reunion stories move Roxy to tears, but they haven't budged Chris's belief that externalizing your consciousness for any reason, even as a hedge against dementia, is a grievous mistake.

"If it stopped there, maybe," she's heard him say, "but it never stops there. The collective is like gravity: Almost no one can withstand it. In the end, they give it everything. And then the collective is that much more omniscient."

Almost no one can withstand the collective; Roxy will be the exception. She has no interest in other people's memories. She wants only to relive her best days—times she knows won't be matched by anything to come.

Today there are four regular D&D players plus a new one, tattooed and gym-bulked everywhere but his face, which has the caved-
in look of a meth head. Chris guides him through rolling the dice
and filling in his character sheet. Roxy isn't surprised when the new
player chooses to become a female Elf; people often seem to pick
D&D characters opposite to their everyday selves. Brawny men play
Dwarves, delicate men play Warrior Barbarians, which has led Roxy
to ponder, in a philosophical turn unusual for her, which one is really
them?

"Depends which world you think is the real one," Chris said, grinning when she asked him once.

Now he beckons her with an empty character sheet and says,
"What do you say, Rox? Is today the day?" She shakes her head. She
would play her opposite, too: a D&D version of her sixteen-year-old
self, a girl with molten ardor roiling in her chest and stomach and
groin, who was unafraid to hold the stare of any man, daring a result.
What would that be in D&D terms, and how can she ask without
embarrassing herself? Roxy lost her virginity at thirteen to her first
boyfriend, Terrence Chen, who was a junior in high school, and then
she dumped Terrence and went in search of men in their twenties
and thirties who could rise to her occasion. She took pride in her
mishaps. She'd been punched! Had her stomach pumped! Yet her
face in the mirror looked dewy and untouched, its birdlike angles
bewitching even to herself. She was gamine, her mother said. There
wasn't an ounce of fat on her body.

Roxy had located Terrence Chen again—the Internet version of
Terrence—when she first moved to Northern California in her early
thirties, in the brand-new millennium. Everyone was finding everyone on the Internet then. Terrence, it turned out, had also moved to
the Bay Area and was a veterinarian in Marin County. He looked
buff and handsome on his website, smiling over a foam of golden
retriever fur, and he appeared also to have several children and a wife
whose hair was the same color as the golden retriever's. Roxy toyed

with the idea of bringing her new rescue kitten to see Terrence the veterinarian, despite the inconvenience of schlepping across the bay to his practice. But no, she decided. Not yet. She needed to swan through the door to Terrence's clinic a clear winner. At that point she was still pretty; Lana and Melora had paid to restore her smile after the loss of several teeth, and to straighten out her nose from a bad break. She was slim and stylish in her thirties, could still dance. But she was also grappling with a heroin habit and had a dozen years behind her that Terrence would likely regard as lost. She needed to at least match and, better yet, exceed Terrence's high life score before casting her somewhat-less-pretty-but-undeniably-pretty self in his path. Fame would do it. Roxy had always believed she would be famous, and others had, too. And when she first moved to San Francisco and tracked down Terrence—almost twenty-five years ago now—fame was not out of the question.

Dungeons & Dragons unfolds glacially. Roxy marvels at the deep absorption of the players, who never seem impatient. It's as if the rest of life has slowed to match the pace of the game. The new female Elf employs sleight of hand and some magical objects to rescue the other players from a band of brigands in an ancient wood. There are no pictures of this wood; it is represented by a hand-drawn map on an old-fashioned sheet of graph paper like the kind Roxy remembers from geometry class. Other hand-drawn sheets represent dungeons, taverns, towns, catacombs, and even outer space: a vast web of inter-connected worlds that can be stored, between games, inside a manila envelope. Sometimes a player will depart one map through a "portal" and emerge onto a different sheet of graph paper, a transition Roxy finds electrifying. From one world to another, *like that!* Whenever a player emerges onto a new sheet, Chris and Molly switch roles as leader. The game is infinite.

Chris and Molly are not in recovery. Nor are they a couple; Chris is with Samantha, and Molly has a girlfriend, Iris. Until last year, Chris led the group with Colin Bingham, his best friend from childhood, who died from an overdose eight months ago. Chris has yet to regain his old lightheartedness since Colin's passing. It shook Roxy, too; Colin was in his twenties, young enough to have returned to mainstream life with hardly a gap to account for. Colin's skin was clear, he still had his teeth. He and Chris grew up together in Crandale, New York, where they played D&D as boys. Molly, too, is a friend from that time. After Colin died, Molly Cooke stepped in to take his place, but Molly is a meek and tentative pleaser, and Roxy is struggling not to hate her.

No player wants the session to end, they never do, and maybe the game's slowness is a form of delay. But at nine, they must cede the meeting room to a weekly gathering of Bright Day clients who are pregnant. Several big-bellied young women wait in the hall as the players file out, raucously crowing over their scrape with the brigands as if it were a real event.

Chris and Molly bring their books and maps to their office, on an upper floor of the same building as Bright Day. Chris's company, Mondrian, hosts gaming sessions at recovery centers all over the Bay Area. The walls of Mondrian's small office are lined with posters of fire-breathing dragons and cloaked assassins, and there are shelves full of books about magical beasts and an iron statue of an orc that Chris found inside an abandoned piece of luggage. But Roxy has gradually come to suspect that gaming is a cover for some deeper business at Mondrian. Mages and Barbarians have their special skills, and so do Former Junkies—one of which is Sense Subterfuge. Roxy *knows*. Her neighborhood is full of double meanings: The newsstand around the corner from Bright Day sells Oxy pills, the flower seller is a lookout, and at Betty's, a nearby lunch counter, you can score heroin from the busboys by prearrangement. Because Roxy is good at Feign Oblivion, another Former Junkie skill, people tend not to guard their words around her. While employing Apparent Inattention and Vacant Stare, she has overheard Chris on his phone discussing *contracts*, *impersonation*, and *mimesis*. She has heard him say, "The demand is overwhelming" and "She has an ear for dialogue." Where Roxy's skills fail her, though, is in knowing what any of it means. Is that the dyslexia? The nature of Chris and Molly's real work is as unintelligible to Roxy as the local drug hidey-holes are to the woman who parks her Mercedes in the O'Farrell Street garage and clickety-clacks toward the Opera House in a floaty turquoise dress. Beyond a certainty that Mondrian's deeper business is legal (no weapons or police avoidance) and unprofitable (Chris's apartment is tiny), Roxy is ignorant. Whatever it is, he is doing it for love.

She steps outside Bright Day for a cigarette. Wind and sunlight tear at the fog. A tingle of underground cables permeates downtown, faintly audible in the morning hush. Gray-white seagulls stalk the sidewalk for debris from last night's party (every night is a party on these streets), lofting away potato chips and pizza rinds in their long yellow beaks.

With forty-five minutes to kill before meeting her drug counselor at ten, Roxy heads for Betty's lunch counter. She hears trotting foot-steps behind her but doesn't turn, suspecting it's Molly. Sure enough, she hears "Are you going to get coffee?" and nods, exasperated. Her resistance to Molly isn't just because she replaced Colin, whom Roxy loved. With her frizzy hair and guileless smile, Molly Cooke is a misfit at Bright Day and in this neighborhood. She has no shell, no cool—is the sort of girl Roxy would have spurned or possibly tormented as a teenager. Molly knows instinctively where she isn't wanted and goes there anyway. Roxy dislikes her, above all, for awak-ening her mean side.

They sit side by side at the counter drinking cups of sour, watery coffee that would tip off anyone with a modicum of Sense Subterfuge that Betty's customers are here to buy something else. Externalizing your consciousness to a Mandala Cube takes four hours, and Roxy has persuaded herself that she might not be able to hold still that long without chemical assistance (Righteous Rationalization) in the form of a few bags that she absolutely will not use unless she has no

choice (Self-Duping). Molly Cooke sips the wretched coffee, oblivious. Her Sense Subterfuge score must be close to zero.

"What was Chris like as a kid?" Roxy asks. She likes to talk about
Chris—imagines sometimes that he's her son, not Bennie's.

"Oh, I was in love with him," Molly says. "He's a year older, which
added to his grandeur."

"Did you play D and D with him?"

"We played with Chris's uncle," Molly says. "And another girl,
Lulu. She came to Colin's memorial."

"I know Lulu!" Roxy says with excitement. "She works for Bennie."

"Lulu was the exotic outsider who lived upstate and was only
around occasionally. We were all in love with her."

"You were in love with everyone," Roxy says slyly. "Was anyone in
love with you?"

"No," Molly says. For a moment she seems far away.

"I'll bet you were a good girl."

"Well, we were all pretty good, even Colin—and he was a 'bad
boy.' There wasn't a whole lot of trouble you could get into at the
Crandale Country Club."

"You hung out at a country club?" Roxy is disdainful.

"We did," Molly says. "We lived whole lives there."

"I would have found some trouble."

Molly laughs—a real laugh, full of wicked delight. "You would've
ruled that place, Roxy."

Roxy smiles, satisfied. She is starting to like Molly better. "I was
a good dancer," she says.

She scores from one of the busboys on her way to the restroom.
There is no betrayal in transacting this business while Molly waits
just a few feet away. The Junkie Grid is like a separate sheet of graph
paper from the one where Molly is sitting, just as Mondrian's secret
work is a separate sheet, and the life of Terrence the veterinarian,
whose hair has now gone white and who recently welcomed his first
grandchild (Roxy has tracked his life online all these years, though

she never went to see him). And yet these many irreconcilable worlds occupy one physical space—like the D&D maps stacked inside a single envelope. How is it possible? Philosophy!

After Roxy's meeting with her counselor, Chris walks her home. Her apartment building is two blocks from Bright Day, up a steep hill. She has to stop halfway and catch her breath. "Smoking," she pants.

Chris looks worried. He worries more about her since Colin's death, and his Sense Subterfuge, which rivals Roxy's own, has been activated this morning. Can he intuit the glassine bags in her pocket? When they're walking again, he asks, "Are you going to the greenhouse today?" and she nods, still too short-winded to speak.

Outside her building, he seems reluctant to let her go. "Come to dinner this weekend," he says. "Sam would love to see you—I'll pick you up."

But Roxy is too excited about Own Your Unconscious (and the glassine bags) to make concrete plans. She hugs Chris goodbye.

The Mandala box is already waiting by her door; Piers, her neighbor, must have brought it in. Roxy has lived in the same studio apartment for almost twenty-five years (her rent paid directly by her sisters; no one trusts her with money), and for the past seventeen of those years, she has shared a wall with Piers. He looks to be in his sixties, gay and sexually active—she's seen men leaving his apartment—but aside from a sister who visits occasionally with her two young grandchildren, Piers is alone, like Roxy. They are friendly neighbors who make the effort to run downstairs when they hear the other's buzzer go unanswered and see a delivery truck outside. They have never entered each other's apartment. Lying in bed watching lavender fog hurtle across the night sky, Roxy can sometimes hear, or even just sense, Piers moving across their shared wall. It will strike her, with force, that he exists even when she can't see him. She struggles to believe that Piers is as real as she is—as full of thoughts and memories and feelings. Yet he must be, and so must everyone else in this low-rent warren of small apartments whose inhabitants range from tech-boom refugees to "lifers" like herself and Piers. How can the architecture contain all those lives? Why doesn't it explode from the pressure?

Chris is troubled by Roxy's lack of intimacy with her fellow lifers. Why aren't she and her neighbors friendlier—*friends*—after decades of coexistence that have included spells of pandemic quarantine? But friendship risks the end of friendship, and Roxy has moved through too many friends in her life. Maybe they all have—maybe being a lifer in an O'Farrell Street apartment building presumes a trail of scuttled friendships. She and Piers are better off remaining amiable strangers than taking the risk of becoming enemies who share a wall.

Artie, the orange kitten she adopted three weeks ago from a Bright Day client who had three of them tucked in the pocket of his hoodie, marauds amid the packaging as she carefully opens her Mandala box, with its distinctive glyph. She arranges the contents on her gleaming wood floor, which she cleans with Windex as if it were a window. After long consideration, she chose "graphite" for her Consciousness Cube: one cubic foot of sparkling material that looks like it was mined from the moon.

Roxy has an intuitive gift when it comes to machinery—might have been a Bix Bouton herself, *if only* . . . but half the world probably tells itself that. Still, she did manage to view her father's consciousness even after Charlene gave her the list of passwords in the wrong order. Roxy wanted to watch her trip to London with her father through *his* eyes, see her sixteen-year-old self in action like a movie heroine. But she ended up tearing off the headset before her father had even left his house to pick her up for the airport. The intimate flux of his thoughts sickened her: of Jocelyn, his strung-out girlfriend, spread-eagled in bed; a loop of electric guitar chords; an itch on his balls; a lawnmower buzz from somewhere; a yen for an avocado-and-Jack sandwich; a wish that he could go to London without Roxy; a seizure of regret at having invited her to come with him—all subsumed by a spasm of rage when he spotted Bowser taking a shit by the pool.

After flinging away the headset, Roxy sat numb and horrified, thinking she might vomit, or die. With a sense of crawling away from a precipice, she reminded herself that the magic of their London trip hadn't begun until she and her father were on the airplane, in first class, and he let her drink champagne. She'd hardly known him before then, being one of his middle children by his middle wife. According to her mother's own bitter report, her sole function had been to lure him away from the first wife, Christine, whom he'd actually loved.

Roxy had always assumed her father had taken her to London to show her off; she had just appeared in two music videos on MTV, a brand-new American invention in 1984. But those wretched moments inside her father's mind revealed a different motive: education. That explained their initial visits to a cathedral and several art museums. Her father would lead Roxy to a painting or an altar, accost it with dubious inquisition, then glance at her expectantly, as if hoping the object had acted upon her in some way it refused to act upon him. "To hell with museums," he said on the third day. Their joint failure brought them closer.

Roxy spreads apart her hair so that each sensor touches her scalp. She feels afraid, and has an impulse to put off the process. But she wants to be done in time for her greenhouse shift at three. She places the Consciousness Cube beside her futon bed and lies down carefully, so as not to disrupt the sensors. Artie climbs onto her chest and wedges his tiny head under her chin like a doorstop. She's heard that you feel nothing during the externalization—can be asleep or awake, it makes no difference. But no sooner does the Cube begin to hum than Roxy experiences a swarm of memories like dust roused by vigorous cleaning. On their last day in London, her father took her to lunch at a fancy French restaurant in a neighborhood full of vintage clothing shops. They sat outdoors, the white tablecloth blinding in the sunlight. Her father gave her his sunglasses. They were entertaining a band: four long-haired English boys hardly older than Roxy, with incomprehensible accents. Her father and the band's manager were making a deal, and the feeling was celebratory. Everyone drank champagne. The drummer nuzzled Roxy's calf under the table and later intercepted her outside the ladies' room, wagging an ampoule full of cocaine. Roxy snorted a bump into each nostril. The drummer tried to kiss her, but his sparse mustache was unappealing, and his breath smelled of pâté. On another day, in another place, Roxy might have done anything—had sex with him in a bathroom stall, as she'd done twice at punk clubs in L.A. But not here. She returned to the table, luxuriating in her father's evident relief at having her back. He put his arm around her and refilled her glass. The sun hammered down, but the champagne, straight from the ice bucket, cracked coldly in her chest.

After lunch, they all took a walk. Her father held her hand. London was heavy and dense and green. She felt grown-up at sixteen, walking beside the two men while the four musicians skulked and horsed around behind them. She swung her father's arm, champagne and cocaine waltzing in her blood. In a park, they stood beside a lake full of swans and toy sailboats. As the musicians tried to push one another in, their manager turned suddenly to Roxy and asked, "What do you plan to do with your life?" Normally, she would have said, *Become a dancer or an actress* or just *Be famous!* (like every other L.A. kid), might have mentioned the MTV videos and several more she was already booked to shoot. But Roxy said, "I want to make my mark," with such crisp finality that both men laughed in surprise. She felt her father's pride, exhilarating and new. Long after the musicians had drifted away, Roxy stayed with her father and the band's manager, walking and talking long into the night. At ten o'clock, the sun was still up. It was the happiest day of her life.

"I want to live with you," she told her father on the plane ride back to Los Angeles. She was still drinking champagne, although he had stopped.

"Won't work, Rox," he said. "I travel too much. And Kiki would miss you."

"She'd be glad to get rid of me."

"Everyone needs a sibling they can be close to."

"I could come with you when you travel. Like now."

"Be fun, wouldn't it?"

He wore his reading glasses. Papers were stacked on his airplane tray, and a pile of cassette tapes he needed to "give a listen" on his Walkman. She understood then that their trip had ended. The perfect harmony she felt with her father, a symbiosis that made her old life obsolete, had been temporary. She started to cry.

"You're tired," he said. "I've worn you out. We've got a long flight, get some sleep."

She did, leaning against his shoulder as he worked. When she woke, the plane was circling Los Angeles and her father was packing up his tapes. Roxy watched him with a sensation of drowning, but she hardened her face and kept her arms at her sides. She didn't see him again for five months.

Back at home with her mother and sister, she was morose and adrift. Kiki received her indifferently; Kiki refused even to see their father, whom she'd deemed "a godless man" on learning from Charlie that he'd seduced Jocelyn while she was in high school. Kiki spent all her time with a Christian youth group; Roxy assumed that, being plain, her sister had no better options. God loves everyone, right? But less than a year after Roxy's trip to London, Kiki ran away with the youth-group leader, who was twenty-six. Roxy remembers the wounded astonishment she felt at being trumped in transgression by her humdrum sister. Their father hired detectives, but they failed to locate Kiki before her eighteenth birthday. She resurfaced a couple of years later, writing letters to their mother from the Far East, where she'd become a missionary. In the end, she married an insurance executive, settled in Connecticut, and had four children who are now adults. She goes by her full name, Krysanne. Roxy has seen her only twice in adulthood, at their father's funeral and, more recently, their mother's. But since all they have in common is their girlhood, about which Krysanne can only repeat, "Thank God I got out," there is little to say.

Getting high, which is hard to accomplish through the methadone (it takes a lot, Roxy has to be careful), gives her a sensation of power and transcendent rightness beyond anything she could have imagined when she uttered those words: *make my mark*. Making her mark ended up not involving any of the things she'd banked on—her dancing, her beauty, her sexual confidence—in fact, all of those succumbed to it. Heroin is her great love, her life's work, and she has given up everything for it, through renunciation or sheer neglect. No one can say she hasn't been steady—or, rather, everyone says that, but only because they fail to grasp that her scarred arms and swollen fingers, her gray teeth and thin hair and stooped, halting gait, are testaments to her fierce devotion. She's outlasted even Jocelyn, whom she used to nod off with at her father's house. Jocelyn got a social work degree in her forties and settled down with a famous guitarist who'd been in love with her since high school. Not Roxy. She will depart this world empty-handed: a sacrifice that only Kiki, in the religious fervor of her girlhood, might have understood.

The Cube chimes sooner than Roxy expects. She sits up, refreshed and wanting to pee, as if she fell asleep. Maybe she *was* asleep, for crossing the room feels different, strange. Good. Beside her futon, the Consciousness Cube is warm as a newly laid egg, Artie asleep on top of it. Roxy slides the kitten onto her bed and lifts up the Cube. It feels heaver: the weight of her past. As she plucks the sensors from her scalp, she feels a corresponding lightness, as if she's been relieved of some internal pressure. She saw a video once about a woman who fell headfirst from a third-story window. Doctors opened up her skull and removed her brain, placing it in a basin of brainy fluid so that it could swell freely without getting squashed against the inside of her skull. That's how Roxy feels: as if her brain has been released from a cell it outgrew.

She texts the greenhouse that she isn't feeling well and can't come in, Effortless Prevarication being another Former Junkie skill. The greenhouse job is a Bright Day program, which means they'll test her urine tomorrow. Fine—she's clean! But she wants to give herself to this aftermath, to understand what has changed. Artie hops back onto the Cube when she sets it down. The Cube is *her*, in a way. It contains the entire contents of her mind: all the things she can and can't remember, every thought and feeling she has had. At last, she is the owner of her unconscious. She knows where everything can be found.

Everything, that is, until the chime. The twenty minutes since won't be saved to the Cube until she reapplies the sensors and updates her externalization. For now, they exist only in her mind. And although Roxy has longed for a Consciousness Cube as a means of traveling backward, it is this diaphanous new present, with its fresh-born minutes, that captivates her. She touches her face, feeling the warmth of her skin against her fingertips. She goes to her window and opens it. Blue sky. Brisk San Francisco wind. A sense of the ocean, although it's nowhere in sight. The satisfaction of one good long breath. She inhales again, even more deeply, and thinks, *I am lucky*.

The movie she's longed to see of her young self in London is the one she just watched in that flurry of memories dislodged by the upload. What more does she need? How could revisiting that time in its unfiltered state improve upon the story her memory has made? What if, like those vile moments inside her father's mind, the truth disappoints?

Roxy understands now why Chris Salazar opposes even the most private, limited use of Own Your Unconscious. The logic of this process pushes *out*. She feels it as a natural force, a current drawing her consciousness beyond the limits of her self into a wider sphere. To converge, to be subsumed—how she longs for this! The prospect shimmers before her: a fulfillment of everything she has wanted in her life. *Make my mark.*

Energized by a need to act before she becomes afraid, Roxy aligns the Cube with her Wi-Fi and sits cross-legged in front of it. She provides the required DNA swipe from inside her cheek and the Cube begins to hum, Artie purring rapturously at the rush of new heat. She feels a whirring deep within her body, the gush of her consciousness pouring onto the Internet: a torrent of memories and moments, many painful—some actually memories of pain—all emptying into a cosmos that writhes and twists like an expanding galaxy. Her father is there, somewhere. Roxy feels their memories conjoin at last, like their two arms swinging on that long bright night. The whole of her past whirls through a portal and vanishes onto a separate sheet of graph paper.

And on this one, a secret new life known only to herself, Roxy will go to D&D and say, to Chris and Molly, "I'm ready to make my character. Will you help?"

i, the Protagonist

Chris Salazar couldn't remember what sort of work he'd envisioned when he first fell under the sway of Sid Stockton, the weirdly charismatic CEO of SweetSpot Networks, during a pandemic Zoom interview, and wound up ditching his editing job for Sid's entertainment start-up, but it definitely hadn't involved filling entire walls with algebra. Yet here he was, two years later, with an aching arm and a racing heart, having run through several dry-erase pens defending his suite of "algebraizations"—a word he would have had trouble defining two years ago but now used upward of eighty times a day (he'd counted).

Why, the professional counters wanted to know (Jarred especially; Stanford '19, like Chris, but a calc major), had Chris algebraized *A Drink in the Face*—

$$a \,(+ \text{drink}) \times (\text{action of throwing drink}) = a \,(- \text{drink}) + {}^i\!/_2$$

—making *i*, the protagonist, the *target* of the hurled drink rather than the hurler?

Without looking directly at Jarred, whom Chris made a point of ignoring, he explained to the group that a drink-hurling protagonist belonged to a different story block, *Hero Delivers Comeuppance to Perennial Jerk,* which Chris had algebraized several months back.

Jarred was dissatisfied; Jarred was always dissatisfied with Chris, and the feeling was mutual. "Shouldn't *i* be squared after the drink lands in his face?" he pressed.

"Having a drink thrown at you is humiliating," Chris said firmly. "Which is more likely to make *i* feel reduced, or *i* halved."

"Yes," intoned Aaron, their boss, a man of so few words that the occasional word he did utter had the cleaving finality of an ax splitting a log.

Chris experienced a jolt of manic exhilaration. He was killing it, crushing it; murdering this meeting; he was destroying Jarred, having powered through an entire set of algebraizations with nary a mathematical change required. These included, in addition to *A Drink in the Face*, which he'd catalogued as 3A*i*m:

- *A Slap in the Face* [3A*ii*r]
- *"You Never Cared for Me." (Shouting)* [3A*viiiy*]
- *"How Dare You?" (Whispering)* [3A*viiiz*]
- *Protagonist Hits Bottom Alone, at Night, on City Streets (with Soulful Music)* [3A*ix*b]
- *Protagonist, Drunk, Drugged, or Hit on Head, Stumbles Through Distorted Landscape* [3A*ix*d]
- *Nighttime Roar Followed by Vacuous Morning-After Hush* (3A*xii*w)
- *Blurred Faces Lean Over Protagonist, Gradually Sharpening* (3A*xi*p)
- *Hand Fumbles from Bedclothes for Ringing Phone* (3A*yiii*n)

When Chris was first assigned the task of scouring movies and TV shows for every possible stock element ("stockblocks"), and then cataloging and converting them into one algebraic system, he'd thought it impossible. He'd been an English major at Stanford; he loved to read and still devoted his scant free time to the practice. But it turned out that representing stock narratives algebraically was easier than he'd expected:

Protagonist in a heightened state: i^2
Protagonist in a reduced state: $i/_2$
Protagonist, excluded by others, feels reduced: $i < (a, b, c \ldots) = i/_2$

i, the protagonist, had even begun to assume the swaggering air of a hero:

i!

Whereas *a, b,* and *c* appeared correspondingly meager—bit players who failed to get that the story wasn't about them and that *i* would invariably triumph. In the world of stockblocks, redemption was guaranteed.

"SweetSpot is going to do for entertainment what MK did for social media!" Sid Stockton had raved during that first Zoom interview, and although Chris nodded in avid accord, he'd had to look up "MK" afterward. It referred to an anthropologist, Miranda Kline, who had mapped "the genome of human inclinations" almost thirty years ago and created algorithms for predicting behavior. She'd become famous for giving social media companies the means to monetize their business back when that was new, although she took no pride in it. The interview clips Chris had glanced through showed a kind of futility creeping into Kline's demeanor over the years. In the most recent, a questioner said, "You seem kind of 'over it' at this point." Kline, a silver-haired woman of seventy-two in a red satin blouse, threw back her head and laughed. "I still enjoy being alive, if that's what you're asking," she said. And then, in a phrase that haunted Chris, "But I'm tired of my history."

Chris surged from the morning meeting in a state of jacked-up jittery glory that felt oddly close to tears. Triumph was premature; he was presenting another set of algebraizations tomorrow morning and wasn't close to being finished. In states of artificial elevation (frequent in this job) he avoided SweetSpot's roof garden—where bees from the company apiary drowsed in beds of lavender—and instead joined the smokers, who lit up outside the building beyond a yellow perimeter line thirty feet from SweetSpot's entrance. The smokers' disdain for their employer and antisocial vibe conformed with uncanny precision to stockblock 1K*ii*p, *Raffish Outsiders*. Chris was noticing more and more such correlations, which had the effect of turning the whole world into a matching game. But they also worried him; what did it mean that much of his life could be described in formulaic clichés?

Chris didn't smoke; his attraction to the smokers was a consequence of his own narrative function—*Enabling Sidekick*—which he'd become sheepishly aware of in his two years of stockblock codification. All his life he'd played supporting roles in other people's dramas (except in D&D games, where he usually played a burly leader), starting with Colin, his best friend from childhood and to this day, and extending to Pamela, his recent ex, whose heroin addiction he'd been unable to fix.

The smokers' most raffish outsider, Comstock, appeared to do nothing *but* smoke; Chris had never seen him inside the building. Husky and leather-clad, Comstock quelled a lurking cough with swigs of Robitussin DM from a bottle secreted among his leather layers (post-pandemic, not even raffish outsiders would tolerate coughing). During a rare verbal exchange, Comstock had told Chris that his job at SweetSpot was in Diagnostics, which he described as "a repair shop where non-Stanford grads get their hands dirty." To which Chris had rejoined, in similar spirit, "And we're the thoroughbreds that can't actually do anything." It was the right answer. He was rewarded with a grin and something approaching eye contact.

"Salutations," Comstock said now, his standard greeting. Then he added, "*¿Qué pasa, hombre?*"

The Spanish startled Chris—was it a comment on his ethnicity? He looked like his dad, who was, in fact, Latino—*self-hating*, Chris liked to needle him, although that was too extreme. But it was fair to say that Bennie Salazar had subsumed his Honduran origins in a *Countercultural Mien* (1A*iii*p) starting in high school, right here in San Francisco. A punk rocker who'd presided over a band unforgivably named the Flaming Dildos, his father had been too ashamed to bring a single friend home to Daly City, where he lived with Chris's grandmother (who lived there still) and one of Chris's four aunts, who'd had a baby while in high school.

Chris would have liked to greet Comstock's *¿Qué pasa?* with a torrent of Spanish, but his father had always insisted he take French. "How long have you worked at SweetSpot?" he asked instead.

"Too long."

"Meaning—a week?"

"Five years."

Chris felt a squiggle of doubt. "Haven't we only existed for three . . . ?"

"I was in it before it was SweetSpot," Comstock said. "Sid and I go way back."

Chris had never met anyone who *knew* Sid Stockton; only others like himself, who had been hypnotized by him. "How come you're stuck in Diagnostics if you and Sid are tight?" he asked.

"I'm *not a team player*," Comstock said. "But Sid can't chuck me— I know where the bodies are buried."

Chris felt a quiver of awareness: a sense of new experience tilting his way. It was the feeling he'd had when he first spotted Pamela at Colin's graduation from Sylvan Shires, an inpatient rehab in the East Bay: a sense that the excitable girl with dangly heart-shaped earrings would lead him somewhere new. Chris had mistaken Pamela for a friend or relative of a graduate, not a person with an addiction. But the feeling had been right: He'd never loved anyone so much. And Pamela had loved him, or seemed to until her relapse, after which point Chris could only fume ineffectually as she nodded off in front of the *Yu-Gi-Oh!* cartoons she liked to watch when she was high, strands of orange hard-candy drool lazing from her mouth. Chris's shouting, begging, and intermittent weeping couldn't touch Pamela in that state; she greeted all of it with tender, blinkered euphoria.

Comstock was talking—which, for Comstock, meant sweeping words in Chris's general direction without looking at him. ". . . take my bike for a . . . Want to come . . . ?"

"Sure," Chris said reflexively, aware that *Raffish Outsiders* seldom repeated an offer. In truth, he couldn't go anywhere—he'd have to work the rest of the day to complete his algebraizations by morning. But there was no need to pull away just yet. He walked downhill beside Comstock away from SweetSpot's blond-wood lobby, which soared invitingly behind plate glass. The block facing theirs was bisected by "Junkie Alley," where Chris had seen people injecting into their groins and necks when he dared to look. SweetSpot claimed it couldn't regulate what took place across the street, but the smokers had a different theory: Management tolerated the dire symmetry because it kept SweetSpotters from venturing outside their cushy citadel.

Comstock's dented black Harley-Davidson was parked amid a bevy of bicycles that looked like cowering fawns beside it. The moment had come for Chris to peel off—or, rather, a succession of moments had come and gone, each having seemed just slightly premature. Comstock tapped the seat of his bike, inviting Chris to experience firsthand its brand-new leather padding. Chris mounted, aware that the moment had now decisively arrived, then was taken aback when Comstock hopped on in front of him with surprising agility for a big man, bringing their torsos into disarming union. Comstock gunned the engine and the bike lurched forward, forcing Chris to seize his acquaintance's warm midriff in order not to somersault backward into the street. They gobbled up a hill and plunged down its backside, pounded by wind and the quaking, shrieking vibrations from the machine. Chris was terrified. He had little experience of physical danger; his parents had taught him, in earnest unison, that his young life was precious, and he had absorbed the lesson.

And yet, when at last he managed to relax even slightly—unclench his teeth, biceps, stomach, legs, and feet and open himself to this journey whose roaring violence should by any rights have left the buildings they passed smoldering in heaps of rubble,

Chris experienced a shocking infusion of joy. He gave himself to the ride—the whiplashing ups and free-fall downs, curves taken at such drastic angles that the pavement fondled his shoulder. He felt elation so pure, so removed from the jittery triumphs of work, that it registered as new. Had he been depressed? A sense of failure had dogged him in the five months since Pamela OD'd in a Starbucks restroom and was revived with Narcan. Her mother drove to San Francisco, helped Pamela pack, and drove her back to Nebraska. Pamela texted Chris that she would be out of touch: "I just need to focus on gtng well..." Who could argue with that? Except that now, according to her social media stories (which Chris monitored more closely than his own), she'd completed another treatment program and gotten matching ring tattoos with an Ultimate Frisbee player named Skyler.

He'd failed, but how? Was it failure to cure Pamela? Failure to be enough—in bed, in life—to keep her from relapsing? The truth felt deeper, weirder: failure to descend alongside her into catastrophe. Compared with Pamela's childhood, savaged by sexual abuse from an uncle now in prison, his own had been laughably easy. Its one sorrow—his parents' divorce when he was eight—had been softened to the point of nullity by the arrival of his uncle Jules to live with them. Jules was a writer with writer's block, which left him with plenty of time to assemble a LEGO Yeti Enclave for Chris while he was at school; to orchestrate biweekly D&D games for Chris and Colin and, when they were older, ferry them to a former Girl Scout camp in New Jersey where ordinary people transformed themselves into Warlords and Dark Elves and bright blue Naiads; where Chris and Colin took turns playing frightened townsfolk or passing peddlers or (best of all) gore-streaked monsters who swarmed unsuspecting travelers on country roads, sending sprays of imaginary blood into hills of real snow.

All of it had left Chris irrevocably, unshakably *well*, cauterized from hardship much the way SweetSpotters were from the wretched squalor of that alley down the block. Losing Pamela had left a shadow of sadness that he'd grown so used to, he'd stopped noticing it. And now it had lifted.

The fact that they were tearing along an open stretch of highway permeated his awareness gradually, then with a seizure of warning. He had to get back! He tried leaning around Comstock's torso to shout in his ear something along the lines of "Dude, where the fuck are you going?" but a rabid wind invaded his mouth, threatening to dislodge the skin from his skull and send it flying into the hills like a pillowcase. He tried rising onto his haunches to bellow the question into Comstock's ear, but this proved impossible because Comstock was wearing a helmet—and Chris was not! So he clutched and endured, reassuring himself that his predicament conformed perfectly to *Straight Arrow, Hijacked by Lawbreaker, Is Unexpectedly Exhilarated* [2P*vii*], a stockblock firmly lodged in the realm of comedy. They were on Highway 101; the East Bay gleamed opalescently to the left while foothills rose overhead on the right, fog tickling their crests. It was a stretch of highway Chris knew from trips to the airport.

Sure enough, they were soon spiraling among terminals at SFO. "What are we doing here?" Chris managed to shout when Comstock idled to check his phone.

"Her plane landed a couple of hours ago. She's pissed."

A moment later, Chris spotted *her* at the curb, unmistakable in black leather, black lipstick, and a look of seething rage. Comstock jerked the bike to where she stood, leaped off, and began kissing her openmouthed while Chris looked primly away. Then came the sound of *her* screaming at Comstock in a language Chris didn't immediately recognize—Russian, maybe? Traffic leaned at the curb, and he heard police whistles. The bike idled beneath him.

"Here, bring it forward a little," Comstock said, and Chris turned to look behind him, certain that Comstock must be addressing an adjacent person who knew how to drive a motorcycle [1Z*iiip*]—but no, he meant Chris.

"I can't drive this thing," Chris sputtered.

"Hop off, then."

Chris did, gladly, then was beset by a sensation of having metamorphosed into stone. Stress and frustration, disguised until now by sheer motion, ambushed him. What the fuck was he doing at the airport? How much time had he lost? The specter of Jarred pouncing on his smallest inconsistency gave him a head rush.

Comstock helped his lady friend onto the bike, and she gunned the engine and shot to the terminal's outer edge. Comstock followed with her huge, battered industrial-plastic gray suitcase. The wheels appeared to be stuck, and Comstock had to drag it over the pavement. Chris identified an obvious logistical hitch: There was no way to carry a third person, much less an oversize suitcase, on Comstock's motorcycle.

"Look, she really wants to drive," Comstock muttered at Chris in his sideways fashion. "Why don't I ride with her and you follow us in a cab with the case."

Chris was at a loss for how precisely to spurn this absurd proposal: *No, I'm going to get in a cab and* not *take the suitcase . . . ? No, I insist on riding your motorcycle with a woman I've never met . . . ?* The absurdity lay in the fact that he'd allowed himself to be dragooned here in the first place.

Chris glowered through the taxi line. At last a driver hoisted the suitcase into his trunk, and Chris climbed into the cab, whaling shut the door to telegraph his outrage. That left him sitting peevishly in the backseat while Comstock, in the role of adult, spoke to the driver. But at last their motley caravan was moving, Comstock's lady friend helmeted and driving while Comstock, bareheaded, held on to her from behind. When they were out of the airport and heading north on 280, Chris felt himself calm down. He had all night to finish his presentation, if it came to that, and plenty of Adderall from Colin, whose drug connections remained impeccable even in his recovery.

Chris scrolled through stockblocks 3B*i*-3B*xii*, which included:

- *Funny Best Friend Gets Serious to Talk Sense into Protagonist*
- *Makeover Montage Followed by Gaping Reaction Shots*
- *Partner Who Spurned Protagonist Comes to the Rescue at Crucial Moment*
- *Crowd Rises to Its Feet in Unexpected Tribute—*

"The hell does she think I'm driving?" the cabdriver said.

Chris looked up, registering the man as an individual for the first time: long gray hair, grizzled tan, tchotchkes swinging from the rearview mirror, a stick of incense on the dash. A *character*. "Your friend thinks he's James Bond," the cabbie remarked. Chris chuckled politely and went back to his list, but the driver soon spoke up again, more insistently. "I can't keep up with them. Just tell me where I'm going."

"I—I'm not sure. He didn't tell you?"

"Told me to follow the bike."

Chris had presumed their destination would be SweetSpot, but on reflection, this seemed unlikely. "Can you just . . . speed up a little?" he asked. "I'm not a hundred percent sure where they're going."

"It's hard on my shock absorbers. And there's a danger the radiator could overheat."

"Look, there's a great tip at the end of this," Chris said, but mention of money prompted a dire revelation: Unless they kept up with the bike, *he* would be the one stuck with the exorbitant taxi fare.

"Feel that jiggling?" the driver said. "That's the motor being taxed. It already needs an oil change, and I spent three hundred and twenty bucks last week on new shock absorbers."

Chris nodded impatiently through this automotive hypochondria. The driver, he realized, was *a*: the bit player who mistakenly believes he's the protagonist. Chris welded his gaze to Comstock's leather jacket and issued ferocious mental commands that he turn around. But Comstock did not turn—perhaps couldn't; perhaps trusted *her* to keep the cab in sight. Who knew what they thought—they were total strangers! He and Comstock had yet to make eye contact!

"Hear that clicking? That low hum?"

"Look, I don't need a blow-by-blow about your cab," Chris said. "I just need you to drive it. If we lose the bike, we're in a mess."

"Not me. I'm not in a mess."

"I don't have my wallet. If we lose the bike, you don't get paid."

Even if true, which it was not, this was an empty threat; he could pay with his phone, obviously, although this boomer driver might not know that. Chris had merely wanted to remind the driver that he was *a,* not *i,* and needed to shut up and do his job. A sullen silence briefly reassured Chris until he realized that *a* had signaled a lane change and was exiting the highway. "What the fuck are you doing?" he roared. The bike had become difficult to see.

"No money, no ride."

"Of course I can pay you. I don't want to, but I can."

But a schism had occurred between *a* and *i.*

$$a \neq i$$
$$a \longleftarrow \longrightarrow i$$
$$i$$

And so it was that Chris found himself alone on a sidewalk beside a stranger's suitcase under a blazing sunset in what he recognized now as Daly City. He permitted himself a howl of frustration, prompting wary looks from commuters leaving the BART station. Then he calmed down. After all, he wasn't the one with the problem, *she* was. Chris hadn't spent a dime, the suitcase was in good order, and according to his phone, he was eight blocks from his grandmother's house. She'd been begging him to come to dinner, and he was starving. Abuela often played chess in the evenings, but a quick exchange of texts confirmed that she was home, moments away from serving chicken stew to Chris's cousin Gabriella, who was visiting from Fresno. This last bit of news slightly dampened Chris's triumph; Cousin Gabby didn't like him. Still, the good fortune of his soft landing buoyed him over eight hilly blocks, dragging the dysfunctional suitcase past identical houses whose individuality came in the form of extreme paint choices—hot pink, sno-cone blue—their psychedelia magnified by the sunset.

Abuela met him at the door of her gray-green house and folded him into a fragile embrace mentholated by the cigarettes she still smoked at eighty-six, despite haranguing from Chris's father. Slender and delicate, she wore only Celine, elegant knits in blue and beige, thin gold chains at her neck. Her hair, from which any rumor of gray had been snuffed, was looped and pinned to the back of her head. She played chess every day, usually all day, and believed in sitting down to battle in full regalia. As a girl in Honduras, she'd been a champion, but as a mother of five in a hostile land, widowed at thirty-five, she'd had to give it up. Only when Chris's father, her youngest, was in high school, "ashamed to come home," as Abuela often complained, did she return to the game, and over time, her tournament winnings allowed her to quit working for the city and buy her small house. Then, in a senior swim-yoga class at the YMCA, Abuela became friendly with a woman whose son was involved with an alternate currency. She began, through him, to invest some of her chess winnings—and finally, her whole net worth—in Bitcoin. She'd cashed out at the top of the market, netting untold millions (untold because she would not tell), some portion of which she'd sunk, anonymously at auction, into a painting by Piet Mondrian. To Chris, the artwork looked unexceptional: white squares and blocks of primary color. But for Abuela, its geometry was a bottomless source of meditative renewal. "When I am lost here, I take myself there," she was fond of saying. "In two dimensions, problems are simplified." The Mondrian hung, uninsured, in her living room; even alarmed, her house had been deemed too vulnerable by every actuary she consulted. Abuela refused to move. "These people don't know a Mondrian from a meringue," Chris had heard her say of her neighbors. "Look at the way they've painted their houses!"

Chris's father refused to sit in a room with an uninsured Mondrian, and this standoff between mother and son meant that for two years, they'd gone exclusively to restaurants when his father visited from New York—often with Chris's stepmother, Lupa, a wildlife photographer specializing in insects.

"Why not enjoy the beauty of my Mondrian"—Abuela pronounced it with a European flourish—"rather than make such a fuss?"

She had posed this question to Chris's father a couple of months ago as the four of them ate at a North Beach restaurant near the old Mabuhay Gardens, a storied, long-defunct punk venue where his father's band, the Flaming Dildos, had played just once, in 1979.

"I don't see beauty. I see a bare spot, and God knows how many millions down the drain, when some hooligan rips it off your wall," his father retorted. Chris and Lupa exchanged an eyeroll.

"Benicio," Abuela scolded. "You are bemoaning an occurrence that has not occurred. What could be more silly?"

"Hanging an uninsured Mondrian on your wall!"

There was a performative aspect to their sniping, a whiff of *Hotheaded Offspring Rails Against Coolheaded Parent* [2P*xix*l] that made Chris doubt whether, without him and Lupa for an audience, they would even bother.

"You know," Abuela said with a sidelong glance at Chris, "*I* ironed his Mohawk. For the punk rock."

"Here we go," his father said.

"On my ironing board. With my Aqua Net. He would have seared his head."

"I remember," Chris said.

"Everyone remembers," his father huffed. "You won't let them forget."

"He looked like . . . like a monster, to scare children," Abuela said, gazing lovingly at Chris's father. "But I did it, why?"

"To make him happy," Lupa finished.

They'd driven past the old Mabuhay Gardens after dinner. The Flaming Dildos had been the first of several opening bands, their set greeted with tossed trash. Chris had searched, in vain, for video footage of it (what a world that was, with so few cameras!). If he had bought into the Collective Consciousness, he doubtless could have viewed the concert from a multitude of viewpoints. But Chris recoiled from Own Your Unconscious—a reaction radically out of step with his cohort. Bix Bouton was a god in Chris's world, but Chris secretly (very secretly) sided with the boomers who viewed Mandala's "memorevolution" with existential horror. It was possibly the only thing he and his father agreed on.

Although the Dildos' set was lost to Chris, threads from it managed to stretch across forty-three years to his present-day life: Scotty Hausmann, the folk hero who'd revived his father's career a couple of years ago, had been the Flaming Dildos' singer. Lou Kline, the late record producer, had attended the Dildos' concert and afterward taken Chris's father under his wing. Lou's daughter Roxy, an unsteady creature who lived in San Francisco, occasionally joined Chris and his father for dinner. But the most staggering connection was one he'd stumbled on just recently when Miranda Kline, the anthropologist, kept floating into his mind unbidden. Digging deeper into her biography, Chris had discovered that she was briefly *married to Lou Kline* in the 1970s! The fact brought a chill of eerie recognition—confrontation, even—as if Miranda Kline were waving to Chris, or winking, from a distance.

Abuela tied a Mondrian-patterned apron over her dress and ladled chicken stew into Mondrian-patterned bowls. Her Mondrian merch included candleholders, vases, umbrellas, tea trays, glasses, place mats, towels, throw pillows, framed posters, coffee-table books, and a needlepoint footstool—all of which comprised, in her mind, a deviously impenetrable camouflage. "No one with a real Mondrian would ever acquire such crap," she liked to say.

"Were you on a trip?" Gabriella called to Chris as she lounged at the dinner table waiting for him to serve her. She was eyeing the suitcase, which he'd set—unobtrusively, he hoped—inside the front door.

"Not mine," he replied.

"Isn't that a no-no? Carrying other people's luggage?" She spoke with a visible quiver of pleasure.

"Not getting on a plane."

Gabriella was heavyset, with a beautiful, brooding face. Her mother, Chris's aunt Laura, had allegedly seethed with resentment at Chris's father for being the treasured baby and only son, pampered and Mohawk-ironed while Laura struggled at home with teenage motherhood. Laura had since prospered, and now had a time-share in Scotland where she spent half of each summer golfing. But her resentment had decanted into Gabriella, who turned it on Chris whenever they met.

"What are you doing at work?" she asked him when they were all seated. "Making apps?"

"Not exactly."

"Isn't that what all Stanford grads do? Make apps?"

"You tell me."

"I wouldn't know. I went to Chico State."

"What do Chico State grads do?"

"Become prison guards. Kidding, kidding," she genuflected, for Abuela had a zero-tolerance policy toward self-pity. And anyway, Gabriella was a successful pharmacist.

"What product is your firm creating, Christopher?" their grandmother asked, regarding him with her calm, perceptive eyes.

"I'm . . . not totally sure," Chris said. He'd never been able to lie, or even fib, to his abuela. "I mean, we're an entertainment company. But what I'm mostly doing is breaking down stories into familiar parts, and then breaking down those parts into smaller parts, which I"—he couldn't bring himself to say "algebraize"—"sort of diagram. I think the idea is . . ."

What was the idea? To make art—or make a *way* to make art—but as far as Chris knew, no product was in sight. He'd tried asking Aaron, his boss, where their work was leading, exactly, but Aaron merely replied, with his axlike finality, "DNA."

"How do you like this work, Christopher?" Abuela asked.

"I love it," he said fiercely.

Gabby had recused herself from their tender exchange by going to the bathroom. Now she stopped to examine the suitcase. "What's in here, Chris?" she called. "I smell hydrochloric acid."

Chris rolled his eyes, but his grandmother rose quickly from her chair.

"Oooh, I'd put that out, Abuela," Gabby said, for their grandmother had finished her tiny portion of stew and was enjoying one of the slender mentholated cigarettes she bought on a black market, now that the FDA had banned them. "We don't want an explosion."

Abuela went swiftly into the kitchen and doused her cigarette under the tap. "Let's move this case outside," she said.

"Let's call the police," Gabby suggested.

"No!" Chris and their grandmother said in unison. Abuela, he knew, was loath to jeopardize the anonymity she believed was protecting her treasure, and Chris had no wish to represent the suitcase's unknown contents before the law.

"Look, I can take it back to the city," he said with a sigh. "I can call an Uber right now." This was pure bluff, an invitation for Abuela to insist that he stay and finish his stew. But he'd miscalculated.

"I think that would be for the best," she said with reluctance. "We can wait for the taxi together, outside. With the suitcase."

"I'll just go finish my dinner," Gabby said. "Nice to see you, Chris." She was grinning, and why not? She'd managed to banish him from the house.

• • •

It was dark when Chris's Uber pulled up outside SweetSpot Networks. He looked for Comstock, but there were no smokers out—in fact, he couldn't recall ever having seen them at night. He'd fantasized during the ride about leaving the suitcase inside the Uber's trunk, but now he shrank from this thought, as he did from taking it to his apartment in the Richmond District. Not that he'd be returning home tonight—he would need to work straight through to get his presentation done by morning. He kept a change of clothes in his cubicle for such occasions, along with Adderall.

He left the Uber without checking the fare—he didn't want to know. As he dragged the suitcase toward SweetSpot's sliding glass doors, he noticed sparks spraying up from where its wheels scraped the pavement. Holy shit! He hefted the suitcase into his arms, aware for the first time of its unnatural weight. It was large enough to hold a compact adult in the fetal position.

"Whoa," said Dieter, one of the night guards, as Chris staggered through the sliding glass doors with his unruly load.

"Do you know Comstock?" Chris panted, the effort of setting down the suitcase causing sweat to leak from his forehead into his eyes. "Guy named Comstock? Drives a Harley? Smokes outside a lot?"

"We'll have to open that," said Frank, the *Bad Cop*.

"Can you just . . . run it through the machine?"

"Machine only picks up certain things," said Dieter, the *Good Cop*. "And anyway, that's too big to go through."

"What's inside?" asked Frank.

"It belongs to Comstock's girlfriend," Chris said. "She's from another country, Russia, I think. I went with Comstock on his motorcycle to pick her up at the airport, but I came back separately in a cab with her luggage."

The guards listened with blank attention, as if awaiting some hook of reason upon which to affix their comprehension.

"I don't like to open someone else's suitcase," Chris said, but this was an understatement: The thought made him light-headed with dread. "Can I just . . . go on up? Leave this here for Comstock?"

"We don't know any Comstock," Frank said.

"Why don't we check the company directory?" Chris said with impatience. "How many Comstocks can there be?"

"There is no directory," Dieter said. "Company's grown too fast. Can you text this Comstock? Or call him?"

"I don't have his number."

A pause opened and hardened. Chris felt the strangeness of his predicament settle over all three of them.

"I'm going to have to ask you to remove that suitcase from the building," Frank said in a more formal tone.

"To the perimeter," Dieter said with apology. "It's the policy."

Without another word, Chris dragged the suitcase back through the glass doors into the dark. Fog toppled in from the sea, swamping the streetlights. At the sound of the automatic doors whispering shut, he felt as if he'd been sealed off from not just *Good Cop/Bad Cop* but the storytelling universe they occupied. His caper had failed to find a comic resolution. Instead, there had been a genre switch, and the madcap adventure had turned serious. Or had this bleakness underlain the caper from the start?

Indifferent to sparks, Chris dragged the suitcase past the yellow perimeter line and stood there, waiting. Frank ambled to the window to check that he'd complied, then returned to Dieter. Chris could hear them laughing.

$$i < (a + b) = {}^i/_2$$

He felt a convulsion of self-loathing at what his dutifulness had cost him: This fucking suitcase was proof. He couldn't bring himself to abandon it, or to open it, or take it home. He could only stand with it and wait for Comstock to return.

Now and then, groups of SweetSpotters approached the building. "You coming up?" asked the ones Chris knew.

"In a minute," he said each time, and they went inside without looking back.

$$i < (a, b, c \dots)$$

There was a long lull, during which Chris's avidity to hear an approaching motorcycle assumed the pitch of an engine roar. Each time, it was nothing. His legs began to ache. He considered perching on top of the suitcase, but its explosive potential held him back. Anyway, Frank would surely get wind of it. Or was it really Dieter? Maybe Dieter was the fuckhead and Frank the henchman. Maybe they weren't even people but machines programmed to animate the stockblocks Chris had been algebraizing these past two years. No degree of depravity seemed out of reach.

Noting the dark turn of his thoughts, Chris reasoned with himself: Comstock still existed. He was somewhere right now—fucking *her*, no doubt. Inevitably they would reappear and reclaim the suitcase. By this time tomorrow, the loose ends of the story would all be tied up—likely with laughter, possibly with newfound intimacy and burgeoning friendship. That's how it went for *Enabling Sidekicks*, Chris knew from experience.

At last, out of sheer exhaustion, he dragged the suitcase across the street and turned into the alley, where the streetlight didn't reach. Sheltered by the dark, he leaned against a wall and let himself slide to the pavement. God, it felt good to sit down. He turned the suitcase on its side and draped himself over it, letting the hard plastic take his weight. He had a clear view of SweetSpot's entrance and would know the instant Comstock arrived. But the longer Chris waited, eyes fixed to the sliding glass doors that occasionally opened to accept or disgorge an employee roughly interchangeable with himself, the more the gleaming interior beyond those doors began to look like an alien place. Chris had been banished, or had banished himself. *I'm tired of my history*. He would never go back.

$$i \neq (a, b, c \dots)$$
$$i \longleftarrow \longrightarrow (a, b, c \dots)$$
$$i$$

The night was filled with sounds of foghorns. Chris had heard they weren't necessary for ships anymore, just a nod to nostalgia. A stockblock. He shut his eyes and tried to decide, from the pattern of tones, whether the sounds were communicative or merely decorative. He wanted them to be real! With his ears thus attuned, he began to perceive faint movements around him, murmurs and sighs and small adjustments at close range. He snapped open his eyes. Now that his vision had adjusted to the alley's darkness, he saw that it was lined with dozens of dozing bodies draped against the walls, singly and in pairs, a few sprawled across the pavement as if they had fallen there or been dropped. An initial clutch of fear soon eased, and Chris relaxed into the company of his new companions. Their faces were reposed in expressions of absolute peace. He tipped back his head to look at the sky, its torn beauty rinsed and salved by fog, and imagined he was seeing their opioid dreams rising into heaven.

DROP

The Perimeter:

After

When I really need to cry my guts out I go in the Ladies Locker Room which is empty on weekdays because the Tennis Moms are already playing tennis and the Golf Moms are playing golf and the Moms With Little Children can't bring them inside the Ladies Locker Room because kids have to be thirteen so this is my first summer of being old enough and something about this place calms me down, maybe the soft carpeting or so many lotions and creams by the mirrors or maybe it's the sound, like someone humming just one note, *mmmmmmmmmmmmmmmmmm* that helps me deal with the fact that Stella my best friend is DROPPING ME AGAIN, this has been going on since fourth grade because the only way not to be dropped by Stella is to act like you don't care and I DO CARE, it's too late to find new friends, the other groups don't want me because Stella is mean and I've been mean trying to stay her friend and just BE POPULAR and BE ON TOP which is the only way not to live in constant danger of what is going on behind your back such as just now at the Snack Shack I was waiting with Stella and Iona for grilled cheese sandwiches and Chris Salazar and Colin Bingham walked by and Stella and Iona SMILED AT EACH OTHER SECRETLY and when I tried to share that smile they both looked away TRYING NOT TO LAUGH which means Stella is HAVING PRIVATE FACEBOOK CHATS WITHOUT ME about Chris Salazar who she has liked forever.

Before, when my family lived next door to the Salazars, Stella was like *Molly, do you ever see Chris Salazar inside his house?* and I was like

No there are trees in between our houses and she was like *Well, do you know where his room is?* and for some reason I was like *No,* but I did know from a cocktail party I went to Before, when we lived next door. Chris's room faces the front and there's a green lamp in his window and now sometimes I walk Biscuit our new Welsh Corgi past our old house at night where we don't live anymore because Mom and Dad are Divorced, and I look for that green lamp to be turned on and then I know Chris Salazar is awake and I might be in love with him too.

After Stella and Iona and I got our grilled cheese sandwiches we were carrying them to the Herb Garden which is where Stella likes to eat and I stopped to fix my sandal and Stella and Iona JUST KEPT WALKING AND DID NOT WAIT FOR ME and when I stood up they were already far away and I would've had to run to catch up with them which is hard to do carrying a grilled cheese sandwich, and I knew they'd be like *Oh. Hi Molly,* not wanting me there, so I went the other way to the Ladies Locker Room to cry.

Why is Stella on top you might ask, well who can understand Popularity although I'm sure it has been studied by Universities, Stella's family is rich but no one is poor around here let's face it, she is extremely pretty with thick brown hair and green eyes but that is not "it" since other girls are just as pretty but they are not electric. Colors are literally brighter when Stella gives you her full attention but also there's this feeling of peace, you don't need to scramble or fight to try to get someplace else because you are THERE, but then again maybe all of that is BECAUSE Stella is popular rather than the reason for her popularity, it is a "chicken-and-egg question" I think.

Back when I was younger Mom would say, "Look, Molly, you have two options: stop caring about Stella or make her come crawling back, and if you pick the latter I will help you." I didn't have the strength to walk away from Stella so Mom planned a Kitten Cap Party in fourth grade where she would help every girl make a kitten cap, Mom is a very good sewer and I invited all of the girls who mattered EXCEPT for Stella and of course she found out and started being nice again, but Mom said DO NOT BUDGE until she gives you Tears and Groveling, nothing less, and on the morning of the Kitten Cap Party Stella came with her mom to our house "wanting to talk," and Mom poured Stella's Mom a cup of coffee although she has privately called Stella's Mom a "superficial dunce," and Stella and I went upstairs to my room and she cried and apologized saying I was her best friend she just liked to hurt me sometimes but that was the last time and PLEASE could she come to my Kitten Cap Party? So I had my Tears and Groveling, and Stella and I came back downstairs holding hands and I said *Mom I want to invite Stella, I'll let her have my kitten cap materials* but Mom said, "Actually, I believe we have one extra!"

That's how it has worked out with crochet squares and another time a treasure hunt but all of that was BEFORE Dad told Mom he wanted a Separation. Brian and I had no idea, it was a school night and we were doing homework but as soon as Dad told Mom about wanting a Separation, Mom went into our Art Supply Cabinet and made a "HOUSE FOR SALE" sign out of pasteboard and black Sharpie and nailed it to a gardening stake and hammered the stake directly into our front lawn in the pitch dark, and when Brian and I heard the racket we came outside and Dad was already out there pleading with Mom, "Noreen, is this really necessary?" and Mom said, "Actions have consequences, Bruce." That was more than a year ago and I still don't know what Actions she meant, now Brian and I live with Mom in an Apartment and Hannah stays in Dad's Apartment when she comes home from College, and when I asked Hannah about Dad's Actions and their Consequences, she said, "Mom is impossible, Molly, have you never noticed that?"

When I'm done crying I soak cotton balls in Witch Hazel and dab my cheeks with them and brush my hair and eat a Jolly Rancher green apple candy from a glass jar. Then I hear two Ladies come into the Ladies Locker Room so I scamper behind the last row of polished wood lockers to hide and I recognize the voices of Stephanie Salazar who is Chris Salazar's Mom and Kathy Bingham who is her Doubles Partner. Kathy is one of the prettiest Moms in the Club maybe THE prettiest, and her husband Clay is one of the richest Dads and they have five children including Colin, Chris's best friend who was recently caught shoplifting tools from Home Depot. I hear Stephanie and Kathy opening their lockers and Kathy obviously thinking the locker room is empty, says: Harriet's backhand just keeps getting worse. She should give up on the lessons.

Stephanie: Or maybe find another pro. I have my doubts about Henri.

Kathy: Henri is a fucking disaster.

Stephanie: He's still new. Who knows if they teach tennis differently in France.

Kathy: That little blonde, Marisol, is so pigeon-toed it's a miracle she doesn't fall flat on her face.

Stephanie: She got some good shots off you.

Kathy: It was the first time I'd seen her play.

Stephanie: Anyway, we won.

Kathy: I wish we'd won by more.

Stephanie: I'm heading out to the pool.

Kathy: Does it hurt a lot, getting a tattoo?

Stephanie: Are you thinking about it?

Kathy: Sort of.

Stephanie: What would you get?

Kathy: I don't know, something symbolic. What does yours symbolize?

Stephanie: Well, the image comes from a piece of Minoan pottery that was made on Crete during the Bronze Age. The Minoans had this beautiful way of representing sea life that I fell in love with in my college art history class, and I got the tattoo in my twenties when I first moved to New York, so probably what it symbolized most of all was a big fuck-you to my parents, who hated tattoos and were scandalized.

Long pause.

Kathy: Where did you go to college again?

Stephanie: U. of Illinois Champaign. You?

Kathy: Harvard. It's kind of amazing we're friends, isn't it?

Stephanie: I'd say we're doubles partners.

Kathy: Nice.

Stephanie: You can take it.

Kathy: You get the chairs, I'll grab us a couple of iced teas.

They leave the Ladies Locker Room together and I sit there trying to understand what I just heard, whether Stephanie and Kathy are friends or not, and if they were joking or not, or whether that was a fight. Then I realize that while I was eavesdropping on those Tennis Moms I COMPLETELY FORGOT about Stella and Iona and I feel much better now, and since feeling strong is the best way to regain my advantage with Stella who also loves gossip about grownups, I rush out of the Ladies Locker Room and gallop over the stretch of grass to the Herb Garden all ready to sing out *Hiya Folks!* but THE HERB GARDEN IS EMPTY and I feel like a horse's ass to use a phrase of Dad's, so I lean down like I just sprinted over to smell the herbs in this Herb Garden which could not be more wrong, I don't care about plants that is Mom's domain although her garden now belongs to the Dunns who bought our old house but Mom calls them "Occupiers" and will not walk past it.

A row of Cypress Trees separates the Herb Garden from the Pool Area and I peek between those trees at the line of kids waiting for the High Dive. Even from the back I recognize Chris Salazar from his darker skin, his Dad is Hispanic which is unimportant of course but everyone knows it, Mr. Salazar is a music producer who discovered Dad's favorite band the Conduits, and he and Stephanie Salazar are divorced. Tatum and Oriole and that group are by the pool but they aren't my direct friends and I can't join them without Stella, it would seem weird and they might be nice but they might also freeze me out the way Stella and I might freeze out one of them if she all of a sudden attached herself to us. So now I am alone and adrift having no idea where Stella and Iona have gone, and this gives me a fading feeling I get sometimes when I think Stella has forgotten me for good, like I'm a particle floating invisibly through space and I might float so far away that I stop existing even to myself. How will I get back? I need somewhere to be or someone to be WITH, but Hannah is at UC Berkeley and Brian is playing baseball and Mom used to come to the club Before, but now she says "That place is full of twits" and her Court Stenography classes take up all her time because she needs to start a Career now that she has been Discarded. So I am ALL ALONE and average-looking at best, I am not one of the dewy girls, I have faded blue eyes that hurt in the sun and my hair is thin and curly like a baby's and I have very thick hair on my legs that is one step away from Tarzan according to Brian, but I do look better when I'm with Stella, that is an objective fact I can see in pictures, you would think I would disappear beside her but it's the opposite, like some of her magic dust floats onto me and sticks.

I walk slowly back to the Snack Shack and get in line for food because it's the only way I can think of to stop floating and attach myself somewhere that can't be questioned or mocked. Kathy Bingham is near the front of the line radiating extreme impatience and crowding the one girl in front of her who looks around my age and somewhat familiar, she must be a Non-Member. This girl gets out of line like she forgot something and walks to the back of the line behind me, and I'm like, *Did you get out of line because of that Lady behind you?* and she's like, *Yeah she was stressing me out,* and I'm like, *Here, at least go in front of me,* and she's like, *Thanks* and I remember now that this girl went to my school a few years ago in the grade below me, and I'm like *Do you live in Crandale?* and she's like *No my Mom just dropped me off for the day, we're friends of the Salazars,* and I realize that she's the girl who STAYED WITH THE SALAZARS when I was nine and she went to our school for three months because her MOM

WAS IN PRISON and she HAS NO DAD, which are unheard-of Facts around here even separately, not to mention combined.

Remembering the Facts of this girl makes me ashamed for her, so I open my phone praying for a text from Stella but there are no texts period so I just stare purposefully at my empty flip phone which is embarrassing in 2011 but Dad says I can't have an iPhone until I'm fourteen, and when the girl in front of me gets to the window she turns around and she's like *What do you want I'll order for both of us* which is a very nice thing to do with the line moving slowly and I'm like *Wow, thanks, I'll have a burger and a Coke* and she orders two hamburgers and two Cokes which is my second lunch since I already bought a grilled cheese but I never even took a bite, I think I left that sandwich in the Ladies Locker Room where food is not permitted! We collect our food and kind of drift together toward Pool Area and her name is Lulu and she is floating too and thank God there is no sign of Stella who would have a good laugh about my *new friend*.

Our Club's pool has a Diving Board plus a High Dive and there is a wide paved Splash Zone where teens congregate and beyond that is a lot of thick grass where grown-ups sit on wooden recliners with soft cushions attached. Stephanie Salazar and Kathy Bingham are on recliners drinking iced tea in their bikinis, they are both Bikini-Wearers which is surprising in Kathy who has five children including twins, she still has a six-pack under what I have to say is a lot of loose skin and in her position I would wear a one-piece. Stephanie Salazar on the other hand looks kind of amazing, she is deeply tanned and there is the dark octopus tattoo on her calf which you don't see every day at the Crandale Country Club, and she lies on her back reading *The New Yorker* and underneath her arm that holds up the magazine I can see little spikes of dark hair that she hasn't shaved in a day or two and is it strange that I'm so fascinated by people's bodies? There are no secrets when grown-ups wear bathing suits they might as well be naked, I have seen various Dads' Testicles dangling inside their swim trunks when I'm lying face-up on a towel and they walk past, they look like overgrown pink grapes and there is no way I will ever have sex with a man whose Testicles look like that, it is a dealbreaker as they say, and I might not have sex anyway, the idea is horrifying.

Lulu and I sit down on the grass and I'm like *I'll pay you back for the burger* and she's like *I charged it, no worries* and of course no one pays for anything at our Club we just sign tickets with little green golf pencils although Lulu is a Non-Member so I'm not sure who will pay. We eat our burgers watching the High Dive where Chris Salazar and Colin Bingham are still diving, Colin is fearless I have seen him belly flop from the High Dive which caused the Lifeguard to jump into the pool but Colin came up laughing, he is a Thrill-Seeker. I ask Lulu where she lives and she says Upstate New York and her Mom has a gourmet store and there are a lot of lakes and she can swim for several miles without stopping. I tell her I came back three weeks ago from Camp in Maine and my Primary Activity was Archery and my Secondary was Beaded Basketing. Lulu points to a pale daylight moon above the trees and she's like *I love the moon I always look for it even in daytime* and I can hear Stella repeating those words in a mocking voice and it reminds me that I need to get away from Lulu before Stella comes back.

So I get up taking our paper plates to throw them away and I go into the Girls Room to pee which is right near the Pool, taking my time so Lulu will get the memo that eating one burger together doesn't make us All-Day Friends and disappear so I can return to my Stella drama which feels dangerous to forget about for too long. When I come back outside I glance at where we were sitting hoping Lulu will be gone, but Lulu is still there and CHRIS SALAZAR AND COLIN BINGHAM ARE SITTING WITH HER. At first I'm too stupefied to even move, Lulu is two years younger than those boys who are fourteen and rising freshmen, but I hustle back over there and sit down with them kind of shyly, the boys are still in their bathing suits with T-shirts on and Colin is flicking water at Lulu who laughs trying to dodge the drops and I notice she has dimples and tiny gold hoop earrings and a sweet laugh and I'm like *Hi* and they're all like *Hi* and Lulu is like *Colin is about to show us his favorite place at the Club, but I didn't want to leave without telling you, Molly,* and I'm nothing short of amazed by her kindness, this is not something you see in my world, kindness and coolness do not go together in girls, being cool means you leave people out, that is the actual definition of the word because if you're nice to everyone, then why should people near you feel special and why should people NOT near you WANT to be near you, and why should anyone assume that the Times they are having without you are worse than the Times they would be having with you?

You coming, Molly? Chris asks and you bet I am, I have few chances to be around Chris Salazar now that I don't live next door to him like I did Before. As we leave the Pool Area Chris passes close to his Mom Stephanie's recliner and he brushes his hand over hers, they don't even look at each other but it's a nice moment of connection as opposed to Colin who doesn't even glance at his Mom although I notice Kathy watching him and after he passes by she flops over on her stomach with a sigh. Colin is skinny with shaggy hair and his eyes are always moving like he's on the lookout for something that is about to happen any second. He's walking backwards in front of us making magician hands like he's hypnotizing us to follow him, and we walk along the bottom of the Grassy Hill that slopes down from the Dining Terrace and when I look up my HEART STOPS BEATING because STELLA AND IONA ARE WALKING TOWARD US FROM THE CLAY COURTS. Yvette is with them in tennis whites being another disciple of Stella's who comes in handy when I am being excluded or punished. Stella calls out *Molly, where did you go? We waited for you!* and Iona makes agreeing chirps and I realize that Stella is trying to reel me back in with this lie because whereas me wandering alone or me hanging out with a Non-Member who is younger and has strange Facts in her life would be pitiful and shunnable, me and that same girl PLUS two Rising Freshman Boys, both of whom are cool, is another story. I have bested Stella through sheer good luck and Lulu's kindness, but I know that I can't push my advantage too far without risking Permanent Exile. The only safe thing to do now is say to Lulu and Chris and Colin, *Sorry—see you guys,* and break off to reclaim my rightful place as Stella's Number One, at which point we'll ditch Iona and Yvette and have a sweet time, the magic of Stella being most intense when we're first reunited and there is a sparkling surprise even to normal things like Shuffleboard or the Bocce Ball Courts or the Tire Swing. Ditching my new group is the only right move in my Stella drama but I can't bring myself to do it, it is a split-second decision—NO—so I just smile at Stella and we keep walking and it feels dangerous to do this, I know I will pay later on but now it's done.

I've been coming to the CCC my whole life, I've had birthday parties here, skating lessons on the Rink in winter, I've played Tennis and Paddle Tennis and had swimming lessons and diving lessons and attended Day Camp, I've been to Mother-Daughter Teas and Father-Daughter Dances and three weddings and one after-funeral lunch and one Sweet Sixteen (my sister Hannah's), I've played Hide and Seek and Capture the Flag and Marco Polo and gone on Treasure Hunts and Easter Egg Hunts and Christmas Carol Sings and Barbeques and Fourth of July fireworks. The Club has barely changed since I was born, there is no Before and After here, in summer there is always the faint *thop thop* of tennis balls and kids' voices tangled with pool splashes and it is a beautiful place, our Country Club, when I'm not fighting for my life. But in all that time I have never been to Colin's Favorite place, which is right alongside the Club's brown painted Perimeter Wall near the Generators which are huge heavy metal boxes that rumble and hum and keep the whole place going I guess but in the blazing August heat they are awful.

Colin pulls out a packet of Merit Cigarettes and offers them around and Lulu and I shake our heads and Chris is like *Bro, these girls don't smoke* and Colin is like *There's always a first time* and he lights a cigarette for himself and takes a big puff and Lulu is like *I will never smoke a cigarette or get a tattoo* and Colin is like *I already have a tattoo I made it myself* and he lifts one leg of his bathing trunks and the word HA is inked on his upper thigh in crude smudgy blue capital letters and I'm like *Does your mom know?* and Colin is like *She doesn't care what I do since I quit tennis, I got sick of wearing white* and Lulu is like *You don't have to wear white on public courts* and Colin's like *Word, Lulu, we're in a bubble here this ain't real life* and Chris is like *That's what a Country Club IS, bro, it's a bubble that's why people want to join them* and Lulu's like *I'll never join a Country Club, I'll be too busy being in Doctors Without Borders* and Chris is like *Are Borderless Doctors invisible? Do they blend into their surroundings like ghosts?* which makes all of us laugh and Colin is like *Serious question: Will you marry me, Lulu?* and Lulu looks like she has a raging sunburn and I realize that LULU AND COLIN LIKE EACH OTHER even though Lulu is a non-smoking non-tattooing long-distance swimmer and Colin is a smoking self-tattooing shoplifter/belly flopper, and Lulu is like *No, you have an unhealthy Lifestyle* and Colin is like *Can Yelatin marry Gwenisphere at least?* and I'm like *Huh?* and Chris is like *Those are their D and D characters, Yelatin and Gwenisphere* and Colin stubs out his cigarette on the Perimeter Fence and his eyes are moving around and he's like *You girls have your bikes, right? Let's take a ride* and then he leads the way back through the club to the Bike Lot and as we're walking I ask Lulu if she likes Dungeons & Dragons which I've never played, and Lulu says yes it's like going inside a different World and her character Gwenisphere is a Spy who can blend into any Situation and find out people's Secrets.

I hesitate before getting on my bike wondering how far I'm pushing things with Stella by leaving the Club altogether but I don't want to find out YET and I don't want to get left behind so I climb on my bike and we zoom out of the Bike Lot with Colin in front and I ride my bike all the time of course, everyone does until they turn sixteen and start driving, but riding with this group is like taking off with a flock of birds heading for parts unknown although what could be un-known in Crandale New York? We ride through a section you might call "the other side of the tracks" which is grittier and more like a city and I don't go there except for pizza with Dad when Brian and I are staying at his Apartment, and we fly across the railway tracks to the Muskaheegee River which has a new path that you aren't supposed to ride bikes on but we do it anyway riding incredibly fast with Colin in front and the hot wind in our faces.

After a while Colin pulls over and we leave our bikes on their sides and walk under some trees onto a small pier in the Muska-heegee River that has so many chemicals you need shots to water-ski there. Chris explains that he and Colin like to smoke weed here because it's isolated, and I'm like *I don't want to smoke weed*, illegal things make me nervous with Dad being a lawyer and very focused on law-breaking, and my sister Hannah plans to be a lawyer too and told me last Christmas, "Mistakes still count, Molly, even if you're young when you make them," and Lulu is like *I don't want to smoke either* which is no surprise since she is opposed to cigarettes and tat-toos but I wouldn't call her a Goody-Goody because she is fierce and proud in her Beliefs, and the boys are like *Is it ok if we do?*

The four of us take off our shoes and sit side by side on the pier with our bare feet dangling above the chocolate-milk-colored water, the two boys on the outside and Lulu and me in the middle with Lulu next to Colin and me next to Chris, and the boys pass the joint behind us so we don't have to touch it and I've never been with peo-ple smoking weed before so this is a new Event in my life and maybe in Lulu's. Further down the river the trees are leaning their branches into the water like another time in History when only Indigenous People lived here, and the boys get red eyes and start to sound kind of slow and I'm like *Hey are your Moms friends?* meaning Stephanie and Kathy who I overheard in the Ladies Locker Room earlier today although it feels like several weeks ago, and the boys are both like *They're doubles partners* which is exactly what Stephanie said to Kathy, which makes me laugh kind of uncontrollably and the boys are like *You must be getting a contact high* and maybe I am!

Finally the boys lie back on the pier facing the sky and Lulu and I laugh together because they seem pretty out of it, and Colin is like *No taking advantage of us, girls* and Chris's eyes are closed but he's like *I'm not sleeping, I'm watching a movie about a big red fireball expanding and contracting* and Colin is like *Dude I've seen that movie many a time* and Lulu is like *Tell us what happens* and Colin is like *It ends with me kissing you, Lulu* and Lulu is like *No, but I will lie down next to you* and Colin is like *Can I hold your hand at least?* So Lulu lies down and she and Colin hold hands and now I'm the only one still sitting up and Chris Salazar's eyes are closed so I can look at him closely, I see his beautiful collarbones and I wonder what would happen if I leaned over and kissed him but I don't know how to kiss and I might be bad at it, so instead I lie back on the pier like the others and the warm breeze sweeps across us and I look up at the shaking trees and I'm so grateful that we left the Club because these Events of the past hour could not have happened there, all of this would be unthinkable in that Place, and I understand now why Lulu will never join a Country Club: because the Life she wants for herself can't happen there. I take hold of Lulu's hand and she squeezes my hand back and I whisper very softly close to her ear *Lulu let's be secret friends and no one will know except us* and she whispers back very softly *Friends Without Borders* and we squeeze our hands hard and that is our promise. And I wonder if I might be in love with Lulu instead of Chris, or maybe I love them both which seems possible on a pier in the Muskaheegee River but nowhere else. I want to move closer to Lulu so our whole Selves are touching but I'm afraid to, so instead I inch toward Chris whose arms are stretched back over his head on the warm pier and my cheek touches his ribs through his T-shirt and I feel his chest moving as he breathes and I can hear the actual sound of his heart, a steady thumping like someone jogging and you think they'll have to stop pretty soon and take a rest, but they just keep going.

There is a discombobulated end to this nice time when I notice Lulu's phone vibrating nonstop and I sit up to find them ALL
THREE ASLEEP and maybe I WAS ASLEEP TOO because the
river is now blue-black and the sky is burned orange and I'm like
Lulu, your phone and she jumps awake like *Crap! My Mom is picking me up after her appointments in the City!* and all of us scramble
onto our bikes kind of groggily with Lulu worried because her Mom
wanted to make the drive Upstate in Daylight and we ride very fast
back to the Club which is not as far away as it seemed going the other
direction. A Silver Minivan is waiting outside the Club Gates and a
voice calls, "Just put your bike in back, Honey" and the rear door lifts
open and Lulu puts her bike inside and climbs in the backseat and
her Mom waves to us looking very normal and not like a Prisoner,
and they drive away and I never get to say goodbye to Lulu or hug her
which I assumed we would do after everything that happened today,
it feels incomplete.

I stand with Chris and Colin feeling close to them now, but our
bond is a bond of missing Lulu, without her there's a hollow between us because even though she's younger and lives Upstate and
has strange Facts in her life she became the core of us in just one
afternoon, it is miraculous. How did she do it?

I'm like *When will she come back?* and Colin is like *Not for a while*
kind of gloomily and Chris is like *Molly, you should play D and D with
us, my Uncle Jules is the GM, he's awesome* and I hesitate because this
will mean being next door to our old house from Before and maybe
even seeing the Dunns its Occupiers, but I say *Yes I would love that.*

Colin and Chris ride away but I'm having dinner at the Club
tonight with Dad and Brian and Great Aunt Francine who used to
jump horses at the CCC back when it was in the actual Country
rather than the Suburbs although now she has a walker and is ninety-
three. I text Mom asking can she please bring me a summer dress
when she drops off Brian and then I leave my bike in the Bike Lot
and walk back through the big iron Gates with CCC in gold script

and the temperature is ten degrees cooler beyond those Gates and the grass is wet from the sprinklers that are still on in the distance, I see their sparkling plumes and hear their pulsing noise.

There are no Kids at the club at this in-between time, even the ones coming back for dinner are home changing clothes, which means there's nowhere I'm supposed to be and no one I'm supposed to be WITH and no way to be left out because there's nothing to be left out OF. I am ALONE AND PEACEFUL and that combination is so unusual, it's like meeting someone for the first time. I take off my sandals and walk barefoot over the damp grass past the Wading Pool where I wore my floaties with Mom and the Playground where I learned how to slide down a slide, all of which was Before, and I slip through a thicket of trees to the Golf Course which is off-limits for safety reasons but it's too dim to golf now. When I emerge from that thicket everything opens up like I've reached another Land, it's like going from Before to After in one second, the sand traps are pink from sunset and the Golf Course grass is warm and spongy under my feet, and I sit down on the grass and I'm like *Hello Molly, it's nice to sit with you here,* actually saying the words out loud but very softly, and I hug my warm knees and look up at the sky and there is the moon Lulu pointed out earlier except it's bigger now and still fragile-looking like it's made out of sugar or paper and could break or tear easily, but already it's brighter than before, and it isn't even night.

Lulu the Spy, 2032

1

People rarely look the way you expect them to, even when you've seen pictures.

The first thirty seconds in a person's presence are the most important.

If you're having trouble perceiving and projecting, focus on projecting.

Necessary ingredients of a successful projection: giggles; bare legs; shyness.

The goal is to be both irresistible and invisible.

When you succeed, a certain sharpness will go out of his eyes.

2

Some powerful men actually call their beauties "Beauty."

Counter to reputation, there is a deep camaraderie among beauties.

If your Designated Mate is widely feared, the beauties at the house party where you've gone undercover to meet him will be especially kind.

Kindness feels good, even when it's founded on a false notion of your identity and purpose.

3

Posing as a beauty means not reading what you would like to read on a rocky shore in the South of France.

Sunlight on bare skin can be as nourishing as food.

Even a powerful man will be briefly self-conscious when he first disrobes to his bathing suit.

It is technically impossible for a man to look better in a Speedo than in swim trunks.

If you love someone with dark skin, white skin looks drained of something vital.

4

When you know that a person is violent and ruthless, you will see violent ruthlessness in such basic things as his swim stroke.

"What are you doing?" from your Designated Mate amid choppy waves after he has followed you into the sea may, or may not, betray suspicion.

Your reply—"Swimming"—may or may not be perceived as sarcasm.

"Shall we swim together toward those rocks?" may or may not be a question.

"All that way?" will hopefully sound ingenuous.

"We'll have privacy there" may sound unexpectedly ominous.

5

A hundred feet of blue-black Mediterranean will allow you ample time to deliver a strong self-lecture.

At such moments, it may be useful to explicitly recall your training:

"You will be infiltrating the lives of criminals.

"You will be in constant danger.

"Some of you will not survive, but those who do will be heroes.

"A few of you will save lives or even change the course of history.

"We ask of you an impossible combination of traits: ironclad scruples and a willingness to violate them;

"An abiding love for your country and a willingness to consort with individuals working actively to destroy it;

"The instincts and intuition of experts, and the blank records and true freshness of ingenues.

"You will each perform this service only once, after which you will return to your lives.

"We can't promise that you will be exactly the same when you go back."

6

Eagerness and pliability can be expressed even in the way

you climb from the sea onto chalky yellow rocks.

"You're a very fast swimmer," uttered by a man still submerged, might not be intended as praise.

Giggling is sometimes better than answering.

"You are a lovely girl" may be meant straightforwardly.

Ditto "I want to fuck you now."

"Well? What do you think about that?" suggests a preference for direct verbal responses over giggles.

"I like it" must be uttered with enough gusto to compensate for a lack of declarative color.

"You don't sound sure" indicates insufficient gusto.

"I'm *not* sure" is acceptable only when followed, coyly, by "You'll have to convince me."

Throwing back your head and closing your eyes gives the appearance of sexual readiness while concealing revulsion.

7

Being alone with a violent, ruthless man, surrounded by water, can make the shore seem very far away.

You may feel solidarity, at such a time, with the beauties just visible there in their bright bikinis.

You may appreciate, at such a time, why you aren't being paid for this work.

Your voluntary service is the highest form of patriotism.

Remind yourself that you aren't being paid when he climbs out of the water and lumbers toward you.

Remind yourself that you aren't being paid when he leads you behind a boulder and pulls you onto his lap.

The Dissociation Technique is like a parachute—you must pull the cord at the correct time.

Too soon, and you will hinder your ability to function at a crucial moment;

Too late, and you will be lodged too far inside the action to wriggle free.

You will be tempted to pull
the cord when he surrounds
you with arms whose bulky
strength reminds you,
fleetingly, of your husband's.

You will be tempted to pull
it when you feel him start
to move against you from
below.

You will be tempted to pull it
when his smell envelops you:
metallic, like a warm hand
clutching pennies.

The directive "Relax"
suggests that your discomfort
is palpable.

"No one can see us" suggests
that your discomfort has
been understood as fear of
physical exposure.

"Relax, relax," uttered in
rhythmic, throaty tones,
suggests that your discomfort
is not unwelcome.

8

Begin the Dissociation
Technique only when physical
violation is imminent.

Close your eyes and slowly
count backward from ten.

With each number, imagine
yourself rising out of your
body and moving one step
farther away from it.

By eight, you should be
hovering just outside your
skin.

By five, you should be
floating a foot or two above
your body, feeling only vague
anxiety over what is about to
happen to it.

By three, you should feel fully
detached from your physical
self.

By two, your body should be
able to act and react without
your participation.

By one, your mind should
drift so free that you lose
track of what is happening
below.

White clouds spin and curl.

A blue sky is as depthless as
the sea.

The sound of waves against
rocks existed millennia
before there were creatures
who could hear it.

Spurs and gashes of stone
narrate a violence that
the earth itself has long
forgotten.

Your mind will rejoin your body when it is safe to do so.

9

Return to your body carefully, as if reentering your home after a hurricane.

Resist the impulse to reconstruct what has just happened.

Focus instead on gauging your Designated Mate's reaction to the new intimacy between you.

In some men, intimacy will prompt callous indifference.

In others, intimacy may awaken problematic curiosity about you.

"Where did you learn to swim like that?" uttered lazily, while supine, with two fingers in your hair, indicates curiosity.

Tell the truth without precision.

"I grew up near a lake" is both true and vague.

"Where was the lake?" conveys dissatisfaction with your vagueness.

"Upstate New York" suggests precision while avoiding it.

"Manhattan?" betrays unfamiliarity with the geography of New York State.

Never contradict your Designated Mate.

"Where did you grow up?," asked of a man who has just asked you the same question, is known as "mirroring."

Mirror your Designated Mate's attitudes, interests, desires, and tastes.

Your goal is to become part of his atmosphere: a source of comfort and ease.

Only then will he drop his guard when you are near.

Only then will he have significant conversations within earshot.

Only then will he leave his possessions in a porous and unattended state.

Only then can you begin to gather information systematically.

10

"Come. Let's go back,"
uttered brusquely, suggests
that your Designated Mate
has no more wish to talk
about himself than you do.

Avoid the temptation to
analyze his moods and
whims.

Salt water has a cleansing
effect.

11

You will see knowledge of
your new intimacy with your
Designated Mate in the eyes
of every beauty on shore.

"We saved lunch for you"
is likely an allusion to the
reason for your absence.

Cold fish is unappetizing,
even when served in a good
lemon sauce.

Be friendly to other beauties,
but not solicitous.

When in conversation with a
beauty, it is essential that you
be perceived as no more or
less than she is.

Be truthful about every
aspect of your life except
marriage (if any).

If married, say that you
have divorced, to give an
impression of unfettered
freedom.

"Oh, that's sad!" suggests
that your interlocutor would
like to marry.

12

If your Designated Mate
veers abruptly toward the
villa, follow him.

Taking his hand and smiling
will create a sense of low-key
camaraderie.

An abstracted smile in return
may signal pressing concerns.

The concerns of your
Designated Mate are our
concerns.

13

The room assigned to a
powerful man will be more
lavish than the one you slept
in while awaiting his arrival.

Never look for hidden
cameras: The fact that you're
looking will give you away.

Determine whether your
Designated Mate seeks
physical intimacy; if not, feign
the wish for a nap.

Your pretense of sleep will allow him to feel that he is alone.

Curling up under bedclothes, even those belonging to an enemy subject, may be soothing.

You're more likely to hear his handset vibrate if your eyes are closed.

14

A door sliding open signals his wish to take the call on the balcony.

Your Designated Mate's important conversations will always take place outdoors.

If you are within earshot of his conversation, record it.

Since beauties carry neither pocketbooks nor timepieces, you cannot credibly transport a recording device.

A microphone has been implanted just beyond the first turn of your right ear canal.

Activate the mic by pressing the triangle of cartilage across your ear opening.

You will hear a faint whine as recording begins.

In extreme quiet, or to a person whose head is adjacent to yours, this whine may be audible.

Should the whine be detected, swat your ear as if to deflect a mosquito, hitting the on/off cartilage to deactivate the mic.

You need not identify or comprehend the language your subject is using.

Your job is proximity; if you are near your Designated Mate, recording his private speech, you are succeeding.

15

Profanity sounds the same in every language.

An angry subject will guard his words less carefully.

If your subject is angry, leave your camouflage position and move close to him to improve recording quality.

You may feel afraid as you do this.

Your pounding heartbeat will not be recorded.

If your Designated Mate is standing on a balcony, hover in the doorway just behind him.

If he pivots and discovers you there, pretend that you were on the verge of approaching him.

Anger usually trumps suspicion.

If your subject shoves past you and storms out of the room, slamming the door, presume that you have eluded detection.

16

If your Designated Mate leaves your company a second time, don't follow him.

Deactivate your ear mic and resume your "nap."

A moment of repose is a good time to reassure your loved ones.

Nuanced communication is too easily monitored by the enemy.

Your Subcutaneous Pulse System issues pings so generic that detection would reveal neither source nor intent.

A button is embedded behind the inside ligament of your right knee (if right-handed).

Depress twice to indicate to loved ones that you are well and thinking of them.

You may send this signal only once each day.

A continuous depression of the button indicates an emergency.

You will debate, each day, the best time to send your signal.

You will reflect on the fact that your husband, coming from a culture of tribal allegiance, understands and applauds your patriotism.

You will reflect on the enclosed and joyful life the two of you have shared since graduate school.

You will reflect on the fact that America is your husband's chosen country and that he loves it.

You will reflect on your shared conviction that your service had to be undertaken before you had children.

You will reflect on the fact that you are thirty-three and have spent your professional life fomenting musical trends.

You will reflect on the fact that you have always believed you would do work of more significance.

You will reflect on the fact that too much reflection is pointless.

You will reflect on the fact that these Field Instructions are becoming less and less instructive.

Your Field Instructions, stored in a weevil inside your skull, will serve as both a record of your actions and a guide for your successors.

Pressing your left thumb (if right-handed) against your left middle fingertip begins recording.

For clearest results, mentally speak the thought aloud to yourself.

Always filter your observations through the lens of their instructional value.

Your training is ongoing; you must learn from each step you take.

When your mission is complete and the weevil removed, you may review its contents before adding your Field Instructions to your mission file.

Where stray or personal thoughts have intruded, you may delete them.

Due to the classified nature of this work, you are strictly forbidden to upload or share any portion of your consciousness for the duration of your life.

17

Pretend sleep can lead to actual sleep.

Sounds of showering suggest the return of your Designated Mate.

Beauties are expected to visit their rooms often to change clothes; a fresh appearance at mealtimes is essential.

The goal is to be a lovely, innocuous, evolving surprise.

A crisp white sundress against tanned skin is widely perceived as attractive.

Avoid overbright colors; they are attention-seeking and hinder camouflage.

White is not, technically speaking, a bright color.

White is, nevertheless, bright.

Delicate gold sandals may compromise your ability to run or jump, but they look good on tanned feet.

Thirty-three is still young enough to register as "young."

Registering as "young" is especially welcome to those who may not register as "young" much longer.

If your Designated Mate leads you to dinner with an arm at your waist, assume that your attire change has been successful.

18
When men begin serious talk, beauties are left to themselves.

"How long have you been divorced?" suggests the wish to resume a prior conversation.

"A few months," when untrue, should be said without eye contact.

"What was he like, your husband?" may be answered honestly.

"From Africa. Kenya" may satisfy a wish to talk about your husband.

"Black?," with eyebrows raised, may indicate racism.

"Yes. Black," in measured tones, should deliver a gentle reproof.

"How Black?" suggests that it did not.

"Very Black" is somewhat less gentle, especially when accompanied by a pointed stare.

"Nice" hints at personal experience.

"Yes. It is nice" contradicts one's alleged divorce and should be hastily amended to "*Was* nice."

"But not nice enough?," with laughter, indicates friendly intimacy. Especially when followed by "Or too nice!"

19

House-party hosts are universally eager to make guests eat.

For most beauties, the lure of food is a hazard; as a short-term beauty, you can eat what you want.

Squab may be consumed by ripping the bird apart with your hands and sucking the meat from the bones.

A stunned expression suggests that your host expected the use of utensils.

The adjacency of his chair to yours may presage a confidence.

Turning your ear toward your host's mouth will save you from having to smell his breath.

Ears must be kept clean at all times.

If your host warns you that your Designated Mate may pose a danger to you, assume that he has left the room.

20

Going to the bathroom is the most efficient means of self-jettisoning.

Never betray urgency, even in an empty hallway.

If you have no idea where your Designated Mate has gone, hold still.

If you find yourself beside a pair of glass doors, you may open them and look out.

Nights in the South of France are a strange, dark, piercing blue.

A bright moon can astonish, no matter how many times you have seen it.

If you were a child who loved the moon, looking at the moon will remind you of childhood.

Fatherless girls may invest the moon with a certain paternal promise.

Everyone has a father.

A vague story like "Your father died before you were

born" may satisfy even a canny child for an unlikely number of years.

The truth of your paternity, discovered in adulthood, will make the lie seem retroactively ludicrous.

Publicists occasionally have flings with their movie star clients.

Discovering that you are a movie star's daughter is not necessarily a comfort.

It is especially not a comfort when the star in question has six other children from four different marriages.

Discovering that you are a movie star's daughter may prompt you to watch upward of sixty movies dating from the beginning of his career.

You may think, watching his movies, *You don't know I exist, but I am here.*

You may think, watching his movies, *I'm invisible to you, but I am here.*

A sudden reconfiguration of your past can change the fit and feel of your adulthood.

It may cleave you from the mother whose single goal has been your happiness.

If your husband has transformed greatly in his own life, he will understand your transformation.

Avoid excessive self-reflection; your job is to look out, not in.

21

"There you are," whispered from behind, by your Designated Mate, suggests that he has been looking for you.

"Come," uttered softly, may communicate a renewed wish for intimate contact.

The moon's calm face will make you feel, in advance, that you are understood and forgiven.

The sea is audible well before you see it.

Even at night, the Mediterranean is more blue than black.

If you wish to avoid physical intimacy, the sight of a speedboat will bring relief despite the myriad problems it presents.

If no words are exchanged between your Designated Mate and the speedboat's captain, their meeting was likely prearranged.

A man known for his cruelty may still show great care while guiding his beauty into a rocking speedboat.

He will interpret her hesitation to board as fear of falling in.

Resist the impulse to ask where you are going.

Try, when anxious, to summon up a goofy giggle.

Locate your Personal Calming Source and use it.

If your Personal Calming Source is the moon, be grateful that the moon is especially bright.

Reflect on the many reasons you can't yet die:

You need to see your husband.

You need to have children.

You need to tell the movie star that he has a seventh child, and that she is a hero.

22

The moon may appear to move, but really it is you who are moving.

At high velocity, a speedboat slams along the tops of waves.

Fear and excitement are sometimes indistinguishable.

When the captain of a boat adjusts his course to commands from your Designated Mate, he may not know where he is taking you.

If your Designated Mate keeps looking up, he's likely using the stars for navigation.

The Mediterranean is vast enough to have once seemed infinite.

A beauty should require no more context than the presence of her Designated Mate.

She must appear to relish any journey he undertakes.

Feign such enjoyment by putting an affectionate arm around him and nestling your head beside his.

Aligning your head with your Designated Mate's will allow you to share in his navigation and calculate your route.

At night, far from shore, stars pulse with a strength inconceivable in the proximity of light.

Your whereabouts will never be a mystery to us; you will be visible as a dot of light on the screens of those watching over you.

You are one of hundreds, each a potential hero.

Technology has afforded ordinary people a chance to glow in the cosmos of human achievement.

Your lack of espionage training is what makes your record clean and neutral.

You are an ordinary person undertaking an extraordinary task.

You need not be remarkable for your skills, only for your bravery and equilibrium.

Knowing that you are one of hundreds should not diminish you.

In the new heroism, the goal is to merge with something larger than yourself.

In the new heroism, the goal is to throw off the scourge of self-involvement.

In the new heroism, the goal is to renounce the modern fixation with being seen and recognized.

In the new heroism, the goal is to dig beneath your shiny persona.

You'll be surprised by what lies underneath: a rich, deep crawl space of possibility.

Some liken this discovery to a dream in which a familiar home acquires new wings and rooms.

The power of individual magnetism is nothing against the power of combined selfless effort.

You may accomplish astonishing personal feats, but Citizen Agents do not seek individual credit.

The need for personal glory is like cigarette addiction: a habit that feels life-sustaining even as it kills you.

Childish attention-seeking is usually satisfied at the expense of real power.

An enemy of the state could not have connived a better way to defang and distract us.

Now our notorious narcissism is our camouflage.

23

After a juddering ride of several hours, you may not notice at first that the boat is approaching a shore.

A single lighted structure stands out starkly on a deserted coastline.

Silence after a roaring motor is a sound of its own.

The speedboat's immediate departure suggests that you won't be returning anytime soon.

Knowing your latitude and longitude is not the same as knowing where you are.

A new remote and unfamiliar place can make the prior remote and unfamiliar place seem like home.

Imagining yourself as a dot of light on a screen can be oddly reassuring.

Because your husband is a visionary in the realm of national security, he occasionally has access to that screen.

If it calms you to imagine your husband tracking your dot of light, then imagine it.

Do not, however, close your eyes while ascending a rocky path in strappy sandals, in total darkness.

At Latitude X, Longitude Y, the flora is dry and crumbles under your feet.

A voice from above suggests that your arrival has been expected and observed.

An empty shore is not necessarily unpatrolled.

The best patrols are imperceptible.

24

A formal handshake between your new host and your Designated Mate may mean that they haven't met before now.

In certain rich, powerful men, physical slightness will seem a source of strength.

The failure of your new host to acknowledge you may indicate that women do not register in his field of vision.

Being invisible means you won't be closely watched.

Your job is to be forgotten yet still present.

A white, sparkling villa amid so much scrabbly darkness will appear miragelike.

A man to whom women are invisible may still have many beauties in his domain.

These neglected beauties will vie for his scant attention.

Among neglected beauties, there is usually an alpha beauty who assumes command.

As you enter the villa, her cool scrutiny will ripple through the other beauties and contract around you.

The sensation will remind you of going as a child to a school, or a country club, where you knew almost no one.

Feeling at the mercy of those around you prompted a seismic internal response.

The will to integrate and thrive among strangers felt deeper than yourself.

You were never childish, even as a child.

Your unchildishness is something your husband has always loved in you.

Once the new children had become your allies, it was wrenching to leave them.

25

A small table and chairs carved into a spindly clifftop promontory are doubtless designed for private conversation.

If your Designated Mate brings you with him to this spot, he may be imperfectly at ease with your new host.

When your new host dismisses his alpha beauty, important business is likely under way.

An alpha beauty will not tolerate her own exclusion if another beauty is included.

If your new host's first acknowledgment of you is a gesture of dismissal, look to your Designated Mate.

Take orders from no one but your Designated Mate.

If your Designated Mate keeps an arm around you in the face of your new host's dismissal, you have become the object of a power play.

If your new host speaks directly into your face, at close range, he is likely testing your ignorance of his language.

If your Designated Mate stiffens beside you, your new host's words are probably offensive.

An uncomprehending giggle is a beauty's most reliable tool for diffusing conflict.

If the men relax into their chairs, your neutralization has been successful.

Your new host has insulted you and, by extension, your Designated Mate.

Your Designated Mate has prevailed in his claim that

you're too harmless to bother sending away.

Congratulate yourself on preserving your adjacency and activate your ear mic.

26

In the presence of business discussion, project an utter lack of interest or curiosity.

Notice where you are at all times.

On a high, narrow promontory at Latitude X, Longitude Y, the ocean and heavens shimmer in all directions.

There may be moments during your mission when you'll sense that critical information is imminent.

It may come in the form of a rush of joy.

This joy may arise from your discovery that the moon, hard and radiant, is still aloft.

It may arise from a sense that you have entered the fantastical realm where childhood stories are set.

It may arise from the knowledge that, when your

task is complete, you will return to the husband you adore.

It may arise from the extremity of the natural beauty around you, and recognition that you are alive in this moment.

It may arise from your knowledge that you have accomplished every goal you've set for yourself since childhood.

It may arise from the knowledge that, at long last, you have found a goal worthy of your prodigious energies.

It may arise from the knowledge that, in accomplishing this goal, you will have helped to preserve American life as you know it.

27

A wave of joy can make it difficult to sit still.

Beware of internal states—positive or negative—that obscure what is happening around you.

When two subjects begin making sketches, concrete planning has commenced.

The camera implanted in your left eye is operated by pressing your left tear duct.

In poor light, a flash may be activated by pressing the outside tip of your left eyebrow.

When using the flash, always cover your non-camera eye to shield it from temporary blindness.

Never deploy flash photography in the presence of other people.

28

Springing from your seat with a gasp and peering toward the villa will focus the attention of others in that same direction.

"What? What did you hear?," uttered close to your face by your Designated Mate, indicates that your diversion is credible.

Wait until their eagerness to know approaches anger; then tell them, faintly, "I heard screaming."

Violent men live in fear of retribution.

Your new host will be the first to bolt toward his house.

Your Designated Mate's glance toward the dock, far below, suggests that his interests are not fully aligned with your new host's.

His immediate preoccupation with his phone may mean that he is summoning the speedboat captain.

Among the violent, there is always a plan for escape.

29

A brightly lit phone will, hopefully, distract its user from a camera flash at some slight distance.

Move close enough to the sketches you wish to photograph that they fill your field of vision.

Hold very still.

A flash is far more dramatic in total darkness.

An epithet followed by "What the fuck was that?" suggests that you overestimated your Designated Mate's phone absorption.

A bright, throbbing blindness suggests that you neglected to cover your non-camera eye.

Distance yourself from involvement in the flash by crying out, truthfully, "I can't see!"

It is hard to safely navigate a clifftop promontory at high speed while blind.

It is impossible to defer said navigation when your Designated Mate is forcefully yanking your hand.

A buzzing presages an approaching speedboat.

Trying to descend a crumbly wooded path in a state of blindness (and heels) will lead to tripping and collapsing.

Receding footfalls suggest that you've overtaxed your limited value to your Designated Mate.

Blind disorientation may prevent you from doing more than calling to him from where you have fallen.

A boat departing at high speed will send a vibration trembling up through the soil.

30

Temporary blindness sharpens one's appreciation for not being blind.

In the aftermath of blindness, an accretion of objects around you may have an almost sensual quality.

The knowledge that you are without your Designated Mate will settle upon you slowly and coldly.

Each new phase of aloneness reveals that you were previously less alone than you thought.

This more profound isolation may result, at first, in paralysis.

If it soothes you to lie back in the dirt, then lie back.

The moon shines everywhere.

The moon can seem as expressive as a face.

Human beings are fiercely, primordially resilient.

The mythical feats you loved to read about as a child are puny beside the accomplishments of human beings on earth.

31

The discovery of another person nearby when you thought you were alone may occasion fear.

Leaping from a supine into a standing posture will induce vertigo.

"I see you. Come out" must be uttered calmly, from the Readiness Position.

When you've expected a man, the appearance of a woman may bring relief, despite everything that you know, and are.

"Why are you here?," uttered by your new host's alpha beauty, is likely hostile.

Reply to abstract questions on the most literal level: "He left without me."

"Bastard," muttered bitterly, suggests acquaintance with the phenomenon of being left behind.

Sympathy from an unexpected source can prompt a swell of emotion.

Measure the liability of shedding tears before you let them fall.

The perfumed arms of a beauty may pour strength and hope directly into your skin.

32

A lavish clifftop villa may look even more miragelike on a second approach.

Sustaining an atmosphere of luxury in a remote place requires an enormous amount of money.

So does coordinated violence.

Your job is to follow money to its source.

A powerful man whose associate has fled the premises after a false alarm is unlikely to be cheerful.

The reappearance of the vanished associate's stranded beauty will likely startle him.

Astonishment is satisfying to witness on any face.

"Where the fuck did he go?" can be deciphered even in a language you don't recognize.

A shrug is universally understood.

An alpha beauty's indifference to the consternation of her mate may mean that he's easily moved to consternation.

It may also mean that he's not her mate.

33

As a beauty, you will sometimes be expected to change hands.

Generally, you will pass from the hands of a less powerful to a more powerful man.

Your job is identical regardless of whose hands you are in.

Advancing further toward the source of money and control is progress.

If your vulnerability and helplessness have roused the interest of an enemy subject, accentuate them.

Dirty, bleeding knees may accentuate your vulnerability to the point of disgust.

They might get you a hot shower, though.

34

Homes of the violent rich have excellent first-aid cabinets.

If, after tending to your scrapes, you are shown to a bathing area with a waterfall, assume you won't be alone for long.

The fact that a man has ignored and insulted you doesn't mean that he won't want to fuck you.

Slim, powerful men often move with catlike swiftness.

Begin your countdown early— as he lowers himself into the tub.

By the time he seizes your arm, you should be at five.

By the time your forehead is jammed against a rock, you should perceive your body only vaguely, from above.

35

If you feel, on returning to your body, that much time has passed, don't dwell on how much.

If your limbs are sore and your forehead is scraped and raw, don't dwell on why.

Emerging from a hot, churning bath where you've spent an indeterminate period of time will leave you shaky and weak.

Remind yourself that you are receiving no payment, in currency or kind, for this or any act you have engaged in.

These acts are forms of sacrifice.

An abundance of diaphanous bathrobes suggests that women often visit this bathing area.

A soiled and tattered white sundress may seem oddly precious when it's all you have.

Keep with you the things that matter—you won't come back for them.

36

If you're shown to a tiny room containing a very large bed, your utility to your new host may not have been exhausted.

At times, you may wish to avoid the moon.

The moon may appear like a surveillance device, tracking your movements.

Sleep whenever you can safely do so.

37

Your abrupt awakening may feel like a reaction to a sound.

In moments of extreme solitude, you may believe you've heard your name.

We reassure ourselves by summoning, in our dreams, those we love and miss.

Having awakened to find them absent, we may be left with a sense of having spoken with them.

Even the most secure houses achieve, in deep night, a state of relative unconsciousness.

A beauty in a diaphanous lavender bathrobe can go anywhere, as long as she appears to be delivering herself to someone.

A universal principle of home construction makes it possible to know which door will lead to the master bedroom.

Linen closets, with doors closed, can resemble master bedrooms.

So can bathrooms.

Bare feet are soundless on stone floor.

A slim, catlike man may still snore.

When trespassing in a sleeping man's bedroom, go straight to his bed, as if you were seeking him out.

38

An alpha beauty who appeared to have no tie to your new host may yet turn out to be his intimate.

Their sleeping entanglement may contradict everything you have previously witnessed between them.

Human beings are
unknowable; hence
the Faustian allure of
consciousness sharing.

A small crib near the bed
suggests the presence of a
baby.

Avoid indulging your own
amazement; it wastes time.

39

Enemy subjects will store
their phones away from
where they sleep.

A beauty's closet is
unmistakable, like a quiver of
bright arrows.

Having located a man's
private space, seek out the
Sweet Spot where he empties
his pockets at the end of each
day.

If his phone is in the Sweet
Spot, consider using a Data
Surge to capture its contents.

A Data Surge must be
deployed only if you feel
confident of an exceptional
yield.

The quantity of information
captured will require
enormous labor to tease
apart and process.

Its transmission will register
on any enemy monitoring
device.

We can guarantee its
effectiveness only once.

40

Reach between your right
fourth and pinky toes (if right-
handed) and remove the
Data Plug from your Universal
Port.

Insert the plug's magnetic
wire into any port on the
subject's phone.

Seat yourself on the floor,
away from sharp surfaces,
and brace your back against
a wall.

A red ribbon has been
tucked inside your Universal
Port; hold this in one of your
palms.

Spread apart your toes and
gently reinsert the plug, now
magnetically fused to your
subject's phone, into your
Universal Port.

You will feel a surge as the
data floods your body.

The surge may contain
memory, heat, cold, longing,
pain, or even joy.

Although the data are alien, the memories dislodged will be your own:

Peeling an orange for your husband in bed on a Sunday, sunlight splashing tossed sheets;

The smoky earthen smell of the fur of your childhood cat;

The flavor of the peppermints your mother kept for you inside her desk.

The impact of a Data Surge may prompt unconsciousness or short-term memory loss.

The purpose of the red ribbon is to orient you; if you awaken to find yourself clutching one, look to your foot.

When your body is quiet, detach the subject's phone and return it to its original location.

41

A Data Surge will leave a ringing in your ears that may obscure the sound of another person's arrival.

A face that brought you relief once may trigger relief a second time.

When an alpha beauty screams at you in an unfamiliar language, it may mean she's too sleepy to recall just who you are.

It may also mean she's calling someone else.

Beauty status will not excuse your appearance where you are not supposed to be.

Prepare to defend yourself at the first sign of physical encroachment.

Your new host lunging at you, shouting, "What the fuck are you doing?" constitutes physical encroachment.

Thrusting your elbow into the tender socket under his jaw will send him backward onto the floor.

The cries of a newborn will lure its mother away from even the physical travails of her mate.

A man disabled by an elbow blow will have little reaction to infant cries.

42

At the revelation of martial-arts expertise, a man who has perceived you as merely a beauty will recalculate your purpose.

An immediate exit is advisable.

A slim, catlike man may well rebound before a hasty exit can be made.

Watch his eyes: He'll be measuring the distance to his nearest firearm.

Kicking him in the foreneck, even barefoot, will temporarily occlude his windpipe.

The alpha beauty of a violent man will know where his firearm is kept and how to use it.

A woman holding a gun and a baby no longer qualifies as a beauty.

No beauty is really a beauty.

Disabling a gun holder will likely hurt the baby she is holding.

As Americans, we prize human rights above all else and cannot sanction their violation.

When someone threatens *our* rights, however, a wider leeway becomes necessary.

Follow your instincts while bearing in mind that we must, and will, hew to our principles.

A woman holding a thrashing baby in one arm may have trouble aiming a firearm with the other.

Bullets do actually whistle in an enclosed space.

If a person has shot at you once and missed, incapacitate her before she can fire again.

We are most reluctant to harm those who remind us of ourselves.

43

There is lag time between getting shot and knowing that you have been shot.

Assuming no artery involvement, wounds to the upper limbs are preferable.

Bony, tendony body parts bleed less but are harder to reconstruct if shattered.

The right shoulder is a bony, tendony part.

When shots have been fired in a powerful man's home, you have minutes, if not seconds, before the arrival of security.

Your physical person is our Black Box; without it, we have no record of what has transpired on your mission.

It is essential that you remove yourself from enemy possession.

44

When you find yourself cornered and outnumbered, you may unleash, as a last resort, your Primal Roar.

The Primal Roar is the human equivalent of an explosion, a sound that combines screaming, shrieking, and howling.

The Roar must be accompanied by facial contortions and frenetic body movements suggesting a feral, unhinged state.

The Primal Roar must transform you from a beauty into a monster.

The goal is to horrify your opponent the way trusted figures, turned evil, are horrifying in children's stories and in nightmares.

Deploy your camera flash repeatedly while Roaring.

When approached by a howling, spasmodic, flashing monster, a woman holding her newborn will quickly step aside.

Discontinue Roaring the instant you're free from immediate danger.

Those stampeding to the aid of a powerful man will barely notice a disheveled beauty they pass in his hallway.

If you're lucky, this will buy you time to flee the house.

Resume your beauty role while running: Smooth your hair and cover your bleeding wound with the sundress scrunched in your pocket.

The fact that you can't hear alarms doesn't mean you haven't set them off.

45

After violence in a closed room, cool night air will have a clarifying effect.

Get to the bottom of a steep dirt path any way you can, including sliding and rolling.

In residences of the violent rich, there will be at least one guard at each port of egress.

In deep night, if you are extremely lucky (and quiet), that guard will be asleep.

Assume, as best you can, the air of a beauty larkishly gamboling.

If running barefoot onto a dock transports you back to your childhood, pain may be making you hallucinate.

Lying on a warm dock near a country club, holding a boy's hand for the very first time, is a sensation you remember after many years.

Hindsight creates an illusion that your life has led you inevitably to the present moment.

It's easier to believe in a foregone conclusion than to accept that our lives are governed by random chance.

Showing up for a robotics course by accident, because of a room-assignment mix-up with your Homer class, is random chance.

Finding an empty seat beside a boy with dark skin and beautiful hands is random chance.

When someone has become essential, you will marvel that you could have lain on a warm dock and not known him yet.

Expect reimmersion in your old life to be difficult.

Experience leaves a mark, regardless of the reasons and principles behind it.

What our Citizen Agents most often require is simply for time to pass.

Our Theraputic Agents are available around the clock for the first two weeks of your reimmersion and during business hours thereafter.

Describing any aspect of your mission to civilians, including mental health professionals or spiritual counselors, is strictly forbidden.

Trust that we have every resource necessary to address your needs.

46

Even preternatural swimming strength cannot propel you across a blue-black sea.

Staring with yearning ferocity from the end of a dock cannot propel you across a blue-black sea.

When your body has been granted exceptional powers, it is jarring to encounter a gulf between your wishes and your abilities.

For millennia, engineers have empowered human beings to accomplish mythical feats.

Your husband is an engineer.

Children raised among natural predators learn to detect irregular shapes and movement in a landscape.

Intimacy with another human can allow you to scrutinize your surroundings as he would.

Along a rocky, moonlit shore, the irregular shape is a right angle pitching in time with the waves, beneath an overhang of brush.

A speedboat has most likely been hidden by your new host as a means of emergency escape.

The key will be inside it.

47

Slither between branches and board the boat; untie it and lower its motor into the water.

Be grateful for the lakes in Upstate New York where you learned to pilot motorboats.

Fluff up your hair with your functional arm and force a wide, carefree smile across your face.

A smile is like a shield; it freezes your face into a mask you can hide behind.

A smile is a door that is both open and closed.

Turn the key and gun the motor once before aiming into the blue-black sea and jamming the accelerator.

Wave and giggle loudly at
the stunned, sleepy guard.

Steer in a zigzag motion until
you are out of gunshot range.

48

The exultation of escape
will be followed almost
immediately by a crushing
onslaught of pain.

The villa, its occupants,
even the gunshots will seem
like phantoms beside this
clanging immediacy.

If the pain makes thought
impossible, focus on
navigation.

Only in specific Geographic
Hotspots can we intervene.

While navigating toward
a Hotspot, indicate an
emergency by pressing the
button behind your knee for
thirty continuous seconds.

You must remain conscious.

If it helps, imagine yourself in
the arms of your husband.

If it helps, imagine yourself
in your apartment, where his
grandfather's hunting knife is
displayed inside a plexiglass
box.

If it helps, imagine harvesting
the small tomatoes you
grow on your windowsill in
summer.

If it helps, imagine that the
contents of the Data Surge
will help thwart an attack
in which thousands of lives
would have been lost.

Even without enhancements,
you can pilot a boat in a
semiconscious state.

Human beings are
superhuman.

Let the moon and the stars
direct you.

49

When you reach the
approximate location of a
Hotspot, cut the engine.

You will be in total darkness,
in total silence.

If you wish, you may lie down
at the bottom of the boat.

The fact that you feel like
you're dying doesn't mean
that you will die.

Remember that, should you
die, your body will yield a
trove of crucial data.

Remember that, should you die, your Field Instructions will provide a record of your mission and lessons for those who follow you.

Remember that, should you die, you will have triumphed merely by delivering your physical person into our hands.

The boat's movement on the sea will remind you of a cradle.

You'll recall your mother rocking you in her arms when you were a child.

You'll recall that she has always loved you fiercely and entirely.

You'll discover that you have forgiven her.

You'll understand that she concealed your paternity out of faith that her own infinite love would be enough.

The wish to tell your mother that you forgive her is yet another reason you must make it home alive.

The thought that your father will never know what he has lost is another reason you must make it home alive.

The need to tell him what he very nearly lost is another reason you must make it home alive.

You will not be able to wait, but you will have to wait.

We have never failed to recover a Citizen Agent, dead or alive, who managed to reach a Hotspot.

50

Hotspots are not hot.

Even a warm night turns frigid at the wet bottom of a boat.

Looking up at scattered, blinking stars can feel like floating above them and looking down.

The universe will seem to hang beneath you in its milky glittering mystery.

Only when you notice a woman like yourself, crumpled and bleeding at the bottom of a boat, will you realize what has happened.

You've deployed the
Dissociation Technique
without meaning to.

There is no harm in this.

Released from pain, you can
waft free in the night sky.

Released from pain, you can
enact the fantasy of flying
that you nurtured as a child.

Keep your body in view at all
times; if your mind loses track
of your body, it may be hard—
even impossible—to reunite
the two.

As you waft free in the night
sky, you may notice a steady
rhythmic churning in the
gusting wind.

Helicopter noise is inherently
menacing.

A helicopter without lights
is like a mixture of bat, bird,
and monstrous insect.

Resist the urge to flee this
apparition; it has come to
save you.

51

Know that in returning
to your body, you are
consenting to be racked by
physical pain.

Know that in returning
to your body, you are
consenting to undertake a
jarring reimmersion into an
altered life.

Some Citizen Agents have
chosen not to return.

They have left their bodies
behind, and now they glitter
sublimely in the heavens.

In the new heroism, the goal
is to transcend individual
life, with its petty pains and
loves, in favor of the dazzling
collective.

You may picture each pulsing
star as the heroic spirit of a
former agent beauty.

You may imagine heaven as
a vast screen crowded with
their dots of light.

52

If you wish to return to your
body, it is essential that you
reach it before the helicopter
does.

If it helps, count backward.

By eight, you should be close
enough to see your bare and
dirty feet.

By five, you should be close enough to see the bloody dress wrapped around your shoulder.

By three, you should be close enough to see the dimples you were praised for as a child.

By two, you should hear the shallow bleating of your breath.

53

Having returned to your body, witness the chopper's slow, throbbing descent.

It may appear to be the instrument of a purely mechanical realm.

It may look as if it has come to wipe you out.

It may be hard to believe that there are human beings inside it.

You won't know for sure until you see them crouching above you, their faces taut with hope, ready to jump.

The Perimeter:
Before

"How do we know that man is really her brother?" Mom asks after dinner one night when Brian and Molly have gone upstairs to start their homework and I'm helping her load the dishwasher.

"What man?" Dad says from his recliner in the study beside the kitchen. "Whose brother?"

"It just seems a little . . . coincidental," she says. "He moves in, and nine months later, boom. The husband moves out."

"Ah," Dad says. Not because he agrees with Mom's latest conspiracy theory—he never does, none of us do—but because he's figured out who she's talking about: our next-door neighbors, the Salazars.

Mom leaves the kitchen and stands beside Dad's recliner, looking down. "They don't look remotely alike," she says. "Do you see any sibling resemblance?"

"We've never been on good enough terms with him for me to get a close look at his face," Dad says.

"I think he's given up on the journalism," Mom says. "He's around the house a lot."

"You're around the house a lot," Dad points out.

"I'm keeping an eye on him."

Dad carefully sets down his newspaper—the equivalent, for Dad, of standing up and staring fixedly into Mom's eyes. "Observe the property line, Noreen," he says. "If you encroach on their property again, I can't protect you. Hannah, are you listening?" he calls to me through the kitchen door. I'm always listening. "You are my witness."

"What if he encroaches?" Mom asks.

A few months after Stephanie Salazar's brother moved in with Mr. and Mrs. Salazar, Mom saw him climbing into their house through a window (he'd forgotten his keys) and called the police to report a break-in. She knew exactly who he was but didn't trust him, she told Dad (who told me), having received hostile looks while gardening near the split-wood fence that separates our yard from the Salazars' yard. What Mom didn't know was that Stephanie's brother was on parole, which resulted in the police taking him away in handcuffs. That night, the Salazars came over to talk to Mom and Dad about Stephanie's brother and his mental health. Bennie Salazar discovered Dad's favorite band, the Conduits, and produced all their songs, so Dad broke out the bourbon and nodded sympathetically while Mom gazed at the window like she was distracted by a sound that no one else could hear. Sure enough, while that conversation was going on, a portion of the fence between our two yards tipped drastically in our direction, violating our "airspace," as Mom put it, and "aggressing" one section of her pink phlox. A few weeks later, Mom dug up one of the fence posts with an electric shovel-drill she rented from Ace Hardware and moved the post five inches onto the Salazars' property. She was giddy when we got home from school. She sang as she cooked and chuckled as she folded laundry. That night, I answered the front doorbell and found Stephanie Salazar's brother standing there, pale and shaking with rage, clutching a tape measure. I called for Dad, and they went into the backyard and looked at the fence post together. Dad agreed that it had been moved and hired a handyman to move it back.

That was two years ago, when I was a freshman. We were all sorry when the Salazars split up, Dad most of all. Bennie Salazar moved to Manhattan, and now we only see him when he picks up or drops off their son, Christopher, who's a year older than Molly. Bennie Salazar waves to us from the window of his sports car. "What a loss," Dad always says.

After Mom and I finish cleaning up, I stay downstairs with Dad, studying for my AP finals, while Mom goes upstairs to help Brian and Molly with the many things they need help with. Brian's cup underwear is uncomfortable and he has a baseball game tomorrow, so Mom drives to the Modell's four towns over that's open late to pick up new cup underwear one size bigger, and afterward she helps Brian with his math (Mom is freakishly good at math). Later I hear Molly crying to Mom about her friend sagas, which are never-ending. I stopped bringing my problems to Mom a few years ago, as she predicted I would. "I can only help you until high school, Hannah, maybe not even, and after that you'll be on your own," she used to say over my objections and denials. But she was right: By high school, I saw Mom differently. Now it's Dad I turn to.

When I was little, I had a fear of dying in my sleep. Mom never said, "That's silly. You're going to live forever, sweetheart, and so am I, and so is our whole family and everyone we love." Instead, she got out her stethoscope, hospital-grade thermometer, and blood pressure cuff and took my vital signs.

"Normal," she said. "You won't die tonight."

According to Mom, you have to be careful or the forces of doom will line up against you. Things are more connected than they seem. The world is cruel and irrational, the strong thrive at the expense of the weak, and happy endings are purely a matter of framing. She emphasized this last point at the end of every fairy tale she read to us:

"We'll see if the prince still loves her when she's middle-aged and has stretch marks, or whether he trades her in for a newer model."

"Yes, the prince inherits his rightful kingdom—until an enemy prince invades it and slaughters them all."

"'Happily ever after' so long as the hundreds of serfs toiling in the fields and scores of servants that make a castle habitable keep slogging away."

"In the real world, there's only one ending, and it isn't happy," Mom has been telling us for as long as I can remember. And when these dire pronouncements made us cry, she would gather us into her arms and murmur, "My beloved children, things are interwoven in ways we don't understand. There are conspiracies. There are plots. I am your mother. You come from my womb. And I will kill anyone I have to kill to protect you."

Nowadays I find it painful to have a mom who's widely perceived as unhinged—a mom my friends laugh at. But when I was young and she was all I knew, I lived inside a force field that shielded me from every danger without concealing it. She made me strong.

Sometimes I think that Mom is like a character from a fairy tale: engrossing until I outgrew that kind of story. Now I want to read other things.

The next night, while Brian and Molly are at the dinner table, Mom says, "He doesn't like me."

"No one likes you," Dad says with that little half-smile that's Dad's version of a grin. "Except us."

"We love you," Molly says.

In the world of moms, ours is solitary. She's not invited to moms' meetings or moms' parties, not included in moms' book clubs or wine tastings or sample sales or theater trips or spa weekends or even moms' round-robins, although she was once a competitive junior tennis player.

"He's a convicted felon," she says.

"Let's not go there," Dad says. "He's a normal person who went off the rails. You of all people should understand that."

"I have never gone off the rails."

"Arguably, you've never been *on* the rails," Dad says with a wink at me.

"Bruce," Mom says very softly. "That is hurtful."

She rises from the table and floats upstairs with her sewing basket, which contains fluffy white yarn for the kitten cap party she's organizing for Molly to win back her monstrous best friend, and several shirts whose labels Brian needs removed because they scratch the back of his neck. You can't just cut off a label with scissors because that leaves a prickly label stub that's worse than the label itself. Mom snips each tiny, nearly invisible stitch that attaches the label to the shirt, using minuscule scissors that have to be special-ordered from Germany and stored in a deionized glass cylinder or they will lose their sharpness overnight.

Brian, Molly, and I clear the table and clean up while Dad sits in his recliner reading *The Wall Street Journal.* In the absence of Mom, the silence becomes oppressive.

"Dad," I tell him, looming over his recliner, "you need to apologize."

"Please don't use that tone with me, Hannah," he replies mildly.

A while later, Molly climbs into his lap, mussing his newspaper, and kisses his cheek—the sort of thing you can get away with when you're nine. "Please say sorry to Mommy?" she coos.

"I'll think about it, pumpkin."

Brian, never a big talker and becoming less so by the minute, stands three feet from Dad's chair and toes the carpet. Finally, he mutters, "Dad."

"Yes, Brian?"

"Come on."

"I beg your pardon?"

"You know."

"What do I know?"

"*Do* it."

"I'm missing the topic of our conversation, Brian."

"Now, Dad."

"Now *what?*"

Brian takes a long breath and screams into Dad's face, "SAY SORRY TO MOM!!!"

Dad slowly returns his recliner to an upright position—the equivalent, for Dad, of springing out of his chair. "I was just about to do that, son," he says, walking calmly toward the stairs. "Thank you for reminding me."

．　．　．

Mom attributes her exclusion by the other moms to the poisonous influence of one pivotal mom: Kathy Bingham, whom Mom refers to as the High Priestess of Bitches. Kathy has five children, all criminally neglected (according to Mom) while Kathy plays obsessive tennis at the Crandale Country Club, where she's been ladies' singles *and* doubles champion for the past eight years. According to Mom, Kathy controls every aspect of ladies' tennis at the CCC with the cutthroat brutality of a racketeering boss. Kathy won't look at Mom, much less speak to her, although Mom insists she's done nothing to warrant Kathy's hatred. "I think it's my hair," she says, and it's true that she bleaches her hair a much whiter blond than the other moms' subtle highlights.

"I'm going to kick the bucket one day, make no mistake," she has told us. "And given what's in the peroxide I'm using, it may be sooner than expected."

When we begged her to stop using the peroxide, Mom said, "Not a chance. Life is all about bargains, and I'm willing to forfeit a couple of years to have hair like Marilyn Monroe."

A few nights later, while Dad is grading my practice SAT test at the table after dinner, Mom says, "Bruce, I'm disturbed by your indifference to the very real threat I face."

Dad pushes back his chair. Dad is a lawyer. "Has he threatened you?"

"He stares at me angrily across the fence."

Dad takes off his reading glasses and looks up at Mom. "Why are you so often by that fence, Noreen?"

"I'm gardening. It's May, peak gardening month."

"Please, just stay on our side," Dad says. "That goes for you *and* the fence."

"You say that a lot, Bruce." Mom uses Dad's name when she is unhappy with him. "I'm starting to tune it out."

"Tune it any way you like. Just don't cross the property line."

"You're saying it again."

"I really can't say it too much."

"Yes, you can, Bruce," Mom says. "You're saying it too much right now."

They stare at each other. Then Mom turns and walks out the back door into the garden. Dad returns to my SAT, pretending not to care, but he can't pull it off. He goes to look out the kitchen window, then strolls briskly through the back door—the equivalent, for Dad, of taking off at a sprint. Through the kitchen window, I see that Mom has jumped the fence between our yard and the Salazars' yard and is standing on their lawn. Her platinum hair shimmers in the dark.

"I'm over the property line, Bruce," Mom calls. "What's going to happen?"

"That's not up to me," Dad says from our side of the fence. "You are beyond the scope of my protection."

"You weren't protecting me in the first place."

"I protect you in ways you're hardly aware of," Dad says, "but I can't protect you from yourself."

I duck away from the window at the sight of Stephanie Salazar coming outside, but I can't resist creeping out our back door and crouching behind Dad's grill, with its floppy rain cover. Stephanie has short black hair and looks nothing like the other moms. A few months after the Salazars first moved in, she became doubles partners with Kathy Bingham, the High Priestess of Bitches. They did a lot of winning until Bennie Salazar moved out, at which point Stephanie and Kathy stopped being doubles partners and also stopped speaking. That led to whispers about whether Kathy had played a part in the Salazars' breakup, but the whispers were very quiet because (according to Mom) no one wants to risk having Kathy rub them out.

Then came last year's singles match between Stephanie and Kathy for the 2006 Ladies' Championship at the Crandale Country Club. The match took almost five hours. Every game went on forever; every set went into tiebreakers that required tiebreakers themselves to be broken. Eventually, scores of people gathered from all over the club to watch. When Kathy finally won, Stephanie dropped onto the court with her face in her fists and let out an animal howl and then began to sob. To everyone's wonderment, Kathy went around the net and knelt beside Stephanie on the clay and put her arms around her—something nobody could believe and later thought they hadn't really seen; it must have been a trick of the twilight. But it happened: I saw it. Kathy pulled Stephanie onto her feet, and they walked to the locker room together. After that, they were doubles partners again. They haven't lost a match.

"Hi, Noreen," Stephanie says, crossing her lawn toward Mom in a friendly way. "Everything okay out here?"

"I'm just making a point," Mom says.

"Well," Stephanie says. "It's a beautiful night."

"True," Dad agrees from across the fence, and it is true: The sky looks dark and clear, and everything smells fresh from a rainstorm earlier in the day.

"Your lilacs are going crazy," Stephanie tells Mom. "God, that smell—I wish I could live in it." She's good at handling Mom—but is she *handling* Mom, I think, or just being nice?

"Thank you," Mom says, and begins edging back toward the fence.

Just then the door to the Salazar house flies open and Jules, the felonious brother, bursts onto the lawn with Stephanie's son, Chris, and a little girl named Lulu who's staying with them for some reason. Jules hasn't changed since I saw him on our doorstep two years ago: He's pale and overweight, his button-down shirt untucked. He looks normal except for his eyes, which are frantic.

"What are you doing out here?" he asks Stephanie. "Why is *she* on our property?"

"We're discussing the lilacs," Stephanie says.

"She's standing on our lawn. There is no reason for her to be doing that."

"Noreen," Dad says, "why don't you—"

"Get off our property," Jules orders Mom. "Now."

Stephanie wheels around on her brother. "Don't speak to her that way, Jules! She's our neighbor. Jesus."

"It isn't your property," Mom corrects Jules. "It's your sister and her husband's property."

"Actually, we're divorced," Stephanie says. "So it is my property."

"I'm her brother," Jules says. "Get off."

"Jules, stop it!"

"There is no sibling resemblance between you," Mom says.

"She's crazy," Jules says to Stephanie. "You're letting a crazy person stand on our lawn. Why?"

Dad and Stephanie approach Mom from opposite sides of the fence. "Noreen, please come back over," Dad says, and I hear in his voice the anxiety he gets when he thinks laws are about to be broken.

"I apologize for my brother's rudeness," Stephanie says.

"He's rude, but he's right," Dad says.

"A sane person!" Jules cries. "Thank you!"

"You're hopeless," Mom tells Dad.

"Noreen, is there something you need over here?" Stephanie asks, and I realize that she *is* handling Mom, and what makes her so good at handling Mom is having to handle her brother on a daily basis. "Because if not, I think Jules would be more comfortable if you—"

"GET. OFF. THIS. PROPERTY!" Jules hollers at the top of his lungs. The sound ricochets between our two houses.

"I will not be screamed at," Mom says fiercely.

"Let her stand there," Stephanie tells Jules. "Who cares?"

"You've lost your mind, Steph. Why do you cut her so much slack?"

"Jesus Christ, Jules, we're talking about a fucking fence," Stephanie says, raising her voice for the first time. "The Middle East is imploding, you've got refugees trying to raise their kids under plastic tarps with no running water—I mean, there are conflicts over space in the world that actually matter, but our suburban split rail is not on the list."

I listen to Stephanie Salazar and I worship her. Dad worships her. Her son, Chris, worships her, as does Lulu. Stephanie is a publicist for rock stars, but she should *be* a rock star.

"If more people respected each other's fences, we wouldn't have those problems," Jules sniffs.

"I give up," Stephanie says, and walks back toward her house. "Chris, Lulu, come on. We're going in." And they do. Stephanie doesn't turn back around. She says she's going inside, and she goes.

There is a long pause. Dad, Mom, and Jules stand like chess pieces in their respective positions. Finally, Dad says, "I'm going in too, Noreen," and I dart back into the house ahead of him.

Dad sits in the study watching the eleven o'clock news but really waiting for Mom. I watch from the kitchen window as she and Jules face off in silence. They look eerie in the dark, like sculptures of people. Jules hasn't moved any closer to Mom. He's afraid of her. And she is afraid of him.

"There's a sitcom version of this story," I tell Dad. "We might even have seen it."

"Sitcoms leave out a lot," Dad says. "That's what makes them funny."

"What's going to happen?"

"I don't know, Hannah," he says. "But I'm getting tired."

By the time Dad and I call good night to Mom through the back door, Jules has gone inside. Mom is standing alone in the Salazars' moonlit yard.

The next morning, Mom shakes leaves from her hair into the kitchen sink before she starts cooking our cheese omelets and making Brian's and Molly's school lunches.

"You slept in their yard?" Dad asks. "You lay down?"

"I dozed."

"You're lucky he didn't call the police."

"Felons don't call the police."

"Are you pleased with yourself? Do you consider this a victory?"

"You need not concern yourself any longer, Bruce," Mom says, "with what I feel."

Mom is suddenly very busy. There are no more non sequiturs about Jules Jones, but now and then a slight smile will drift onto her face when she flicks her eyes in the direction of the Salazar house.

"What?" Dad asks after one such smile.

"What?" Mom rounds her eyes in exaggerated innocence.

"I sense something afoot that may not be permissible by law."

"Well, if that is true," Mom says slyly, "and in no way am I suggesting that it is—aren't you better off, as a lawyer, not knowing about it?"

One evening, after Mom picks us up from Girl Scouts (Molly), baseball practice (Brian), and Yearbook (me), she detours to one of the malls and says, "I need to grab something at Ace Hardware."

"Can I come?" Brian asks. He loves Ace Hardware.

"I'd rather you didn't, just this once."

After a very long time, she emerges with an awkward, bulky bag wrapped so that we can't see what's inside it. She asks me to move into the backseat and places the bag beside her in front, with a seat belt around it.

"What did you buy?" Brian asks.

"Personal items."

"So personal they need a seat belt?" I ask.

"That's so the thing doesn't beep."

"You never tell us anything anymore," Molly says.

"I never did," Mom says. "You told me things."

"We're lonely," Molly wails. "We feel left out."

"Yeah," Brian says.

Mom swivels around to face the three of us in the backseat. "The world is a lonely place," she says. "I've never tried to hide that from you."

A week after my AP exams, Mom looks out the back window during dinner and says, "He's watching us."

We all look out. The days are getting longer, and the sky is still bright. There are robins all over our lawn. "Where?" I ask.

"He's inside his house, looking at us inside our house."

"He doesn't have the power to do that," Dad says. "It's not physically possible."

"There may be machinery involved."

Dad sets down his fork—the equivalent, for Dad, of rising to his feet and clearing his throat. "I feel like I'm losing you, Noreen," he says. "Things aren't getting done. The laundry is in a massive pile. I don't have any socks."

At the mention of laundry and socks, Mom's wandering attention visibly engages, so Dad pushes on and the rest of us join in: My pale green hoodie isn't in my closet and Molly's hand puppets have holes in the tops and Mom hasn't called the Seattle Seahawks to see if they'll sign Brian's jersey and return it if she includes a preposted envelope and our burger buns weren't toasted and she hasn't bought chocolate chips to make blondies for Molly's Girl Scout party and she's missed two vet appointments and now Fizzy hasn't been spayed and it seems like she might be in heat and we're missing a lightbulb in the downstairs bathroom and there aren't any double-A batteries for the Wii remotes and the Ping-Pong table is sagging and wasn't she going to get the lawn guy to take a look at those yellow patches, and wasn't she going to figure out where those three screws Molly found on the kitchen floor originally came from? And the kitchen counters are supposed to be resealed every six months—has that happened? Because they're staining more easily when we spill dark liquids on them like coffee or berry juice, and we're all out of cheese and low on kitty litter and the sewing basket is getting kind of full and the wood glue she used to help Brian make that ramp for science class hasn't held, they should have used nails like he told her in the first place and could they repair it with real nails tonight?

Mom sits up straight in her chair, her eyes dilated. "Yes," she says. "We can."

"It's two years since she threw out that lovely husband of hers," Mom says when the invitation arrives. "That's something to celebrate?"

"You have no idea whether she threw him out," Dad says. "Maybe he stormed out. Maybe she's having this party to reward herself after two rough years."

"Believe me, he was pushed out. And that so-called brother of hers is behind it."

"You are not a credible source."

But a day or two later, Dad is the one who returns to the topic while Mom is reorganizing the kitchen cupboards and I'm doing homework on the computer in the study.

"Noreen, in light of all that has transpired," he says, "I think it is essential that we go."

"Go?"

"To Stephanie's party."

"*I* should go?" Mom asks.

"That is what I mean by 'we.'"

"Bruce, can't you see that this is a trap?"

"It concerns me when you speak in that way."

"You should be concerned!"

"It concerns me not only because it is delusional, but because we tend to project our own states of mind onto other people. So the fact that you believe our neighbors may be plotting against you suggests that you may be plotting against them."

"Electrifying our fence will only hurt them if they touch it," Mom says.

"You are not electrifying our fence."

"Not yet—I need to read a little more about electrostatic energy," Mom says. "But I've bought all the materials."

Dad shuts his eyes—the equivalent, for Dad, of burying his face in his hands.

"You go," Mom says. "The kids and I will stay home."

"No, Mom," I call to her from the office, where I've been eavesdropping. "We're going. Our friends will be there."

"You call them friends, Hannah," Mom lashes out, confronting me from the doorway with hands on hips. "But your connection to them is situational. Years from now you'll look back and marvel at what you could have seen in most of these people."

"You're probably right," I say, because Mom's predictions have turned out to be right a surprising number of times. "But in three weeks, when the party is, they'll still be our friends."

Stephanie's cocktail party is on a warm evening in mid-June, close to the end of the school year. My AP exams are done and the scores haven't come in yet and the sky is still pale summer blue. I've always loved parties with every age included, even before my friends and I started getting drunk alongside the parents. Here it is, the world that made me: a fantasy I get to believe in for one more year, according to Mom. This, too, is a fairy tale, and after I grow up, these parties will become part of the lost mythical land of my childhood.

Mom waits for us at the kitchen table wearing a black dress with big white polka dots—an odd choice for a person who claims not to want to be noticed. She holds a seltzer bottle in each hand.

Dad comes downstairs in one of the dapper bow ties he always wears to parties. "I'm guessing they have seltzer," he tells Mom.

"*He* may be serving," Mom says. "And I will not accept a drink from that man."

All of us leave our house through the front door as if we're walking to church. I go ahead with Dad, our arms linked. We descend our pebbled driveway and then turn back up the white paving stones that lead to the Salazars' front door.

"We could have just climbed over the fence," Mom says. Dad gives her a severe look, and she smiles. "Kidding."

The front door is open. People are milling around just inside it, the women in bright summer dresses, the men in seersucker shorts or patterned golf pants, holding gin and tonics. They all work in the city, and everyone knows which ones are richest. We'll never be rich-rich, according to Mom, because lawyers can only bill by the hour. "But when the bubble bursts, and I'm guessing it'll be soon," she's been saying lately, "your father will still have a job."

It's hard to imagine Bennie Salazar in this crowd, with his brown skin and wild hair, but until two years ago, it was his house. *What a loss.*

Stephanie greets us at the door in a sleeveless salmon-colored dress. Her shoulders are hard and tanned: all that tennis. "I really appreciate your coming, Noreen," she says, removing the seltzer bottles from Mom's clenched fists. "Can I bring these to the bar and pour you a glass?"

"Thank you," Mom says stiffly. "I would like that."

Dad vanishes. A few minutes later I hear him laughing, which means he's drinking bourbon. Brian and Molly have gone upstairs to where the kids are. The High Priestess of Bitches, Kathy Bingham, reigns by a window in a white sleeveless dress, her taut shoulders a paler version of Stephanie's. Mom averts her eyes from Kathy with a flinch, and I can't bring myself to leave her.

"I don't see your brother anywhere," Mom remarks to Stephanie as a bartender fills a glass with seltzer from one of her bottles.

"Ah," Stephanie says heavily. "I think Jules may sit this party out."

I feel Mom's whole body tense, the way Fizzy's does when a hawk lands in the tree behind our house. "And why is that?" Mom asks carefully.

Stephanie lowers her voice. "I made the mistake of inviting his ex."

"His ex!" Mom is fascinated. "Which one is she?"

"Over there." Stephanie gestures with her elbow, not turning her head. "In the blue knit dress. Her name is Janet Green—Kramer now. She and her husband moved to the area recently, and she doesn't know many people. Jules was fine with it, but now that she's here, he's very unhappy."

Janet Green/Kramer is long-waisted and deeply tanned, with highlighted brown hair and a lopsided grin. She looks like any other mom. But I can't help thinking, as I watch her sip from a glass of white wine: Crazy Jules was in love with that woman. They were *together*. It makes Janet Green seem profound, mysterious.

"Difficult breakup?" Mom asks.

"Devastating for him. It brought on everything: his breakdown, the assault . . ." Stephanie shakes her head. "What was I thinking."

"Is Jules here?" Mom asks. "In the house?"

Stephanie is instantly wary. "He wants to be alone, Noreen."

A crush of people comes through the front door, and Mom and I follow Stephanie toward them. But as soon as Stephanie starts greeting her guests, Mom veers toward the front staircase. "Mom!" I say, and manage to catch Stephanie's eye. She hurries back over. Mom has already mounted the steps, but Stephanie seizes her arm and forces her to turn around. "Noreen," she says, looking up at Mom from the stair below, "for whatever reason, you put Jules on edge, and he can become dangerously unstable when he's on edge. I'm asking you: Please leave him alone." She looks hard at Mom's face. Then she goes to greet her guests without looking back.

Mom continues up the stairs. "You just promised," I say, clambering after her.

"I promised nothing," Mom says. "I never spoke."

On the second floor, she begins knocking on doors and immediately shoving them open.

"You have to wait after you knock," I hiss. "That's the point of knocking."

"Hannah," she says, not slowing her pace, "you're becoming more and more like your father."

"Good," I retort. "I want to be a lawyer."

Mom charges up a smaller staircase to the third floor, which reverberates with sounds of running feet from the attic, where the kids are. There are only two doors on this floor. Mom pounds on the first, and we hear a guttural cry from within: "No!"

She flings open the door. Jules Jones is poised barefoot in the middle of the room in what looks like a martial-arts position. At the sight of Mom, he shrieks, as if confronting a demon. "You! Get out."

He's wearing khakis and a lavender button-down shirt with dry-cleaning folds still visible, as if he dressed for the party before changing his mind. A single bed is tucked in one corner of the room. By the window, a big desk is strewn with books and papers and a laptop.

"Relax," Mom says. "I come in peace."

"Like hell you do." Jules bolts to the window and squints down at our two yards. He's begun to resemble the Crandale dads, but only to a point, the way Mom somewhat resembles the other moms without ever fully blending in.

"I haven't touched the fence," she says. "I swear."

"Your oath means nothing to me," he says. "Less than nothing." He peers again through the window, as if unable to stop himself. I notice a tape measure on the windowsill—the same one he brought to our house when Mom first moved the fence post two years ago.

"Let's go down and measure it," Mom says. "Come."

Jules shakes his head. "I can't right now."

"Of course you can. So what if your ex is down there? You have a whole new life now."

"No," Jules says. "She has a new life."

"Come on, years have passed since you were with that woman. And frankly, she isn't aging well."

There is a long pause. "I wanted us to have kids," Jules says. "But she had them with someone else."

"So? You can have them with someone else, too."

"Are you mocking me?"

"Listen to me, Jules," Mom says. "I have important things to say to you."

She moves closer and he eyes her mistrustfully, sweat beading on his pale forehead. Suspended between sounds of pounding feet above and laughter below, the room feels strangely still.

"I have three children," Mom says. "This is Hannah, my oldest. She'll be gone in a year, and the others will go soon enough. They're the best and only thing I've managed to do in this world. I'm friend-less, and God knows how long Bruce will stick around after Hannah goes. I'm not the woman he married, as he often reminds me."

"Mom, stop it," I say. But I see that she means it, and feel a torque of dread.

"If I can do this, anyone can," Mom tells Jules. "Certainly you can. You have skills, a trade, a place in the world."

Jules seems to register my presence in the room for the first time. Then he looks back at Mom. I watch him see her: a thin, anxious woman with bleached-blond hair, in a polka-dotted dress.

"You moved the fence," he says. "That's what this is about."

"Let's go," Mom says.

Jules seizes his tape measure and they leave the room side by side, with me close behind. "Are you . . . writing an article?" I ask, to ease the silence. "I saw a lot of papers on your desk."

"A book," Jules says bleakly. "About the Conduits' lead singer, Bosco Baines. He's on a concert tour that's supposed to kill him, but he keeps not dying."

"You could kill him," Mom suggests, and Jules gapes at her. "Kidding," she says.

On the second floor, I stop and let them go on without me. They seem not to notice. Like Stephanie, I've done all that I can do. Now I turn away, like she did.

The Salazars' entertainment room has a huge-screen TV with surround sound where Bennie Salazar used to play concerts of artists he'd worked with. He invited Dad a few times to watch old Conduits shows, and Dad came back grinning and smelling of bourbon. Now Chris Salazar and Brian and the other boys are doing Wii on that screen, and Molly and the girls are playing board games. My friends are sprawled on an L-shaped couch, a mix of girls and boys drinking cans of soda laced with gin and vodka they've swiped from the bar. Someone hands me a can, and we talk about college visits and summer internships. Soon we'll be seniors.

I keep going to the window to check on Mom, but the garden is so far down that I have to stand on a footstool to see her. "What's Hannah looking at?" someone asks.

"My mother," I say, and they all laugh.

The first time I check, Mom and Jules are squatting in the dirt with the tape measure extended.

The second time, they're both standing up, holding glasses of seltzer.

The third time, they're leaning against the fence side by side, looking up at the sky. It's electric with twilight.

The secret to a happy ending, Mom used to tell us, *is knowing when to walk away.*

Once I've seen Mom leaning against the fence with Jules, I force myself not to look again.

See Below

1

Joseph Kisarian ⟶ Henry Pomeranz
CLASSIFIED

Dear Mr. Pomeranz:

As I conclude my leave of absence, it is incumbent upon me to report my ongoing concern over the mental and physical health of my wife, Lulu Kisarian (Citizen Agent 3825), who completed her mission nearly two years ago.

Some of the difficulty arises from the several surgeries Lulu has undergone to repair damage from the gunshot wound to her right shoulder (she is right-handed), a hindrance to caring for our eight-month-old twins, whom she can lift only with difficulty. But my deeper worry is her mental state. She is convinced that spyware remains within her body, citing the following symptoms as evidence:

- A tendency to think aphoristically in the second person, as required for her mission's Field Instructions (e.g., "Laundered socks will vanish despite your best efforts to track them"; "Reading books about babies sleeping may not result in your babies sleeping more").
- A persistent wish to return to her mission, despite its agonies, as if to a mythical land from a dream or a book.
- A conviction that she—and I—would have been "better off" had she perished at the end of her mission rather than returning.

We have availed ourselves of every in-house resource in terms of therapy and body scans, but Lulu's present distrust of our institution renders these assurances null. I understand that, after the exposé last fall and resulting suspension of the Citizen Agent program, seeking outside consultation is doubly impossible now. Yet this leaves us in a bind.

Lulu's wariness and anxiety prevent our employing child care of any sort. The staunchest reassurance about vetting and references for babysitters or day-care programs prompt her to quote from her own indoctrination: "Your lack of espionage training is what makes your record clean and neutral." And of course she is right.

The secrecy of Lulu's mission has distanced her from old friends, and she avoids the company of other new mothers. For these reasons, my return must be conditional. I am not concerned for the children's physical safety or Lulu's own; I would not return at all if such were the case. But if her suffering and discomfort do not abate, I will have to take an indefinite leave to assist her.

Sincerely,
Joseph Kisarian

Henry Pomeranz → Joseph Kisarian
What a shit show, Joe. I'm so sorry.

Joe → Henry
There are beautiful moments with the babies, but Lulu is not herself.

Henry → Joe
Anything I can do to help? Other than file this letter?

Joe → Henry
I wish there were a way for her to communicate

with other Citizen Agents. I believe her isolation is damaging.

Henry → Joe
Cuts across too many security firewalls, as you well know.

Joe → Henry
I helped to build them, yet I can't remove them.

Henry → Joe
She thinks we're using her to watch you? Is that it?

Joe → Henry
Her words on the subject are guarded, as if an enemy were listening. And this creates distance between us.

Henry → Joe
Christ.

Joe → Henry
My hope is that, on her own, Lulu will find a solution that she can't when I'm beside her day and night. I have enormous faith in her resources.

Dolly Peale → Joseph Kisarian
Dear Jojo,

I'm looking forward to being in the apartment and helping Lu with the babies the first two weeks you're back at work. But I'd also love your advice on how to become closer to Lu. There is a gap between us that must have to do with her service, which I know she can't discuss. But looking back, I wonder if this gap had already appeared before she left. I am racked by worry and guilt over choices I made long ago, and wondering what I can do to help Lu—and us.

I trust your instincts and will follow your advice.

Love, Dodo

Joseph Kisarian → Dolly Peale
Dear Dodo,

Lulu has basked in your love the whole of her life,
and that is what matters. Please ease your mind. Your
help with the babies will be invaluable, giving Lulu time
to (hopefully) reconnect with old friends online, and
perhaps even in person. I'm so grateful to you for this.
Omar and Festa adore their grandma, as do we.

Love, Jojo

2

Lulu Kisarian → Kitty Jackson
Dear Kitty Jackson,

We haven't seen each other in decades, but we are
not strangers. You may remember me as the 9-year-
old girl who accompanied you on a secret visit to X,
then ruled by General B, with my mother, Dolly Peale,
26 years ago (!). My mother and I have celebrated
your many professional triumphs since that strange
and otherworldly journey.

I'm writing very much out of the blue, I know.
I've had a craving to reconnect with you ever since I
returned two years ago from a hard overseas stint of
my own that made me think about our trip to X and
imagine what it must have been like for you. But also,
last week I watched your most recent film, *Dazzle
Me Sideways,* with Jazz Attenborough. I need very
urgently to correspond with Mr. Attenborough. Can
you please help me get in touch with him?

Awaiting your reply, Lulu Peale Kisarian

Ashleigh Avila → Lulu Kisarian
Dear Ms. Kisarian,

Ms. Jackson thanks you for your recent email.
She is, unfortunately, not able to make introductions
to fellow actors, and suggests that you write to Mr.

Attenborough via his publicist, or perhaps his social media accounts.

With best wishes, Ashleigh Avila

Lulu Kisarian → Kitty Jackson
Dear Kitty,

I am not some crazed fan deserving of an assistant's reply. I am the daughter of Dolly Peale, the publicist who single-handedly revived your career in 2008. I am also a 35-year-old professional with many years of successful music industry work behind me, including helping to produce Scotty Hausmann's Footprint Concert fourteen years ago.

I am asking, politely and respectfully, for your help in reaching Mr. Attenborough. It is not a lot to ask, considering what my mother did for you.

Awaiting your reply, Lulu Kisarian

FWD: Ashleigh Avila → Kitty Jackson
See below. Polite "no"?

Kitty → Ashleigh
Just realized who she is. Will handle.

Kitty Jackson → Lulu Kisarian; bcc: Ashleigh Avila
Dear Lulu,

Wowowowowowowowowow . . . is it really you?!? So sorry you got caught in the snares of my manager/publicist/assistant/mama bear, who tries to make things (and people) disappear without my knowing they ever existed!

I've spent the past fifteen minutes catching up on your achievements. Scotty Hausmann's Footprint Concert . . . What????? SOOOOO IMPRESSED!!! I've pretended that I was AT that concert, but I'll know better than to try that with you! I trust your mom is

alive and well? Send news! And tell me, of course, how
I can help.

   Xxxxoooo Love, Kitty

Lulu ⟶ Kitty
Dear Kitty,

   It's exciting to hear back from you in a voice
I remember as yours. I'm still recovering from a
period of overseas service that has left me with a
reconstructed right shoulder. It has brought me to
a state of reckoning that I somehow think you will
recognize: I can't return to the life I had before, but I
can't move forward without resolving some unfinished
personal business.

   All of which leads me to Jazz Attenborough.
Maybe, as a starting point, you could tell me what
he's like as a person? He seems not to give interviews,
which makes it hard to get any sense of him online.
Because of our shared history, your impressions would
mean a lot to me.

   Awaiting your reply, Lulu

Kitty ⟶ Lulu; bcc: Ashleigh Avila
Dear Lulu,

   You've made me think back on that crazy voyage
to X for the first time in soooooo long. But wait a
sec . . . how could I have been a grown-up 26 years
ago when I'm only 26 now? ;-) Can't deny it, your
mama saved my ass. Please give her a big smackeroo
from me.

   So, Jazz. He's a notorious dog, as you probably
know. Hardly a spring chicken but still sexy and in
great physical shape. Like most die-hard flirts, he's a
liar: told me HE was the reason I'd been offered the
costar role (later found out he'd pushed for Anne
Hathaway). Also said he'd been trying for years to

work with me (false). But once the bullshit was out of
the way, I adored him. We both love the Conduits and
no matter what song I named, he could sing every lyric
in perfect tune!

More you want to know? Anything you can tell me
about WHY you want to know? Holy crap about your
shoulder. Do you have kids btw?

xxxxooooKitty

Ashleigh Avila → Kitty Jackson
Unless you have a death wish, DO NOT EVER
write an email like that again. If this "Lulu" person
even is who she says she is—and we have no idea—God
only knows what she's up to. "Overseas service"?
"Reconstructed shoulder"? WTF!!! Bottom line: she
forwards your musings about JA to five friends and
your career ends.

Kitty → Ashleigh
Calm down. It takes more than that to sink a career.
Remember, I've done it once.

Ashleigh → Kitty
Yeah, and you were 22 and gorgeous then. Now you're,
um, 51 and gorgeous. [Insert empty flattery about how
incredible you look for your age.]

Kitty → Ashleigh
Honesty appreciated. Now go fuck yourself.

Ashleigh → Kitty
Btw, just spent some time searching your visit to X in
2008. No reference to any Lulu, but I do see mention
of "publicist Dolly Peale." Did you know she's the same
one who did time in 2007 after her lighting fixtures
melted and dumped boiling oil on 700 people????

Kitty → Ashleigh
Get up earlier. That's WHY she took the job of
whitewashing General B's atrocities. Kid to feed,
etc.

Ashleigh → Kitty
Ever consider a book/doc about that history?

Kitty → Ashleigh
Signed multiple nondisclosure agreements. Also have
a bad memory (was drinking heavily then).

Ashleigh → Kitty
General B died two years ago, so those agreements
would be void. Own Your Unconscious would solve
the memory problems. Worth considering a doc? The
untold story of Kitty Jackson's love affair with General
B, and X's resulting turn toward democracy??? Could
give you a huge boost!!!

Kitty → Ashleigh
Ah yes, a year has passed since your last documentary
brainwave. Should have expected another. [Insert
empty reassurance that I support your creative dreams
and have total faith in your filmmaking genius.]

Kitty Jackson → Jazz Attenborough
Hi Jazzy,
    Hey, what happened to our plan of eating oysters
and drinking white wine when shooting was finished?
Guess you say that to all the girls you sing along
with.
    Unrelated topic: a music producer friend of mine,
female, has asked me to put her in touch with you.
May I?
    Xxxxoooo Love, Kitty

Jazz Attenborough → Kitty Jackson
Darling, please tell her no. Oysters and white wine any
time. In Belize until end May. Hugs, JA

Lulu Kisarian → Kitty Jackson
Dear Kitty,
    To your other question, I have eight-month-old
twins, a boy and a girl named Omar and Festa. They
are beautiful living creatures who make me cry a lot,
maybe because THEY cry a lot, being babies, and also
my shoulder injury.
    Would you be willing to pass along contact info for
Jazz Attenborough so I can approach him directly? He
will never know it came from you, I promise.
    Awaiting your reply, Lulu

Kitty → Lulu; bcc: Ashleigh Avila
Twins!!!! OMG I hope you have mega nannies. As for
me, I currently keep eight horses. I guess you could
call them my babies. Not sure I have JA's email, will
search but not optimistic.
    xxxxooooLove, Kitty

Ashleigh Avila → Kitty Jackson
Kitty please just give her JA's contact. If you decide
to pursue the documentary idea we'll need her, and
especially her mother, to cooperate.

Kitty → Ashleigh
Can't. I already asked JA and he said no.

Ashleigh → Kitty
He'll never make the connection. You're less on his
mind than you think.

Kitty → Ashleigh
I may be more on his mind than YOU think!

Ashleigh ⟶ Kitty
!!!! What'd I miss?

Kitty ⟶ Ashleigh
I NEVER kiss and tell, as you should know by now.

Ashleigh Avila ⟶ Lulu Kisarian
Dear Ms. Kisarian,
    I hope you won't take it amiss that my client, Kitty
Jackson, has bcc'd me on your correspondence. Here is
Jazz Attenborough's personal contact, but you didn't get
it from me! And Kitty would be furious with me if she
knew I was going around her, so please do not tell her!
    With best wishes, Ashleigh Avila

Lulu ⟶ Ashleigh
Dear Ashleigh,
    Thank you so much! I hereby disavow any
knowledge of where this information came from.
    Gratefully, Lulu

Ashleigh ⟶ Lulu
Dear Lulu,
    Now that we have our own line of communication,
and I've familiarized myself with the remarkable history
you and Kitty share, I have an unrelated question:
what would you and your mother say to the idea of a
documentary about your trip to X, Kitty's relationship
with General B, and its geopolitical consequences?
    With best wishes, Ashleigh

Lulu ⟶ Ashleigh
Dear Ashleigh,
    I'm doubtful that my mother would be willing, as
it was a VERY low moment of her life. We haven't
spoken about it in years.
    Lulu

Ashleigh →Lulu
Understood. Let me know if you get anywhere with
JA, and if I can help in any way.
   With best wishes, Ashleigh

Lulu Peale →Jazz Attenborough
Dear Mr. Attenborough,
   It is urgent that I speak with you for reasons that
will become clear as soon as I explain. But it must be
in person. I live in New York but am willing to travel
anywhere. Please say that this is possible.
   Awaiting your reply, Lulu Peale

Eric Platt → Lulu Peale
Dear Ms. Peale,
   Unfortunately Mr. Attenborough is unable to
respond to the many people who wish to communicate
with him directly. On behalf of his team, I wish you
well in your future endeavors.
   Sincerely, Eric Platt
   3rd Assistant to Jazz Attenborough

FWD: Lulu Kisarian → Ashleigh Avila
Dear Ashleigh,
   See below. I think this qualifies as "getting
nowhere." I would appreciate any ideas you might have
about how I can reach Mr. Attenborough, although my
reasons are personal and I cannot share them.
   Awaiting your reply, Lulu

Ashleigh → Lulu
What is your ideal outcome?

Lulu → Ashleigh
A private in-person conversation with him.

Ashleigh ⟶ Lulu
What about interviewing him in the guise of a
journalist? Your music background could make it
credible.

Lulu ⟶ Ashleigh
I thought of that, but he doesn't seem to do interviews.

Ashleigh ⟶ Lulu
He turned seventy last week: tough milestone for a
movie star. I'm wondering if we could propose a "special
interest" topic (i.e., wine, cigars) that would resonate.
Will dig a little. Meanwhile, would you please ask your
mother about the General B documentary idea?
     Warmly, Ash

Lulu Kisarian ⟶ Dolly Peale
Hi Mom. Thanks so much for the visit and help.
Omar and Festa miss you already. Listen, I've been
contacted out of the blue by a representative of Kitty
Jackson asking if we would be willing to participate
in a documentary about our trip to X with Kitty in
2008. Obviously a horrible idea, but this person is now
helping me with something else (a job possibility), so
I'd like to pretend for the moment that we're open to
doing this. Ok to put you in touch with her to bluff for
a bit?
     Love, Lu

FWD: Dolly Peale ⟶ Joseph Kisarian
Jojo, see below. Any idea what this "job possibility"
might be?

Joseph Kisarian ⟶ Dolly Peale
None. But Lulu has seemed noticeably better since
your visit! If duplicity isn't too uncomfortable for you,
perhaps it will be temporarily justified here? ☺

Dolly → Joe
Duplicity is all too comfortable for me (former publicist, remember). See you Saturday in time to babysit for your date night!
   Love, Dodo

Lulu Kisarian → Ashleigh Avila
Dear Ashleigh,
   My mom is willing to speak with you about the documentary. However, before I put you in contact with her, I need to make something crystal clear: my mother does not know, and CANNOT know, that I'm trying to meet with Jazz Attenborough. I need your 100% guarantee that his name will not be mentioned between you.
   Awaiting your reply, Lulu

Ashleigh → Lulu
Guaranteed. And to close our circle of secrecy, a reminder that Kitty has no idea we're strategizing about how to get you into a room with JA and would be pissed at both of us if she found out.
   Warmly, Ash

Ashleigh → Lulu
Separate thread: speedboats!! JA collects them and likes to ride them along the SoCal coast at extreme speeds (3 run-ins with Coast Guard in past 10 years). An interview/article about speedboats has a remote chance of being welcomed by a newly septuagenarian movie star striving to maintain sex appeal and fend off grandpa roles. Thoughts?

Ashleigh Avila → Kitty Jackson
Dearest Kit Kat: Lulu, Dolly, etc., are totally on board to participate in a doc about your relationship with General B and your positive impact on humanity!

PLEASE give it some thought. Gentle reminder: I
have nothing to gain from this. My only concern is
your future and your wish to fend off grandma roles.

Kitty ⟶ Ashleigh
You lying bitch, don't pretend you don't want a
production credit.

Ashleigh ⟶ Kitty
Well, I am producing the film.

Kitty ⟶ Ashleigh
Reality check: there is no film. There was no
"relationship" that I'm willing to discuss. I am a middle-
aged B-list actress, and you are one more NYU film
school grad who's gone on to do squat.

Ashleigh ⟶ Kitty
C-list. Fuck you, too.

Ashleigh ⟶ Kitty
Bitch I am actually angry with you.

Kitty ⟶ Ashleigh
Lmk when tantrum ends. Asking myself if I really
need an assistant, esp. one who knows nothing about
dressage?

Kitty ⟶ Ashleigh
Hell-oo-ooo. Still tantruming?

Kitty ⟶ Ashleigh
Asking myself: if we're not speaking anymore, why am
I paying you?

Ashleigh ⟶ Kitty
Because no one else would put up with your sorry ass.

Kitty → Ashleigh
I love you, too.

3

Lulu Kisarian → Jules Jones
Dear Jules Jones,

I am a longtime admirer of your work, especially *Suicide Tour*, the most amazing book-length work of rock-and-roll journalism I've ever read. I'm also a family friend: your sister, Stephanie Salazar, worked with my mother, Dolly Peale, for many years, and you taught me to play Dungeons & Dragons with Chris and Colin (RIP) in a game I joined occasionally. I led Bennie Salazar's marketing team starting in college, helping to produce Scotty Hausmann's Footprint Concert among many others.

I'm writing now with an out-of-the-blue request: would you have any interest in interviewing Hollywood icon Jazz Attenborough about his passion for speedboats? I'm well aware of your dislike of celebrity culture, but Attenborough is apparently a huge Conduits fan, knows all their lyrics, and will doubtless have read *Suicide Tour*. Please let me know.

Awaiting your reply, Lulu Peale Kisarian

Jules Jones → Lulu Kisarian
Dear Lulu,

I remember you. Dimples, right? Wasn't your character a spy?

Couple of questions:
1. What publication is seeking an interview with Jazz Attenborough?
2. Whom are you representing?

Yours, JJ

Lulu ⟶ Jules
Dear Jules,

I left out that information because I feared that
the answers might not please you. Honest reply: there
is no publication yet. My goal is to pitch this project
to Jazz Attenborough AFTER you have signed on. In
other words, your name and clout are essential to the
success of this undertaking.

Hoping flattery and curiosity will outweigh
frustration and impatience.

Awaiting your reply, Lulu

Jules ⟶ Lulu
You still haven't answered my second question: What
is your part in all this? Is it a moneymaking venture for
you (hard to believe)?

With candor on my side, cursory digging reveals
that your husband is Joseph Kisarian of National
Security. If this "story idea" is a ruse to pry into my
life, please just say so. I have mental health issues that
make me prone to paranoia, and I cannot manage
uncertainties in this realm. If government agents want
to question me, they are welcome, anytime.

Yours, JJ

Lulu ⟶ Jules
Dear Jules,

Sorry for alarming you! This has nothing to do
with NSA or Joe, who recently returned to work
after a 9-month leave of absence for the birth of our
twins (now 8 months old). This journalism project
is "moonlighting" for me (note that it is 3am!), and
Joe is not even aware of it. He has plenty else on his
mind.

I have private reasons for wanting to meet with Jazz
Attenborough, but they won't mean anything to him,

which is why I'm taking this extremely roundabout route.

    Awaiting your reply, Lulu

FWD: Jules Jones → John Hall
See below. If Jazz Attenborough were willing, are there advantages for me? I'm fully on target to meet my book deadline and this would not interfere.
    JJ

John Hall → Jules Jones
Sure: remind the world before pub that you can do f-ing anything, incl ride speedboats w/celebs (despite having done time for hating/assaulting them). Lux/ high-end mags best exposure imo. Happy to shop.

Jules → John Hall
Danger of hypocrisy?

John Hall → Jules
You're too old for hypocrisy. I'd play it as tongue-in-cheek self-conscious eminence.

Jules → John Hall
You told me writers are never old.

John Hall → Jules
Only until 70. After that, everyone is old.

Jules Jones → Lulu Kisarian
Dear Lulu,
    My agent is willing to pitch this idea to high-end luxury magazines once we have approval from Jazz Attenborough. I presume you have some way to reach him?
    Yours, JJ

Lulu → Jules
Dear Jules,

I have contact info for both Jazz A and his 3ʳᵈ (!) assistant, but a query from me will lead nowhere. I've already tried.

Another late-night thought: would Bosco of the Conduits possibly want to be part of this? I have no idea what he's up to these days (he's alive, right?), but given that Jazz A is a rabid Conduits fan, having Bosco involved might be the thing that persuades him. Or are these the crazy 4am notions of a woman with a weevil left in her brain by the government agency she almost died for? Hitting "send" before I start deleting.

Jules → Lulu
Dear Lulu,

Next time, DELETE. I cannot stomach talk of weevils. I have been scanned for invasive hardware multiple times by an underground "cleaner." Even in jest it causes me too much anxiety to read such musings, and invokes the specter that you are part of a government plot to invade my brain.

Re Bosco: Weird idea. Need to think that one over. Yes, he is alive.

JJ

Lulu → Jules
Dear Jules,

Is there a way to reassure you of my good intentions while also promising you that I would not joke about such a thing?

Awaiting your reply, Lulu
P.S. Would you be comfortable sharing contact info for the dry-cleaning service you mentioned? I have a dress that is badly stained, and I'm desperate to restore it to its former state.

Jules ⟶ Lulu
I think we should meet in person (assuming that you are not sharing your consciousness to the collective). You are in NYC, correct? Happy to come to you sometime next week.

JJ

Ashleigh Avila ⟶ Dolly Peale
Dear Dolly Peale,

I was thrilled beyond belief to learn from your daughter, Lulu Kisarian, that you are willing to participate in a documentary about Kitty Jackson's relationship with General B and its historic consequences. Now I'm wondering how many players from 2008 we can round up? I'm imagining you, Kitty, Lulu, the photographers who captured images of General B and Kitty together, and military and political experts who can speak to General B's resulting pivot toward democracy.

What we're missing is someone from General B's circle who can describe events from that side. Might you be able to dig up your contacts from the former regime and see if any are still alive and reachable?

With best wishes, Ashleigh Avila

Lulu Kisarian ⟶ Ames Hollander
Dear Ames Hollander,

The journalist Jules Jones passed along your email. I understand you have a dry-cleaning business that specializes in removing deeply embedded stains. I have a friend in need of this type of cleaning. How can I put him in touch with you?

Awaiting your reply, Lulu Kisarian

Ames Hollander ⟶ Lulu Kisarian
Dear Lulu:

Please have your friend contact me via Mondrian,

a more secure network that will make him jump through several hoops to ensure our communication is private.

Ames Hollander

Lulu ⟶ Ames VIA MONDRIAN
Hi Ames, it's Lulu Kisarian. How can my friend describe his dry-cleaning problem if he is being surveilled from within?

Ames ⟶ Lulu VIA MONDRIAN
Lulu, please advise your friend to CLOSE HIS EYES while typing out his dry-cleaning needs, and to press "send" BEFORE opening his eyes.

Ames Hollander

Lulu ⟶ Ames VIA MONDRIAN
Ok short vrsion sory for mistakes I was ctzn agent for six months incl data surge gunsht wound and hotspot rscue suspect I am still being monitrd can sense other eyes looking thru my eyes other ppl listning inside my head is agony would do anything to stop this inclding endmy life but wld hurt others too much we have twins eight months need cleaning please husband Joseph Kisarian works for NSA it may be him they are spying on

Ames ⟶ Lulu VIA MONDRIAN
Dear Lulu,

I can absolutely help your friend with those stains, but I'm upstate and only in New York City a few days each month. My cleaning shop is hard to find, but since Jules has been there before, I will make the appointment directly with him. Please have your friend deal with Jules directly going forward.

Thanks for the referral!

Ames Hollander

Jules Jones → Bosco Baines
Dear Bosky, long time. Belated thanks for the ice
cream, which I look forward to each Xmas more than
I like to admit. Not sure how your chocolate chips
manage to be melty, not waxen. Ah, the wonders, the
mysteries.

    How is your health? Assuming good, I'm curious
whether you might be in the market for a gonzo
journalism caper involving travel, speedboats, and
a movie icon who apparently knows all your lyrics.
Thoughts?

    Yours, JJ

Bosco → Jules
Health excellent. New hips and new knees have me
feeling frisky. Lost 80 pounds in the past ten years, eat
your heart out. This caper is expenses-paid I take it?
Be fun to see you again, old man, even on a speedboat.

Jules → Bosco
Commencing starvation diet. Downloading abs app.
Caper is still pie in the sky, but that's how all good
things begin, right?

    Love you, old man, JJ

4

Eric Platt → Jazz Attenborough
Dear Mr. Attenborough,

    We have received an interview query too
intriguing to reject out of hand as I normally do.
Potent elements: Bosco from the Conduits; Jules
Jones (author of *Suicide Tour*), and speedboats. Any
interest?

    Sincerely, Eric Platt
    3rd Assistant to Jazz Attenborough

Jazz Attenborough → Eric Platt
Sounds like a hoax. You've checked it out?

Eric → Jazz
Dear Mr. Attenborough,
    Sorry, got overexcited. Will check now.
    Sincerely, Eric Platt
    3rd Assistant to Jazz Attenborough

Jazz Attenborough → Carmine DeSantis
New 3rd assistant a disaster. Please find another.

Carmine DeSantis → Jazz Attenborough
Will start looking, but background checks take time.
Have you read the scripts?

Jazz → Carmine
Remind me?

Carmine → Jazz
Grandpa; Santa; Undersea Cave-Warlock.

Jazz → Carmine
No, no, and no. Want sexier roles. How can I get
paired with younger stars?

Carmine → Jazz
Grandpa, Santa, Undersea Cave-Warlock!!

Jazz → Carmine
Facelift?

Carmine → Jazz
Too obvious. Stick with craggy.

Eric Platt → Jazz Attenborough
Dear Mr. Attenborough,
     It all checks out. The people are real. I've spoken
with the writer, Jules Jones, who has remained close
to Bosco Baines (of the Conduits) since writing about
him in *Suicide Tour*. Could be great publicity for you.
     Sincerely, Eric Platt
     3rd Assistant to Jazz Attenborough

Jazz → Eric
Forward to Carmine, he will handle. 1st and 2nd
assistants too busy.

FWD: Eric Platt → Carmine DeSantis
Dear Mr. DeSantis,
     Please see below my correspondence with Mr.
Attenborough regarding a possible interview to take
place on one or more of his speedboats. I've spoken
to the writer and it all checks out. I think it could be a
great way to burnish Mr. A's image as a silver alpha.
     Sincerely, Eric Platt
     3rd Assistant to Jazz Attenborough

Carmine → Eric
Silver alpha, I like that. Haven't seen 70 y/o Jazz in
swim trunks lately, have you?

Eric → Carmine
Yes, he'd just finished swimming when I came for my
interview. Looks great for a senior: well tanned, well
muscled, abundant gray chest hair, stringy/beef jerky
abs.

Carmine → Eric
Can chest hair be dyed?

Eric ⟶ Carmine
Yes. My girlfriend is a makeup artist. She does it with a toothbrush.

Carmine ⟶ Eric
Tell the writer yes. One problem: Jazz wants me to replace you. If you'll oversee the logistics, I'll present them as my own.

Eric ⟶ Carmine
With all due respect, Mr. DeSantis, why should I settle for that?

Carmine ⟶ Eric
Ok let's have it: hopes and dreams in five words or less.

Eric ⟶ Carmine
Screenwriter/Director

Carmine ⟶ Eric
I hereby pledge to read your next script and represent you if I like it.

Eric ⟶ Carmine
Thank you, Mr. DeSantis! Could you please include a quick witness signature?

Carmine ⟶ Eric
You're learning fast.

Jules Jones ⟶ Ames Hollander VIA MONDRIAN
Dear Ames,
    While I appreciate your trust, I need to get out of the middle of this. I'm anxious about weevils for the first time in a year, and I have too much on my plate to deal with a breakdown right now.
    Yours, JJ

Ames → Jules VIA MONDRIAN
Dear Jules,
    Fear of weevils outweighs incidence by 5,000 to 1,
which is why they are classified as a *Terrorist Weapon*
rather than a *Surveillance Tool*. That said, there may
be a slight possibility of a breach in our friend's case,
so I'm moving her to the top of my NYC list. I knew
her husband a little from my own dealings with NSA
(great guy), but the government has a strict rule against
outside cleaners, so there is no way he can be involved or
even know about this. You are the obvious person, Jules.
Will throw in a "tune-up" scan for you, if that helps.
    Ames Hollander

Jules → Ames VIA MONDRIAN
Fuck. Going for a run. Too anxious to continue this
convo and trying to lose weight.

Carmine DeSantis → Jazz Attenborough
Jazzy, I strongly suggest you do the speedboat profile
with Jules Jones (SUICIDE TOUR) and Bosco
(CONDUITS), and have taken the liberty of answering
"yes" on your behalf.

Jazz → Carmine
How long have we worked together, Carmine?

Carmine → Jazz
My whole career, 23 years.

Jazz → Carmine
If I've had a single motto, from day one, what has it
been?

Carmine → Jazz
I know I know, "No reunions." But I thought that only
meant with angry ex-wives and feckless offspring.

Jazz ⟶ Carmine
It means everyone.

Carmine ⟶ Jazz
Well you've never met Bosco Baines or Jules Jones,
so it will be a reunion for THEM but not for you.
On another note, why fire 3rd Assistant when his
suggestion ended up checking out?

Jazz ⟶ Carmine
Don't like to flip-flop. Replace.

Eric Platt ⟶ Jules Jones
Dear Mr. Jones,
    I'm pleased to relate the news that Mr.
Attenborough is willing to participate in the speedboat
interview with you and Bosco Baines after his return
from Belize next month. As security on his property
is tight, can you give me a sense now of how many
people would be present? The crew must be minimal,
and we'll need signed affidavits from each person
present stating that the day will be deleted in full from
any uploads to the Collective Consciousness.
    Respectfully, Eric Platt
    3rd Assistant to Jazz Attenborough

Jules ⟶ Eric
Dear Eric,
    Excellent news. We are a no-frills crew consisting
of myself, Bosco, a photographer/videographer, and
my pal Lulu, a seasoned music producer and jack-of-
all-trades.
    Yours, JJ

Eric ⟶ Jules
Mr. Attenborough has fired me, capriciously, but
Mr. DeSantis has quietly retained me to oversee this

project. Long-shot question: Any chance your friend Lulu would be willing to pose as Mr. Attenborough's new 3rd assistant until this shoot is complete, to free up Mr. DeSantis from playing middleman? Mr. DeSantis will assure Mr. A of background checks, etc.

Respectfully, Eric Platt
3rd Assistant to Jazz Attenborough

5

Lulu Kisarian ⟶ Jazz Attenborough
Dear Mr. Attenborough,

Lulu Kisarian, here, your new 3rd Assistant. I look forward to performing whatever tasks you need me to perform—and of course, meeting you in person when you return from Belize. Many thanks for the honor of working for you.

Respectfully, Lulu Kisarian

Jazz ⟶ Lulu
You are hired on a trial basis. I trust you have a thorough knowledge of my work?

Lulu ⟶ Jazz
I've seen all of your movies.

Jazz ⟶ Lulu
Attaching three scripts for you to read and cover as a test. Please convey results to me, rather than 1st or 2nd assistants, so I can personally evaluate your work.

Dolly Peale ⟶ Arc
Dear Arc,

I wonder if this will ever reach you—I think it's been ten years since we were last in touch! All is well here; more people are moving upstate, and they seem to love cheese. I have a specific question for you, but asking now, when we haven't communicated in so long, feels too transactional even for me. Thinking of the aftermath of our mad escapade for General B, I am overwhelmed with fondness, sweet memories, and curiosity about your life. Send news if by a miracle you see this!

Affectionately, Dolly Peale

Arc → Dolly Peale
Ah, Dolly, what a singular pleasure to hear from you. Memories indeed.

I am blessed to report that my family and I are well. My daughters have both married and I am a grandfather thrice over. The recent political changes in our country, while generally salutary, have not benefitted me personally. I am too closely associated with the general's misdeeds, and am no longer permitted to travel abroad, which is largely why I have not been in touch. While I miss being in government, my manufacturing business remains sound, and the prolonged peace and economic stability of our nation are of course good for all.

How is Lulu? And . . . your question?

Sending very fondest thoughts, Arc

Dolly → Arc
Dear Arc,

How wonderful to hear from you! Lulu is well, and I'm the grandmother of beautiful 8-month-old twins, Omar and Festa.

I think you have more or less answered my question, but here goes: there is interest in a documentary about Kitty Jackson's "relationship" with General B. The idea is to give Kitty's career a boost (she's 51, to save you the math) by portraying her as a hero in X's turn to democracy. You and I would be the villains, though; our plan to rehabilitate the general's image with their

phony liaison would have to come out, along with
the purely accidental nature of General B's political
"awakening." As you can imagine, I dread all of this. It
would also require that you travel to the USA. What is
your gut reaction?

Affectionately, Dolly

Arc → Dolly
Dearest Dolly,

"Gut reaction" is such a very American phrase:
grotesque, yet somehow apt. Mine includes a
recollection of the deep and dark silence beside
the lake where you live, and the pointed fir trees
surrounding it. Their pine scent was both sweeter and
saltier than any I have smelled before, or since.

All of which is to say that I would return to
the USA immediately—would in fact already have
returned—were I not fettered as I am. Alas, I cannot.
Were the filmmakers permitted to come here to X
(highly unlikely), I would gladly participate.

With the utmost respect, Dolly, I must gently
correct your account of our shared motives for
bringing together General B and Kitty Jackson in
2008. Did we not engineer an appearance of romantic
involvement between them as a "Trojan horse" to
compel an end to the general's depredations? That
was my plan, certainly—and yours, too, as I recall you
saying quite explicitly. If you will probe the recesses of
your memory (perhaps you have externalized it, like so
many?), I am confident that these laudable details will
return to you.

Widespread recognition of our unorthodox and
successful scheme to bring democracy to my country
would improve my standing with the current regime, and
I would relish the chance to speak of it "on the record."

Sending very fondest thoughts, Arc

Dolly Peale → Ashleigh Avila
Dear Ashleigh,
   I have made contact with the man who served as
my liaison with General B's regime in 2008. Though
theoretically willing to participate, he is sadly out of
favor with the current regime and unable to leave the
country. He will begin the process of requesting a
travel visa, but it may be slow. Stay tuned.
   All the best, Dolly

Ashleigh → Dolly
Dear Dolly,
   INCREDIBLE that you've found this person and
he is willing!!! And don't lose hope: I have a close
friend who emigrated from X as a kid and has family
in the current regime! Will ask her to query about
permission to shoot INSIDE of X, which would
be a thousand times better for original locations
and atmosphere. Not sure I've mentioned that I'm
trained as a documentary filmmaker (MFA/NYU)?
I have experience with permissions logistics and
enough interested funders that overseas travel might
work.
   With hope and expectation, Ash

FWD: Dolly Peale → Joseph Kisarian
Jojo, HELP! See below: I have made a horrific blunder
by admitting that Arc is alive and willing. I'm terrified
of making a wrong move and thwarting Lu, but this
"documentary" must be shut down before further
steps are taken! Please advise!
   Love, Dodo

Joe → Dolly
Dodo, please do not be upset! Remember my motto:
"If everyone is still alive, whatever it is can be fixed."
   You will see for yourself this weekend that Lulu

has made enormous strides! She is sleeping well, and
I have heard her laugh, really laugh, for the first time
since her return from service. There are flashes of the
old Lulu: buoyant and bright with the merest hint of
subterfuge. She is up to something, our Lulu, and it is
bringing her joy.
    Love, Jojo

6

Bosco Baines ⟶ Bennie Salazar
Hey Pal,
    Jules has got me mixed up in some journalism
scheme involving Jazz Attenborough (big Conduits
fan, who knew?). The idea is that Jazz and I will ride
around in his supersonic speedboat next month in LA,
and Jules will write about it, and people will video and
meme and stream it, and then old-timers will start
broadcasting their memories of our original greatness
a millennium ago, and we'll get famous all over again.
Wondering if we might hitch that caper to a minor
Conduits relaunch; new-take-on-old-songs kinda
thing? Just askin'.
    Love you baby, Bosky

Bennie ⟶ Bosco
Bosky baby!! Great to hear from you. Thanks again
for the ice cream, although the teen and her voracious
friends devoured most of it. Will look at our Conduits
numbers and give this some thought. The most tuneful
stuff could be aces acoustically. How's the voice?
    B

Bosco ⟶ Bennie
Honestly not sure. Will knock out a few scales and see.
Been living clean, so that's something.
    Bosky

Bennie → Bosco
Just checked, and the numbers are surprisingly strong
on Conduits classics. Timing good too: your original
fans are mostly still alive, and I'm told there's a solar
system's worth of Conduits memories in the collective.
A fresh take on the old material could lead younger
people to it. Let's conference in a day or two so Melora
and I can take a listen to the voice.

Bosco → Bennie
Need a little more time to limber up.

Bennie → Bosco
Ok, but just to be clear, Bosky, a re-recording needs
to be GREAT to work at all. Anything less will be
comedy, not the good kind.

Bosco → Bennie
Was Melora bcc'd on that?

Bennie → Bosco
Very funny. Melora is a resourceful business partner
with whom I enjoy a rich creative collaboration, as well
as the youngest daughter of my beloved mentor, Lou
Kline.

Bosco → Bennie
Then why'd she steal your company and make you
move to LA and be her lackey?

Lulu Kisarian → Jazz Attenborough
Dear Mr. Attenborough,
    Enclosed please find my test coverage of the three
scripts you sent, attached and copied below in order of
ascending quality:
    1. GRANDPA GRUMP, comedy
    You play a grumpy grandpa softened by a prank-

filled weekend with five grandkids who help you to
solve a cold murder case. We have all seen this movie a
thousand times. As you've never played a grandfather,
I would hesitate to put yourself in that category for
the sake of this formulaic project.

2. SANTA SENSATION, comedy

You play an alcoholic Macy's Santa who recognizes
a woman bringing her grandsons to sit in his lap as the
girl he loved in high school—now conveniently a widow.
There are some cleverly written scenes of drunken
Santa tracking down his true love (for whom he will
sober up, of course), but you spend much of the movie
looking buffoonish.

3. MERMANCE, fantasy

Terrible title, but the Undersea Cave-Warlock
role has possibilities. You play a powerful wizard, and
there is a romance with a MerQueen that could
be compelling with the right actress. If done well,
the undersea landscape might be beautiful and
otherworldly. Worth considering.

Sincerely, Lulu Kisarian

3rd Assistant to Jazz Attenborough

Jazz ⟶ Lulu

Test passed. Will give the cave-warlock a look. Meanwhile,
please update me on the interview to take place after my
return. It involves speedboats, which I collect.

Lulu ⟶ Jazz

You have upwards of 40 speedboats, I believe.

Jazz ⟶ Lulu

Impressive homework. I rarely discuss my speedboat
collection.

Lulu ⟶ Jazz

Honestly it has never felt like homework.

FWD: Jazz Attenborough → Carmine DeSantis
See below. Concerned that new 3rd assistant may
be a nut. She seems a bit TOO keen. Who reviewed
background check?

FWD: FWD: Carmine DeSantis → Eric Platt
See below

FWD: FWD: FWD: Eric Platt → Jules Jones
Dear Jules,
    Please see below. Can you ask your friend Lulu to
take it down a notch (not that he'll be satisfied then,
either)?
    Thanks, Eric

Bennie Salazar → Alex Applebaum
Hey Alex,
    Long time, baby! Listen, there's a chance Bosco
and I may record a few Conduits classics acoustically
during a trip he's making to LA in a few weeks. I have
no idea what he sounds like—or, frankly, looks like!
Would you be able to drive up there soonish and
work with him a little? He's being cagey about letting
me listen, and the reason may be that he sounds
like shit. Need to know before I start thinking about
musicians etc.
    Best, Bennie

Alex → Bennie
Dear Bennie,
    What a joy to hear from you!
    Bosco . . . Lord is he still kicking? Seems the
Suicide Tour was really a longevity tour! Glad to be
involved and timing good . . . we are just finishing our
semesters.
    More soon, Alex

Alex Applebaum ⟶ Bosco Baines
Dear Bosco (if I may):

I teach Sound Analytics at Queens College and am a longtime collaborator of Bennie Salazar's, starting with Scotty Hausmann's Footprint Concert fourteen years ago. Bennie mentioned that you may be re-recording some Conduits classics acoustically and I begged to be involved. I play serviceable piano and guitar and would be honored to work with you in any way that might be helpful.

Your fan, Alex

Bosco ⟶ Alex
Good timing. Would love your help. Voice a bit wonky, must confess.

Jules Jones ⟶ Ames Hollander VIA MONDRIAN
I've resigned myself to bringing our friend to your clinic next week, but how?? She has 8-month-old twins and distrusts babysitters. I am afraid of infants, which are unpredictable and do not like me.

JJ

Ames ⟶ Jules VIA MONDRIAN
Is there someone you trust unconditionally who could come along and help with the babies? Ideally a person with children?

Jules ⟶ Ames VIA MONDRIAN
Two options: My friend Noreen, a little unstable but a hyper-involved grandma of many. Or my sister Stephanie, rock solid but grandma to just one, far away.

Ames ⟶ Jules VIA MONDRIAN
Let's go with Stephanie.

Alex Applebaum → Bennie Salazar
Dear Bennie,

I made time this weekend to visit Bosco before
he changed his mind. He lives on a small dairy farm
(beautiful yellow cows with long curved horns). I didn't
recognize him—he is thin, I kid you not, and extremely
fit! Showed me his weightlifting setup in an old barn.
He looks more like Bosco of yore than at any time
since 2000 (albeit with wrinkles and silver hair).

Here's the oddball part: his voice is higher than
before. It has a scratchy texture (polyps I'm guessing)
that I've come to feel adds some depth to the quasi-
falsetto of his singing.

Summary: Looks great, moves well, voice a bit high
but I think we can work with it. Recording link below.

Alex

Bennie → Alex
Quasi-falsetto? What the hell? Listening now.

7

Stephanie Salazar → Bennie Salazar
B,

I'm not sure what it says about my life that the
only person who will appreciate the day I've just had is
the one I divorced almost thirty years ago. Not gonna
worry about it, too eager to spill.

Jules messages me asking if I'll meet him in lower
Manhattan in a couple of days to help him with "a
project." It's urgent, but nothing is wrong. He's been
working on his new book and in good health (down
15 lbs!), so I agree, no questions asked.

Two mornings later, he meets me outside an
apartment building in Tribeca in a cold sweat: gray
face, collar soaked. I say Jules, do we need to go to
the hospital? He says no, everything is fine, he's just
anxious. Tells me the next couple of hours will seem

strange, but there's nothing wrong. Oh, and my job is
going to be minding a pair of 8-month-old twins!

We go inside the building and ride up in an elevator.
Jules opens the apartment door and I find a beautiful
boy and girl buckled into a double stroller, just starting
to whimper. There are some toys around, so I drop
to the floor and start shaking a rattle and they quiet
down. Meanwhile Jules goes into another room and
comes back leading by the hand (out of sight of the
babies) a woman with a black hood covering her entire
head and one arm in a sling! She seems calm and even
waves to me with her good arm, which is the only
reason I don't call 911.

Jules motions for me to lead the way out of the
apartment with the stroller. He's ordered a car with
two infant seats. The hooded woman stays out of sight
until I've buckled in the babies. Then she slips into the
front seat wearing a wide-brimmed hat and sunglasses,
so the hood just looks like a face mask. No one says a
word. The twins fuss a little at first, but some rattling
from me distracts them.

We pull up outside a seedy bar near Penn Station.
I can hear Jules wheezing like he's having a panic
attack. I buckle the twins back into their stroller and
Jules motions for me to lead the way into this crappy
bar. I'm thinking this can't be right, but the bartender
catches my eye and jerks his chin toward the back. I
roll the stroller toward a grimy, crusty door that I'm
assuming will lead into a biohazardous restroom, I can
almost smell it, but I brace myself against the door and
push it open.

Then it's like we've gone through a portal in one of
Chris's old video games: We're inside a medical clinic
and a buff military-looking guy in a surgical mask
greets us in friendly silence. We follow him into a room
that's totally dark except for a glowing purple ring in
the middle of the floor. I'm trying to interpret this

scene: Is it a game? A performance? A test? But Jules
is morbidly serious and no one says a word, so I keep
quiet and roll with it.

Jules and I sit on a bench against the wall with the
stroller. The twins are mesmerized by the purple ring.
The military guy leads the hooded woman into the
center of this ring and takes off her sunglasses and
hat, but leaves on the hood. Then he disappears. I hear
a humming sound and a mechanical arm begins to
raise the ring slowly up from the floor. It moves from
the woman's feet over her shins, her thighs, her hips,
her torso, and finally her head. The purple light has a
stupefying effect; the twins fall asleep instantly and I
feel Jules slump against me and I'm sort of entranced, I
guess, just staring at that purple light.

When the ring has moved up over the woman's
entire body, the purple light goes out and the military
guy reappears and leads her to a chair. Then he sits
down behind a screen and spends a long time studying
it. The only light in the room is a blue-green glow on
the guy's face, and all I can see above his mask are his
eyes.

Finally the lights gently rise, and the guy stands up.
He looks around and sees that I'm awake. When our
eyes meet, he says, "You don't get motion sickness,"
and I realize it's the first voice I've heard since I met
Jules that morning.

"Never," I say.

He goes to the woman in the chair and gently pulls
off her hood. She's asleep too. The guy crouches beside
her chair, close to her face, and says, "You're clean,
Lulu. There's nothing."

She starts upright, and that's when I recognize
her: it's Lulu. As in OUR Lulu, Dolly's daughter. IT'S
LULU!!

Then it's like a spell breaks: the twins start to wail
and Lulu leans over the stroller kissing them both and

she's crying, too. She looks haggard, and one arm
kind of hangs at her side like she can't use it properly.
Jules introduces the military guy as "A," a "cleaner,"
meaning one of those people who scan for weevils.
He's promised Jules a scan (not his first, apparently),
which of course turns up nothing.

    Lulu and I waited with the twins in another room
while Jules had his turn in the purple ring. I asked
about her injured arm but she was vague and evasive.
It was hard for her to stop crying, which was strange to
see. I think of Lulu as so capable and stoic. Poor thing,
she's clearly been through something terrible, but I
didn't want to pry. I wonder if Chris knows.

    Ok, that was my day. How was yours?

    S

Bennie → Stephanie
Steph, you're sure this wasn't a dream?

Stephanie → Bennie
What was the one rule I made when you first lured me
into bed? AND it was in our marriage vows.

Bennie → Stephanie
I know: no making each other listen to our dreams.
But . . . Lulu and Jules? When did they reconnect?

Stephanie → Bennie
Apparently they're collaborating on some kind
of celebrity interview involving Bosco, in Los
Angeles . . . !?

Bennie → Stephanie
Interesting. I'm already aware of that project from
Bosco himself. Didn't know Lulu was involved.
Coincidence, or do all roads start to converge after
age 70?

Jules Jones → Stephanie Salazar
Sis what can I say? Life not possible w/o you.
      Your loving Bro, Jules

Stephanie → Jules
Anytime. You know that.

Jules → Stephanie
Wish you'd taken up Ames on his offer of a scan. They
are VERY hard to come by.

Stephanie → Jules
Unless someone wants to infiltrate the Westchester
Senior Ladies' Tennis Circuit, I think I'm safe.

Jules → Stephanie
Doesn't it ever occur to you that another entity might
be looking out through your eyes and listening through
your ears or uttering words through your mouth?

Stephanie → Jules
Nope. But it has occurred to me that buying a
fluorescent ring and offering "scans" would be a lucrative
racket. Has "Ames" ever actually found a weevil?

Jules → Stephanie
He had one in his own brain!

Stephanie → Jules
Whaaaaat?

Jules → Stephanie
I saw it. Looks like a narrow, pointed pill bug with
flexible synthetic scales.

Stephanie → Jules
I wish I could unknow that.

Jules ⟶ Stephanie
He was in Special Operations, then worked as a
contractor doing stuff the military didn't want to
touch. Bottom line: If you ever find yourself thinking
that a mass human extinction event would be good
for population control, you might want to get
checked out.

Stephanie ⟶ Jules
Uh-oh. I think that all the time.

8

Ashleigh Avila ⟶ Dolly Peale
Dear Dolly,
    INCREDIBLE NEWS. My friend from X has put
me in touch with a media relations person in the inner
circle of the current regime. They're willing to let us
shoot the documentary there. It's officially a go!!!!!!!
Funding is fully in place—oversubscribed, in fact. Let's
talk schedule.
    Wow, right?! Ash

FWD: Dolly Peale ⟶ Joseph Kisarian
Jojo, see below. I am beside myself. Ashleigh will be
livid when I pull the plug, and obviously the last thing I
want to do is to undermine Lu's opportunity, whatever
it may be. But what choice do I have? Waiting will only
make it worse. Help!!
    Love, Dodo

Joe ⟶ Dolly
Last night, Lulu planted tomato seeds in small pots on
our windowsill for the first time in three years. I was
moved to tears when she showed them to me. We
must not disrupt her fledgling happiness.

Dolly → Joe
Ok, so how do we end this without angering or
disrupting anyone? Can we say National Security
won't allow it . . . ??

Joe → Dolly
That is untrue. We would welcome closer relations with
the new regime in X.

Dolly → Joe
Wait—what???? Are you suggesting that Lulu and I
should actually GO TO X and make this documentary?

Joe → Dolly
I can easily take another short leave to care for the
twins while you are gone.

Dolly → Joe
Jojo, that is OUT OF THE QUESTION. My part in all
of it was deplorable, not to mention that I would have
to revisit the boiling oil catastrophe.

Joe → Dolly
Are you not the one who first explained to me that
Americans love redemption stories precisely because
they are so irrevocably tainted by original sin?

Dolly → Joe
This isn't a redemption story! It's a story about how
I sank so low that I took a job camouflaging the
atrocities of a genocidal dictator!

Joe → Dolly
Are you not the one who told me a good publicist can
turn a violent coup into a humanitarian rescue mission?

Dolly → Joe
But I'm not a publicist anymore—I'm a gourmet
grocer. My good name is everything to me.

Joe → Dolly
Are you not the one who told me that celebrity is
a neutral amplifier—positive, negative, it makes no
difference?

Dolly → Joe
Gosh, Jojo, I'm amazed that you've memorized so many
of my pronouncements. And flattered, I will confess.

Joe → Dolly
I sensed that a day would come when recalling your
words would prove essential.

9

Ashleigh Avila → Kitty Jackson
Amazing news, Kit Kat:
 I have all of the pieces in place for the
documentary, the most important being the
cooperation and even—dare I say it?—ENTHUSIASM
of the present regime in X. You have many fans in
the inner circles of government there. Not only do
they love your movies, but they regard you as having
been pivotal to General B's "conversion" (might
also be "gelding" or "enlightenment," depends on
the translation). Of course they're hoping you'll be
willing to share new "intimate" information about
General B, now that your legal fetters are gone—the
more shocking the better, obviously, not that I would
EVER encourage you to exaggerate or lie (perish
the thought!), although being dead, the general can't
exactly contradict you and I've verified that there is no
Mandala Cube in the picture . . .
 Finally, they asked whether you'd be interested in

riding some rare stallions from a wild herd that roams their beaches. Short video below; note the naturally curly manes!

Please let me know that I can move forward on this. XxxxooooAsh

Kitty → Ashleigh
Let me get this straight: I'm being asked to provide salacious details about General B, thus outing myself as a prostitute, in exchange for the chance to ride a curly-maned horse. And the person engineering this is NOT an enemy bent on my destruction, but my trusted helpmate and longtime confidante/publicist whom I PAY to protect my reputation and interests.

Am I missing anything?

Ashleigh → Kitty
Yes, you spoiled bitch, you're forgetting a couple of things that will accrue to YOU (since no one else really matters) by doing this:

1. Massive exposure as a person willing to do ANYTHING for the sake of democracy—a Citizen Agent before her time, if you will—and a woman so bewitching that she was able to convert/enlighten/geld a mass-murdering despot and thereby transform a volatile region and save the lives of millions.

2. A shot at an exponential rise in cultural status that would place you among the first-namers whose ranks you have zero chance of joining otherwise because a) you're too old, and b) you were never that good an actress in the first place.

These are the opportunities I've created for you. Spurn them if you like, but know what you are giving up, you twat.

Kitty → Ashleigh
You made me cry. I hate you.

Ashleigh → Kitty
Yes or no?

Kitty → Ashleigh
Yes if I can be as far away from you as possible.

Ashleigh → Kitty
That is guaranteed.

Lulu Kisarian → Jazz Attenborough
Dear Mr. A,

Could you please let me know how many people can comfortably ride in your speedboats, so that we can finalize plans for the article/photo shoot with Bosco of the Conduits and Jules Jones, the author of SUICIDE TOUR?

Sincerely, Lulu Kisarian
3rd Assistant to Jazz Attenborough

Jazz → Lulu
Nothing about a speedboat ride is "comfortable" unless you enjoy crashing violently over the tops of waves, as I happen to. The real question is: will these elderly gentlemen be able to handle it? My boats are extremely long, so space will not be an issue.

Lulu → Jazz
Dear Mr. A,

I will warn the elderly gentlemen, but their struggles might make you look more at ease. Appearing to advantage in a watery environment could also be helpful pre-publicity for the Undersea Cave-Warlock role, should you end up taking it.

Sincerely, Lulu Kisarian
3rd Assistant to Jazz Attenborough

Jazz → Lulu
You like me in this role. Why? (five words or less)

Lulu → Jazz
You'll play the romantic lead.

Jazz → Lulu
How romantic can it be if the MerQueen is not young?

Lulu → Jazz
That depends on the actress. Kitty Jackson is
in phenomenal physical shape (prizewinning
equestrienne), and I've been told that her reputation
will soon have a boost.

FWD: Jazz Attenborough → Carmine DeSantis
See below. What is 3rd assistant talking about re Kitty
Jackson?

Carmine → Jazz
There is buzz about a Kitty Jackson doc involving these
events from 2008. See link below.

Jazz → Carmine
Why was I not given this background on Kitty before
working with her on DAZZLE??

Carmine → Jazz
As it is common knowledge, I gave you credit for
knowing it.

Jazz Attenborough → Lulu Kisarian
Need to find a new manager. Carmine is hopeless.
Would prefer not to involve 1st or 2nd assistants, as they
know him well. Ask around and get me some names.

Lulu → Jazz
Dear Mr. A,

I'm sorry, but as Mr. DeSantis hired me, it would be awkward for me to work on replacing him.

Sincerely, Lulu Kisarian
3rd Assistant to Jazz Attenborough

Jazz Attenborough → Carmine DeSantis
Need new 3rd assistant. Lulu is hopeless. Also pls accept Undersea Cave-Warlock role in MERMANCE, contingent upon Kitty Jackson accepting the role of MerQueen.

10

Alex Applebaum → Bennie Salazar
Dear Bennie,

Good news first: The voice work with Bosco has gone well. Warm milk, in abundant supply here (more cows than people, as they say), seems to calm the raspiness. I've rearranged the Conduits' 15 greatest hits to accommodate his higher range.

Bad news: Bosco on his own will sound, at best, good (not even very good).

Bosco tells me that Jazz Attenborough (as in, the actor) is planning to attend his recording session. Huge fan apparently. Attenborough appeared in musicals early in his career and his singing voice was strong and clear (see below for recording links). What if we invited Attenborough to sing with Bosco?

Even if Attenborough agrees and sounds good (big ifs), any shot at greatness will have to be supplied by the accompanist and the context/moment, à la Scotty Hausmann's Footprint Concert. Ah, where are Scotty and Lulu when we need them?

Alex
P.S. Where ARE Scotty and Lulu these days (serious question)?

Bennie Salazar → Jocelyn Li
Hi Joc

   Listen, I have a proposal for Scotty that is really
a proposal for both of you. Bosco is coming to LA to
record some Conduits classics acoustically, and I'm
wondering if Scotty would be willing to accompany
him on slide guitar?

   xxB

Jocelyn → Bennie
Hi Bennie, he says sure. We love the Conduits! I had
a HUGE crush on Bosco back in the day (don't tell
Scotty). xxJoc

Bennie → Jocelyn
Aces. Ok if Jazz Attenborough (yep, THAT one) joins
on vocals?

Bennie Salazar → Jocelyn Li; Alex Applebaum
Joc, Alex,

   Putting you two together to work out details
of this recording session. Jocelyn and I are high
school bandmates (along with Scotty) from that cult
sensation the Flaming Dildos. Joc has a beautiful
singing voice, as I was reminded recently when we sang
karaoke together. Alex was the silent partner in the
Footprint Concert and thus instrumental to Scotty's
world fame and the resurrection of yours truly's career.

   So here we are, conniving once again to bump
Scotty's reputation, along with Bosco's and—let's be
honest—my own and that of everyone else over 60
striving for cultural relevance in a world that seems to
happen in a nonexistent "place" that we can't even find
unless our kids (or grandkids!) show it to us. The only
route to relevance at our age is through tongue-in-
cheek nostalgia, but that is not—let me be very clear—
our ultimate ambition. Tongue-in-cheek nostalgia is

merely the portal, the candy house, if you will, through which we hope to lure in a new generation and bewitch them.

The thing that changes everything: isn't that always the goal?

Ok, enough rhetoric. Can you two take it from here?

B

11

Bennie Salazar → Stephanie Salazar

Steph,

I now find myself in exactly the position you were in a few weeks ago: eager to tell the story of a day whose twists only you will appreciate. Does this mean we should've stayed married? (Kidding! Your tennis career wouldn't have happened with me around, and Lupa somehow puts up with me.)

We decide to do the recording at Lou Kline's old place (now Melora's, but she was on the road) because it's got the private beach and dock and lets us go directly from a speedboat ride into a recording session. I wasn't sure if Jocelyn would be willing to go back to Lou's house—talk about bad vibes—but she was game to return as a survivor. So she and Scotty arrive around noon and Lupa and I are already there with Alex, a sound guy I've worked with on and off since the Footprint. We break out the Jägermeister in Scotty's honor and have a toast at Lou's big table with the piles of wax in the middle (It's still there, can you believe it?) under the chandelier with all those candles in it. Scotty's in great form—the new teeth are a big improvement over that bright-white set, and he's a happy man with Joc. I had a good feeling even before Scotty started playing the new arrangements on slide, but when I heard them, I thought holy shit: they actually sounded better, more contemporary and just all-around better, than the originals. I knew then that it was going to be great, no matter what Bosco and Jazz Attenborough sounded like. We'd already done it.

We've got the teen and her girlfriends with us and they're lounging around Lou's pool in their bikinis because apparently Jazz Attenborough's name still means something to the 15-year-old set (good sign!). Eventually we all go out onto the deck overlooking the ocean and sure enough, a long black cigarette boat zips into view, the kind you'd expect to be delivering bricks of cocaine outside Miami. It's going so fast it's a blur, but Lupa's brought along the camera she uses to shoot insects in flight, and she takes blasts of the boat and then breaks them down into stills so we can zoom in and see everyone. The scene is intense: in one, Bosco is midair with a Munch-like howl on his face. There's one of Jules puking over the side of the boat, and then he disappears. Can't find him anywhere!

Jazz Attenborough has a kind of wolfish grin, like he's enjoying pushing everyone to the brink of death or possibly beyond it (where the hell is Jules?). After a while they tear away and reappear in a different boat, this one even longer, canary yellow. On the yellow boat, Lulu and Jazz Attenborough get into a serious conversation that distracts Jazz to the point that he slows the boat down and we're able to see everyone clearly. Jules is back, looking very white. Attenborough hands over the steering to Lulu and sits down with a kind of blank expression. Lulu knows her way around a speedboat, and they take another few turns before finally heading in to Lou's dock.

I'm wondering if we'll have to carry Bosco and Jules off the boat, and I'm also wondering if Bosco will have screamed his voice away. But Bosco and Jules come off the boat bellowing, pumped, both in swim trunks (Jules wore a T-shirt and you're right, he's slimmed down!), both of them roaring at the top of their lungs. It's a geezer fest. The photographer and videographer follow them off the boat, and the teens are whispering and giggling, a little cowed by these ancient alphas, and now everyone's just waiting for Jazz.

He comes last, with Lulu. I know she's in her thirties and a mom, but in the company of these geezers she looks 21 again. Jazz keeps turning to her, checking on her, worrying over her injured arm, and my stomach is starting to turn (you know his rep). Then he takes Lulu's hand to help her off the boat and their faces line up for a second, and I realize that it's EXACTLY THE SAME FACE. Dimples, cheekbones, chin. Think about it, Steph. She's basically a clone of him.

There's more, as I'm sure you've heard from Jules. But I'm going to stop there and let you digest.

Love, B

12

Lulu Kisarian → Chris Salazar and Molly Cooke, VIA MONDRIAN

Hey you two,

I don't think I've seen either of you since Colin's memorial (ten years ago, can that be?), but I think of you both a lot, especially that day when we rode away from the country club on our bikes and fell asleep on the pier. It is one of those way stations that I keep coming back to, maybe because of Colin. Still can't believe he's gone.

Anyway, I'm contacting you now at the suggestion of Ames Hollander, who recently gave me some invaluable cleaning help. Small world, great minds, all roads, etc. Who needs a Collective Consciousness?

I'm thirty-five, unemployed, and looking for a way to make the world better, not worse. I know something of your work from Ames Hollander, and from the grapevine, and from the ether (and from your mom, Chris, who brought me lunch recently). If you'll have me, I would love to work for you.

Awaiting your reply, Lulu

Lulu Kisarian → Joseph Kisarian
Joseph my love,

The general's compound is a ruin, but they let us walk
through it.

A tree with enormous waxy leaves has thrust itself
through the middle of the room where Mom and I
slept.

They've named a holiday after Kitty and filmed her
riding a wild stallion into the sunset. They're going to
put her on a postage stamp.

Kitty and my father are planning to make a Western
together. Horses and speedboats apparently have
more in common than you'd think.

In deep night, when I listen to sounds of the rainforest,
I feel like I've returned to my mission.

The landscapes are nothing alike.

I see now that the place I've been yearning for is my
own imagination.

It was with me before and will be always. It's in every
children's book.

Kiss our babies for me a thousand times, and
remember to water the seedlings.

I'm counting the seconds until I see you next week.

BUILD

Eureka Gold

1

It was billed as one of those old-fashioned snowstorms, the kind that had been predicted throughout Gregory's twenty-eight years but never quite panned out (according to his father), always devolving into rain or half-rain, icing up or turning prematurely to slush, and leading, at the Sunday family dinners Gregory sporadically attended, to nostalgic reveries from his father—who'd walked New York a lot before he got famous—about what *real* snowstorms used to be like: the softness, the silence, the transformation of a frenzied city into a plush, whispery terrain.

"You say that every single time, Dad," Gregory would huff. "Word for word."

"Do I?" His father always seemed surprised.

Now, from his waterbed, Gregory could hear his roommate bustling around their small common area preparing a spate of last-minute weed deliveries to ease people through *snow quarantine*. "Guess who's on my list," Dennis called. "Athena."

"No way," Gregory said.

"Third time. She's way into the antique thing."

Dennis sold vintage weed: Humboldt Homegrown, Eureka Gold, weed from back in the day when marijuana was leafy and harsh and full of seeds but delivered a high that was the weed equivalent of vinyl: "whorled" and "crosshatched," "sonorous" and "plump" (Dennis's MFA in poetry served him well in these marketing descriptions)—in other words, *authentic* in ways that the bloodless, odorless tinctures that passed for weed nowadays were not.

"How is our Athena?" Gregory projected, with effort, toward his open bedroom door. In the weeks since a mysterious fatigue had confined him to his bed, Gregory and Dennis had perfected the art of conversing between rooms.

"Unchanged," Dennis said. *"Topical. Fearsome."* He popped briefly into Gregory's doorframe.

"Poison," Gregory said.

"Aaaaaant." Dennis made a buzzer noise. "Word-casing."

"True," Gregory reflected. "'Poison' is no longer toxic."

"'Toxic' isn't toxic," Dennis said.

"'Toxic' is anodyne," Gregory agreed. "'Robust' is limp. 'Catalyze' fails to react."

"The 'silos' and 'buckets' are empty," Dennis said.

"What about 'empty'?" Gregory said. "Is 'empty' empty?"

"'Empty' is supposed to be empty," Dennis said. "'Empty' fails by being full."

"But does 'empty' convey *enough* emptiness?"

They could do this all day.

It was Athena who had first made them aware, in the workshop where Gregory and Dennis met, of word-casings and phrase-casings: gutted language she likened to proxies. "Find the eluder," she instructed her rapt graduate students, narrowing gold-flecked eyes at them across the seminar table. "I want words that are still alive, that have a pulse. Hot words, people! Give me the bullet, not the casing— fire it right in my chest. I'll die gladly for some fresh language."

She meant their prose, not their conversation, but Gregory and his peers strained for fresh ways to say, in workshop, that a piece of writing was powerful ("coiled," "obsidian," "hegemonic") or flat ("waxen," "kerneled," "coffee grounds"). Athena was the author of *Gush*, a collection of erotic essays that had roused her students of every gender to a state of manic lust before they'd ever seen her. She was known to have sex with the ones whose work she admired. Gregory was first in their workshop to be anointed; after lavishly praising his novel in progress, Athena rewarded him with a blow job among the stacked canvases of an art gallery where a debauched book party was in progress. The murky, drunken encounter left Gregory convinced he was in love with Athena, but he knew, from friends who'd taken her class the semester before, that the sex would happen only once. Gregory bore his unexceptionalism with dignity, he hoped, but a later recipient of Athena's largesse went to pieces, professing his love for her in class and then fleeing home to Stockholm. The incident reached the ears of NYU's administration, and Athena was quietly fired. But her new book of essays, *Flout*, hit several bestseller lists, and Gregory heard she'd landed a faculty job at Columbia.

The snow began to fall shortly after Dennis left to make his deliveries, soggy clumps that dropped past Gregory's window like an unsavory load being dumped. He imagined his father's critique, then felt a small jolt—as if he'd leaned against a wall that turned out not to be there. His father had died two months ago, of ALS. The complaints about climate-compromised snow were over; Sunday dinners were over; the family home in Chelsea would soon be over, his mother having already declared that she planned to sell it. "I'm not in the museum business," she'd said.

The apartment Gregory and Dennis had shared for the past year was on the eleventh floor of an East Village high-rise. From his waterbed, Gregory could see a slice of sky and eight floor-to-ceiling windows in the building across the street. Since the onset of his exhaustion, he'd begun tracking—often while afloat between sleep and alertness—an array of human lives unfolding behind those windows. He'd watched a man masturbate to his laptop while his wife/partner fed their toddler daughter in the next room (Wanker Man). There was Garden Lady, who tended to twelve linked glass globes that covered her window, each containing a separate plant. Cocaine Couple, middle-aged lesbians, did lines late at night and frenetically cleaned their apartment until Corporate Cog, who slept with a gun under his pillow in a generic bedroom next door, battered the wall for them to stop.

Right now, only the Skins were visible: a male and female around Gregory's age who spent hours sitting on a white leather couch wearing Mandala headsets. They always held hands, which meant they were likely using Mandala's new Skin-to-Skin™ tool that let people access each other's consciousness directly if their flesh was touching. "The End of Aloneness," the advertising said—now you could share another person's suffering and confusion and joy immediately and wordlessly. But the Skins tended to bellow in unison, which made Gregory think they were using Skin-to-Skin to watch streamers who broadcast their perceptions in real time, using self-implanted weevils. Social media was dead, everyone agreed; self-representations were inherently narcissistic or propagandic or both, and grossly inauthentic.

Gregory's father was credited—and blamed—for ushering in this new world, although Mandala disavowed weevils (recycled military devices sold on a black market) and vehemently condemned their use. Gregory had declined even the ritual "baseline" upload to a Mandala Cube, now customary at age twenty-one as a hedge against brain injuries. In this, he was part of a fractured resistance whose symbolic leader was Christopher Salazar, an enigmatic West Coast figure a decade older than Gregory. Salazar's not-for-profit, Mondrian, ran a network of role-playing games at Bay Area drug treatment centers but was also widely credited—and blamed—for coordinating a web of bafflers and proxies that helped people to elude their online identities, sometimes for years. Everyone loved a rivalry, and Mandala vs. Mondrian had been cast by the media as an existential battle whose very terms were decided by which camp you belonged to: Surveillance vs. Freedom (Mondrian); Collaboration vs. Exile (Mandala). Gregory's older brother, Richard, who was Mandala's heir apparent, had persuaded their father to mount a PR campaign the year before to remind the world of what miracles Own Your Unconscious had performed in its nineteen years of existence: tens of thousands of crimes solved; child pornography all but eradicated; Alzheimer's and dementia sharply reduced by reinfusions of saved healthy consciousness; dying languages preserved and revived; a legion of missing persons found; and a global rise in empathy that accompanied a drastic decline in purist orthodoxies—which, people now knew, having roamed the odd, twisting corridors of one another's minds, had always been hypocritical.

Gregory was startled from a doze by Dennis's premature return. His bike had skidded in the snow and dumped him in a puddle, soaking his delivery backpack. The weed was safe in airtight cases, but some of his trademark red velveteen bags had to be swapped. Dennis was flustered and rushing; he needed to finish his deliveries in time to report to the vegan kitchen where he worked at night. On weekends, he had a third job, sorting books that had been donated to the public library. In the year since they'd finished their MFAs, Dennis had grown scrawny and frantic, gnawed at by student debt. He had time to write poetry only in the wee hours after the restaurant closed. Gregory sometimes heard him pacing their common area in darkness, occasionally activating his phone flashlight to scribble a line.

"I'll deliver to Athena," Gregory said.

Dennis appeared in the doorway looking astonished; Gregory hadn't left the apartment in over two months. "Seriously?" Dennis said. "You'll be saving my ass."

Gregory wanted to save his friend's ass, but what had prompted his ambitious offer was a sudden, tidal urge to see their former teacher. It wasn't sexual. He was too drained even to fantasize, and had heard an unsettling rumor (which he'd not repeated to Dennis) that Athena had once been male. His craving to see her had more to do with the fact that those two years of graduate school, of writing workshops and literature classes, had been the happiest of his life. He'd hauled boxes for a moving company, read two books a week, and begun the novel that Athena and some others, too, had liked. Alone by choice on Saturday nights, writing by an open window in his studio apartment, Gregory had experienced a kind of euphoria: a swelling, bursting, yearning hunger that had something in common with lust but included everyone, from the revelers outside his window to the carousers down the hall. He was where he wanted to be, and needed nothing else.

"You'll give her a shock," Dennis said. "She asked about you and I filled her in. Hope that's okay."

"Athena asked?"

"Babe, everyone asks," Dennis said, which of course was true. It had gotten around who Gregory's father was, although he never mentioned the connection. "She wanted to know if you were writing."

"What did you say?"

"Said I didn't know. Are you?" He sounded dubious.

Gregory had stopped writing on the day he learned of his father's diagnosis. What began as an interruption had hardened, in the eight months since, into renunciation. He doubted he would ever resume. Still, he pretended sometimes that *he* was the omniscient narrator of the scenes he witnessed through the windows across the street: a novel about the secret lives of adjacent New Yorkers. He'd titled it *Contiguous*.

"I'm writing in my head," he said.

Dennis laughed. "Don't try that on Athena."

Gregory extracted himself from his waterbed and wavered beside it, acclimatizing himself to verticality. In the bathroom he steadied himself on the sink to brush his teeth and splash cold water in his face. He'd showered that morning with the help of a "shower chair" Dennis had bought at a medical supply shop and assembled (having told Gregory, "You stink, babe"). In the mirror, Gregory appeared more or less normal, he thought: a tall, formerly athletic (now slightly gaunt), ethnically ambiguous male in dire need of a haircut. Gregory had the Affinity Charm, according to his father, which was a fancy way of saying he'd been taken for Greek, Latino, Italian, Native American, Jewish, Asian, and Middle Eastern, as well as Black and white, depending on some alchemy of perceiver and context. But it *wasn't* alchemy, his father always insisted—it could be predicted with algorithms created by Miranda Kline, an anthropologist he invoked with annoying frequency in what had turned out to be the final years of his life. Even Richard got sick of hearing about her (Gregory could tell, although Richard wouldn't say it). It was as if Kline were a departed relative their father wanted them to honor. One fact about her did interest Gregory, unrelated to her theories: Kline had successfully eluded ten years ago, in the mid-2020s, back when eluding was new. She had never been found.

Gregory's parka hung on a peg by the door, his woolen beanie still in the pocket—the same he'd been wearing when he collapsed on the street five days before his father's death. Dennis watched him lace up his boots. "It's that easy?" he said.

"You haven't felt it from my side," Gregory said, and they laughed—it was a joke among their friends that Gregory's consciousness, being marooned inside him, was an unfathomable mystery.

Gregory had been taking a short walk the day he'd passed out, to escape the vigil at his childhood home. A shrunken, crumpled version of his father lay inert on his parents' king-size bed, little more than a head with sensors attached to upload his consciousness to a blue Mandala Cube. Everyone else had managed to seem essential in the crisis: Gregory's two sisters and brother, even his mother's old friend Sasha was there from California, taking messages and brewing pots of tea while her husband, Drew, ran interference with the doctors. Gregory alone had no role. Each day he feigned industry before slinking miserably to his childhood bedroom and sorting through old Magic cards. Each morning he felt a greater dread of returning to Chelsea and resuming the charade. Too many people loved his father. There were too many siblings, too many rooms in the house, too many visitors: an endless worshipful parade of friends and colleagues and favored journalists and devotees seeking wisdom, insight, comfort. No one wanted to let him go. Well-wishers gathered outside the Chelsea house in the sleet and rain; they chased away the haters (most of whom went silent once the vigil began) and held up cloth banners that could be seen from the windows. "We love you, Bix." "Thank you, Bix." "Don't leave us, Bix." Dozens of intricate paintings of mandalas.

Gregory had just bought a bottle of mango juice and was chugging it outside a Seventh Avenue bodega when he noticed a bright ring throbbing in his middle vision. Next he knew, he was on the pavement gazing into the worried faces of strangers. At St. Luke's Roosevelt, where he went by ambulance, he received a diagnosis of low blood pressure, likely from undereating. Dennis met him there, and they rode the subway home—Gregory's family had enough to deal with. But the next morning he awoke too weak to cross the room. The distance from his waterbed to the Chelsea townhouse seemed to divide and subdivide infinitely, and a weight of impossibility thrust him back. He told himself that his presence at the house made no difference—one more, one less—but he knew that nothing short of paralysis could excuse his absence from his father's deathbed. And so he was paralyzed, peeing into bottles for the first two weeks, cared for by Dennis when he was home, unable to attend the funeral.

After the funeral, doctors came: the kind who drew blood and the kind who asked questions about suicidal ideation (too exhausting to contemplate). His sisters, Rosa and Nadine, came, flopping onto one side of Gregory's waterbed and causing tidal waves that nearly pitched him off the other. They uttered long paragraphs that amounted to "We're worried" and further paragraphs that amounted to "You're depressed."

"I just need to rest," Gregory said.

His brother, Richard, was too buried in Mandala business to visit (translation: was punishing Gregory for his absence). His mother came, of course. Gregory was her youngest and had breastfed for so long that he actually remembered doing it. She watched him intently, her scrutiny eroding her respectful distance from his bed. "What, Mom?"

"What?"

"You're staring at me."

"What else would I do?"

"I don't know, read a book. Look at your phone."

"I'm here to see you."

"'See' doesn't have to be constant. Or literal."

"I'm a literal lady," his mother said. "Fine, I'll look out the window." She did, and Gregory shut his eyes and let himself drift, but when he opened them, she was watching him again. "Dad loved you," she said. "And he knew you loved him. I'm concerned that you've lost track of that."

Gregory nodded. Though well-intentioned, her words were a dreary reminder of what all of them knew but none of them said: Gregory hadn't been close to his father. Technology, wealth, fame— to Gregory, these were features of a world where the things that mattered to him, namely books and writing, counted for nothing. He'd recoiled from all of it, starting early. His sisters and brother went from private schools to Ivy League, but Gregory insisted on moving to public school in sixth grade. He used his middle name, Cyrus, as a surname, initially at the behest of his father's security team (it reduced the risk of kidnapping); later, because he preferred it. He paid his own way through Queens College by going part-time over six years and working construction. His father, he knew, had been wounded by these choices. Gregory was nine in 2016, when Own Your Unconscious was released, and he'd announced to his father immediately that he would never use it. ("Come on, laugh it off," he'd overheard his mother say. "He's a little squirt.") But Gregory's father cared what he thought. "I love books. You know that, right?" he'd reminded Gregory over the years, at one point dragging out a crumbling paperback *Ulysses* as proof of his literary seriousness. But nothing could change Gregory's belief that Own Your Unconscious posed an existential threat to fiction.

And yet that whole time, Gregory had nursed a parallel certainty that he and his father would one day be close. He'd even carried a mental image of that communion: laughing with his father like two peers talking about a play they'd just watched. And then, out of no-where, his father was sick—dying of an illness he'd known about for months and could no longer hide. Gregory tried not to ask himself when Richard had been told. During his father's telescopic decline, he and Gregory had had the essential conversations—You-know-I-love-you Yes-and-I-love-you—but they'd been forced, rushed, and there was no mistaking the relief in his father's face when Richard entered the room. Gregory had waited too long. He'd squandered his chance, and now the chance was gone.

2

He made it to the Upper West Side on three different subways. There was a bad spell when he couldn't get a seat on the 2 and hung sway-ing from a bar with his eyes shut until one opened up. At 110th and Broadway, he stepped out into heavy mounting snow that accentu-ated the tree-starved concrete landscape. The address Dennis had given him was on 107th, toward Central Park. As Gregory walked, the grand old apartment buildings above and around him began to look strangely familiar—not from his own memory, he realized, with a start, but from his father's! His father had played certain sections of his consciousness for Gregory and his siblings, usually to illustrate a point or teach them a lesson—although, lately, it had occurred to Gregory that maybe what their father wanted was just for them to know him better. One such memory was the night he'd conceived of Own Your Unconscious. The stated lesson was that inspiration could come from any direction; that they should never give up. They'd watched as a family, sprawled together on his parents' huge bed, wearing individual headsets. Gregory was ten. His father first showed them what he called the Anti-Vision: a vacancy where a new idea refused to appear. For several moments it filled the screen, depthless and white. Gregory was fascinated. Was it really empty?

Then the Anti-Vision gave way to Upper West Side streets as his father searched for an address, dry leaves tumbling over his boots.

"Can you go back to the Anti-Vision?" Gregory asked.

But the Anti-Vision wasn't the point. Their father fast-forwarded through parts of the professors' meeting and his cringy interactions with Rebecca, the pretty graduate student—first on the subway, then in the East Village, where they chased and fled each other in the dark. Gregory's sisters tore off their headsets in agony.

"Oh my God, Daddy! You were such a dork!"

"I believe the word is 'flirt,'" their mother said, jabbing their father with a toe. "Little did I know!"

Their father activated the thought-and-feeling portion of his consciousness just before the moment of revelation. Gregory felt him straining to remember a boy who'd drowned, then felt the roar of his frustration at the inaccessibility of his memories. But amid that frustration was a tiny fillip—a hiccup, almost—of possibility. "There. *That!*" their father said as they peered through his eyes at the rippling dark river. "Can you feel that instant when it happens? I only knew later." And Gregory felt it—a sensation like dropping through a trapdoor without noticing, yet, that everything is different.

"Can I see the Anti-Vision again?" he asked, and everyone groaned.

Another night, their father played for them his return to the professors' apartment. The lesson here was the importance of coming clean and expressing gratitude, even when it was hard or—in this case—contentious. A professor named Fern kept interrupting as he tried to explain why he'd worn a disguise the first time. "You lied to us once," she said. "Why should we trust you now?"

"Shut up," Gregory's sisters yelled at her from beneath their headsets. "Let him finish."

Gregory's father ended by thanking the group for having occasioned an idea that would direct the next phase of his work. The host, Ted Hollander, who turned out to be an uncle of their mother's friend Sasha, erupted, "How marvelous! We helped you to shift a paradigm without knowing who you were or what you were grappling with! You were right not to tell us; fame is distracting."

"Feels a bit biblical, doesn't it?" said English-Accent Guy. "We took in a weary traveler, and lo, he turned out to be Christ our Lord. Lucky us!"

"We didn't *take him in*," said Kacia, the Brazilian animal studies professor. "We were all strangers, remember?" Gregory's father ended up hiring Kacia a few months later, and she'd come to lead a division of Mandala.

"It almost feels like we were a focus group for Bix, not a gathering of peers," said Portia, Ted's wife.

Rebecca spoke up a little shyly. "This whole experience has helped me finalize my dissertation topic," she said. "*Authenticity* as problematized by digital experience. So thank you all."

She and their father had never met again, but Rebecca Amari had gone on to write many books—in fact, it was she who'd coined the term "word-casings" in *Eating Our Tails: Craving Authenticity in a Hyper-Mediated World*, which Athena had assigned in workshop.

"You should interview my son Alfred," Ted told Rebecca. "He's obsessed with authenticity. He screams in public just to watch people react."

"Wow," said Rebecca. "Definitely."

"What do you want from us?" Fern demanded of Gregory's father.

"He wanted to join a discussion group," Ted said. "And after one meeting, he overcame a mental block. I say more power to him."

In that instant, Gregory felt his father's joy: a giddy infusion of promise alongside a faint cadence of thought: *I've got it. I've got it. I've got it.* He was about to change everything, yet again, but no one knew it yet.

"What bothers me," he said, "is that I might've derailed this group."

"If we let ourselves get derailed, that's on us," said Broken-Glasses Guy. "We're supposed to be professionals."

"We're supposed to be professors!" said English-Accent Guy with an arch glance at Rebecca.

"I can go anytime, no hard feelings. Do you want to finish tonight's session without me?"

There was a long pause. "Why does everyone look at me?" Fern asked.

"Stay," Ted said. "Please."

3

Athena opened her door wearing a long dark purple kimono. The apparition of Gregory on her threshold disrupted her cool demeanor only slightly, like a faint tinkling of glassware. "He walks," she said. "He moves. He lives."

"Hi, Athena."

"He talks."

Gregory handed over Dennis's red bag and said, "Hey, do you mind if I sit down a minute?" During the walk, his head had begun to feel like a balloon floating above his body.

"Shoes off, please," Athena said, and went inside.

He left his boots in the onion-smelling hallway and padded into Athena's apartment, which was small and high-ceilinged with faded abstract oil paintings on the walls and a radiator hissing in one corner. She poured each of them a glass of scotch at a small freestanding bar. Dave Brubeck played on an old-fashioned turntable. As Gregory lowered himself onto a cushioned window seat, he experienced a flash of imagination that felt like memory: white guys in 1950s turtlenecks lounging in an apartment like this one, sipping martinis as they engaged in earnest literary debate. The apparition roused a shiver of awareness, as if he'd glimpsed a shaft of light from another dimension.

Athena brought her scotch and an ashtray and sat down beside him, her long legs exposed between folds of kimono. Tattoos of the Seven Dwarves encircled her calves. She looked the same: thick dyed-black hair; short bangs, long flickering eyes. Her blackberry-dark lipstick was so invariable that Gregory suspected her lips were tattooed. She had just the one name, surely not the one she was born with, and struck him as a person without origins, who had made herself up from scratch. The rumor about her sex only heightened the breathtaking quality of Athena's self-genesis.

"How's Columbia?" he asked.

"I love it. My students are *native*."

"At writing?" He couldn't resist.

Athena narrowed her eyes. "Yes, at writing," she said. "I had to sign a behavior contract to get the job. Plus, I'm in a monogamous relationship."

Gregory indicated surprise.

"His name is Barney. He's sixty-two. I had to agree to stop sharing to the collective before he would sleep with me."

"Was that hard?"

"Hell yes," she said. "My life felt like it was made out of disintegrating straws. But now I like it. *Incognito*. I think I'm done with the collective. Sorry, Bix." She raised her eyes heavenward.

"Oh, he'd approve," Gregory said. "His Cube is programmed to delete if anyone tries to share it to the Collective Consciousness."

"But he invented it!"

"Yeah, but only as an extension to solve specific problems. I don't think it ever occurred to him that people would choose to hand over their minds to the counters or stream their perceptions with weevils."

"Age," Athena mused.

"He wasn't that old. Sixty-six."

"I'm sorry about your dad," she said. "I should have said that first. It must be so hard. Ack, sympathy-casings. But I mean it."

She took Gregory's hand and held it with intention, studying his fingers and knuckles and palm as if telling his fortune. Athena's hands were smooth and hot, the nails lacquered magenta and filed to sharp points. Each time one of those points grazed him, Gregory experienced a flicker of arousal that felt akin, somehow, to that imaginative flash of martinis and turtlenecks. Desire—that was what his lassitude had extinguished. Desire for anything.

Athena released his hand and opened her red velveteen bag. "Shall we?" It wasn't really a question.

Gregory didn't like being stoned; it untethered his mind too much, detaching him from the people around him and occasionally even from himself. But his fleeting arousal—his desire to feel *desire*—argued in favor.

The joint crackled and spat like wet firewood as Athena took a first long toke. "Jesus," Gregory said, waving sparks away from his eyes.

"Seeds," Athena croaked, passing it to him. "Eureka Gold: It's cloned from an actual crop grown by Beats in California in the 1960s. The whole forest burned up in the early '20s. Space travel: We're going to a real place that doesn't exist."

Intrigued, Gregory took the joint and inhaled a vapor so noxious that his affronted lungs ejected it in an explosion of coughing. "You *paid* for this?" he gasped, wiping his eyes.

"It's harsh," Athena conceded. "But wait for the high. It's . . . effortless. Cordial. Like ripe peaches."

Ripe peaches brought to mind Athena's magenta talons pressing the skin of a peach almost to the point of bursting it, releasing the juice, but not quite. She passed him the joint again, and Gregory's lungs grudgingly accepted a small hit.

"Did your dad record himself? At the end?" Athena asked.

Not the topic he was hoping for. "Of course."

Thousands of people had uploaded (and, more recently, streamed) their deaths, hoping to grant survivors a glimpse of what lay beyond. But the "successful" attempts had all been fakes.

". . . And?"

"And nothing," he said. "The light went out."

He knew these facts from his mother, having been asleep in his waterbed at the time of his father's passing. But there had been a Beyond of sorts—an unexpected aftermath. Last month, his father's longtime lawyer, Hannah Cooke, an unflappable personage their father had admiringly referred to as "The Vault," summoned the family to her midtown office. Gregory attended remotely. In the meeting, Hannah disclosed the news that Bix Bouton had directed an enormous bequest to Mondrian, Christopher Salazar's not-for-profit. Over gasped objections from Gregory's siblings, Hannah laconically explained that in their father's final year, when his ALS was known only to Lizzie, he'd been gripped by an imperative to contact Miranda Kline, the anthropologist. Kline hadn't been heard from since eluding a decade before. But Bix had recently attended the wedding of Sasha's son, Lincoln, a high-level counter, and quietly enlisted Lincoln's help to find Miranda Kline. Lincoln traced her digital trail to Brazil, where it turned out she had died the year before, in 2034, at age eighty-four. Lincoln next tracked down Lana Kline, the daughter Miranda remained close to until her death. It was Lana who arranged a meeting with Christopher Salazar, who had helped her mother to elude back when eluding was still new. Bix met several times with Salazar in the last months of his life, unbeknownst to anyone, even Lizzie.

Gregory's siblings blared their disbelief and lobbed questions at the Vault (who calmly asserted her ignorance of anything more than what she had told them): Several times where? Several times when? Had Salazar been inside the Chelsea house? What common interests could their father possibly have had with him? Did this mean Bix had been working against his own interests—their interests, the interests of Mandala? Did it mean he regretted Own Your Unconscious? Had he renounced the Collective Consciousness? What had he and Salazar talked about? Had Salazar brainwashed their father in order to swindle him? Richard, normally the mildest of the four of them, shouted a demand for proof, his face wet with tears.

Their mother sat quiet throughout. Abruptly, she stood, startling even Gregory, who was watching on his phone. She was sixty-one and fashionable, having begun designing clothes when Gregory was in high school. "You're forgetting yourselves, children," she said. "Your father was a private man. We're not owed an explanation for anything he did."

"That story is bullshit," Richard yelled—the first time Gregory had ever heard him curse. "There is no way Dad would've met with Salazar and not told me. No. Way."

"Apparently, there is a way," their mother said. "And given your reaction, I'm not surprised he kept it to himself."

Gregory was glad not to be in that room. He, too, had wept while listening to the Vault, but not for the same reason Richard had. What pained Gregory was the thought of a dying man trying to repair, and atone for, a world he had inadvertently wrought. Gregory had never known that man, and wanted to.

Recalling all of this now, from within the warm orb of Eureka Gold, Gregory found himself newly, deeply affected. A dreamy silence had overcome the room, and in the vibrations of that silence, he identified a truth: He and his father were alike, after all.

"Are you writing?" Athena asked, startling him.

"Not a lot," Gregory admitted, which sounded better than *Not at all.* "I've been too drained."

"Maybe not-writing is what's draining you," she said. "Maybe you've severed your energy source."

"I've been thinking a lot," he said, to scuttle the topic.

Athena turned to him. "Finish your fucking book, Gregory," she said mildly. "It's been bloody years."

"Are you trying to piss me off? Or is it happening by accident?"

She shrugged. "I'm your writing teacher. What did you expect?"

There were many possible answers to that question, none especially kind. Gregory summoned a defiant memory of Athena going down on him among the stacks of canvases, but her teasing golden eyes seemed, in retrospect, to proffer an identical goad: *Finish your book!*

Now she glanced at her phone and stood up. "Barney's here," she said. "Out you go."

In the lobby he passed a silver alpha with a handsome goatee, brushing snow from a baguette. He decided to take the C downtown and fumbled through blizzardy wind to Central Park West. Once there, he stepped inside the park. The wind dropped magically away. In the stillness, Gregory noticed that every twig and branch held a delicate stack of snow. Snow swarmed like honeybees in the golden glow of the old-fashioned streetlamps; it slathered tree trunks and sparkled like crushed diamonds at his feet. He heard a whispering noise and saw two people glide from among the trees on cross-country skis. A lavender lunar radiance filled the park. It was a world from childhood: castles and forests and magic lamps and princes scaling walls of brambles. *That* world.

He would tell his father!

No. And with that thudding refrain, the drag of Gregory's exhaustion returned. He looked around for a bench but saw just snowdrifts and occasional human shapes blurred by the falling snow into shadows, or ghosts. Two people were lying down, making angels. Now, there was an idea: Gregory let himself fall backward into a drift that caught him like a featherbed, so light and dry that he couldn't feel its cold.

He found himself staring up into a gray-white void. It disoriented him: Was he looking up or down? Only near his face did its contents reveal themselves in spiraling motes of cold that pricked his eyeballs and twanged in his throat when he inhaled. There was something familiar about all of it. He'd done this before: lain on his back in a snowstorm, gazing into a depthless, empty sky. But when? It must be déjà vu. And then, with a rush of comprehension, Gregory recognized his father's Anti-Vision: that bleak blank vista that had harried and tormented him, driven him in disguise to this same neighborhood twenty-five years ago. The Anti-Vision had never been an absence—the opposite! It was a density of whirling particles. His father just hadn't gotten close enough.

Gregory gazed, transfixed, as snow swarmed down upon him like space junk; like disarranged flocks of birds; like the universe emptying itself. He knew what the vision meant: human lives past and present, around him, inside him. He opened his mouth and eyes and arms and drew them into himself, feeling a surge of discovery—of rapture—that seemed to lift him out of the snow. He wanted to laugh or shout. *Finish your book!* Here was his father's parting gift: a galaxy of human lives hurtling toward his curiosity. From a distance they faded into uniformity, but they were moving, each propelled by a singular force that was inexhaustible. The collective. He was feeling the collective without any machinery at all. And its stories, infinite and particular, would be his to tell.

Middle Son (Area of Detail)

There's no mystery about this creature: a human boy. Eleven years old, a little shrunken-looking in his beige uniform, nothing to hook your gaze if he isn't your brother or son, but all eyes on him now because he's the one at bat, bases loaded, his parents and two brothers in the stands, his mother wringing a lump of yarn because it's agony watching him hit (or try to hit, he never hits), her emotions cliché to anyone who's read a book or seen a movie about children playing sports and how their mothers feel, and yet—how is this possible?— fiercely specific: a wish to pluck him from that spot and spirit him away to a place where she can protect him; a craving to hold him like she did when he was newly born and smelled like milk (his first smile, a tiny sputter of lightning across his face, a thing she often recalls); a hope that he won't be dwarfed forever by his older brother, who moves through the world as if it were a receiving line; a plea to someone, something, that her boy's uniqueness, so manifest to her lovestruck eyes, be revealed to all: a singularity that, were there justice in the world, would rearrange the present scene and cause a beam of light to fall directly onto his head.

But no beam—no sun, even. A cloudy dusk in late spring in an Upstate New York suburb interlocked with many others, around a city like many other cities. At night, from the window of a plane, their lights look like seams of gold ore in black rock. And among the tens of thousands of suburbs surrounding some three thousand American cities, there might be, from April onward, seven or eight hundred boys standing at home plate at any particular time, each emulating the batting stance of whatever hero's poster hangs above his bed, and a throng of parents, some ringing cowbells, some getting nasty—stories of bad parental behavior are part of a picture that turns generic the instant you cease to have a stake in it, as in: The boy at bat is your boy.

His name is Ames Hollander. Middle son, squashed between godliness above and eccentricity below. People forget his name. They forget he exists—that he can see and hear and remember like they can. His mother frets, knitting the brown V-neck sweater he'll reject in winter when she presents it to him (*No one wears knitted sweaters, Mom!*): How can the love and dread she feels for her middle son be converted into something tangible, something that can help him? One horror of motherhood lies in the moments when she can see both the exquisiteness of her child and his utter inconsequence to others. There are so many boys in the world. From a distance they look alike even to her, especially in uniform.

It's 1991, and a lot of things that are about to happen haven't happened yet. The screens that everyone will hold twenty years from now haven't been invented, and their bulky, sluggish predecessors have yet to break the surface of ordinary life. No one in this crowd has ever *seen* a portable phone, which gives to this moment the quality of a pause. All these parents gathered in the fading light, and not a single face underlit by a bluish glow! They're all *here,* in one place, their attention burning toward home plate, where Ames Hollander stands looking smaller than usual, compressed by the grim facts that have converged upon him: two outs, bases loaded, bottom of the ninth, the visiting team ahead by three. The game is surely lost, yet the possibility of victory still exists, should the batter—Ames, that is—manage to hit a home run. And although Ames is the last player on the home team likely to manage such a feat (he hasn't hit once all season), every home team member and home team parent is seized by wild, irrational faith that he can. They wrote him off three games into the season, but now they scream his name and stamp their feet on the chilly metal bleachers in a communal howl of conviction.

Strike one. Didn't swing. Possibly didn't even see the ball.

Like every team, this home team has a story that would render comatose anyone without a stake, but for those who do, its minutiae are inexhaustible fodder for passionate, intricate discussions over beers (the dads, mostly) or telephones attached to walls, their coiled rubber cords knotting and tangling when extended to their full length so that moms can talk behind closed doors without their sons hearing. Over beers or twisted cords, these conversations have certain identical refrains:

1. The sons of present company don't get enough playing time and/or are in the wrong positions.
2. The coach rewards his own son beyond his abilities.
3. Present company excepted, parents are overly invested in the team and its performance.

Strike two. Swinging, at least.

Ames is oblivious to these parental confabs. What he does feel, in the form of amorphous bouts of unease, is his own precarious suspension between childhood and whatever comes next, and between two brothers who jostle him from above and below, barely leaving him room to breathe. People's eyes slide over Ames and settle on Miles, two years older, whose advantages are so laughably clear (better athlete, better student, better-looking) that he's actually *kind* to Ames, no more threatened by him than a king would be by his valet. Or they settle on Alfred, the "baby," already making an art of his quirky displeasure. There are moments when Ames's own startled face in the bathroom mirror looks unnervingly blank, like nothing. Should he exist? What could he be worth, if he is nothing to himself? There is a perilous quality to these thoughts, a dizzy weightlessness like the moment of releasing the rope they all use to swing out over the lake from "the cliff" at the abandoned summer camp—shut down after a boy died *swinging from that very cliff* (the myth so much more fun than the truth: declining enrollments and an embezzling bookkeeper). But from somewhere deep within Ames, an answer rises to his rescue: He is special, and that specialness is a secret. The void he sees in the mirror is a disguise of invisibility that conceals a volcanic strength. So immense are the doubts Ames's inner voice must quell that his self-advocacy approaches the titanic. He is awesome in the thunderous sense of that word—not the vague, ubiquitous positivity it will soon assume in casual conversation. He can do it, whatever it is! Of course, he can't always do it, but when he doesn't (hit the ball, for example), the failure lies in some hindrance to the cataclysmic power of his swing; it was thrown off by the wind, a light in his eyes, an itch on his hand—there is always a reason Ames doesn't hit when he doesn't hit (which is always), making each nonhit a freak exception to a norm he alone expects.

When the ball leaves the pitcher's hand, Ames feels that slow-motion hyperawareness that always follows a pitch: the ball advancing; his parents side-by-side on the bleachers yet somehow always far apart; Miles scrutinizing, preparing a catalog of Ames's missteps; Cecily, a teammate's sister and his secret crush, blowing soap bubbles near first base that float into a twilight sky whose dab of moon can barely hold its own against the throbbing heavens beyond it; the skeletons of Onondaga Indians who once presided over the forest whose last crimped vestige this baseball field now occupies, curled and humming deep below. Ames swings and connects: He hits the ball as predicted (by him), *smashes the hell out of that ball* (his father's voice in his head), an event fraught with shocking sensations—not at the fact of hitting, which he expected, but at the feeling of hitting, which is entirely new: the violence of it, pain forking up his arms; and the sound, a *crack* like stone splitting open. A white flash of ball hangs briefly alongside the moon (though Ames can't see this, he's too busy running) before vanishing beyond the field for a grand slam that clears the bases, bringing three runners home, plus Ames, and winning the game 5–4. Ames knows none of this yet—*Just keep running*, their coach often harangues them, *don't stop to enjoy the view—*

so Ames runs and runs, unaware that the pounding din he vaguely hears is the sound of people cheering.

It became a myth, that hit, a topographical feature that glowed in certain psyches for the rest of their lives, melding with the geography of fairy tales. Talked about in middle school by Ames's teammates; bragged about in high school by Miles, who absorbed the triumph as his own (a family is a team!); sulked over by Alfred, who could find no toehold against the purity of bat hitting ball. It's tempting to build a version of Ames's life in which that hit was a "turning point," empowerment at a crucial moment, etc. (stockblock 3M*iis*), but that would be phony, as nine-year-old Alfred already likes to say. The hit's worldly reach lasted only as long as that season, another four weeks during which Ames's teammates chanted his name, futilely, whenever he was at bat. The next spring a new coach came in who hadn't seen Ames hit; who could see only what he could see, which wasn't much, and cut him from the team. The hit was a fluke, a random eruption of power that Ames alone knew he possessed. He carried that knowledge with him into high school, then the army (over his parents' passionate objections), where, in boot camp, he hit the hearts on the human dummies far more often than the other recruits. You might say that Ames had been a gun awaiting firing since his childhood.

He turned twenty-one just days after 9/11, already an army sharpshooter; was recruited to Special Ops and, eventually, in his early thirties, weary of the tech nerds who were ascendant, and eager to make some real money, retired to work for a private contractor known to handle "targeted killings"—tactically expedient but harder to justify militarily. Reaching these targets required feats of superhuman endurance, alone or in small teams, navigating submersibles and then scuba diving to shore; scaling mountains or rappelling down cliffs; fast-climbing from choppers that swung away into the night the instant he let go. He worked in deserts and forests and cities, sleeping in a hammock strung up inside the bellies of hollowed-out transport planes on overseas flights. Humming danger followed by fleeting clandestine triumph—no worldly thrill could match that cycle. Ames had one shot, maybe two, before a hammer of security fell; if the planned exit should fail, then capture. Death. His own possible extermination was a shadow partner that accompanied him throughout his work. No one stayed lucky forever.

He felt baffled by people who lived the other way: Mark Tucker, whom he'd played Nintendo with, now a father of three who kicked aside rubber balls to welcome Ames into his living room. Ames grew bored, sleepy. He drank a glass of lemonade on Mark's cat-shredded couch and wondered what to say to a man who spent his weekends coaching girls' ice hockey. Ames had no spouse, no lasting relationship; felt a dull distance even from his mother, the person he was closest to. And she felt this, too. Long divorced, a real estate agent whose social life included lovers (occasionally married), Susan was haunted by the gap between the sensation of three boys climbing her torso like a tree, combing sticky fingers through her hair, muttering into her ears—and the constraint of adulthood: *How are you, honey? You look a little tired. Is there anything I can do? How about a hug for your old mom?* If she'd had an inkling, back then, of the ache this constraint would cause her, she would never—*not once!*—have said, "Let go of me, boys, I just need a minute," and shaken them off. She would have held still and let them pick her clean, understanding that there would be nothing better to save herself for.

Closing his eyes, Ames could view a sequence of bodies whirring with their last moments of life: soaping a flabby back in a shower; carefully removing skin from a mango; feeding crumbs of toast to squabbling sparrows; struggling to right a window shade, belly exposed by an uplifted shirt. At the time, such glimpses had meant no more to him than the development of a target. But unbeknownst to Ames, those flashes of humanity were collecting inside him. There came a day in 2023 when he'd crouched in a tree for several hours, tracking his target in glints through windows and waiting, with reptilian patience, for him to come outside. At last the man did, sat down in the sunlight with a book of poems, a small gray cat fumbling into his lap. Ames hesitated. Through the man's thinning hair, he caught a glitter of perspiration on his scalp, and all at once, it was not his right to take this life. The discovery arrived incontestably as night: a recognition, at forty-three, of what his work had forced him to become.

And so he returned to the Upstate New York town where he'd grown up. His mother had just listed their old house for the third time since she and his father divorced more than twenty years earlier. On a lark, Ames went to the open house: young couples with children, professors at the college where his father used to teach. Wandering among strangers through the rooms of his childhood felt like returning to Oz or Ali Baba's cave: the laundry chute where he and his brothers sent messages up and down in a basket on a string; the garage smelling of walnut rinds and gasoline; his own room, where the "x" he'd carved with a penknife inside his closet door was there, under layers of paint. How could anyone live here but him? Ames decided, on the spot, to buy this memory palace (he knew the broker, after all) and begin his new life where he'd begun the first.

So Ames moved back into the family house and married and began having kids—filled the living room with rubber balls that had to be kicked aside by visitors approaching the worn-out couch, and the years flew away like calendar pages blown by the wind in old movies, his wife mopping his sweaty brow when he woke up screaming. But there's a false bottom under this happy ending, a hollowness around the words. Can you hear it? There was no wife (although he did track down Cecily, his childhood crush, online: an unrecognizable mother of four now living in Tucson). There were no children except the ones Ames imagined he heard when he sat in his father's old study: a snuffing and sighing from the hallway that made him wonder if a house somehow retains the memory of everything that has happened inside its walls—in which case three curious boys still prowled outside that office door, their smudged fingers streaking the paint as they listened, listened, for the beating of their father's heart. There was a point beyond which the trappings of conventional life became hard to assume, and Ames had passed that point. His mother understood. In the kitchen where she'd packed his school lunches thirty years before, they played Scrabble and gin rummy; in the family den, they watched nature shows about puffins and pandas, and she knitted sweaters he actually wore. Even as Susan mourned the life he might have had, she was relieved to have him back and kissed the thinning hair at the crown of his beautiful head each time they said goodbye. And maybe we should end here, at this conjunction of love and sorrow between a mother and her middle son (P2l*iv*), but that's too easy—another false bottom—because there's more.

Four years after his return, in 2027, Ames decided to have the government-implanted weevil removed from his brain. He knew the device was dead—knew, as any insider to the world of intelligence knows, that surveillance requires too many resources to waste on people who don't matter. Yet he wanted it out. A small surgery with an overnight stay for observation, and then! Rejuvenation! A buoyant renewal that could be explained psychologically, as a by-product of having been cut open and sewn back up. Online forums were crammed with testimonials from former soldiers and spies about the salutary effects of removing defunct weevils to treat depression and PTSD. Among civilians, terror of weevils was rampant in the post-pandemic years, a figment of the mass psychosis that characterized that dark time in American life. Ames spent months designing a low-frequency imaging device. With the help of his cousin Sasha's husband, Drew, he built a prototype: a machine to salve the dread of paranoids and ease the minds of people who felt unlike themselves; whose dreams had gotten strange; who believed they were being watched from within or used to watch those around them; who could no longer concentrate; and with each stroke of solace (and, a handful of times, detection) he was able to provide, Ames felt a step nearer to absolution.

And maybe here is where we should end—Ames renewed, Ames with a girlfriend he met on the job, Ames hosting his brothers and their families each August at the old house, where they roasted a suckling pig in the backyard. Why follow him all the way to his final years in an upstate nursing home, the last of the Hollander brothers to survive? We have these facts—creamed spinach, Go championships, a Jamaican nurse named Annalise who would have been Ames's true love had they not been fifty years apart in age (she said so, too, her firm hands holding his shaking ones), a robin's nest outside his window one spring containing four blue eggs, "H-a-p-p-y B-i-r-t-h-d-a-y" spelled out in sparkling cardboard letters across the door to the common room the day he turned ninety. Thanks to Bix Bouton, that genius, all of this is in our reach.

Even so, there are gaps: holes left by eluding separatists bent upon hoarding their memories and keeping their secrets. Only Gregory Bouton's machine—this one, fiction—lets us roam with absolute freedom through the human collective.

But knowing everything is too much like knowing nothing; without a story, it's all just *information*. So let us return to the story we began: Ames rounding the bases to a roar of jubilation that approaches the meteorological. People charge onto the field as he crosses home plate: a throng of ecstatic parents and teammates and siblings mobbing him in a way that would be frightening if not for their merry faces. His teammates hoist him into the air like ants lofting a stick and carry him around the bases a second time before they set him down and dump a cooler of Gatorade over his head.

Miles towels off Ames's lime-smelling hair because Miles loves winning and a family is a team, and the coach gives a lecture to the radiant boys and their radiant families about patience and hard work and *believing in yourself*, and there are hugs and goodbyes among the giddy parents, but Miles insists they can't leave, not without finding the ball—*Come on, it's our trophy!* So the Hollander family stays on after everyone else has driven away. In the hush, they circle the field to its farthest perimeter and disperse among the whispering pines in that scrap of ancient forest. They browse separately among pine needles in the deepening dark until their mother finds it—she's expert at finding their lost things (she finds two baseballs, in fact, a few feet apart, and hastily shoves one under a bush before shouting, "Got it!").

Trophy recovered, they walk to their station wagon, the only car left in the lot, crossing asphalt that glitters like stars under the parking lights. Miles has commandeered the lucky ball, tossing it into the air and catching it. Ames walks between his parents holding both their hands, Miles and Alfred right behind, an orb of happiness enclosing them as they move together into the sonorous black aquatic night.

When they reach the car, his father pulls off Ames's baseball cap and kisses his sweaty head.

"What now, slugger?" he asks. "Anything you want."

Acknowledgments

With each book, I become more dependent on the people who help me to do this work—or perhaps just more keenly aware of how dependent I've always been!

First and always, David Herskovits—for decades of reading, conversation, and everything.

Our sons, Manu and Raoul Herskovits, for luring my attention into realms essential to this book.

My mother and stepfather, Kay and Sandy Walker, for believing in me always.

My agent and partner, Amanda Urban, and her teams at ICM and at Curtis Brown: Sophie Baker, Ron Bernstein, Felicity Blunt, Daisy Meyrick, and Charlie Tooke.

My editor, Nan Graham, and everyone at Scribner: Dan Cuddy, Ashley Gilliam, Erich Hobbing, Jaya Miceli, Katherine Monaghan, Sabrina Pyun, Stuart Smith, Kara Watson, and Brianna Yamashita.

My splendid UK team at Corsair Books: James Gurbutt, Hayley Camis, Emily Moran, Phoebe Carney, Nico Taylor and Marie Hrynczak. Alex Busansky, Ken Goldberg, Barbara Mundy, and Dr. George Carlo for expertise legal, tech-historical, academic, and military.

Finally, my readers, some of whose frank perceptions I've been relying upon for decades. In addition to my writing group, to whom I've dedicated this book, they are Monica Adler, Genevieve Field, James Hannaham, David Herskovits, Don Lee, Gregory Pardlo, Gregory Sargeant, Ilena Silverman, Deborah Treisman, Kay Walker, and Stephanie Weeks.

About the Author

Jennifer Egan is the author of six previous books of fiction: *Manhattan Beach*, winner of the Andrew Carnegie Medal for Excellence in Fiction; *A Visit from the Goon Squad*, which won the Pulitzer Prize and the National Book Critics Circle Award; *The Keep*; the story collection *Emerald City*; *Look at Me*, a National Book Award Finalist; and *The Invisible Circus*. Her work has appeared in *The New Yorker*, *Harper's Magazine*, *Granta*, *McSweeney's*, and *The New York Times Magazine*. She recently completed a term as president of PEN America. Her website is Jenniferegan.com.